Is he re...
preci...

Her Pregnancy Surprise

Three exciting, intense romances from three
beloved Mills & Boon authors!

In March 2010 Mills & Boon bring
you two classic collections, each
featuring three favourite romances
by our bestselling authors

HER TYCOON LOVER

On the Tycoon's Terms by Sandra Field
Her Tycoon Protector
by Amanda Browning
One Night with the Tycoon
by Lee Wilkinson

HER PREGNANCY SUPRISE

His Pregnancy Bargain by Kim Lawrence
The Pregnancy Secret by Maggie Cox
Their Pregnancy Bombshell
by Barbara McMahon

Her Pregnancy Surprise

KIM LAWRENCE

MAGGIE COX

BARBARA McMAHON

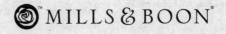 MILLS & BOON®

First published in Great Britain 2010
Harlequin Mills & Boon Limited,
Eton House, 18-24 Paradise Road, Richmond, Surrey TW9 1SR

HER PREGNANCY SURPRISE
© by Harlequin Enterprises II B.V./S.à.r.l 2010

His Pregnancy Bargain, The Pregnancy Secret and *Their Pregnancy
Bombshell* were first published in Great Britain by Harlequin Mills & Boon
Limited in separate, single volumes.

His Pregnancy Bargain © Kim Lawrence 2004
The Pregnancy Secret © Maggie Cox 2006
Their Pregnancy Bombshell © Barbara McMahon 2005

ISBN: 978 0 263 88099 1

05-0310

Printed and bound in Spain
by Litografia Rosés S.A., Barcelona

HIS PREGNANCY BARGAIN

BY
KIM LAWRENCE

Kim Lawrence lives on a farm in rural Anglesey. She runs two miles daily and finds this an excellent opportunity to unwind and seek inspiration for her writing! It also helps her keep up with her husband, two active sons, and the various stray animals which have adopted them. Always a fanatical consumer of fiction, she is now equally enthusiastic about writing. She loves a happy ending!

CHAPTER ONE

'YOU said *what*?'

Even the anonymity of the phone could not disguise the natural authority in his most famous client's voice or, at that moment, the irritation and astonishment that had crept into the distinctive deep tones.

It had been a good idea *not* to have this particular conversation face to face, decided Malcolm, who was starting to feel uncomfortably like a man stuck between the proverbial rock and hard place. Yes, the analogy worked—if his sister was the rock, Luc could easily be considered a hard place.

Eyes slightly narrowed, Malcolm summoned an image of the younger man's startlingly good-looking face. The sharp jutting cheekbones, an aggressively angular jaw a wide, mobile mouth capable of issuing painfully blunt comments, and deep-set eyes. He gave a mental shudder as he considered those penetrating, spookily pale grey eyes. No doubt about it, Luc definitely constituted a hard place...a *very* hard place!

When Malcolm had initially met the first-time author of the sexy action thriller that had landed on his desk, he hadn't been able to believe his luck. Luc wasn't only incredibly photogenic, he was articulate and witty. Malcolm's visions of women snatching the book off the shelves after they'd seen his new client charming the pants off the public on the chat-show circuit were dashed when the guy had calmly announced that he was a writer, not a salesman.

Luc had spelt out his conditions to Malcolm. He wasn't available for interviews or photo opportunities; in fact he wanted to remain anonymous. If the books weren't good enough to sell on their own merits, so be it.

Malcolm's argument that one unfortunate experience at the hands of the press was not sufficient reason to make a disastrous business decision had not impressed Luc who, never one to take anyone's word for anything, had had a clause inserted in his contract.

Malcolm injected a note of desperate *bonhomie* into his voice. 'I was sure you'd love to come for the weekend so I sort of, well, I...I said you would.'

Perversely the silence that greeted his confession was more nerve-shredding than a tirade of angry abuse might be—Luc didn't get loud when he was mad.

The words 'soft but deadly' sprang unbidden into Malcolm's head.

'It'll all be very casual. No need to dress up. Charming woman, my sister—everyone loves her parties.'

Luc squinted up at the wall he had just painted. It really hadn't looked that *blue* on the label and the room was north facing...too cold. It would have to go.

'Have you developed a sense of humour, Mal? Or have you gone totally insane?' The latter explanation seemed much more likely to Luc.

'I know how you get after you've delivered a book.'

'Relieved...?'

'A weekend in the country is just what you need,' pronounced the editor firmly.

'I live in the country,' came the deceptively gentle reminder.

'No, you live in the back of beyond,' Malcolm corrected with an audible shudder in his beautifully modulated voice. 'I'm talking about Sussex; they have pavements there.'

The observation made Luc smile, but Malcolm, on the other end of the line, didn't have the comfort of seeing the warmth it lent his lean, dark features.

'Only recently someone persuaded me that what I needed

was a place in town…losing touch with reality, someone said, I seem to recall…? Now who was that? Oh, I remember—*you*!'

'Good company, excellent food…' Malcolm had a rare talent for selective deafness, which came in handy at moments like this. 'You like old things, don't you…? My brother-in-law was a great collector and they tell me the house is Elizabethan in parts, a moat, the whole thing,' he finished vaguely before producing his winning argument. 'Ghosts…!'

'I beg your pardon?'

'They have a ghost—several, I expect. Never seen them myself, of course, but…people doing psychical research come to look in the cellar and they open to the public on bank holidays so it must be something special.'

At the other end of the line the thought of the landed gentry brought a disdainful sneer to Luc's face. Personal experience had not given him a rosy view of the families who had once divided the wealth of the country between them. His father had worked on an estate as a forester until the titled owners had decided to turf him out of his tied cottage.

A job and home lost in one fell swoop, and all his dad had done was tug his forelock respectfully when they had explained that tourists were a more cost-effective way to utilise their resources. It was the meekness, the way he had accepted his fate that had filled Luc, then ten, with seething anger.

He had resolved on the spot that he would never bow and scrape to anyone. This resolve had been hardened into grim resolution as he had watched the defeated droop of his father's shoulders become permanent over the months that had followed.

He had been more adaptable than his father, who had struggled to fit in the large industrial town they had moved to. It hadn't been an accident that he'd lost the country burr that had made him the obvious target of bullies in the inner-city school.

Luc was a survivor.

Malcolm continued. 'Gilbert left my sister pots of money. Do you shoot, Luc?'

'*Shoot?*' Luc ejaculated in a tone of disgust. 'What is this—*Gosford Park*?'

'I meant clays,' Malcolm hastened to explain amiably.

'The only thing I shoot are editors who accept invitations on my behalf.' A spasm of curiosity crossed his handsome face. 'I'm interested—you knew I wouldn't agree, so why on earth did you say I would?'

'I knew you wouldn't like it, but I just heard myself saying it.' Impossible of course to make someone like Luc understand. 'You don't know my sister,' Malcolm added darkly. 'When she wants something she's relentless, like a dripping tap.'

'Sounds like a delightful hostess,' Luc interjected drily.

'She's an enormous fan of yours. You'd be treated like royalty, I swear.'

'I have no desire to be treated as royalty and I would be a major disappointment as a house guest...'

'As a favour to me...?' his editor cajoled.

'She can have an autographed copy of my next book.'

'She already has one, your signature is really *very* easy to fake.'

Malcolm decided that Luc's reluctant laugh was a sign the younger man was mellowing and pressed his advantage.

'Laura's been on at me for ages about you. Now, with Megan being thirty next month, and the lawyer chap breaking his leg last minute...' A huge sigh reverberated down the line.

'Who or what is Megan?'

'My niece, lovely girl...not married.'

An expression of amused comprehension crossed Luc's lean face. 'Am I invited because your sister is looking for a mug to partner her daughter?'

'Megan is a lovely girl,' Malcolm protested. 'Great personality. Takes after her father in the looks department, of course, but you can't have everything.'

Luc listened in growing amusement to the flow of confidences…from the moment he had walked into Malcolm's office he had *wanted* to dislike the other man. He represented everything Luc despised, from his accent to his privileged background. Yet Malcolm also possessed charm, he was basically a very likeable guy and, as Luc had learnt, despite his vague attitude, no pushover when it came to business.

'Do all the members of your family live in a previous century?'

Malcolm Hall's voice took on an ill-used quality as he responded to this incredulous query. 'Well, really, Lucas, I don't think it's much to ask considering what I've done for you. You really can be selfish, do you know that?' he complained.

Luc didn't resent the observation; he considered it was essentially true. He didn't enjoy money for its own sake, but he did enjoy the freedom it gave him. He considered himself a lucky man that doing what he enjoyed enabled him to live life on his terms.

It hadn't felt like it at the time, but with hindsight Luc recognised that losing his business the way he had had been one of the best things that had happened to him. If it hadn't been for his embezzling ex-partner he would never have shut himself in a room and worked for three weeks solid on the novel he had always *meant* to finish.

'I suppose I could tell Laura you have flu…'

'You can tell *Laura* anything you like, so long as it isn't I'd love to come to her party.' He liked Malcolm but that didn't mean he had the slightest intention of enduring a weekend being nice to people he had nothing whatever in common with.

It hadn't required enormous powers of deduction to discover where he lived, just a sneaky look in her uncle's address book.

Lucas Patrick, the best-selling author of a string of commercial and critically acclaimed novels, resided in the penthouse apartment of a warehouse conversion beside the river, the one that had won a whole bunch of awards the previous year. It was an address that didn't appear on the flyleaf of his numerous novels, but then neither did a suitably moody-looking black-and-white snapshot of the author.

Was the man genuinely allergic to publicity or was it a clever marketing ploy? Megan was not sure, but what was indisputable was that his point-blank refusal to promote his books had boosted his sales and turned him into an enigmatic hero-type figure not unlike the one that featured in his books. And Uncle Malcolm had been no help; the only thing he had let slip was that his most famous client was single and young.

If, when he went public, the writer turned out in the end to have middle-aged spread or a receding hairline there were going to be a lot of disappointed fans out there, her own mother included! she thought with a wry smile. Megan hoped he was presentable—it would make her idea a lot easier to pull off.

She paused, her finger hovering above the appropriate button, seized by last minute doubts about what she was doing. Last night this had seemed a truly inspired idea. In the cold light of day she didn't feel quite so confident that she was doing the right thing…she was even starting to wonder if it might not be a little crazy…?

But then desperate circumstances, she reminded herself, called for desperate measures!

What was the worst that could happen…?

Nothing as bad as what was going to happen if she didn't take some drastic action. Last Easter's efforts were still indelibly etched in Megan's mind. It had been totally excruciating and obvious to everybody but the hostess herself that the investment banker she had invited for the weekend as a potential husband for her spinster daughter was gay.

Megan loved her mother dearly, in fact she would have been the perfect parent if it weren't for her unswerving devotion to marrying off Megan!

Laura Semple had a simple philosophy—no woman could be happy without a man.

The conversation they had had over breakfast that very morning was more or less the same one they'd been having ever since Megan had decided not to marry the ever-so-suitable Brian four years earlier. Brian, who had turned out to be, not caring and protective in a charming, old-fashioned way, but a fully-fledged, possessive control freak who wanted her to account for every minute of her day and who got jealous when she talked to another man—*any* man.

Megan considered herself to have had a lucky escape, a view not shared by her mother.

'Of course I'm proud of what you've achieved, darling, but you can't tell me you're happy…not *really* happy.'

'*You* don't have a man, Mum.'

'That,' Laura rebutted firmly, 'is not the same thing at all. I'll never love a man the way I did your father.'

Megan saw the tears in her mother's eyes before she turned her head.

'There are lots of different loves.' Her own throat thickened with emotion as she gently squeezed her mother's hand. 'And actually I am happy.'

Her claim met with polite but open scepticism.

'I *promise* you, Mum, I'm perfectly content.'

'"Content" is a very middle-aged word, Megan,' her mother disapproved with a sigh.

'Maybe I'm one of those people that are born middle-aged...?'

'Oh, I know you put a brave face on it,' Laura continued, ignoring this flippant interjection. 'But, no matter what they say, no woman is totally fulfilled without a man.'

Megan bit her tongue and carried on smiling, past experience had taught her it was a waste of breath to argue this particular point.

'In your case a strong man I think,' Laura mused. 'One who isn't intimidated by your brains. Now *Lucas Patrick* doesn't sound to me like a man who is likely to lack confidence. The way he coped when his plane went down in the Andes...'

'That was his hero. He writes *fiction*, Mother,' Megan reminded her parent. 'He doesn't spend his life scaling impregnable peaks, busting international drug cartels or fighting off beautiful women who want to ravish him.'

'I am perfectly able to distinguish fact from fiction,' her mother retorted with dignity. 'But your uncle says he's scrupulous about his research and he *never* asks his hero to do anything he hasn't himself.'

'I seriously doubt if that includes crash-landing a plane and walking away without a scratch,' Megan muttered under her breath, then added in a louder voice, 'And the fact is you wouldn't know him from the man who delivers the milk. He'll probably turn out to be a regular anorak.' Her brow furrowed. 'And why on earth is he coming to one of your country weekends...?'

'I was a man short and your uncle Malcolm is his publisher; he's coming along with him. Well, he *was*—it turns out your uncle can't make it, but he says that Lucas is looking forward enormously to meeting us.'

'So you've only Uncle Malcolm's word that he's coming...?' In her experience, to stop his sister nagging her uncle would promise literally anything. 'Was Uncle Malcolm sober at the time...?'

'Don't be rude,' Laura reprimanded. 'And if you possess a skirt, pack it for the weekend, dear, do. You have very pretty legs—in fact you really are a very pretty girl, or would be if you took a little more effort. First impressions *do* count, Megan.'

Back to the task in hand, Megan squared her shoulders with resolution and, with a deep breath, she pressed the button. This idea might be a long shot but she just *had* to try. If Lucas Patrick was game she had figured out a fairly foolproof way to get her mother off her back *and* keep her happy.

A voice over the intercom responded almost immediately.

'About time too…' It was a deep voice, a bit gravelly at the edges and decidedly cranky which didn't bode too well for her plans.

'This is—'

'Yeah…yeah, you're here now. Just bring it up.' There was a buzz and the glass door swung open.

Megan shrugged and walked inside.

The lift rose smoothly and quickly, giving her no opportunity to change her mind. She knocked on the ajar door to the penthouse and heard the same impatient voice.

'Just bring it in—the money's on the table. If there are no extra anchovies don't take the tip.'

Oh, God, he's expecting a pizza and he's got a woman who wants him to pretend to be desperately in love with her!

Megan cleared her throat and looked curiously around the vast open-plan living space. With its steel support columns and lofty vaulted ceiling, it wasn't what she considered homey. She couldn't imagine coming here after a tough day, kicking off her shoes, pouring a glass of wine and switching on the telly. No, this was strictly bachelor territory and a rich bachelor at that, she thought, but then by all accounts the owner was worth a small fortune.

It was hard to gauge his taste as what furniture there was

was covered in dust-sheets. Her nose wrinkled; the place was permeated with the smell of paint and turps.

She cleared her throat and projected her voice to reach the invisible and grouchy presence. 'Mr Patrick, I'm afraid…' As the word left her mouth a lean, broad-shouldered figure materialised in a doorway.

Megan was pretty hopeless when it came to ages but she put this hunk somewhere in his early thirties. He was also tall, well over six feet, and dressed in tatty paint-stained jeans and a tee shirt that was clean but looked as though it had shrunk in the wash. The shrinkage meant it was impossible *not* to notice how well-developed his lean torso was. The tee shirt also revealed an inch or so of lean, flat belly and gave a glimpse of the thin line of dark hair that disappeared suggestively beneath the loose waistband of his jeans.

His dark flyaway brows drew together above a strong aquiline nose as he frowned suspiciously across at her.

'Who the hell are you?' he demanded as he dragged a hand through his collar-length sable hair that gleamed with health and was liberally speckled with blue paint. The jagged ends that rested on the nape of his brown neck suggested he hadn't seen the inside of a hair salon for some time.

This was the sort of guy who had women falling out of upper-storey windows to get a better look at him.

His presence undetected at first Luc had had an opportunity to study his intruder. Dressed casually as she was in jeans, there was nothing to distinguish this young woman from any number of others you saw in the street, except perhaps that this one appeared to carry herself with a certain air of quiet assurance.

She was tall and slim with hair like warm honey and candid china-blue eyes, which widened as they met his. The colour was so dramatically intense it could almost constitute an assault on the senses, he decided. The eyes had the sort of impact that made you not notice at first that her nose was undistinguished and her jaw slightly too determined. As far as he could tell she wasn't wearing any make-up, something she could get away with because her skin was smooth, the colour of milk and flawless.

Despite the fact she wasn't his type Luc felt his interest sharpen.

Megan's generous mouth tightened. Being a fairly direct person herself, she could appreciate the characteristic in others, but his question hadn't been brusque, more downright rude!

Clearly she had not made a favourable first impression on the decorator...she'd have to do a lot better with his employer if this wasn't going to be a total waste of time and energy.

'I'm Dr Semple.' Somehow what was meant to be a simple statement of fact emerged sounding pompous, but men this good-looking always made her feel slightly defensive... not that she had ever seen a man *this* good-looking.

His dark brows soared and the corners of his wide mouth twisted...something definitely cruel about that mouth, Megan decided, raising her glance hurriedly to eye level as something deep in her stomach twisted.

She sounded as cool and sure of herself as she looked. Luc liked her voice and found himself wondering what she would look like flustered. That hair spread out around her flushed... *Don't go there, Luc.*

He spread his expressive hands wide, inviting her inspection. 'Do I look like I have need of a doctor?' she heard him demand with vitality leaking out of every gorgeous pore.

He looked, from the top of his dark head to his... Her eyes dropped and her tummy did a crazy little back flip as she registered that his feet were the same even, toasty brown as the rest of him—at least the bits she could see. Not that she had any desire to see any more—what she was seeing was quite enough!

No doubt he'd be standing there oozing the same level of self-assurance if he had been bare all over.

Megan lowered her eyes quickly as the image that accompanied this maverick thought brought a lick of heat to her pale cheeks.

'I'm not that sort of doctor,' she mumbled. With thoughts like hers it was just as well—she'd have been struck off!

When she looked up a moment later he was still surveying her in unfriendly silence. The moment and the silence lasted too long for her comfort. His expression remained vaguely hostile as he brushed a hand carelessly along his chiselled jaw—God, but this man had perfect bones!—leaving a faint smudge of paint against his olive skin.

For no logical reason she could figure, she found herself wondering what he would do if she licked her finger and wiped the offending mark away from his smooth, blemish-free skin. She took a deep breath, horrified by the direction of her wilful imagination.

It was time to take control here.

CHAPTER TWO

Luc had obviously reached the same conclusion and he got in before Megan.

'I don't know how you got in here, *Doctor*, but I'd like you to go back the way you came.'

Or else—unspoken but definite, the warning hung in the air.

It wasn't his threatening posture that bothered Megan, it was the illicit and inexplicable little shiver that traced a path up her spine. Good looks, even ones as spectacular as his, she could take in her stride. At a subconscious level she recognised it was the earthy, sensual quality that he possessed in abundance that had her standing there like some inarticulate teenager.

She blinked, determined to rectify any false impression she had given that she was a brainless bimbo. Actually she had forgotten to breathe, which might account for the dizzy sensation; she took a deep, gulping gasp and immediately felt a little better.

'Well, unless your short-term memory is shot to hell you ought to know...you asked me in,' she reminded him.

A flicker of something that might have been surprise flickered behind his sensational eyes for a split second before shoulders that any athlete would have envied lifted fractionally. 'And now I'm asking you to leave.'

This was no invitation—it was an order.

Megan's chin went up the same way it had been doing, if her mother was to be believed, for twenty-nine years whenever she had been told what to do. 'I came to see Mr Patrick.'

The grey eyes narrowed but stayed like lasers on her focused face. The dark rings surrounding his irises highlighted the pale metallic colour of his eyes.

Did he ever blink…?

He gave another graceful shrug. 'Well, as you can see, I'm the only one here.' He placed the towel he had been holding on a dust-cloth covered table and picked up a bottle of mineral water. He unscrewed the top and raised it to his lips.

So she'd been dismissed…? Did he actually think she was going to leave just because he told her to…? The angry glow in her eyes became distracted as she watched the contraction of muscles in his brown neck as he swallowed, there was a faint sheen of moisture on his skin. She looked away.

'Is Mr Patrick likely to be home soon?'

'Are you a friend of his or just a groupie?'

Her outraged attention swung back to his mocking, handsome face. His insulting cynicism brought an angry flush to her face, or did that rise in temperature have something to do with the beads of moisture he brushed off his sensual lips…?

'I hardly think that's any of your business,' she retorted haughtily. 'Perhaps you'd like to carry on with whatever Mr Patrick is paying you to do, other than eat pizzas.'

He looked amused. 'Even a humble painter is allowed a lunch break, *Doctor*. Would you like me to give the boss a message?' he offered, casually looping the towel around his neck. The action revealed another inch of smooth, hard flesh.

Megan swallowed and lowered her gaze. 'It's personal.'

'You wish.'

Pale grey eyes clashed with turbulent blue.

'I'll wait,' she announced frigidly. Other than physically remove her, he couldn't do much about it, and if he did come over heavy handed she'd stick him with a lawsuit for assault before he could blink!

'Suit yourself,' he drawled. 'But then I'm sure you generally do.' This woman had spoilt and privileged written all over her, from her smooth voice to her assured manner.

Just as Megan's bottom made contact with the dust-sheet-covered chair there was a sudden upheaval beneath her that sent her with a startled shriek to her feet.

A bundle of spitting fury struck out at her with sharp claws as it hurtled across the room like a ginger flash of lightning.

'Ouch!' she yelled. 'That thing scratched me.' Rolling up the right leg of her jeans revealed a long, though admittedly shallow, scratch along her calf.

'That thing is called Sybil and you did sit on her. Poor cat,' he crooned to the cat from the flat downstairs.

Megan wasn't surprised to see the animal respond to his velvety croon, and in lightning transformation. *That voice…!* She could imagine any number of women who were old enough to know better purring if he used that voice on them.

'Is the skin broken?'

'I'll live,' she replied, rolling down her trouser leg. Superficial or not, the scratch stung. 'Do you have any idea when he'll be back?'

'Who?'

Megan gave an impatient grimace. 'Mr Patrick.'

'Oh, him…he'll be back in the country some time next month, I understand.'

Megan, her high hopes dashed by the casual revelation, felt her face fall. 'But he has to be back before then,' she protested.

'Really…?'

'He's spending next weekend in the country with us.'

'Maybe it slipped his mind…?'

Megan, who had flopped disconsolately into the cat-free chair, cast him a look of scorn. 'Or maybe Uncle Malcolm lied through his teeth,' she muttered half to herself.

Look on the bright side, she told herself, no eligible suitor equalled not being paired off with anyone, and it always had been a long shot.

The bad news was there would be other weekends!

'Malcolm Hall is your uncle?'

Megan shot him a startled glance and began to sneeze. 'You know him?' She felt another sneeze building and began to ransack her bag for tissues, she found the packet just in time.

'We're not members of the same club,' she heard him drawling scornfully when her sneezes subsided. 'And I don't play golf…but they let us unskilled labourers into quite a few places these days.'

Megan gave her pink nose a last angry scrub, her china-blue eyes snapping with anger. Where did this man get off automatically assuming she was some sort of snob? There was only one person here guilty of judging by appearances and it wasn't Megan!

'In my book decorators aren't unskilled, although…' she allowed her gaze to travel significantly over his paint-stained person '…in your case…'

'I'm helping out a friend.'

'So what is your actual day job?'

'I do a bit of this, a bit of that,' he revealed casually.'

'You don't have a regular job?' Megan's voice lifted in amazement—like most of her friends, her life revolved around the demands of work.

Luc found the fact she was looking at him as though he were a rare specimen amusing. 'I don't starve and I don't sponge.'

Megan was immediately embarrassed. 'I never imagined that you…it really isn't any of my business how you live your life, Mr…'

'Not being tied down to a nine-to-five routine gives me time to write. Some of my work is even now sitting on your uncle's desk.'

'You want to be a writer?' That would explain his instant

recognition of her uncle's name. Though he had to be incredibly naive if he thought the work of every unknown who sent in an unsolicited manuscript ended up on her uncle's desk. You had to produce something very special indeed to get that far.

Much more likely his work was languishing at the bottom of a pile on some junior's desk. Being a naturally kind person, Megan didn't have the heart to explain the brutal facts of the publishing business to him.

'Is there any reason why I shouldn't be a writer?'

Her eyes swept over his tall, impressive figure. The truth was he exuded so much vitality and energy Megan couldn't imagine him doing anything that required long periods of physical immobility.

Megan smiled sunnily and had the satisfaction of hearing his teeth grate. 'Listen, I don't know the first thing about publishing and I have no influence with my uncle but if you're serious about writing I think it would probably be a good idea to find yourself an agent.'

'Anybody you could recommend…?'

'Afraid not.'

'Maybe you should see a doctor,' he observed with a grimace as she began to sneeze loudly again.

'Look, I'm not in publishing, but good luck and don't worry—' Megan sniffed '—I'm not ill. I'm allergic to cats,' she explained as she got to her feet.

'Now, if you'll excuse me…?' She nodded, and slung the soft leather satchel she carried over her shoulder and smoothed down her jacket.

The long, lean, intensely aggravating stranger didn't step aside to let her pass. Instead he tilted his head back slightly to look curiously down at her and asked, 'What kind of doctor are you?'

'I'm a research chemist.'

'Interesting,' he said, looking and sounding as though he meant it.

'It has its moments.' Her bag hit her thigh as she hitched it on her shoulder and she winced as the fabric of her jeans rubbed against the fresh scratches on her leg.

'You should put some antiseptic on that; cat scratches can get infected. If you like I've got some…'

An image of those long brown fingers moving over her skin flashed into Megan's head. The reaction to the image was immediate and intense; the surface of her skin broke out in a rash of goose-bumps; her skin tingled; her sensitive stomach muscles contracted violently.

Her wide eyes lifted and collided with a steel-grey interrogative stare. There was a silence. The electric tension in the air had to be a product of her imagination, but it felt disturbingly real.

'That won't be necessary,' she replied huskily. 'But thanks for the offer.'

Adopting a brisk, decisive air, she stepped forward. She caught her lower lip between her teeth and hesitated when he didn't move. There was room to edge past, but that would mean touching him. The desire to get away from this man's disturbing presence was strong, but her reluctance to make physical contact was stronger. 'I'm sorry to have held you up…'

'So Lucas Patrick is a friend of yours…?'

'Actually I've never met the man in my life,' she admitted. 'Now if—'

'You're a fan, then?' he theorised, talking across her. 'If you leave your address, perhaps he'll send you an autograph.'

'Do I look stupid enough to give a total stranger my address?' she demanded.'

The dark, satanically slanted brows lifted, but Megan had no more intention of responding to the gesture than she did the quivery demands of her oversensitive tummy muscles.

'And I don't want his damned autograph,' she grunted, blushing darkly.

'Then you don't like his books?'

'I've read some of his earlier ones, I can see why he's popular,' she observed diplomatically.

'But not with you?' he suggested shrewdly.

'I think he's slightly overrated.' Unfairly she vented her antagonism towards this man on the absent and talented author.

She expelled a silent breath of relief as he finally moved aside to let her pass. As she did so she lifted her head as a thought occurred to her. 'Have you actually *met* Lucas Patrick?'

'In passing.'

Megan's eyes widened. He didn't seem to appreciate this put him in a pretty unique category. 'Really—! And how did he seem?'

'*Seem?*'

'What was he like?'

'He seemed a pretty ordinary sort of guy to me,' he divulged disappointingly.

'Then is he…what does he look like?' She shook her head. 'No, on second thoughts, don't tell me, leave me with my illusions—though if you happened to nod when I said balding, or paunchy, that wouldn't be totally out of order, would it?'

'I thought your uncle was his editor?'

'He is, but Uncle Malcolm's lips are sealed when it comes to Lucas Patrick,' she admitted regretfully.

'And you're curious…?'

A grin of pure mischief spread across Megan's face. 'A girl always likes to know ahead of time what her future husband looks like.'

'Future *husband*…?'

The look of horror etched on his dark, dramatically perfect face could not have been more heartfelt had she just announced her intention to marry him. Megan loosed a gurgle of laughter. 'A joke,' she placated.

'He might not think so,' the tall stranger observed as he scanned her amused face.

'Then he has no sense of humour,' Megan proclaimed.

'You still haven't said what brought you here…'

Halfway to the door, Megan turned back at the sound of his voice. Why not? the reckless voice in her head suggested. You're never going to see the man again. Maybe there was something in that old maxim that it was easier to discuss things with a stranger.

'My mother wants me to be happy.' She began to experience a familiar tightness in her chest and she sat down cautiously on the arm of a chair.

'And that's a problem?' Luc watched her fumble in her bag.

'She believes no woman is complete without a man.'

'And you don't have one.'

Megan's chin went up. 'I don't *want* one,' she rebutted firmly. Her fingers closed over the inhaler she never went out without and she gave a sigh of relief. 'At regular intervals she tries to set me up with someone she imagines…'

'Is good breeding stock…' came the straight-faced suggestion.

Megan's eyes narrowed. 'Will make me happy,' she corrected and raised the inhaler to her mouth. The relief was almost immediate. 'This is why I avoid cats,' she said, anticipating his question.

'You have asthma?' he queried, watching the rapid rise and fall of her chest.

'A little,' she admitted. She went to rise but a large hand fell on her shoulder, anchoring her to the spot. Her eyes slid from his brown fingers to his face.

'Take a minute to get your breath,' he suggested, actually it was more than a suggestion, it was a quiet command.

Normally Megan didn't respond well to commands but on this occasion she found herself strangely willing to let it pass. His concern, even though unnecessary was oddly comforting.

'Can I get you anything? A glass of water?'

She nodded; her throat felt oddly achy and constricted.

Without a further comment he left and returned with a glass of water. He stood there, arms folded across his chest while she drank. Megan was very conscious of his silent presence. He wasn't the sort of man you could forget was there.

'Thank you,' she said politely, handing back the empty glass. Their fingers touched briefly during the exchange; the contact did uncomfortable things to Megan's pulse.

'Can I call anyone for you?'

'Gracious, no!' Very conscious of her warm cheeks, she forced a smile but didn't meet his eyes. 'I'm fine.'

'Despite a matchmaking mother.'

The comment brought her head up. 'I've tried everything to put her off,' she admitted ruefully. 'Nothing works.'

Head tilted a little to one side, a frown deepening the line between his flyaway brows, he scanned her face. 'What are you…thirty…?'

The almost-spot-on estimate disconcerted her; she had enough female vanity to feel peeved.

'Sorry, have I touched a nerve?'

Megan glared at him. 'No, you haven't,' she denied angrily. 'I have no problem with being thirty…actually, *almost* thirty.'

'Good for you,' he interposed with silken gravity. 'Don't you think at *almost* thirty it's time you told your mother to mind her own business?'

Megan coloured angrily. He made it sound so simple, but then it probably was, if you had no problem trampling all over the feelings of people you loved. 'Oh, why didn't I think of that? Of course, it might be because I don't want to hurt my mother.'

His shoulders lifted in a disdainful shrug. 'Well, if you don't mind people running your life...?'

'My mother doesn't run my life!' she flared.

'No?'

Megan clenched her teeth. 'No, she doesn't. She has had a tough time the last few years,' she informed him, swallowing past the emotional lump in her throat. 'She isn't some cold control freak, she is just a caring mum who wants to see her daughter happy and settled.' She dragged a frustrated hand through her hair and gave a dejected sigh. 'Unfortunately happy and settled for her equates with a man and marriage, which is why I had this idea...a sort of line-of-least-resistance thing.'

Luc watched as she gazed abstractedly into the distance, her smooth brow furrowed.

'Least resistance...?' he probed softly.

She nodded. 'If I could get one of the prospective grooms to pretend to be smitten, Mum would be happy and leave me to get on with more important things.'

Luc's deep-set eyes widened slightly as comprehension struck home. 'And what do you consider important?'

'My job.'

'You can't live and breathe your job.'

'My work is very demanding; it leaves no time for relationships. '

'So you're married to your career.'

She frowned; he made her sound freaky. 'I've nothing against marriage, but I don't think I'll ever find a man who is willing to take what little I would have to give.'

'You don't have a very high opinion of men.'

'I'm a pragmatist.'

'You think you were being pragmatic when you came here to ask Lucas Patrick to...*pretend to be smitten*...?'

A mortified flush mounted Megan's cheeks—when he said it, it sounded even more off the wall. 'I didn't say that.'

'But that's what you came here for?'

'It's not as crazy as it sounds.'

'Did I say it was crazy? I'm just wondering…what was going to be in it for him?'

CHAPTER THREE

MEGAN frowned. *'In it…?'*

'As in what would he get out of it?' Luc looked into her bewildered face and laughed. 'You thought he'd do it out of the goodness of his heart.' His mobile lips lifted cynically at the corners. 'You really never have met Lucas Patrick, have you?'

'And unlike you I'd prefer not to bad-mouth him in his absence.'

For some reason her angry reproach caused him to laugh. It was a deep, warm, uninhibited sound that made Megan's pulse rate quicken. 'Just bad-mouth his books…?'

She wrenched her appreciative stare from the mesh of fine lines around his smiling grey eyes and frowned. 'Don't put words in my mouth,' she warned him.

The stern warning brought Luc's attention to her lips; she was attempting to compress them into a thin, disapproving line. As he contemplated the soft, cushiony contours it took considerable self-discipline to prevent his thoughts diverting into a carnal direction.

'And I'm sure Mr Patrick has survived worse than anything I might say about him. And actually,' she added, 'I happen to think that he's quite a talented writer.'

'But you were willing to overlook his dubious literary talent in the interests of a quiet life?' he questioned.

The soft charge brought a guilty flush to her cheeks. She squared her shoulders and sighed. 'All right, I admit it was a pretty daft idea, but as the man isn't here it's fairly academic, isn't it?'

'Maybe…'

'There's no *maybe* about it,' she rebutted morosely.

'Would I be right in assuming that nobody at this house party, including your mother, has ever met Lucas Patrick...?'

'Well, no, since Uncle Mal won't be coming I don't suppose...but I don't see what that has to do with anything, Mr...what is your name anyhow?' The weirdness of discussing such personal things with a total stranger whose name she didn't even know suddenly struck Megan forcibly.

A slow, wolfish grin split the nameless stranger's lean, dark face, revealing a set of white even teeth and causing her stomach to flip. Not only had she lost all control over what came out of her mouth, she had lost control of her nervous system as well!

'To cut down on confusion, perhaps it's better if you just call me Lucas...?' he suggested smoothly.

'*What*...?' Megan's impatient expression vanished as her eyes snapped open to their fullest extent. God, he couldn't be saying what she thought he was...*could he*...?

She scanned his face with suspicion. 'What are you suggesting?'

'I'm suggesting that you need a face to fit your fantasy lover.' He adopted an expression of enquiry. 'Is there anything wrong with this one?' His fluid gesture indicated his own lean face.

Megan looked at the golden toned skin stretched across the perfect arrangement of strong angles and intriguing hollows and went perfectly pale.

'You're insane.' Despite her attitude of total conviction, there was a small voice in her head that said it could just work...

'I'm assuming you weren't expecting Lucas Patrick to actually marry you...?'

'Don't be absurd,' she breathed faintly. Like a hypnotised rabbit, she couldn't take her eyes off his face. That voice in her head was getting louder.

'Did you have a time factor in mind...?' When she

looked back at him blankly he spelt it out. 'How long did you imagine this fake romance had to last? Six months or so?'

'I hadn't really thought that far ahead.'

His disturbing eyes glittering from beneath the sweep of long, curling ebony lashes, he slanted her a sardonic look.

'Oh, I guess so,' she conceded crossly. 'If you're suggesting anyone is going to believe you're a famous author…' She gave a forced laugh.

'Nobody has the faintest idea what Lucas Patrick looks like.'

'They may not know what he looks like—' she deliberately trailed her eyes along the long, lean lines of his athletic frame; about midway she lost her scornful air '—but I think they might know what he *doesn't* look like,' she finished hoarsely.

His self-satisfied air intensified as he surveyed her heated cheeks. 'If I had claimed to be him when you walked in you'd have been none the wiser.'

'Nonsense! Of course I would,' she instantly rebutted indignantly. 'What do you take me for?'

A look she couldn't quite decipher flickered at the back of his steely, dark-lashed eyes. 'Someone who thinks they can tell, just by looking at a person, who he is…or should I say what he does? The two seem to be the same thing as far as you're concerned.'

'Of course I can't.'

'And neither can anyone else. The fact is you assumed I was the hired help because of the way I'm dressed. If I came out of the bedroom with a stethoscope around my neck you'd have assumed I was a doctor. It's all about props.'

'This is all academic…I'm not going to invite a total stranger into my home.'

'Afraid I'll steal the silver?'

She shook her head and refused to respond to this taunt. 'This isn't going to happen. Even if you did carry it off…'

'I will,' he promised.

His smug smile made her frown. 'Even if you did my mother is never going to believe I'm attracted to you.' Then she would be wrong wouldn't she?

'What's wrong with me?'

'You're simply not my type.'

'What is your type?'

'Shall we drop this subject?'

'Because you find it uncomfortable?' The idea seemed to amuse him.

'I find *you* uncomfortable.' Too much information, Megan, she told herself not liking the thoughtful expression on his face. Recalling his earlier cynical comments, she asked, 'What do *you* get out of it?'

He smiled. 'Your uncle Malcolm looks at my manuscript.'

So that was it. 'If you've written a load of rubbish, nothing I say is going to make Uncle Malcolm publish you.'

'It isn't rubbish; it's good.'

'You're very confident.'

He didn't deny her accusation. 'I just need a break and you need a lover.'

'A *fake* lover.'

'I'm applying for the job…?'

Megan clutched her head and groaned. 'I must be mad!'

'You won't regret this,' he promised, extending his hand.

Megan, who was pretty sure she would regret it, allowed her fingers to be enclosed in his firm grip. A shot of heat zapped through her body.

She was regretting it already. She carried on regretting it and questioning her sanity during the next twenty-four hours. In the end it didn't matter.

Her fake lover was a no-show.

CHAPTER FOUR

THE day was grey and drizzly, there had been no buyers for a brisk walk, so Megan hadn't had company when she'd walked the dogs. She was still in her muddy shoes and outdoor clothes when a noisy Land Rover drew up onto the gravelled forecourt right beside a Porsche and a Mercedes. She stopped towelling the muddy terrier and got to her feet, her heart pounding—*please let it not be him...!*

'I wonder who that is?' her mother asked with a frown. 'I do wish you'd fetch the dogs in through the kitchen when we've got guests,' she remonstrated gently. 'Hilary will have hysterics if they go within ten yards of her...tiresome woman,' she added to herself. 'Down, Fred,' she added sternly to the large dog who had planted his damp paws on her stomach.

'I can't imagine who it is,' Megan replied, her heart thumping madly in her chest.

Her mother looked at her sharply. 'Are you feeling all right, Megan?' She considered her daughter's face with a frown. 'You look a little flushed.'

'Me? I'm fine, absolutely fine!' The cheerful smile she pinned on her face felt as though it was about to crack...or was that her face? 'I'll go and see who it is, shall I?' she added brightly.

'Would you, dear?'

Megan was already running across towards the vehicle, her boots crunching on the gravel. Seconds later she arrived breathless and quivering with tension.

'You're late!' she fired as the tall figure stepped with lithe, fluid ease from the disreputable-looking four-wheel drive. 'I thought you weren't coming.' If she was honest

32

she had been relieved when she had thought he wasn't honouring their bargain.

'Something came up,' he revealed casually.

'And it didn't occur to you to let me know,' she quivered accusingly.

One dark brow angled sardonically. 'Don't you think you should wait until we are irresistibly attracted before you get possessive...?' he suggested mildly.

The sarcasm brought an angry sparkle to her eyes. 'This might be a joke to you, but—'

'Not a joke,' he interposed. 'But I don't see any reason we can't make the best of it. We might even enjoy ourselves...'

'*Enjoy?* Are you insane?' Then, transferring her attention to the off-roader, she continued without missing a beat. 'Is that yours?'

If I had an ounce of foresight, she thought, I would have considered the question of transport and hired him the sort of car people would expect a best-selling author to drive around in. If I had any foresight I wouldn't have done this at all.

'No, I stole it on the way here,' he returned, straightfaced. His dark eyes moved from the tendrils of hair that curled damply around her fair skinned face to her wide, anxious eyes. 'Is that a problem?'

Megan tore her attention from the Land Rover and cast him a look of seething dislike...as she did so she immediately realised that nobody would notice if he rolled up riding a child's tricycle!

'Oh, my God...' she groaned, grabbing agitated handfuls of damp hair. '*Look at you!*'

She followed her own instructions and allowed her glance to travel down the long, lean length of him once more. It was a cue for a heat flash to consume her all over again.

He was sheathed from head to toe in black. The leather, age-softened jacket he wore was moulded to truly fantastic shoulders. It hung open to reveal a plain white tee shirt that clung to his powerful chest and lean, washboard belly. His dark moleskins followed the muscular contours of long, powerful thighs. God, was that a hole in the knee…? She despaired that a tiny glimpse of flesh could make her break out in a sweat.

This was never going to work.

'What's wrong with me?'

Nothing, if you liked being hit over the head with sex appeal.

'*Everything!*' she snapped in a doom-laden drone.

His mobile mouth quirked at the corners; he didn't appear particularly chastened by her pronouncement. 'Harsh.'

'You might have made an effort to look less…' *Sexy.* Her eyes slid from his as she added huskily, 'More…like a writer. And you could have shaved; you look like you haven't been to bed.'

He lifted a hand to the strong curve of his jaw covered with a layer of dark stubble and grinned. 'I haven't.' He had had an idea for his next book; when inspiration struck, he listened. He had worked through the night to get it down on paper.

'Spare me the details of your conquests,' she begged.

'Relax, nobody knows what this particular writer looks like.' Persuasive as his argument was, it didn't stop her feeling as though she had made a terrible mistake. 'And isn't this the way they want your writer to look…?'

'*Want?* That's the problem—nobody actually really *believes* he looks like a Byronic hero. You look too good to be true—they'll smell a rat.' But he wasn't true, was he? He was a fake. He was also quite simply the most impossibly good-looking male she had ever seen.

'Why, thank you.'

'Look, if you're not going to take this seriously drive away now,' she instructed. This was almost certainly going to go wrong. 'No,' she added urgently. 'Drive away anyway. This was a very bad idea.'

'Chill out,' he drawled, looking infuriatingly laid-back.

The suggestion made her see red. 'Chill out? *Chill out!*' she repeated in a shrill squeak. 'Easy for you to say. If this goes wrong people aren't going to think you're the desperate sort of woman who has to resort to hire a lover!' she declared with a groan of self-recrimination.

He scanned her anguished face, with deep-set eyes that revealed none of his feelings. 'Presumably they'll just think I'm a gigolo,' he cut back. 'Actually I wasn't aware that sleeping with you was part of the deal, but what the hell?' His sensual mouth formed a wide smile that didn't touch his eyes. 'I'll throw that in for free.'

There was a lengthy silence while Megan cleared her head of disturbing images and sounds: A darkened room, soft groans, intimate murmurs, two sweat-soaked bodies intimately entwined…. She tugged fretfully at the neck of her sweater as she fought for breath. Inch by inch she fought her way back to control…or something that passed for it.

'God, don't go sensitive on me,' she begged, still haunted by the humiliating memory of the suffocating white-hot excitement she had felt when she had imagined— She caught her breath sharply. Don't go there, Megan, she told herself sternly.

'You know I wasn't speaking literally,' she contended calmly, meeting his eyes. 'I've simply realised I can't go through with it. Late in the day, I know, but don't worry— I'll still have a word with Uncle Malcolm. He'll look at your manuscript, I promise.'

Megan heard the crunch of gravel behind her and looked over her shoulder. Her mother was advancing towards them. When her attention flickered back to her co-conspirator he was shaking his head.

'I don't want charity. I'm perfectly prepared to fulfil my side of the bargain.'

Megan looked at him with frustrated incomprehension.

His body curved towards her. 'Smile, sweetheart, and try and remember you've just found the man of your dreams.'

'Nightmares, more like.'

He laughed and touched her cheek with the back of his hand. It was so light it barely constituted a brush but Megan experienced an electrical thrill that travelled all the way to her toes. She stepped backwards, her nostrils flared as she tried not to breathe in the warm male fragrance that made her stomach flip. 'Well, I suppose we'll just have to make the best of it.'

'Is this a friend of yours, Megan?'

Megan, her hands held up in front of her, backed farther away from the tall, handsome figure who was the object of her mother's obvious appreciation.

'No—whatever gave you that idea?' The sharpness of her tone brought her mother's frowning attention to her own face. 'I've never seen him before in my life.'

He spared her a sideways look of amusement as he advanced towards her mother with his hand outstretched. 'You can know some people for years and never really know them, others you can know seconds and there's a rapport—' He broke off and gave a self-conscious laugh. 'Does that sound crazy?'

Megan was staggered to see her mother looking as though he'd just said something profound instead of something profoundly silly.

'Not at all, I know *exactly* what you mean!' Laura exclaimed.

'I think it's dangerous to go on first impressions,' Megan inserted drily.

'You're not a romantic?'

'My daughter is a cynic, Mr…'

'I'm Lucas Patrick.'

Megan drew a deep breath and squared her slender shoulders. Well, that was it! With those words he had committed them both for better or worse...she suspected the latter.

Laura took an audible deep breath and pressed her hand to her mouth. Megan felt a fresh spasm of guilt to see her mother's childlike delight.

'Of course you are.' She laughed. 'Why, this is marvellous.' A faint furrow appeared between her delicately arched brows. 'My brother told me you had flu...'

'Mal's prone to exaggeration, but then you'd know that.' Laura nodded happily. 'I had a head cold, that was all.' He looked around expectantly. 'Where is Mal?'

'Didn't he mention he couldn't make it?'

'No, that's a pity.'

Megan, who was amazed at how he had immersed himself in the part he was playing, watched with unwilling fascination as a troubled expression of suspicion spread across his handsome features.

'He did...you *were* expecting me...?' he pressed.

'Of course we were,' Laura the perfect hostess responded without skipping a beat. 'We just weren't sure when you'd be here, were we, darling?'

'No, we weren't.' Megan glanced at her watch, how many hours of this did she have to endure? The irony was this was a situation of her own making.

'So long as I'm not imposing.'

'Gracious, not at all. Actually we've been thrilled at the prospect of having you stay. Haven't we, darling?'

'*Thrilled,*' said Megan obediently.

'Megan has read all your books, haven't you?'

In full charm mode, his eyes crinkled delightfully at the corners, he turned his attention briefly to a squirming Megan. 'I think you've embarrassed...' he gave a quizzical look of apology '...Meg...?'

'Megan.'

The lack of animation in her response earned her a reproachful glare from her mother. God, he seemed to be enjoying himself…! If he wasn't a con man he'd missed his calling, she decided grimly. A man like that could convince a girl of almost anything, especially if she wanted to believe it! This was something worth keeping in mind the next time her hormones went haywire, she told herself.

'Megan will show you to your room, won't you, darling?'

'Thank you, Megan.'

'My pleasure,' she replied with equal insincerity.

'Please call me Luc,' he invited them.

'I have a French friend called, Luc,' Laura commented.

'My grandfather on my mother's side was French.'

'I knew there was something Gallic about you the moment I saw you…French men have such style,' Laura observed. 'Is your mother alive, Luc?'

'No, she died when I was nine. She named me after her own father, my grandfather.'

Behind her mother Megan shook her head and telegraphed a warning with her eyes. Her fake lover smiled back enigmatically.

'Do you speak French, Luc? I'll get someone to bring your luggage in…'

'No need, I travel light,' he said, extracting a rucksack from the back seat of the Land Rover.

'How refreshing,' Laura said, as though she were used to guests turning up carrying a rucksack that looked as if it was about to disintegrate. 'Show Luc up to the red room, Megan, then bring him down for tea… Then you can meet the other guests. Megan shot Lucas a questioning look.

'A quick shower and I'm all yours,' he promised.

Ignoring her mother's hissed instruction to, *for God's sake, smile, he's gorgeous*, she stalked towards the house with a face like thunder. She kept a tight-lipped silence until they reached the kitchen. Reaching the door that led to the back staircase, she turned and found that he was no longer at her shoulder but standing some yards away looking around the vast room.

'There really are an amazing number of original features intact,' he observed, opening the door of an original bread oven set in an alcove of the cavernous inglenook.

'Save it for my mother,' Megan, in no mood to discuss the architectural merits of her home, snapped. 'Did you have to lay it on with a trowel?' she demanded. 'Why on earth did you say you spoke French?'

'I didn't say I did.'

'You implied.'

'I do speak French.'

'Oh! And what was all that stuff about a French grandfather...?'

'My grandfather was French.'

Which was probably where he had inherited his dark Mediterranean colouring. 'You're not meant to be *you,* you're meant to be Lucas Patrick.'

'I am Lucas Patrick,' he contradicted.

Megan sighed. 'There's such a thing as overconfidence. Let's just hope the real Lucas Patrick isn't a litigious man.'

'You're an awful worrier, aren't you? Do you always assume the worst?'

'I only worry when there's something to worry about.' She scanned his dark face resentfully—he wasn't meant to be enjoying this. 'Aren't you even *slightly* nervous?'

'Not especially.'

'Well, you should be. From now on say as little as possible and follow my lead. Do you understand?' she asked him sternly. It was about time, she decided, to remind him just who was in control here. Her lips curved in a self-derisive smile; had she ever felt less in control in her life?

'Perhaps if you could write it down for me?'

'Very funny.' She sniffed. 'Come on, I suppose I'd better show you to your room. We'll take the back stairs.'

'Anyone would think you were ashamed of me,' he reproached.

Megan dished up a repressive glare but wasn't surprised

when he didn't look unduly subdued. 'There are six other people staying other than you. There's…'

When they reached the room her mother had allocated to him, she decided not to mention it was next to her own and that all the other guests were in a different wing entirely—she asked him to repeat the names of his fellow guests.

He ran his fingers across some carving in an ancient beam above the low doorway. 'Is this a test?'

'Were you actually listening to me?' she asked suspiciously.

'I was listening; your voice is like honey.'

Megan, her hand on the door handle, stilled. She was certain she had misheard what he had said. *'Pardon…?'*

'You have a beautiful voice. It flows…' His hands moved in an expressive fluid gesture before he sighed. 'I could listen to it all day…' Her voice was part of the reason he was here. Her voice—his eyes dropped—her legs and, yes, her mouth.

'Will you stop that? It isn't funny,' she croaked crossly.

His glance moved upwards to the full soft pink contours of her lips. Yes, they had all been factors—they and the fact he thought that the sexy and stuck-up Dr Semple needed to be taught a lesson. You really shouldn't judge by appearances.

'Of course what you actually say isn't always riveting,' he conceded in an attitude of regret as he ducked to enter the bedroom. He looked around with interest.

'Not bad!' He walked over to the canopied half tester and patted the mattress. 'Firm, but I like that.'

Megan responded to the fact he was looking at her body and not the bed when he said this with an irritated air. Actually she would have welcomed some irritation at that moment, if he said the things his seductive eyes managed to convey he could probably be arrested.

He fell back onto the bed and, crossing one leg over the

other, tucked his hands behind his head so that he could look at her. 'Where's your room?'

'Next door,' she admitted reluctantly.

'Handy.'

Her eyes narrowed. 'The moment you begin to believe that, you're out of here.'

To her intense annoyance he seemed to find her threat wildly amusing. Maybe, she thought darkly, it was the idea of any woman saying no to him that struck him as funny…?

'My mother is a firm believer in propinquity. I am not,' she told him drily. 'Perhaps we should lay down a few ground rules.'

'I should tell you I'm not big on rules,' he confided, stifling a yawn.

'Now there's a surprise.'

'In fact,' he admitted. 'I see a rule and I feel this almost overwhelming desire to bend it a little,' he returned, stretching with languid grace.

Megan felt her stomach muscles clench and looked at him in frustration. Without trying he could drive her crazy. What was going to happen if he took it into his head to try? It didn't bear thinking about.

Her expression fixed she braced her hand on the back of a chair covered in faded tapestry. One day she might be able to work out why she had ever thought this was a good idea. Right now that day seemed awfully far off.

'Why am I getting the idea you're not taking this seriously…?'

'I get the idea you take everything much *too* seriously,' he retorted, looking at her curiously. 'What do you do when you're not looking down a microscope?'

'I avoid men like you.' Actually she had never met a man like him. Were there any other men like him…?

'Have you seen the ghost?'

Her eyes narrowed suspiciously. 'How do you know we have a ghost?' she wanted to know.

'Don't all old places like this have a ghost…or several…?'

'I suppose they do,' she admitted. 'But I've never seen one.' And frankly a ghost would scare her less than this incredibly sexy man did. 'Now, seriously, we should lay down some ground rules.'

His head went back, revealing his strong brown throat as he laughed. Oh, God, she thought, he really is just too attractive, in a dangerous what-the-hell-is-he-going-to-do-next sort of way.

'Right, forget the rules, just keep it simple. If in doubt say nothing; better still, let me do all the talking.'

'Won't that make me appear as if I don't have an opinion of my own?'

'That's the way I like my men.'

'Under your thumb.' He extended his aforementioned digit towards her.

He had nice hands, she noticed, but then he had nice everything. 'I like the strong, silent type…' she crisply corrected. 'If in doubt just look enigmatic,' she advised. Her frown deepened as she scanned his face. 'Do you think you could do that?'

'I could.'

'But are you going to do?' Or was he going to make a total fool out of her?

'Is this suitably enigmatic…?'

'You're a natural,' she assured him drily. This was all going to go terribly wrong.

'Relax,' he advised. 'This is going to be fun.'

'If you think this is fun you have a seriously warped mind. Now just try and remember,' she pleaded, 'you're a famous author.'

'I'm a famous author,' he repeated solemnly. 'Do you believe me?'

'I know you're not…I don't count.'

'Believe me, by the end of tonight I'll be so good even you will believe I'm a famous author.'

'Let's not get too ambitious.' She glanced at her watch. 'I've got to get changed for dinner.' She extended one denim-covered leg to prove the point. 'I'll come back for you in half an hour. Don't,' she added, wagging a warning finger at him, 'move until I get here.'

Of course he did.

CHAPTER FIVE

THE French doors had been open all through dinner and the guests had drifted out onto the terrace to sip their drinks and chat. Despite the unpromising start the day had produced a perfect summer evening, warm and balmy, spoilt only by an unexpected shower, which was brief but heavy.

Luc and Megan were caught out in the open when the heavens opened. By the time they reached the shelter offered by the leafy canopy of the ancient oak tree it had stopped raining.

Luc, grinning, shook his head, sending droplets of water everywhere. 'There's something exhilarating about a summer shower.'

Easy for him to say, she thought.

Casting a resentful glance from under her lashes at Luc's classically perfect profile, she pondered the unfairness that made him look incredible with his hair plastered damply to his skull. The moisture that clung to his naturally dark skin only served to emphasise the healthy glow.

She had gone for a vintage look tonight. With a sigh she looked down with distaste at her silk calf-length skirt; it clung damply to her legs. The chiffon overskirt with its beading detail might well be ruined—pity, it had been her favourite. She could feel the excess moisture from her wet hair running in a cold trickle down her neck, she didn't even want to think about what it looked like.

Luc, his back set against the gnarled tree trunk, watched as she ran her hands down her bare arms to remove the excess moisture that clung to her pale smooth skin. She had great arms; like the rest of her body they were toned and firm.

At least the cotton halter-top wouldn't be ruined by the rain, Megan thought, concentrating on the positive. Which was more than could be said for her hair…negative thoughts refused to be *totally* banished.

'Have you ever danced?'

A line forming between her feathery brows, Megan lifted her head to look at the tall figure standing in the shadows. '*Dance?* What on earth are you talking about?' She glared up at him, bristling with suspicion.

Luc registered the antagonistic glitter in her eyes, but didn't comment on it. 'You're very graceful.'

Megan felt her cheeks grow hot. 'Don't be ridiculous.'

'I was simply making an observation. You carry yourself like a dancer. I was wondering if you trained at some point…?'

'Me, a dancer!' She looked at him as though he had gone mad. 'I'm a research scientist.'

'Does being a boffin preclude you having a sense of rhythm?'

She dealt him a look of exasperation. 'I don't dance. I…well, I did have a few lessons when I was a kid,' she conceded. 'Singing lessons too. They were meant to help my asthma.'

'Did they?'

'Well, it got a lot better.'

'You're shivering,' he observed as a fresh shudder ran visibly through her slender frame. 'I'd offer you a jacket except…' his grin made him appear almost impossibly attractive '…I'm not wearing one.'

Megan watched him place his hand flat against his chest. A shaft of agonising awareness shot through her—she was conscious of every crease and fold of the white cotton that clung like a second skin to the broad expanse of his chest. She was even more painfully conscious of the shadow of body hair sprinkled over his broad chest and the suggestion of muscular definition.

Drawing a deep breath as she struggled to regain her composure, Megan developed a deep interest in his shoes.

'You can have my shirt if you like.'

Her stomach flipped over at the thought of wearing something that was still warm from his skin, something that still bore the scent of his body.

An awful thought occurred to her. Did he know that she had just been mentally removing it? Had she been *that* obvious?

'I don't like.' It wasn't just cold that made her teeth chatter violently, it was images of Luc standing there stripped to the waist, his golden skin gleaming his... Stop this, Megan! This was not the time or place to explore her darker emotions!

'Do you want to go back to the house?' she asked him abruptly.

'What's wrong with you?' Luc enquired, scanning her rigid face.

After his performance tonight Megan couldn't believe he had the cheek to ask. Of course she had known when she had gone back to his room and found it empty that she had made a terrible mistake. When she had come downstairs and found him surrounded by a laughing, admiring crowd who were hanging on his every word all her worst fears had been realised.

'Nothing's wrong with *me*.' She sniffed.

'I thought tonight went very well.'

Megan released a laugh of bitter incredulity at this self-congratulatory comment. 'I noticed you were enjoying yourself.'

It would have been hard to miss it!

And to think she had been concerned that he might find himself a little out of his depth during dinner. The gathering had been typical of her mother's weekends. A diplomat, a poet and his lawyer wife, an actress...least said about the voluptuous Hilary, the better! A retired headmaster, and someone who had written a number one rock ballad, then entered politics.

Far from being out of his depth, her fake lover had been totally at ease. His ability to converse on a wide range of subjects with authority and ease had astounded her and impressed the hell out of everyone else.

Of course she had already known that he was intelligent. Two seconds in his company revealed that. Now she knew that, though he might have no formal education to speak of, he was widely read and amazingly erudite with a sharp wit and deadly charm. Her lips pursed; the recollection of his *deadly* charm reminded her of how angry she was.

'Come on, let's walk in the sun. It might warm you up.'

'I'm not cold,' she denied, wrapping her arms around her trembling body.

'Well, I am.'

After a short pause she followed him back out into the evening sun.

'Are you going to tell me what I've done to make you mad?'

'You need to ask?'

'I just did.'

'It might have slipped your memory that the reason—the *only* reason you are here is to establish that you find me irresistible. It might be a start if you had deigned to notice I was alive,' she ground out grimly.

Until he had asked her to take this stroll outside he had acted as though she were invisible. If she hadn't wanted to get him alone long enough to give him a piece of her mind, she'd have told him where he could stick his stroll!

His dark shapely brows moved towards his equally dark and at that moment damp hairline. 'I haven't forgotten why I'm here.'

Megan's lips tightened. His dismissive attitude really got under her skin. 'So ignoring me and spending the entire evening talking to someone else's cleavage is your idea of seeming interested? *Interesting technique,'* she admired with heavy sarcasm.

The memory of his humiliating fascination with the actress's breasts increased the angry tightness in her aching throat. She'd probably hear that woman's awful laugh in her sleep tonight, she decided, thinking of the shrill, jarring sound. Why was it that every single time men went for *obvious*…?

Not, of course, that she gave a damn if he fancied the redhead—after all, that hardly placed him in a unique category. Hilary was the sort of woman who demanded and got male attention. No, Megan's legitimate grouch was the fact he wasn't fulfilling his end of the bargain. Her acting as an introduction agent for him, a fact she had every intention of pointing out, was not part of the deal.

For a moment her angry eyes met his before her lashes swept downwards and she turned and backed away.

'Calm down, *chérie*.' He laughed, catching her arm and swinging her back.

Her shrill, 'I am calm!' made him laugh again.

'Not so as you'd notice.' The first time he'd seen her he'd wondered what she would look like without her upper-crust reserve intact and he had had ample opportunity to find out today. 'Unreasonable and ratty is actually not a bad look for you.'

Something in his voice brought Megan's eyes back to his face. 'I am neither unreasonable nor ratty!' She regarded him with simmering dislike. 'I just don't like wasting my time,' she enunciated clearly.

'I haven't been wasting anything.'

His patronising tone made her teeth clench. 'Certainly no opportunity to chat up anything in a low-cut top.' And if he thought that cleavage was natural he was in for a nasty shock.

'What we've established tonight is that you mind me showing an interest in another woman.'

His smugness made Megan want to scream.

'Your reaction was perfect,' he commended calmly.

'I didn't react,' she told him frigidly. Actually, now that she reviewed her behaviour during the interminable dinner, she had to concede that maybe her conduct hadn't been quite as adult as it might have been, but, in her defence, she had had a lot of provocation.

'God, and to think I thought you had no sense of humour. Everyone there was aware of the friction.'

Megan inhaled deeply. *'Friction…?'* she parroted.

Her cheeks turned a deeper pink as she looked significantly at the long brown fingers still curled over her bare upper arm. The fingers stayed where they were. God, but he had to be the most insensitive, thick-skinned man she had ever had the misfortune to encounter! The idea of respecting personal space was obviously a foreign concept to him.

Megan decided to bravely rise above it all. Rather than participate in an unseemly struggle, she forced herself to stand there passively even though his fingers felt like a white-hot brand against her skin.

'You would have said black if I had said white. In fact I'm not sure you didn't!' he added wryly. 'But don't worry—like I said, that's no problem. We're going to have a turbulent relationship—a classic case of opposites attracting. I predict a lot of really epic rows in public and some epic making up too.'

'If you try to make up with me you'll end up in traction,' she promised. 'And actually opposites don't attract, they end up making each other miserable. And just for the record,' she added grimly, 'I realise that you think you're God's gift, but, trust me—the only thing I minded tonight was not being given value for money.'

'Well, let me remind you, *chérie*, that you haven't bought me.' His narrowed gaze suddenly turned molten silver as he scanned her angry upturned features. 'You're giving me

something I want and I'm giving you something you want…
or I could if you let me.'

The suggestive drawl in his deep, musical voice sent a
surge of heat through Megan's rigid frame.

'That remains to be seen,' she gulped. Unable to bear the
contact for another moment without crawling clear out of
her skin, she tugged her arm free of his clasp. 'And don't
keep calling me *chérie*! I am not your darling and I have a
name,' she said, standing there rubbing the invisible imprint
of his fingers on her flesh.

'And claws…' he observed in a soft, sibilant voice that
made the invisible downy hairs on her skin stand erect.

Luc's silvered glance touched her small hands, which
now hung tensely at her sides, balled tightly into fists. Her
incredible eyes, shadowed in the fading light, were fixed on
his face and her body language screamed hostility.

Against all the odds he experienced a surge of protective warmth. The reaction was inexplicable, but amazingly
strong.

'Chemistry, like ours, usually produces a few sparks…a
lot if you're lucky,' he added as an amused afterthought.

'Not for me it doesn't,' Megan rebutted firmly. She
frowned. She hoped he wasn't forgetting this was all make
believe. It would be very embarrassing if she had to remind
him.

Her frown deepened.

'You don't like sparks…?'

She didn't smile in response to his teasing tone, but looking at him standing there, so incredibly gorgeous, made her
more conscious of the curious little ache, actually not so
little, inside her. If she was honest not so curious considering he was just about just about the most attractive man
on the planet.

'I'm not a combustible person,' she told him before con-
sulting the slim watch on her wrist. She had no intention of
apologising just because she wasn't some sort of smoulder-

ing sex bomb like Hilary. 'We ought to be heading back, people will be wondering where we've got to.'

He smiled thinly. 'They're meant to wonder what we're up to. It's all part of my master plan.'

'Don't you think under the circumstances you ought to consult me about your master plan?' she queried tartly.

'What, and lose the advantage of surprise?'

'Surprise?' she repeated, a groove appearing above the bridge of her nose as she worriedly pondered his meaning.

'You're really not a very good actress.'

'That's because deceit doesn't come as easily to me as it does to you,' she retorted. 'And,' she added, 'I don't think I want to be surprised…actually, I *know* I don't want to be surprised, especially by you.' Fortunately Luc didn't appear to have registered her unwise addition.

'Don't worry, I can think on my feet. I'm actually thought to be quite good at improvising.'

'It's the thought of you improvising that worries me.'

He slanted her an amused look. Megan pursed her lips and glared back coldly. She couldn't share his light-hearted approach; this fly-by-the-seat-of-your-pants thing just wasn't her. Unlike him she wasn't the type of person who got a buzz from living close to the edge. The constant fear of being caught out didn't give her an adrenaline rush, just a sick feeling of dread in the pit of her stomach.

'There is one thing I wouldn't mind knowing…' he admitted with a frown.

The corners of his sensually sculpted lips twitched as his glance dropped. 'You're not a bad-looking woman…' came the verdict after several uncomfortable moments.

Megan batted her eyelashes. 'Wow, thanks!'

Underneath the gushing insincerity she was badly spooked by the way her body instantly reacted to his slow, insolent perusal. Could you class the strength leaving your shaking lower limbs and the ignition of a hot burning flame deep in your belly as *spooked*? Or was it something more serious? She was thinking terminal blind lust here...

The acid interjection brought an answering flicker of humour to his deep-set eyes but didn't deflect him from his purpose.

'So I'm assuming that there are men in your life.'

Megan was continually amazed and *increasingly* aggravated by his apparent belief that being a co-conspirator gave him the right to delve into all personal aspects of her life. She watched his expression grow reflective as he focused his thoughts on the subject of her love life.

'Men compose half the population; it would be hard to avoid them even if I wanted to.'

Luc acted as though she hadn't spoken—something she had noticed he had a habit of doing—as he continued. 'But you don't bring them home to meet Mummy. Now I wonder why...?' One dark brow elevated he turned his speculative gaze upon her face. *'Married...?'*

Megan stiffened in outrage. 'You th...th...think that I would go out with a m...m...married man?' she demanded.

Luc silently studied her rigid chalk white features for a moment before shrugging. 'Apparently not,' he observed drily. 'I've got a mate...your classic commitment phobic who only dates married women. I thought that might be your problem.'

'That you have that sort of mate does not surprise me.'

'He's a reformed character since he met the love of his life. So if they're not married...what's the problem? Not the right social class? Don't they know which fork to use?'

The amazing thing was he didn't even seem to be aware he'd insulted her!

Megan fixed him with a look of seething dislike. If she still had some of the power that the ancestors he despised had enjoyed and, she was the first to admit, abused, she would have wielded them in this instance.

Contemplating having him shipped off to some distant colony, preferably one infested by insects that would bite his smooth, sleek hide, brought a grim smile to her lips. As she contemplated the vee of smooth olive-toned skin visible at the base of his throat her smile wobbled.

For some reason she found herself thinking about an infamous female ancestor of hers. The scandalous Lady Edith who was reputed to have enjoyed the services of several lusty local lads, one of whom was said to have fathered her son who had inherited the estate. Edith, with her shameless appetites, would have had different methods of taming a stroppy male. She would have undoubtedly considered the banishment of Luc, with his sleek, dark and incredibly sexy looks, a waste.

Edith would have found a place for him in her bed.

'Does a bit of rough do it for you?'

The disturbing mental image of Luc tumbling amongst silk sheets with the sloe-eyed lady who looked down haughtily from a painting in the library vanished in a flash. Megan released a long sibilant hiss of fury.

'Go jump in the lake,' she urged pleasantly.

Luc grinned at her venom. 'It's a reasonable question,' he protested.

'My personal life is none of your business,' she told him frigidly.

'It is if you have a secret boyfriend hovering in the background somewhere,' Luc retorted. 'If someone is likely to try and knock my lights out I'd like to know about it.'

She gave a disdainful laugh. 'So this is about you being scared, is it? I should have known,' she sneered scornfully.

He sighed. 'My secret is out.'

'Well, you can relax. Your pretty profile is not in any danger.' Actually he looked, in stark contrast to herself, totally relaxed, especially considering the barrage of abuse she was aiming at his dark head.

'No jealous boyfriend lurking…?'

She half turned then with a hard laugh flung over her shoulder.

'No boyfriend full stop. And before you progress to the painfully predictable male, *you-must-be-a-lesbian* line…I'm not.' She stopped dead and frowned. 'I've not the faintest idea why I'm explaining myself to you,' she admitted angrily.

His shoulders lifted. 'Don't look at me, but go on—I'm finding it educational.'

Megan fixed him with a narrowed resentful glare. It was actually good advice—*looking at him,*…even hearing his deep drawl, was a recipe for stress and mental disintegration.

'I have no time for a boyfriend. As I have already told you, at this point in my life I want to concentrate all my energies on my career.' It made Megan so furious, if she had been a man her decision would not have caused any raised eyebrows.

'*And…*' he prompted when she stayed silent.

'There is no *and*,' she told him crossly.

'A love life or a career is not generally considered an either-or decision.'

'For me they are.'

'Aren't women meant to be big on multitasking?'

'That rumour was undoubtedly started by a man who was more than happy for his partner to run herself ragged trying to do all the things he didn't have time for.'

Luc looked amused. 'You could be right, but you were engaged so you couldn't always have felt that way.'

Unconsciously Megan's hand went to her cheek.

'How did you know about Brian?'

'Your mother told me; she was pretty gutted that you chucked him.'

'She got over it.' Frankly she didn't care if he thought she was a cold, heartless bitch.

'No job is a substitute for sex.'

The way Brian did it, it was. 'Did I say I was celibate?'

His brows lifted sardonically. 'Your mother thinks you are.'

Megan flushed. 'This is the twenty-first century, Luc,' she told him, injecting scorn into her voice. 'Does everything have to be about sex?' When did I start panting? Megan pressed a hand to her throat and made a concerted effort to slow the shallow, rapid character of her breathing.

Knuckles pressed to the slight indent in his chin, Luc pretended to consider the matter. 'Yes.' Eyes that seemed scarily *knowing* zeroed in on her face.

Now she wasn't just panting as if she'd been running a marathon, she was sweating too. Did everybody find his mouth as fascinating as she did? Megan wondered as she watched one corner drop in a cynical smirk.

'Few things in life are constant, but sex is,' he contended in a throaty purr that ought in a fair world to have been preceded by a 'there are flashing lights in this film' type warning for the susceptible.

Megan was definitely susceptible! The moisture between her aching thighs was ample evidence of that.

'It doesn't really matter what decade or, for that matter, what century; it doesn't change. Scratch the surface of the most sophisticated male and you'll find a man who is thinking about sex. Take me, for instance…'

This smooth suggestion wrenched an instinctive croak of protest from Megan's throat. He angled a questioning brow at her flushed, uncomfortable face.

'I don't think I will, if it's all the same to you. You may be right about men, they probably haven't evolved beyond the Neanderthal, but women—of course, I can only speak personally—can rise above their hormones. We've learnt how to work the system like men have been doing for years. A man doesn't date a woman with the primary intention of settling down and starting a family. Why should it be different for a woman?'

'So you're telling me that any sexual needs you have are satisfied by no-strings one-night stands.'

Megan wasn't, she had been blustering, but she was quite prepared to take the credit for this idea. In reality the idea of emotionless sex was not something she warmed to, but he didn't need to know that.

'You have a problem with that?' she gritted belligerently.

'Men and women are driven by very different biological needs. A man has the basic urge to impregnate a woman, to nurture.'

'That's remarkably sexist...' But sadly probably essentially true...is that me talking or my conditioning? In the end does it really matter? I am, and I don't do casual sex.

'No, that's a biological fact,' he stated bluntly. 'I'd say if you try to act like a man you stand every chance of being badly hurt.'

'On the contrary it's women who fall in love with men and idolise them who get hurt when they...' Aware that her comment had awakened a speculative gleam in his eyes she checked her emotional flow abruptly and began to examine her linked fingers.

'Who did you idolise?'

'We were all young and stupid once.'

The silence between them lengthened.

'What's through there?'

Relieved that he had dropped the subject, she turned and saw him lifting the latch on a tall wrought-iron gate half hidden in the ivy-covered wall.

'It's an entrance to the workshops,' she replied absently, 'but this isn't the way back to the house. Where are you going now?'

'What's the hurry?' he asked, skimming her a questioning look before pushing the gate open to reveal a courtyard.

CHAPTER SIX

MEGAN followed Luc into the attractive flower-bedecked courtyard, her heels clicking loudly on the wet cobbled surface. 'It used to be the old stables.'

'And now it's...?'

'A bit of a tourist attraction.' She saw him lift his hand to his eyes to peer into the darkened window of the forge. 'That's Sam's studio.'

'Sam...?'

'He was a bus driver, now he makes terrific wrought-iron stuff to order.'

A local potter had approached her father ten years earlier with a view to him renting her workspace. The idea had snowballed...

'And the others...?' Luc's expansive gesture took in the rest of the quadrangle.

'There are about ten workshops here now all used by local artists and craftsmen,' she told him proudly. 'They double as workspace and a shop front. There's a really marvellous community feel about the place. People can come and watch them work and, if they like it, buy what they see. There are also occasional workshops where you can learn to throw a pot, that sort of thing. Local schools frequently come. It's proved rather successful.'

So much so that the planning authorities were considering an application to extend the operation into the adjoining granary providing tearooms and an art gallery.

'Very enterprising.'

'It's a non-profit-making operation,' she added defensively. Wanting to gain his approval just a little too much. 'We charge a nominal rent and—'

'Hold up,' he interrupted. 'I may think the aristocracy is an anachronism in this day and age, but that doesn't mean I assume that they are *all* out to subjugate the masses.

'That's remarkably open-minded of you, L...'

'Luc,' he prompted, watching with a glimmer of a smile in his deep-set eyes as she bit her lip. 'It is my name.'

'You don't have to *live* the role you—' She broke off and gave a grimace as a stab of pain shot through her right ankle.

'Are you all right?'

Megan waved aside his concern and flexed her right foot. 'Fine, just turned my ankle, that's all.' She frowned at the heel that had got jammed in a crevice in the uneven cobbled surface. She pulled but it didn't budge. She swore softly under her breath. 'These things are lethal,' she complained.

'But very sexy.' His lashes lifted and the glitter she saw reflected in the platinum depths of his eyes made her heart thud.

Flushing, Megan lowered her gaze and let the skirt she was holding, gathered bunched in her hand, fall with a damp, silken slither to the ground.

'I'm not prepared to cripple myself in the pursuit of wolf-whistles...*normally*,' she added drily.

Megan had no self-esteem issue, she knew that some men found her attractive, but even while she had been carefully selecting her outfit earlier she had been aware that, no matter what she wore, it wasn't going to make her look drop-dead gorgeous. It was a fact of life that men who looked like Luc were not generally seen with women who looked the way she did, so tonight she had made an effort.

'I haven't inherited my mother's fashion sense or, for that matter, her figure.' Forgetting for a split second whom she was talking to, she pressed her hands flat to her nicely formed but not impressive bosom.

Luc's eyes followed her gesture and his lips twitched. There was no hint of apology in her gesture, just the merest suggestion of wistfulness. 'You look fine to me.'

The notion that he might have thought she had been fishing for compliments brought a deep flush to her fair skin and a look of horror to her face.

'I can do without your approval.' Do without, but wouldn't it be nice to have it…? Megan's glance dropped as the thought surfaced unbidden to her mind.

His heavy sigh—a mixture of resignation and irritation, brought her head up.

Eyes holding hers, he set his shoulders against the wall behind him. With his weight braced on one leg, he crossed one ankle over the other. The man, she admitted, could slouch like nobody else she had ever met.

'Do you actually want this thing to work?'

The question startled her out of her contemplation of his effortlessly elegant body language. 'Of course I want this to work. Why wouldn't I?'

His lips formed a twisted smile as he scanned her face. 'Good question. Well, if you do want a result it's going to require a bit of effort.'

Effort? Did he have any idea how much effort she was making? 'What do you mean "effort"?'

'Well, for starters you're going to have to put some work in on the adoring love slave front…'

The awful Brian had expected if not demanded his bride-to-be's uncritical adoration as his due, and he had received it. That was, until Megan had woken up to the fact that he was an inadequate creep, and furthermore she didn't love him. Megan fixed Luc with a glare and tossed her head, a disdainful sneer twisting her lips.

'What's wrong with your face?' he asked, watching her rub the left side of her face. His eyes narrowed; it wasn't the first time he had noticed her doing that. The first time had been…when…?

Megan's hand fell self-consciously away. She tried to turn but her foot held her fast. 'Damn…damn,' she cursed.

'Did he hit you?'

An expression of total shock chased across her pale features as she focused on his face. His expression was blank.

It wasn't the reminder of that contemptuous backhander that Brian had delivered when she had explained that she would not be giving up her job or marrying him that brought the look of dismay to her face, but this man's startling perception. It was almost as if he could read her mind at times.

'Pardon…?' she faltered.

'You heard me,' he intoned grimly.

'Once,' she admitted, because one look at his face revealed he wasn't going to let this one go.

Brian had said it wouldn't happen again, but Megan had seen the mask slip and had recognised his tearful apology for the lie it had been. In a weird way it had been a relief; it had been much easier to walk away with a clear conscience.

Luc struggled to keep his expression neutral; it wasn't easy. He couldn't remember the last time he had felt anything like this sort of blinding rage, this desire to rip someone limb from limb, and laugh while he was doing it.

'Why didn't you tell your mother the scumbag hit you? She talked like he was the second coming.'

'It would have upset her and…I suppose I was… ashamed—? Irrational, I know, but I'm not a victim.'

For a long painful moment Luc looked down into her face. His shoulders lifted. 'No, just a stubborn idiot,' he gritted. 'Not all men are vicious bullies.'

'Oh, God, I know that!' she exclaimed. 'Don't run away with the impression I'm emotionally scarred or anything. Damn, damn thing…' she addressed her curse to her shoe.

'What are you doing?' Her voice was high-pitched with alarm as he hunkered down in front of her. She stiffened as Luc took hold of her ankle. Megan swayed like a sapling caught in a strong gust of wind then, eyes half closed, mouth slightly open, she took a series of shallow breaths and she forced herself to remain still.

'This situation requires a light touch.'

Well, he had that, she was forced to concede as slither after shivery slither of sensation sliced like a knife through her helplessly receptive body. It was no longer possible for her to ignore the heat, specifically the heat between her thighs. When his fingertips brushed against the fine, almost invisible denier that covered the skin of her calf she had to bite her lip to stop herself gasping out loud. The situation made it hard to think straight—actually, it made it hard to think full stop!

'It's stuck fast,' came his oddly muffled verdict after a few moments.

The dull thud in her ears made his voice seem to come from a long way off to Megan.

'Tell me something I didn't know,' she grunted, trying desperately to marshal her thoughts.

The man kneeling at her feet lifted his head. In the fading light she didn't see the lines of darker colour scoring his high slashing cheekbones, she could just see his eyes…and his mouth and…*oh, God*—!

'You should take them off.'

Anything you say. God, please let me not have said that out loud! She ran the tip of her tongue nervously over her dry lips. 'What…?' she croaked.

'The shoes,' he replied. 'You should take them off. The stockings too,' he added as an afterthought.

'How did you know?' She stopped and shook her head blushing deeply. Far better, under the circumstances, *not* to know how he knew when a woman was wearing stockings and not tights.

'Don't worry, I don't have X-ray vision.'

'I wasn't worried.' The knot of heat low in her belly made it hard for her to concentrate on what she was doing and a second later she found herself standing in one shoe, teetering awkwardly to one side without having any clear recollection of how she had got to be in that position.

'For God's sake…' His voice impatient, Luc caught her hands in his and placed them firmly on his own shoulders. 'Hold onto me.'

It was either that or fall down in an ungainly heap.

'Give me a minute,' she heard him say. 'That's it.' Hazily she saw him rise, her shoe minus the heel in his triumphant grasp. 'The shoe's a write-off, I'm afraid.'

She shook her head; the loss of a shoe was the least of her problems! Her response to this man was less easy to dismiss. In the gathering dusk it was impossible to read the expression on his lean, hard-boned face.

'It doesn't matter.' Awkwardness made her voice abrupt. Minus her heels she only just topped his shoulders. The illusion of being small and dainty was one she shouldn't in this enlightened age of equality have found attractive…*Shouldn't…!*

The impressive shoulders on which her hands were still hanging, quite unnecessarily, flexed and she felt the powerful muscles clench.

She uncurled her fingers. As if reluctant to lose the contact, her fingertips trailed slowly down the front of his open necked shirt. She felt his lean, hard body tense before she lost contact. It made her cringe to imagine that her action might have been interpreted as deliberately provocative, because she had no control whatever over her actions.

'I suppose we ought to go back.' The thread of reluctance she heard in her own voice made Megan's eyes widen in alarm. Anyone listening would have been excused for assuming she wanted her pulse to carry on racing too fast…that she wanted to prolong the moment.

And you don't…?

'You could be right.' she heard him concede. 'Do you always do the right thing, *ma chérie…*?'

Just this once Megan let the endearment pass, when he said it in that deep smoky voice of his it sounded like a caress.

With a sigh she lifted her head, her eyes meshed with enigmatic silvered orbs that made her heart pound slow and strong… Luc; the name might be no more real than his supposed attraction for her, but strangely fitted him.

He really was the most incredible-looking man!

'I try to.' She gave a shaky little laugh as her eyes slid from his. 'I won't waste my breath asking you the same thing.'

Luc looked like a man for whom *not* doing the right thing was one of life's guiding principles. Was the danger part of his attraction? Had she been playing it safe for so long that she couldn't resist what was dark, dangerous and available?

'I try to do what comes naturally.' His explanation was not soothing. 'We should definitely go back, only first…' Luc's dark head bent as he framed her face between his hands. She felt his breath fan her cheek as he fitted his mouth to hers. Megan's eyelashes fluttered against her cheek as her hand came up to cover one of his.

She murmured his name; the sound was lost against his mouth. The pressure of his lips was gentle but insistent; his mouth was cool and firm against her own.

Luc drew back, his lashes lifted from the angle of his knife-edged cheekbones as he examined the passion-flushed features of the woman who stood in the circle of his arms. He gave an almost imperceptible nod of satisfaction.

'*Now* you look like a woman who's shared a few illicit kisses in the moonlight.'

She was floating; she was on fire, every inch of her skin was prickling with the heat of desire. His words had the same effect as an icy shower.

'There is no moon and I will not be used by you or anyone else!' she declared in a low, passionate voice.

'I wasn't using you; I was kissing you and,' he added with a slow, contemplative smile, 'I was enjoying it.'

'How nice for you that you're happy in your work. Next time maybe you might like to ask whether I *want* to be kissed,' she told him, dragging a hand across her mouth. The symbolic gesture just reminded her of how sensitised and tender her lips felt.

Luc, no longer languid, looked suddenly incredibly furious. 'Are you suggesting I kissed you against your will?'

'Not *exactly*,' she conceded, her glance dropping guiltily from his outraged face.

'Good,' he bit back, not sounding much mollified. 'Because I don't need a signed affidavit to know when a woman wants to be kissed. I know and you wanted it.'

The shocking sound of her hand connecting with his cheek resounded across the courtyard. Megan's hand went to her mouth as her eyes travelled from the livid mark developing on his lean cheek to his eyes, they told her nothing more than his blank expression.

'That was unforgivable,' she said, totally contrite. The fact that physically she was much weaker than him was in her eyes no excuse for her loss of control. She felt deeply ashamed. 'You're right.' Humiliation sat like a leaden weight in her stomach. 'I *did* want you to kiss me.'

'You did?'

She nodded; his expression was as unrevealing as his tone. 'That's why I was so angry...not with you,' she hastened to assure him. 'With me.'

It was ironic—she had been busy getting het up worrying that Luc was getting too immersed in his role, when in reality *he* wasn't the one getting reality mixed up with fiction; she was the one letting her fantasies take control!

Luc watched as her slender shoulders sagged.

'Obviously this thing is not going to work; it's not your fault.' Luc, after all, had done everything she had asked of him. 'It's me.'

'You wanted me to kiss you...?' A muscle in his hollow cheek clenched.

Megan looked at him, her frustration showing. Had he not heard anything she had said after that? She hoped he had; she didn't much fancy grovelling all over again. In fact she refused to, she decided with a spurt of defiance.

'Well, I wasn't exactly averse to it,' she admitted gruffly. 'I appreciate you were doing what you thought I wanted.'

'I was doing what I *hoped* you wanted,' he contradicted, sliding his hands down her slender back until they came to rest on the firm curve of her bottom. His grin flashed out minus the edge of cool dispassion and mockery she had grown accustomed to. 'Now I know…'

'Know what?' She gave a startled gasp as he drew her towards him until their hips collided. She inhaled sharply as hot desire zapped through her body; he was rock-hard against the softness of her belly. An energising wave zapped through her body, her knees sagged and Luc took up the slack ably, wrapping one strong arm around her ribcage.

'Know you want this.' He ground his hips gently against her abdomen. Megan's head fell back bonelessly as the silent groan locked in her tight throat struggled to escape. Mutely, she nodded. Not pretending any more, felt strangely liberating.

His big hand cupped the back of her skull, drawing her face up to his. Looking into his platinum-grey eyes made her dizzy.

'This is quite spectacularly crazy.'

She tried to swallow but couldn't. She couldn't stop shaking, tremors that ran like febrile shudders through her entire body. Insane it might be, but she could actually *feel* his voice. No man had ever excited her this way…up until now she had thought she wasn't capable of feeling this way. What if it never happened again?

The thought spurred her into direct action. 'I don't do crazy, Luc.' Her lashes lifted and she looked him straight in the eyes. 'But I could learn.'

Luc's nostrils flared as he sucked in a startled gasp.

CHAPTER SEVEN

MEGAN'S head dropped. God, she'd been too direct...she'd shocked Luc and small wonder! Her comment had been only slightly less subtle than screaming, *Take me!* Just because you fancy the socks off him doesn't mean he feels the same way!

Teeth clenched, she resisted the hand that curved under her chin and his soft but firm instruction, 'Look at me, Megan.' Until finally with an exasperated sigh she allowed her face to be tilted up to his.

The mixture of embarrassment and defiance faded from her face as she looked at him. He was smiling a smile so fierce so sweet that she felt as if she'd melt. His fingertips ran along the curve of her jaw and she turned her head into his hand and kissed his palm.

'I'll teach you,' he rasped.

This time there was nothing vaguely tentative or gentle about his lips or the probing tongue that slid between her parted lips. Electrified, Megan kissed him back with a driven desperation. Whimpering softly into his mouth, she wound her arms tightly around his neck.

Her mind had stopped functioning. She was simply responding to the primitive need that made her plaster her aching breasts against his chest, pressing her hips into his. She couldn't get close enough to him. She had no idea of how long they stood there kissing with a frenzied, frantic desperation.

At some point they must have stopped kissing long enough to end up standing beneath the porch of one of the stable workshops.

'My God, don't stop!' she pleaded, her self-control a dim

and distant memory by the time his mouth lifted from her own. She lifted her dazed, passion-glazed eyes to his dark face. 'You're...I feel...' She struggled to articulate the hunger that coursed like a forest fire through her body.

'My God, but you're incredible,' he breathed, scanning her face with blazing eyes.

Megan felt his hand slide under her skirt at the same time her back made contact with the ivy-covered wall. His heavy, warm body pressed her into the hard surface.

'Oh, my God!' she groaned, biting her lip.

She felt the pressure ease. 'Am I hurting you?' he asked thickly.

Megan slid her hands under his shirt across his satiny hard skin. She released a shuddering sigh as the muscles contracted under her questing fingers. She felt him suck in a deep breath as the fabric parted. Squirming, she pressed her aching breasts against his bare flesh.

She ran the tip of her tongue over the outline of her swollen lips. 'You're killing me.'

A low feral groan that made her hot skin break out in a rash of goosebumps emerged from Luc's throat as he responded to the sexual challenge glittering in her eyes. 'That's not what I want to do to you.'

'What do you want to do?' she asked in a throaty whisper.

'This, for starters.' His fingers reached the bare skin above the lacy tops of her hold-ups and she let out a deep moan as her stomach muscles contracted violently.

'You're...you're...'

'What am I?' he prompted throatily.

Impossible to resist. Megan shook her head, the ache between her legs intensifying as her eyes dropped down the length of his incredible body. She was aware of every hard inch of him. She wanted every hard inch of him.

Megan blinked to bring his face into focus; her breath was coming in shallow, uneven gasps. The skin was drawn tight across his high cheekbones. His dark lashes lifted, revealing an almost feral glitter of raw hunger in his eyes.

'You're to die for.'

A grin of savage male triumph spread across his face. 'Not just yet, Megan,' he responded, loosing the tie of her halter top with one hand while touching the dampness between her legs with the other.

He was breathing hard and fast but Megan, who was doing the same, didn't notice. She was conscious only of the heat in her blood and Luc stroking her, driving her crazy in a beautiful, mindless way.

Yanking down the neck of her halter top to her waist, he dropped his molten gaze to the pouting contours of her small pink-tipped breasts. The cool air felt like velvet against her sensitised skin. His tongue as he moved it across each erect nipple felt like fire.

She felt like fire.

She reached for him, touching the hardness through the material of his trousers. Luc's breath started to come even faster. Megan moaned softly as she felt his hard male body surge against her hand.

After a few seconds he took her hands in his and holding them above her head, pressed her into the wall. 'I can't give you slow and sweet,' he admitted, sliding a finger inside her. Megan's body arched as she gasped and sobbed his name. The muscles in her thighs were trembling violently.

'I'll take whatever you have. So long as I feel you inside me in the next ten seconds I don't care…I don't care about anything!' she declared wildly.

'Hush,' he soothed, kissing her mouth. 'I will…I will,' he promised throatily. Megan was vaguely conscious of the sound of him adjusting his clothing as she kissed him back and told him she loved everything about him.

She felt him against her soft belly, hard and aroused; she had no time to feel concerned about *how* aroused before he thrust up into her, filling her with his thickness.

'My God,' he rasped, his breath hot against her neck. 'You're so tight.'

She was in a state of mindless pleasure as he moved inside her, slowly at first, then faster and harder the way she wanted, the way she told him she wanted. The tremors began to build inside then burst into an incredible orgasmic release just seconds before she felt Luc's hot release inside her.

They sagged to the floor together in an exhausted tangle of limbs. Utterly spent, her knees still trembling, Megan let her cheek rest against his bare chest. The whorls of dark hair tickled her nose. Luc's arms were around her, and she closed her eyes and listened to the thud of his heartbeat... Gradually it slowed to a steady thud. His skin was hot and slightly damp; the faint scent of the cologne he had used earlier mixed with the musky male scent of his body.

The intimacy was like nothing she had ever experienced in her life.

Luc placed his hand under her chin and lifted her face. Megan waited for the embarrassment she had expected to feel to surface; it didn't. The most conventional sex with Brian had left her feeling embarrassed and always self-conscious.

'I've dreamed about doing that since the first moment I saw you,' he told her. 'But then,' he said, stroking her hair back from her face, I expect you already knew that.'

'No,' she said honestly. 'I didn't even know I wanted to do it until just now.'

Luc laughed at this disingenuous confession and got to his feet.

Shyly she took the hand he offered and let him heave her to her feet. She tilted her head back to look into his dark features. 'Is it possible to fall in love with someone you don't know?'

Immediately Luc's dark features clenched. He looked as though she had just slapped his face.

Megan gave a shaky laugh. If you could die from sheer embarrassment she would be stretched out right now. 'That was rhetorical, no answer expected or required…in case you were wondering…'

'Turn around,' he said abruptly.

Megan did as he asked and felt his fingers brush against the bare skin of her back as he fastened her halter top. She shivered and he swore softly and fumbled the knot.

'What's wrong? I didn't mean me…I…oh, God…!'

He kissed the nape of her neck, then, hands on her shoulders, spun her around. His eyes burned as though lit from within.

'What's wrong is you make me…' He made a visible effort to control himself, then with a sigh of frustration dragged a hand through his hair. 'I think it would be a good idea if we got back to the house.'

'Of course.'

As they neared the house she could hear the sound of laughter and voices; someone was playing the piano, and not very well. There was woodsmoke in the air so she assumed that the fire in the enormous grate had been lit. The drawing room with its panelled walls and views out over the lake was her favourite room but the thought of going into it now made her cringe inside. There was simply no way she could act as if nothing had happened between her and Luc.

Megan shook her head and started to back away. 'I can't go in there.'

Luc overruled her. 'Of course you can,' he said, grabbing her hand. As he was pulling her towards him the automatic sensors on the exterior light kicked in.

She began to smooth down her clothes nervously. 'I look a mess,' she fretted. 'This skirt…'

'You look gorgeous.' Megan knew she had never looked gorgeous in her life. She opened her mouth to tell him that she didn't need to hear pretty lies when her eyes collided with his.

'And don't worry about the skirt—I'll be taking it off for you as soon as we can decently make our excuses,' he promised throatily.

A shiver ran through her from the top of her head to her curling toes. Megan doubted *decency* had ever been used to describe a more indecent plan. 'You think you're going to spend the night with me?' At least her embarrassing introduction of love had not put him off totally.

'Don't you?'

She felt his hand on her cheek and her head lifted. Their eyes met, and Megan was overwhelmed, not just by the stab of sexual desire that nailed her to the spot, but by the totally unexpected tenderness in his eyes.

She felt tears prickle at the back of her eyes and blinked rapidly; her throat literally ached with emotion. This is crazy—I don't even know the man! Actually the only thing she knew for sure about him was he was a good liar…*and an even better lover*.

'I wasn't sure you'd want to…?'

'I've wanted you since the first moment I saw you.' He wound a damp honey coloured curl around one long brown finger. 'I wanted to pull you down onto the sofa and make love to you right then.'

Megan began to shake. She was still blinking in a bemused fashion when a loud, familiar voice suddenly rang out.

'There they are…'

Luc lifted his hand and waved to the figure standing at the window. 'No escape now,' he said without looking at Megan.

Her mother had obviously been waiting for them. 'Where did you two get to?' she demanded as they stepped into the hallway. She focused on her daughter and gave a wince.

'Your hair, Megan...' she rebuked with a despairing shake of her head.

'I like it that way.'

The comment brought both women's attention to Luc's face.

'You do?' Laura said in a startled voice.

Megan assumed that Luc did something to confirm his strange taste to her mother, but she didn't trust herself to check it out for herself. How could anyone look at her and not *know*? She felt as though her shame were written all over her face except that, bizarrely, she didn't feel any shame at all.

'What happened to you?'

Good question. Megan took a deep breath.

'And where are your shoes?'

'Slight mishap—we got caught in the rain,' she said, lifting a self-conscious hand to her tousled head. 'I'll go and fix this.' If only other things could be fixed with a brush and hairdryer. What had happened to caution, and why... *how* did she feel so elated?

'Never mind about that now, it's fine, come along in,' Laura urged, shepherding them across the hall. 'You'll never guess who is here...'

'Who?' Megan didn't much feel like playing guessing games or being polite to guests, but she managed to feign interest.'

Her heart just about stopped when Luc suggested silkily, 'The real Lucas...?' His hand shot out to steady Megan as she stumbled. 'Oops! Watch your step there, Megan.'

'He has such a delightfully dry sense of humour,' Laura observed.

'He is so, *so* dead,' Megan added with a fixed smile. Her reproachful eyes lifted to his face. The innocent expression she encountered was about as believable as a sincere politician. 'You won't be laughing then,' she predicted grimly as she brushed the restraining fingers from her arm.

'What did you say, darling?'

Megan lifted her voice and said in a flat monotone, 'I said he's a laugh a minute.' She ignored the rumble of soft laughter at her elbow and deliberately didn't look at him.

A second later as Laura pushed open the drawing-room door she learnt who the mystery guest was. Horror immediately froze her to the spot. Megan was no coward, but suddenly she wanted to take to her heels and run!

Her scam was about to be exposed in the most horrifying way. Would she be facing public humiliation and litigation or was the author going to see the funny side of this? Did he possess a sense of humour? It wasn't as if they had harmed his reputation—maybe he might even be flattered, as someone who looked fairly ordinary might be if they found themselves being played by Brad Pitt in the film of their life story.

It was, admittedly quite a maybe.

Megan wasn't sure if she was going to throw up or faint. She angled a quick glance at the tall man beside her. He was looking at her uncle Mal, effortlessly projecting his usual unbelievable level of cool and charisma. If she had been the author with a taste for privacy she might have considered paying Luc to be her public face, but the real Lucas Patrick might not see it quite the same way.

'Uncle Mal, this is quite a surprise.' Megan wondered why the presence of her uncle should explain her mother's suddenly bright eyes, and air of barely suppressed excitement.

The figure who had risen from his seat at the piano as they'd entered came towards her. Handsome despite his thickening middle and thinning hairline, Malcolm…looked very like his younger sister.

'Oh, yes, your uncle turned up,' her mother said, dismissing her brother with a slightly irritated shrug. 'But it was Jean Paul that I was talking about.' She drew forward with a flourish the old family friend Megan had known since she was a child.

The distinguished, silver-haired Frenchman smiled at Megan. 'You look very lovely tonight, Megan,' he said with smooth Gallic charm.

Her uncle was less smooth but also complimentary. 'Megan, my dear girl, you do look well,' he told his stricken-faced niece before his glance moved past her to the tall figure who stood with one hand lightly touching her shoulder. His smile was replaced by a look of puzzlement.

'I didn't believe it when Laura said my most famous client had turned up on her doorstep,' Malcolm remarked, shaking his head.

Megan, feeling physically sick, interposed herself between the two men in an instinctively protective gesture. She couldn't let Luc take the blame, not when this had been her idea. Two bright patches of colour appeared on her cheeks.

'I can explain…' She paused, hoping for some inspired explanation, one that would let her emerge *not* looking like a duplicitous idiot who had to bribe someone to pretend to be her boyfriend.

There was no inspiration.

'It was my idea…'

'To show me the art workshops,' Luc completed smoothly for her. Hands thrust casually in his pockets, he stepped forward.

At a time like this I can admire his bottom…I've clearly become a candidate for intensive therapy, she decided despairingly.

'The flu turned out to be just a head cold, Mal. I popped a bit of vitamin C and here I am. I've been made to feel every bit as welcome as you said I would be. All that was missing was you.'

To Luc's amusement Malcolm shifted uncomfortably from one foot to the other, looking more like a guilty schoolboy than head of one of the most successful publishing houses in the country.

'Sorry, I was…urgently, called away…business…only got back this morning. Naturally when I heard you were here…' He leaned towards the younger man and murmured, 'What the hell are you up to, Luc?'

'A very good question, Mal.' His attention drifted momentarily towards Megan. He didn't elaborate.

Megan looked from one man to the other, she pressed her fingers to her temples to relieve the growing pressure. This didn't make sense.

'You know one another…?' she said blankly.

'Of course they know one another,' said her mother, who was standing a little apart from them. She scanned her daughter's pale face with a frown. 'Are you feeling all right? Heavens you've not caught this wretched cold bug, have you?'

Megan wasn't feeling *all right*. She doubted she had ever felt less all right in her life! She lifted her gaze to Luc. 'So you are Lucas Patrick, the writer…?'

He nodded.

'Who else would he be?' Laura asked.

The man I just made love to?

'A man who needs warming up,' responded Hilary huskily. Her hungry eyes announced to everyone that it was a task she was only too willing to take on! 'You look frozen, Luc!' she purred.

Megan watched in seething silence as the voluptuous woman trailed her scarlet-painted fingers slowly down Luc's chest. She felt sick.

'You feel cold too, darling.'

Luc looked directly at Megan over the redhead's glossy head. The expression in his deep-set eyes said, *Save me!* Megan smiled back heartlessly. Save him! Hilary could eat him alive as far as she was concerned!

In the distance Megan was vaguely conscious of her

mother asking if she had had a knock on the head. Someone else suggested that what she needed was a good stiff drink to warm her up.

Good idea, Megan thought, reaching for the decanter of brandy on the bureau. In one smooth motion she filled her glass to the brim and lifted it to her lips.

When the fiery liquid was pooling in her empty stomach, she became aware that nobody was talking. They were all looking at her.

'You know, I feel better already,' she said, angling a hard, accusing glance towards the silent figure who stood just to her right.

It had all been a mistake; she felt the anger like a tight fist in her chest. He has done this to me, she thought hating him as much as she had wanted him earlier.

'No, actually I do feel a bit hot and headachey now I think about it.'

A maternal hand was immediately clamped to her forehead. 'I don't think you have a temperature, but you can't be too careful.' Laura watched with a fixed smile as her daughter refilled her glass. 'Perhaps you should go and lie down…?'

'You know, I think I might.' Megan drained the glass and set it down with elaborate care on the table. 'Lovely to see you, Jean Paul. Catch up later, Uncle Mal,' she called out cheerily. She kissed her mother's cheek. 'I'm sure I'll feel better after a quick nap.'

She didn't say anything to Luc. She knew if she did that all the fury seething inside her would explode.

CHAPTER EIGHT

MEGAN didn't close the curtains. The moon had appeared and the leaded window was open. The soft breeze blowing through ruffled the heavy brocade curtains and cooled the warm, sticky night air.

She had slept in this room most of her life and she knew every creak and groan the ancient building could make. So when she heard a soft creak, Megan knew immediately that someone had stepped on the uneven floorboard just outside her door. That creaky floorboard had saved her from being caught reading under the covers on more than one occasion.

Mum, come to check up on me.

Sometimes, Megan decided, hiding your head under the bedclothes really was the only sensible thing to do. Before she did exactly that she twitched one of the drapes on her half-tester bed closed.

Lying there, eyes tightly closed she heard the door open. Though she strained her ears Megan couldn't hear footsteps on the polished oak floor. Pretending to be asleep when you knew someone was in the room watching you had seemed a lot easier when she was ten, she reflected as she did her best to keep her breathing even and relaxed.

The silent presence she sensed seemed to stand beside the bed for a very long time. It seemed as if hours had passed before she heard the door latch softly click closed. She exhaled a gusty sigh of relief.

'Thank goodness for that!' she breathed, rolling onto her back. With a soft grunt she pulled herself to her knees and drew back the curtain. It was as she pushed wayward strands of hair from her sticky, too-warm face with her forearm that Megan realised she wasn't alone.

Her midnight visitor was still there.

For a split second she just froze at the sight of the tall intruder standing with his broad shoulders set against the panelled oak door. The paralysis only lasted a fraction of second before a massive rush of adrenaline was released into her bloodstream. Megan was out of the bed and standing there her body ramrod stiff.

Luc didn't think he had ever seen anyone radiate loathing quite so effectively as Megan did at that moment. So maybe convincing her he had always intended to come clean might not be easy…?

Easy? She's going to call you a lying bastard!

My God, had he messed up! It wasn't that he had *intended* for things to go that far before he told her the truth not doing so had been one of the stupidest things he had ever done and he was totally prepared to admit it. The fact was, for the first time in his life he had let sexual hunger overrule common sense.

Megan watched as he lifted a hand to his forehead in languid mocking salute. The colour seeped out of her skin only emphasizing the sapphire shimmer of her eyes.

This was all a joke to him. God, but she had been such a fool! She had knocked back God knew how many decent men who liked her for a man who hadn't stopped lying to her from the moment they had met!

First Brian, now Luc—am I doomed to go through life being attracted to lowlife scumbags—? It was a deeply depressing thought, though, if she was honest, nothing she had felt for Brian in or out of bed resembled the passion that this man was capable of wakening in her. She had never hated Brian, or for that matter loved him. Whereas she hated Luc and…

'You lying, conniving rat!' she blasted.

I will not love him…I will not.

She stood there hating him, and hating even more the hot

liquid tightening low in her pelvis and the inner knowledge that if he touched her she would be lost.

Her eyes slid of their own volition over his lean, muscular body. He was perfect, but it wasn't simply his physical perfection and startling male beauty that had her hooked, but the aura of raw sexuality that hung about him. She shivered. Everything he did, the slightest gesture, the way he turned his head, fascinated her.

'A touch hypocritical coming from someone who was pretending, very badly, to be asleep.'

He levered himself casually from the door frame.

'I thought you were my mother.'

'That makes it all right, then.'

She ground her teeth, knowing that if she opened her mouth without counting to twenty she would be shrieking like a fishwife in two seconds flat. She didn't want to risk getting incoherent or, worse, start bawling her head off. Megan wanted to tell him exactly what she thought of him.

'I'm assuming you're a little annoyed with me because I didn't tell you who I was—?'

'You're incredibly perceptive for a lying rat.'

'Do you think we could keep the rat references to the minimum? Can't stand the things.' 'He rubbed his forearm vigorously as he admitted with a grimace, 'They make my skin crawl.'

'*You* make my skin crawl,' she retorted childishly.

'No, I don't.'

The rippling sensation as all the muscles in her abdomen tightened wrenched a tiny grunt from her dry throat. His voice had a tactile quality that was like a caress.

Megan had never believed that violence solved anything, but as he stood there radiating total confidence she wondered if on this occasion it might not be the way to go. Even if it didn't solve anything, wiping that arrogant smirk off his face might make her feel better.

She took a deep, calming breath and told herself to rise above the provocation. Don't sink to his level.

'You like my skin, Megan.'

She started to shake her head until her eyes connected with Luc's. A slow, guilty flush spread over her face.

'Not the man inside it, I don't.' The skin, however, the smooth skin with its incredibly satiny texture, still, to her immense shame, exerted a strong tug to her senses.

His face tautened with anger.

'It wasn't my inner beauty you were interested in earlier.'

The awful thing was his mortifying observation could be equally true now. A fact hard to miss when no matter how hard she tried she couldn't stop her gaze straying to the point where the material of his shirt gaped, allowing a tormenting glimpse of flat brown belly.

He had been wearing the same shirt earlier. Megan had a horrible suspicion that she might have had something to do with that missing button.

Luc's jaw clenched as he bit back the oath that rose to his lips. 'If you stop sniping for thirty seconds I might be able to explain. I was going to tell you who I was, but—'

'But you thought it was a shame to waste the opportunity of a few more make-a-fool-of-Megan moments,' she inserted bitterly.

'I didn't want to make a fool of you, but you've got to admit you were phenomenally patronising when you rolled up at my place…'

'I was not patronising!' How could you be patronising when you were faced with a man who was, not only intimidatingly perfect and off-the-scale sexy, but quite obviously capable of delivering killer put-downs in his sleep?

'You wrote me off as the hired help, nice body but not much between the ears, the moment I walked in.'

'Your body isn't that good,' she lied. 'And I never thought you were stupid.' The intelligence in his eyes had been the first, well, maybe not *first* thing, but it had definitely been one of the first things she had noticed about him.

'Admit it,' he challenged. 'You're an intellectual snob of the worst kind.'

Her face got hot with anger at this totally unjust assessment. 'And you decided to teach me a lesson? That's why you came here pretending to be someone you're not.'

'Can you deny you needed a lesson? And I came here pretending to be me...'

'Being pedantic doesn't make you any less a total sleaze. Tell me, because I'm curious, what part of my lesson involved having sordid sex with me?'

'You seemed to enjoy sordid at the time,' he rebutted with brutal accuracy.

Megan flushed bright pink. 'Carry on thinking that if it makes you happy.' Without taking her eyes off his face, she reached for the bedside lamp; the lamp toppled and fell to the floor with a loud crash.

Megan didn't try and retrieve it. It wasn't as if the room wasn't bright enough—the moonlight streaming in through the window made the room as bright as day. The moon was so bright that she could see things she'd have been happier not seeing. Things like the shadow of body hair through his shirt...something that she was trying very hard *not* to see.

Besides that, this wasn't an occasion when moonlight was appropriate. Moonlight suggested romance and lovers.

'Are you going to pick that up?'

'No!' she snapped as he bent down. His head lifted. 'Leave it,' she snarled. 'You've got a cheek, I'll give you that. How dare you creep into my room? Get the hell out before I call for someone!'

Luc effected innocence. 'I thought we had a date?'

Her hands balled into fists. 'You must be joking!' she hissed. 'What you did was sick.'

'Stupid maybe,' came Luc's grim-faced admission.

Suddenly Megan wanted to cry. 'You're a cold, callous

bastard, and I'm so glad I entertained you.' Her feathery brows twitched. 'Do you generally have to pretend to be someone else to get a woman to sleep with you?'

Luc was starting to look exasperated. 'Look, I really regret what happened tonight.'

'Why—was I that bad?' In case he thought she was seeking reassurance, she added belligerently, 'You should know that I happen to know I was great.'

'You were great and then,' he drawled, 'you opened your mouth.' Even as he spoke an image flashed into his head of those soft, moist lips running over his naked skin. His eyes half closed, Luc's respiration started to come significantly faster as his body responded with painful urgency to the steamy image of Megan kneeling in front of him. It was so real that his long fingers flexed as he imagined himself winding them into the silky honey tresses as she knelt before him.

He touched the back of his hand to the beads of sweat along his upper lip and struggled to regain some control of his imagination.

Dear God, Luc, he told himself, you're acting like a teenager with his first rush of hormones!

'You seemed to think I was great too. In fact I seem to recall you saying you thought you were falling in love with me…?'

Megan froze. *'I did not!'*

'I could say *did too*, but not being five any more I won't. I'm prepared to give the benefit of the doubt…'

This man was quite simply unbelievable!

'The fact is I'm not happy with unquestioning adoration. I hate clingy women.'

'Do I look like I'm suffering from a case of adoration?'

'For crying out loud, woman!' he grated, an expression of seething frustration on his lean, strong-boned face. 'I came here to apologise but you make me so damned mad.'

His heavy-lidded glance slid downwards from the twin beacons of her blazing blue eyes.

At about the same moment Megan awakened to the uncomfortable fact she was standing there in a skimpy, short nightie. Her discomfort would have been ten times worse had she realised that the moonlight had rendered the fabric virtually transparent.

Luc was not similarly unaware and hadn't been since she had leapt from her bed. He was painfully aware of the outline of her slim, supple body. As much as he tried not to let them, his eyes were continually drawn to the gentle upward tilt of her rosy-tipped breasts and the strategic darker shadow at the apex of her long legs.

Megan resisted the urge to tug down the hem, and endured his scrutiny impassively. It isn't what you wear, it's the way you wear it—isn't that what Mum always says? Of course her mother, who bought sexy silk pyjamas half a dozen at a time from her favourite designer, would never have been caught wearing a cheap chain-store nightdress.

'Was it all a joke to you?' Megan asked.

His smoky gaze returned to her face; his manner was uncharacteristically distracted. 'Of course it wasn't a joke… I didn't expect tonight to go the way it did.'

'Well, I don't believe you,' she countered furiously. 'I think you planned everything. I think you're a cold, callous, manipulative snake.'

'Right, then, I don't suppose there's anything more to say.'

He's going now…say something. 'Fine, you know where the door is.'

Face like stone, Luc turned. 'See you around, Megan.'

'Not if I see you first,' she hissed.

The moment the door closed she crumbled.

CHAPTER NINE

MALCOLM, wearing silk pyjamas and a dressing gown, looked relieved when he saw Megan.

'I thought for a second you were your mother. I've been outside to have a couple of puffs on a cigar. You couldn't sleep either, huh?' He looked sympathetically at Megan, who was seated at the long scrubbed table in the cavernous kitchen.

Megan shook her head and nursed her mug of tea, which had gone cold while she'd sat there. She summoned up a weak smile and hoped her face had recovered from the worst of the tear damage. 'Bad night, Uncle Mal?'

'I never sleep in the country. Quite frankly I don't see how anyone does. It's so darned noisy,' he complained, dragging himself up a chair.

Despite her bleak frame of mind Megan was amused by his comment. As a country girl born and bred she couldn't let this comment go unchallenged.

'What about London traffic?' Even she, a sound sleeper—*normally*—found that hard to cope with sometimes.

'You can tune out traffic noises—wild animals making all sorts of unearthly noises through the entire night you cannot. Frankly, it gives me the creeps. Mind you, it's not as bad here as where Luc lives.' He gave a shudder. 'You have the sound of the sea to cope with there as well. God, the sound of the sea has to be the loneliest sound in the world.'

'That's really quite poetic, Uncle Mal.'

'Yes, I thought so too,' he agreed, looking pleased. 'Is there any tea in the pot?'

She shook her head. 'No, it's cold,' she said. 'I thought Luc said he lived in London.'

'Told you that, did he? Not like Luc to tell you anything beyond name, rank and serial number. He must have taken a shine to you.'

Megan laughed uncomfortably and said lightly. 'I doubt it.'

'No, the London place is a new thing. When he isn't traveling—a bit of a gypsy, our Luc is. You never know when he'll have the urge to take off. It's in his blood.'

Megan, who had heard the Land Rover revving up at three in the morning, lowered her gaze to the cold depths of her mug. She had seen the note on the hall stand addressed to her mother in a strong scrawl. It wouldn't be long before Malcolm discovered that Luc had taken off again…and good riddance!

'Normally he buries himself out in the wilds of the country, some place with a name I can't pronounce…Welsh. Not big on his fellow man, is Luc, but then,' he reflected, 'who can blame him under the circumstances?'

'What circumstances would those be?' Megan enquired.

'Said too much,' said Malcolm, looking alarmed.

'No, you've not said enough,' Megan corrected forcefully. She was sick to the back teeth with all this secrecy.

Malcolm sighed heavily. 'You're very like your mother sometimes,' he said. 'Now you must promise that what I tell you stays between us…?'

Megan gravely nodded.

'Luc had a successful business, engineering, he had a partner and, to cut a long story short, the partner had been draining the firm of funds for ages. The chap finally did a runner and left Luc to face the music.'

'Music…but I thought you said it was the partner…?'

'True, the only thing he had done wrong was trusting the wrong man. The police were very good, he said.'

'The police were involved!' she exclaimed.

'Sure, there was a full investigation and Luc was totally vindicated. It might have stopped there but one of the investors killed himself when he realised his life savings were down the toilet. Apparently the guy was pretty unstable to begin with, but when someone leaves a couple of kids and a pretty widow the press are not going to mention that. The press did a real job on Luc.'

The information was a lot for Megan to take in at once. 'Why don't I know about any of this?'

'It happened during your dad's last illness. Luc has changed a lot since then too; he doesn't look much like he did…short hair, sharp suits…people forget.'

'But Luc doesn't,' she said quietly.

'God, no!' exclaimed Malcolm. 'Luc isn't the forgiving and forgetting type.'

'Him and me both,' Megan gritted. No matter what had happened to Luc in the past, nothing made what he had done to her excusable.

'Relocation?' Megan repeated blankly. She had been finding it pretty hard to concentrate all day. It hadn't quite sunk in yet even though she had done the test twice—to be sure. It hadn't really been necessary—deep down she had already known, even before the little blue line had appeared.

There hadn't been symptoms as such, just a *feeling*. She had told herself that she was worrying unnecessarily, dates meant nothing, her cycle had always been pretty erratic.

She was still in denial. Of course she knew it happened, but not to her! The situation had been complicated by the fact that an old school friend was staying with her that week. Sophie was just about her best friend in the world, but confiding in her wasn't an option. Sophie had been married five years and had just completed her second lot of IVF treatment—how could you tell someone who was desperate to have a baby that you'd got pregnant accidentally?

'The quotes to bring the building in line with health and safety regulations have proved prohibitive.'

Megan struggled to concentrate on what her boss was saying.

'This a prime site for development and, apparently, it's economically more viable to sell and move out of the city.' He sighed. 'It's a charming part of the world, not far from a village called Underwood. I don't suppose you know the area…?'

'Actually I was brought up not far from there,' Megan admitted.

'Excellent. Well, you don't have to make any decision now, but we're very keen not to lose key staff like yourself. I think that once you've had a chance to examine the details, you'll find that the relocation package we're offering is generous—very generous indeed.'

For two days afterwards she pretended nothing had happened. On the third she took some of the leave she had accumulated and went home, it seemed the natural thing to do.

Her mother was away when Megan arrived at the house. The housekeeper, Elspeth, whom Megan had known since she was a child, explained that she had gone to Paris for a break.

'Do you know when she'll be back?' Megan asked.

'I couldn't say,' came the less-than-forthcoming response.

Another time Megan might have pressed the subject, but she had other things to think about. Maybe she was reading too much into the way Elspeth spoiled and fussed over her during the weekend, or maybe the older woman had inherited some intuitive powers from her Celtic forebears; either way Megan wasn't allowed to lift a finger. It was actually rather comforting to be fussed over.

The ancient walls of her childhood home had a strangely soothing effect upon her; the moment she walked through the door she experienced a strange sense of peace. Was it her condition that made her look at the beauty of her surroundings with different eyes? While she was walking in the woods one morning she came to a decision: she wanted her child to be brought up here where she had.

Laura returned on Sunday.

'You look incredible,' Megan told her as they took tea together in the pretty morning room. 'I really like your hair that way.'

'You don't think it's too…young…?'

'You are young, Mum.' Normally Megan would have picked up on her mother's tension immediately, but on this occasion she herself was distracted. Should she just come out with it, or would it be better to let her mother have a good night's sleep before she broke her news?

She took a deep breath…there was no good putting it off.

'Mum…'

'Megan, there's something I have to tell you…'

'Same here,' Megan said with a strained smile. 'After you…'

Laura got up and walked over to the low mullioned window. For the first time Megan registered her parent's unease. 'You know I went to Paris?'

Megan nodded. 'Yes?'

'I stayed with a friend.'

Her mother, her discomfort evident, was looking anywhere but at her. A knot of cold fear tightened in her stomach.

'That was nice,' she said, clenching and unclenching her white-knuckled hands as she worked up the courage to ask what she had to. 'You're not…ill, are you, Mum? If you are,' she added quickly, 'you mustn't panic. We can cope with whatever it is.'

When Laura turned and saw her daughter's face a grimace of self-recrimination crossed her own. The fear that lurked behind Megan's composed expression, she had seen before. At her lowest ebb, during her husband's illness and after his death, Megan had been a constant source of strength and comfort to them both, but sometimes Laura had seen that look…a shadow, really… It had made her feel guilty for relying so heavily on Megan.

'Gracious, no, I'm fine,' she assured Megan quickly.

Megan released a sigh of relief; nothing her mother had to say could be worse than what she had been imagining.

'Well, that's all right then. Who did you stay with? Anyone I know?'

Laura came and sat on the sofa beside her daughter. 'Jean Paul Legrand, you remember him…?'

'Tall, silver-haired, sexy French accent.' Laura gave a strained smile as her daughter reeled off the Frenchman's distinguishing characteristics. 'The dishy lawyer whose wife Dad went to college with.' Her brow creased. 'Didn't she die?'

'Yes, three years ago.'

'How is he?' She only had the vaguest recollections of how he'd looked that weekend a few weeks earlier. A few weeks…it felt like a lifetime ago.

'He's fine. Actually…' Laura sighed and caught Megan's hands. 'The thing is, darling, this isn't the first time I've stayed with Jean Paul and actually what I'm trying to tell you… Oh, my, this is very difficult.'

'Whatever it is it can't be as difficult as what I have to tell you,' Megan promised, her fingers tightening encouragingly around her mother's.

'Jean Paul has asked me to marry him and I've said yes.'

Megan's jaw dropped. Her mother getting remarried—it had been the last thing she had expected to hear. It was the last thing she had expected to happen! For the first time for a week she stopped thinking about her own situation.

'Marry…I didn't even know you were *seeing* him!' she exclaimed. Belatedly aware of her mother's anxious expression, she expelled a gusty sigh and pinned a suitably pleased smile on her face. 'But it's marvellous!' she cried, enfolding her mother in a bear-like hug.

Megan felt helpless when her mother began to cry.

'You mean that?'

Megan nodded. 'Of course I do.'

Laura released a shuddering sigh. 'I was so worried that you'd think I was being disloyal to your father's memory…I always said I would never get married again.' She lifted her head from her daughter's shoulder and accepted the tissue that Megan offered with a watery smile.

'Dad wouldn't have wanted you to be alone, Mum,' she said quietly. 'He was the last person who would have wanted you to live in the past.'

Laura sniffed and searched her daughter's face. 'You *really* don't mind?'

Megan shook her head. 'Of course I don't mind. I just want you to be happy. You love Jean Paul…?' It felt incredibly strange to be quizzing her mother on her romantic life. She noticed her mother looked as awkward as she felt.

'He's a lovely man—' Laura's self-conscious smile faded as her manner became solemn '—but he knows…' She shook her head. 'I made it quite clear to him that I wouldn't marry him if it upsets you.'

'So you want my blessing—? There's a bit of role reversal for you,' Megan teased, but her mother didn't smile.

'Yes, I do.'

'Then you have it.'

'Thank you, darling. It isn't the same as it was with your father…but, yes, I am very fond of him and he makes me laugh and feel young again.'

'Then I already love him,' Megan said fondly. 'Have you set a date?'

'We thought…well, there doesn't seem much point waiting under the circumstances.' She met her daughter's eyes and blushed. 'Neither of us are getting any younger…' she added quickly.

'So when…?'

'Next month.'

Megan let out a soundless whistle. 'Wow, you two don't let the grass grow, do you?' Despite her light-hearted tone Megan was beginning to be concerned that her mother was rushing into this.

'The thing is, Megan, Jean Paul's practice is in Paris. I'll be moving there. This place…it's such an enormous responsibility for you with your busy life.'

'Paris isn't very far, you mustn't worry about this place,' Megan said firmly. 'Actually, I might be around a lot more. The company is relocating to nine miles from here, of all places. So I'll be on hand to keep an eye on the old place.' Head tilted to one side, she scanned her mother's face. 'There's something else, isn't there?'

Laura nodded. 'Yes, there is.'

Megan's brows lifted. 'Well, go on,' she prompted, kicking off her shoes and drawing her knees up as she curled up cosily on the sofa. 'It can hardly be any more shocking than learning I'm about to have a new stepfather.'

Laura sighed and placed her interlinked hands on her lap. 'This is very embarrassing,' she groaned, closing her eyes. 'I'll just have to say it.'

'I wish you would,' Megan remarked. 'My imagination has gone into overdrive.'

'The thing is, Megan, I'm pregnant.'

A bubble of laughter escaped from Megan's throat. 'So what's really up?'

Her mother bit her lip and looked hurt. 'I'm not joking, Megan.'

Megan's jaw sagged. Her imagination, even in overdrive, had not produced this possible explanation.

'I know what you're going to say,' Laura rushed on, avoiding eye contact with her open-mouthed daughter. 'I can't be; I'm too old. That's what I said to the doctor when

he told me,' she admitted. 'But it seems I can be and I am…
actually I'm twelve weeks.'

'What does…does…Jean Paul say?' Does he know?'

'Of course he knows—it's not like I wouldn't tell him, is
it?' her mother rebuked gently and wondered at her daughter's guilt-stricken expression. 'Actually Jean Paul is being
marvellous about it, worried about my health, but everything's fine, I'm very fit. Marilyn couldn't have children,
you see, and this will be his first so he's very excited….'

Megan, her voice shaky, interrupted the flow. It still
didn't seem possible. 'You're *really* pregnant?'

Her mother nodded. 'Yes, I'm having a baby.'

Megan looked at her. 'Me too, Mum,' she said with a
high laugh that trembled on the brink of hysteria.

Laura's eyes widened. She scanned her daughter's face
and Megan nodded. 'It's true, I am.'

'Oh, my God!'

Suddenly mother and daughter were in one another's
arms, tears streaming down their cheeks.

Later when they were both cried out Laura turned to her
daughter. 'Now let's get practical. I'm assuming that Luc is
the father.'

'Why would you assume that?'

'Really, Megan! He couldn't take his eyes off you…I'm
assuming you had a falling out…?'

Megan nodded.

'You are going to tell him?'

'I don't know where he is…he's not in London.'

'Malcolm will know. I'll ask him.'

'No,' Megan replied. 'I'll ask.'

CHAPTER TEN

UNCLE MALCOLM had been reluctant to tell Megan where Luc was so she had been forced to tell him why she needed to see him.

'So you see I have to tell him, but,' she hastened to assure him, 'I'm not going to ask anything of him. It's my decision to have the baby...'

'Well, *obviously* you will have the baby.'

Megan inclined her head slightly in agreement. How obvious it had been had been something that still surprised her. Maybe there was a point with most women, even those like herself who had never even considered motherhood, when your body told you it was the right time.

Or maybe wanting to bear the child of the man you love has something to do with it...?

Megan gritted her teeth and ignored the sly voice in her head. 'And obviously he or she will be my responsibility and mine alone...'

'I expect Luc will want a quiet ceremony....'

Megan her cheeks still tinged with colour, looked at her uncle with exasperation. This she could do without! She couldn't afford to start thinking happy families even for one second...it was her duty to stay sane.

'Didn't you hear what I said? I want nothing from Luc.'

'I heard you, but that's plain silly. A child needs two parents.'

And a pregnant woman needs the loving father of her baby at her side. But that just isn't going to happen, Megan, so live with it.

'In a perfect world,' she agreed. 'However, lots of women

93

bring up children on their own.' And she was determined
to make sure her child lacked for nothing. Even if Luc didn't
want to take an active part in his child's life—a definite
possibility—she would make sure that he or she felt loved
and wanted.

'Lots of women don't have a choice,' her uncle rebutted.

'This argument sort of presupposes that Luc is going to
ask me to marry him. Not very likely…we hardly know one
another.' Which made the fact she had fallen in love with
a man who was virtually a stranger all the more ludicrous.

'There's plenty of time to get to know someone after
you're married.'

'You have a unique take on marriage, Uncle Malcolm.'

'And I think you'll find that Luc is actually quite tradi-
tional in a lot of ways.'

And he hates *clingy* women.

What man wasn't going to be horrified to discover that a
woman he had had casual sex with once was carrying his
child?

'Well, it doesn't really matter what Luc wants,' Megan,
calm on the outside but a mass of conflicting emotions inside, told her uncle. 'Because I don't want to get married.'
Not to a man who didn't love her, at any rate.

'You'll change your mind,' Malcolm predicted confidently before reflecting, 'I admit I didn't think so at the
time, considering he had writer's block for the next six
months, which threw the schedule all to hell, but it's turned
out lucky under the circumstances that Grace wanted the
divorce last year.' He appeared not to notice the spasm of
shock that crossed his niece's face.

'Luc is married…? But—' She stopped abruptly, biting
her lip so hard she broke the skin. But what, Megan? Why
shouldn't Luc be married? Most men his age are or have
been.

'*Was,*' Malcolm inserted with a worried look at her pale

face. 'He *was* married. They married when he was incredibly young, but they'd been apart for years. They'd just never bothered getting a divorce.'

Megan, who had a thousand questions, had pressed him for details, but Malcolm had infuriatingly clammed up, and advised her to ask Luc himself. And she was *really* going to do that! Of course you turned up on man's doorstep and said, Sorry, but I'm having your baby, and then asked him about the woman he actually loved.

Some things you didn't need to ask. She was no expert on marriage or divorce but Megan did know that people didn't *forget* to get a divorce. It wasn't the sort of thing that slipped your mind! It didn't take a genius to work out that couples who didn't legalise a split didn't do so because they hadn't given up yet. Luc and his wife had been leaving the door open for a reconciliation, and from what Malcolm had let slip it had been Luc's wife Grace who had finally closed that door.

Luc hadn't been able to work…*Grace*… Was this woman, whom Luc obviously still loved, as elegant and graceful as her name? Having discovered a previously untapped streak of masochism in her nature, Megan tortured herself on the trip to Wales imagining what the other woman looked like.

It was a long and tiring trip. She couldn't ring to let him know she was coming because Malcolm said he didn't have a phone at the cottage and always turned his mobile off when he was there. The cottage turned out to be not *quite* as isolated as her uncle had suggested. It hadn't been easy to find, though, and the last couple of miles proved the most challenging to her navigational skills.

After travelling a mile down a single track lane that was surrounded by high hedges that made it impossible to see anything, being suddenly confronted with an incredible view of the stormy sea took Megan's breath away. She stopped the car and wound down the window to take it all in. The salty tang filled her lungs as she gazed at the scene: white-crested waves crashing onto the pebbly foreshore.

With a sigh Megan turned off the ignition; there was no point putting off the inevitable.

Cautiously—the track was full of potholes—she negotiated the path down the steep slope that led to the solitary habitation. The cottage, set on a rocky outcrop of higher ground, was situated just above the rocky seashore. The high tide lapped up against a low wall, which appeared to be the only defence against the sea. The low whitewashed building was not large, but its walls looked sturdy enough to withstand the worst the harsh elements could throw at it. It looked old enough to have been doing just that for a couple of hundred years at least.

A mud-spattered four-wheel drive Megan immediately recognised stood on a small level area in front of the cheerily red-painted front door.

Megan turned off the engine and pressed her hand flat to her chest. When your heart felt as if it were trying to escape from your chest it probably was not a good time to recall stories about apparently healthy people who dropped dead from undiagnosed heart complaints.

Maybe I should rethink this plan…? Maybe I should drop it altogether.

Calm down, Megan, you know exactly what you're going to say. 'Just a courtesy call—I'm going to have your baby.'

Oh, dear…! Considering she had been working on the intro for the last three hundred miles, that could do with some work.

She felt physically sick as she lifted the door knocker and let it fall. When nobody replied she walked around the building peering in the windows. There was no evidence of life. Was this a sign? Was some higher authority telling her she should go home? There did seem something awfully confrontational about rolling up on a man's doorstep and telling him you were carrying his child.

Megan wasn't a confrontational person by nature.

Sure, a letter was impersonal, but was impersonal such a bad idea in this instance? The impersonal method actually had a lot to recommend it—a letter was much neater and there would be much less opportunity for her to make a total fool of herself and do something embarrassing like burst into tears.

After a brief struggle with herself, Megan decided to give it another half-hour and then return to the village she had passed through a few miles back and see if they had a room for the night. Even if she didn't see Luc she was in no condition to drive back home tonight.

Sitting in the car, she felt stiff and cold; within five minutes she lost all feeling in her extremities. Rubbing her hands together, she turned on the engine. The warmth blasted out by the heater going full throttle and the music on the radio had a predictably soporific effect.

Megan was gently dozing off when the door of the car was wrenched open without warning. It stayed open as, hands pressed on the roof, Luc bent down until he was on eye level with Megan. She thought she had committed every detail, every impossibly symmetrical detail of his face to memory, but now his dark, hard-edged face was within inches of hers she realised that he was far, *far* more beautiful in the flesh.

Thinking about flesh had not been a good move. Her stomach muscles quivered and shifted as images crowded in her head of smooth, sleek skin sheathing tight hard muscles. She had read that pregnancy could kill a girl's libido stone-dead…it turned out she wasn't one of this number!

'It's a very nice place you have here.' Did those terminally stupid words come out of my mouth? This really wasn't how this scene had played in her head.

'And you just happened to be passing?'

His deadly irony brought a flush to Megan's pale cheeks.

'I would have phoned.'

Luc lifted a hand to his dark, wind-ruffled hair. It curled onto his neck. It didn't look to Megan as though it had been cut since she saw him last. 'I don't use a phone for a reason…I don't like to be disturbed by uninvited guests when I'm working.'

She let her eyes slide over his olive-green waterproof jacket that was open at the neck to reveal a black sweater. Her examination moved lower, over his long legs encased in moleskins, and ended on his walking boots. He looked lean and fit, leaner maybe than the last time she had seen him…

She watched, unwillingly riveted as he lifted a hand to his wind-ruffled hair. His face, too, seemed thinner, with the strong bones and angles seeming more pronounced. His eyes were the same, though…an illicit little shiver ran down her spine as she diverted her gaze to a point over his shoulder.

'Are you working now?'

'I'm a writer. Writers are always working,' Luc lied calmly. He hadn't written a word since he'd got down here. 'For me a walk along the beach usually focuses my thoughts nicely.' Recently they had only been on Megan's eyes, her smell, her sweet softness… Of course this obsession would pass. The irresponsible part of him suggested he enjoyed it while it lasted. But it was easier to ignore that irresponsible voice when she was three hundred miles away.

Everyone, he told himself, determinedly ignoring the ache in his groin, knew that recognising you had a problem was part of the cure.

And Luc had recognised he had a problem with Megan from day one.

'Inspiration strikes when you're least expecting it.'

Like love, Megan thought, and gave a disbelieving sniff. 'What do you do, carry a notebook and jot things down? No wonder you've got so many friends,' she muttered under her breath.

Did he ever invite any of those selected few, and she was

thinking female here, to this place? Did they spend week-ends cosily shut away from the world together? What was there to do but walk on the beach and make love? Her hands clenched as she imagined those steamy lovers' trysts.

'No need for notes; I have an excellent memory.'

His excellent memory was at that moment recalling the huskiness of her voice as she had called his name and said she'd never have enough of what he was doing to her. Never have enough of him, and begged him… He drew a deep breath and stopped thinking about the liquid heat of her tight around him.

He was obviously an individual who was drawn to un-suitable women; first Grace, and now Megan. Was it ge-netic…?

A man had to learn by his mistakes and Luc had made this mistake once before. At least last time he'd had extreme youth and rampant hormones to blame. This time around he was old enough and bruised enough by life to be able to know that instant attraction and great sex were not enough. There had to be more.

What that *more* was he had yet to figure out.

A shocking idea was forming in Megan's head. My God, had she been part of his research for his latest book? The idea made her feel physically sick. 'Well, if I ever discover someone who resembles me in one of your books I'll sue,' she told him fiercely.

'I thought you didn't read my stuff.'

Megan shrugged at the taunt and watched as Luc, one hand braced at the base of his spine, straightened up and rotated his shoulders, as if the position he'd been hunched in had put a few kinks in his spine.

'Only when my train is late,' she retorted, grabbing her bag off the passenger seat and preparing to make best use of the fact he wasn't guarding her exit.

'Don't even think about getting out,' he growled.

Megan stopped dead and lifted her glance to his. Luc's

expression held more hostility than she would have thought possible.

He hates me… She swallowed past the emotional thickening in her throat and lifted her chin. So she hadn't expected him to open the champagne, but neither had she expected this level of antagonism.

'I'm going to do more than that,' she promised him, flashing a smile that ached with insincerity.

Not a single muscle moved in his stony expression. 'Just turn the car around and go back home, Megan.' He ran a hand over his jaw, his attitude now more weary than hostile. 'We have nothing to say.'

That's all he knows! 'My God, you're rude!'

He blinked as he looked into those stunning blue eyes that shone with disgusted condemnation. 'I'm the rude one?' he bit back. 'That's rich—you're the one who just turns up on my doorstep uninvited. If you want to take up where we left off you can forget it…I like to make the first move.' And he would if he let her within ten feet of him; along with common sense, the self-control he was so proud of deserted him around this woman.

Making the first move…now *that* she remembered. Actually she remembered everything and it made it hard for her to think this close to him.

Luc's brows knitted in a dark frown as he looked at her.

'Look, we always seem to be yelling at each other!' Megan said, noticing just how tired she was feeling.

'You were the only one yelling.'

'I had reason to yell. You lied and cheated your way into my life. Looked down your nose at my family and friends and then accused me of falling in love with you!' A flush of mortification washed over her skin as she recalled their parting.

She might have been able to forgive him if she hadn't realised that his diagnosis had been spot on. She had been in love with him.

'Anyway you had plenty to say then,' she reminded him grimly. 'And now it's my turn, and I didn't drive all this way to go back without saying it. And if you think for one second that I'm going to turn around just because you say so, then you're wrong.'

She was aware that Luc was watching her as she got out of the car. His silent scrutiny was partially responsible for her inelegant exit; the rest was down to the intense exhaustion that had hit her like a brick wall. Her brain felt even less nimble than her feet, which was not a good thing considering the importance of what she had come here to tell him.

She lost her balance and almost fell as she stepped away from the car. Saving herself without making use of the steadying hand Luc shot out, Megan tilted her gaze up to his and saw his lips twist in a wry smile as his hand dropped to his side.

He didn't say anything; he didn't do anything, except look enigmatic and gorgeous enough to make the average woman weep.

She took a deep breath.

'I have been driving for hours; my back hurts.' She grimaced as she pressed her hand to the base of her spine. 'I need a cup of tea and I need a bathroom, the latter fairly urgently.'

'I suppose you'd better come in.'

The grudging invitation brought a twisted smile to Megan's pale lips. 'How can I resist when you ask so nicely?' Not resisting Luc was what had got her in this position to begin with.

CHAPTER ELEVEN

MEGAN followed Luc inside the cottage, her low-heeled shoes clicking on the flagged floor. The interior layout was a surprise to Megan. The internal dividing walls were gone, creating one large open-plan living area that used up the entire ground-floor space. The original flagged floor had been retained, as had the vast inglenook, but the modern kitchen appliances and stylish Swedish wood burner were very sleek and state-of-the-art.

The heat being thrown out by the wood burner made Megan reach for the scarf that was wrapped around her throat.

'Bathroom…?'

'Up there,' he said, a beat behind.

Megan followed the direction of his nod and walked towards the wrought-iron spiral staircase. It wasn't until she reached the upper floor that she realised that the stairs opened directly into a room. The faint scent of the male fragrance Luc used hung in the air; it made her nostrils flare and sensitive stomach muscles tighten.

So this, she thought, releasing a long sigh, was Luc's bedroom, her pulse rate suddenly going through the roof.

Luc's bedroom was a place she had dreamed about a lot lately but she hadn't expected to find herself there. Furnished in a minimal style she recognised immediately from downstairs. Again the internal walls had been knocked out to make a space that was almost as large as the room below. The roof though was open to the rafters and light flooded in through the window.

Either Luc had just had a spring-clean or he was very neat; there wasn't a dirty sock or crumpled shirt in sight. In fact there was nothing much in sight beyond a couple of vibrant rugs on the oiled oak floor, a chair, a set of bookshelves and a bed—a large bed.

Megan swallowed. A *very* large bed, she thought, staring at the smooth sheets and simple throw.

She was looking around for the bathroom when she saw the wall.

'Oh, my God!'

Up to this point her back had been turned to it, but now she could see that the wall was covered, *entirely* covered from ceiling to floor in photos. Black-and-white prints that overlaid each other in a gigantic collage.

Even to her uneducated eye it was obvious that she wasn't looking at snapshots. The subject matter was diverse. They ranged from stormy seascapes and wild mountain scenery to pictures of old wrinkled men sitting around a chessboard, pipes in hands, and women with babies on their backs and water-pots on their heads, to children with even older faces searching rubbish dumps for food.

Faces frozen in time or starkly beautiful places, the pictures all had a quality, not just great lighting or inspired subject matter, but an indefinable *something* that made the observer stand and stare. Megan did. Despite the urgency of her errand she stood for a long time just looking.

If Luc had taken these himself he was not only very well travelled, but incredibly talented.

She finally managed to tear herself away, her mind still filled with the images she had seen and Megan had to open several doors before discovering the bathroom. Was Luc's mind as organised as his storage space? Unlike his bedroom, the bathroom was neither spartan nor rustic.

Megan looked around curiously and liked what she saw. It was tiled in pale cream stone tiles, which reflected the light flooding in through the roof windows. The bath, a freestanding decadent French slipper job that could have held half a football team. The bathroom in her flat could have fitted into the state-of-the-art shower cubicle.

'So this hasn't started well,' she admitted to her reflection in the mirror. 'That means things can only get better.' With the best will in the world Megan couldn't inject an authentic note of optimism into her voice.

When she went back downstairs Luc was in the kitchen area at the opposite end of the room. He had taken off his outdoor clothes, including the heavy sweater he had been wearing. He stood there in the dark moleskins that clung to the long line of his well-developed thighs. The rolled up sleeves of his pale blue shirt revealed the subtle sinewed strength of his forearms and the even tone of his dark skin.

Would there ever come a day when she would be able to look at him and not be paralysed with lust? Megan forced herself to release the air trapped in her tight chest.

He didn't look up even though he must have heard her come down.

Perhaps he was hoping that she'd go away if he pretended she wasn't there?

She watched as, very much at home in the kitchen, he rattled around in a competent manner in a cupboard, then walked over to a sink and filled a kettle. Even doing something mundane he was always a pleasure to watch and she was glad of anything that delayed the moment she would have to reveal why she was here.

She shifted her weight from one foot to the other and her elbow caught against the wall. She winced as pain shot up her arm. She rubbed it and realised that Luc was watching her.

'Find what you needed?'

She nodded and he returned to his task. 'Did you take the photos upstairs?' She did feel a need to break the lengthening silence, but she was also genuinely curious.

'Yes, did you like them?'

She nodded and then realised he wasn't looking at her.

'Very much, you're very talented.' Multi-talented, it would seem. 'Did you train?' He could easily have made his living out of them. It must have been hard to make the choice between writing and becoming a professional photographer.

'No, I've always taken photos. When I was making a living doing something that bored me rigid it was the only thing that kept me sane.'

'Why were you doing it if you hated it?'

Luc, who was taking a carton of milk from the big American-style fridge, had his back to her.

'I had my own business, and I was doing it for the same reason most people do jobs they don't like.' He turned, his mocking gaze sweeping across her face. 'Money.'

'And did you make a lot?'

'Yes, I made a lot of money.' His long, curling lashes lifted from the slashing curve of his cheekbones. 'And then,' he added, pinning her with a mocking stare, 'I lost it.' He had sold everything he had to pay off the creditors and clients that his partner had stolen from. 'All of it and then some.'

Aware that she wasn't supposed to know about his business, she said, 'That must have been terrible.'

'I thought so at the time.'

'I don't think I could do that,' she mused.

'Do what? Lose money?'

'Do something I hated just for money.' The look she directed towards him was tinged with reproach. 'Especially if I was as talented as you are.' With no talent for anything artistic, she had always envied people who were.

His expressive mouth twisted in a derisive smile. 'You could, believe me you could. Job satisfaction is nice, but so,' he added drily, 'is eating. I like to eat, most people do, and relatively few have the luxury of being able to pick and choose what they do. It's easy to turn up your aristocratic little nose when you've never had to worry about money. You've always had the cushion of Daddy's millions.'

A mortified flush travelled over Megan's fair skin. She swallowed hard. His scalding derision was well deserved. She was deeply ashamed that she had sounded like a spoilt little rich girl.

Actually her strict parents had never overindulged her. They had gone out of their way to teach her the value of money, but Luc was right, she reflected with a repentant shake of her head—she didn't know what it was to worry about money. Compared to many, her life had been easy.

'You're right, that was a really stupid thing to say.' She heaved a sigh. How many women who had found themselves in her present situation had not had the luxury of choice?

It was a sobering thought. Sadly money did make a difference. 'I do appreciate that I'm incredibly lucky, you know,' she told him huskily.

The cynical sneer faded from Luc's face as he stood there for a moment, recognising the unmistakable glow of genuine penitence shining in her blue eyes. The line above the bridge of his masterful nose deepened.

Megan got the impression that for some reason her response had surprised him...disappointed him even...as though he *wanted* her to do something he could disapprove of. She almost instantly dismissed this fanciful idea.

'The photos really are very good, you know. Have you ever though of exhibiting any?' she wanted to know.

'Have you been talking to Malcolm?'

Megan froze guiltily. 'No, yes...well, he didn't want to tell me you were here. Why do you ask?'

'Oh, I thought maybe he had sent you here as his advocate.'

She shook her head. Her instincts told her to drop the subject but her curiosity wouldn't let her. 'Advocate for what?' she asked.

'Oh...' he shrugged carelessly... 'his latest money-making

project. Ever since Malcolm saw my gallery upstairs he's been nagging me to publish a book of them.'

'And you don't want to?' It sounded like a great idea to her. 'If Uncle Malcolm says there's a market for that sort of thing, I'm sure he's right,' she ventured tentatively.

Her earnest defence of her uncle brought an amused, 'Are you *sure* he hasn't got to you?'

'No, he hasn't, but if he had I'd have told him the best way to get you to agree was to let you think it was your brilliant idea to begin with.'

He looked at her, startled for a moment, then the stern lines of his face melted into a grin.

Megan grinned back. 'I did a psychology module in my first year at uni,' she explained.

Her laughing eyes meshed with his, the moment of harmony didn't last long. At almost the exact moment that Megan recognised the atmosphere had changed, that the air between them throbbed with unspoken and dangerous things, Luc stopped laughing. Megan touched her tongue to the perspiration beading her upper lip and the pupils of Luc's eyes dramatically dilated. She saw him swallow before his dark head angled away from her.

'Tea or a beer?' he asked, not looking up.

'Tea.' If he could act as though nothing had happened so could she. Maybe she was the one who had started reading sex into everything because she was obsessed—not Luc.

'Do you mind if I sit down?' She didn't wait for his response; if she didn't sit down soon she would fall. Her knees were shaking. She presumed it was a reaction to the confrontation—she hated confrontations. It couldn't be good for the baby for her to feel this terrible. In an unconsciously protective gesture her hands went to her still-flat belly.

She sank into the soft chair and tried to think calm thoughts…it was an ambitious plan. Her brain was firing off questions one after the other in rapid succession; there was no let-up from the anxiety-inducing bombardment. How would Luc react? Was he going to be angry? Shocked, obviously—heaven knew she had been! Was he even going to believe her?

When Luc approached, mugs of tea in hand, Megan saw his bare feet. Her stomach muscles fluttered. How could she, how could *anybody* find bare feet erotic? Now hands, yes. Luc had the most beautiful hands, expressive hands with long, sensitive fingers… This time the tightening of her stomach muscles was vicious.

Catching the direction of her fixed gaze, Luc offered a curt explanation of, 'Under-floor heating,' before he nudged an open laptop to one side and set a mug of hot tea on the rustic oak coffee table.

Megan ran her fingers across the oiled surface of the wood. The cottage was filled with natural materials and textures and it was all very tactile and sensual. But nothing she had seen in the cottage made her want to reach out and touch more than the man who took a seat opposite her.

Megan nodded her thanks as her fingers closed around the hot, steaming mug, and pretended she was looking at the flickering images of the screen saver while she was actually greedily observing him fold his long length with fluid grace into a Kelim-covered sofa opposite her. Something in her stomach twisted painfully as she looked at him.

The feeling didn't go away when she stopped looking.

Luc glanced at his watch.

The pointed gesture brought a resentful sparkle to her eyes. This was about the single most momentous moment in her life and he didn't even bother disguising he couldn't wait to see the back of her. Deep down she knew it was irrational to feel angry. Luc didn't have the faintest idea why she was here—not that anything excused this boorish display of bad manners.

'I'm so sorry if I'm keeping you from something more important,' she drawled sarcastically.

'Only a couple of thousand words.' Luc, who hadn't been

able to write a word since he'd arrived at the cottage, lied. He leaned forward and rested his chin on the platform of his interlocked fingers.

Megan shivered as his silvered appraisal moved over her.

'You've lost weight,' he judged with a disapproving frown.

'A little,' she admitted.

'It doesn't suit you.'

Megan let the brutal observation pass; she recognised a perfect opening when she heard it. Then again, he wasn't in the best of moods—perhaps she should wait. Wait until when you give birth...? Tell him, Megan, *now...now...*the voice in her head prompted urgently.

As she opened her mouth her heart was beating so fast she could hardly breathe.

'Don't worry, I'll be putting the pounds on again soon,' she said, fixing her eyes firmly on her hands clasped neatly in her lap.

There was a silence, which got longer until, frustrated to the point of screaming, Megan lifted her gaze to his.

'You were supposed to ask *why*!'

'Why what?'

'Why will I be putting on weight...?' she prompted.

A flicker of amusement momentarily lightened the wariness in his eyes. 'Why will you be putting on weight, Megan?' he asked obligingly.

'I will be putting on weight because that's what people do when they're pregnant, which I am...pregnant, that is.'

There, it was out! She ought to be feeling a sense of release, but what she was actually feeling was sick...very sick. She pressed a hand to her mouth and waited, her eyes half closed, for the waves of nausea to pass.

When the imminent danger of throwing up had passed, she swallowed and opened her anxious eyes. Luc hadn't moved a muscle since she had blurted out her news. She gave a frustrated sigh. Whatever he was feeling, she wasn't going to see it here—a granite rock face would have been easier to read than those strong symmetrical contours. It was actually his total *lack* of response, his eerie stillness, that revealed he had even heard what she had said.

'With your baby…obviously.' She coloured. Maybe it wasn't *obvious* at all to him?

It was possible that he thought she acted with equal wanton abandon with every man that took her fancy…

On the brink of making a disastrous confession, Megan bit her tongue. Luc didn't need to hear how special he was, and the fact that she had never felt that way with any other man was something that ought to be kept on a need-to-know basis, and he *definitely* didn't need to know!

'Don't worry, I'm not here to make a scene,' she told him, gruffly earnest. 'I just thought that you had the right to know. And,' she added, 'it's not the sort of thing that's easy to say in a letter. Actually it's not the sort of thing that's easy to say full stop,' she added in a dry undertone. Belatedly she realised this comment might have come over as a little light on empathy. 'Or hear,' she tacked on generously.

Luc's vibrant complexion had acquired a grey tinge as he lost the last shred of his habitual cool. She'd been prepared for shaken, but Megan got seriously alarmed when he suddenly buried his face in his hands. His classical profile was hidden from her view, but she could hear the laboured sound of his breathing from where she was sitting.

After a few moments his head lifted and she was relieved to see his colour was improved. 'A *baby*…?'

She nodded, sympathetic to his traumatised condition.

He shook his head from side to side in the hope the action might kick-start his numb brain.

'So you weren't taking the pill…?' He saw the pain flare in her eyes and thought, Good move Luc, let her think you're blaming her, you insensitive bastard.

'I'm afraid I didn't think…I should…'

'Neither of us thought, Megan.' His expressionless voice cut into her disjointed stream of self-recriminations.

Megan lapsed into unhappy silence. Through the mesh of her lashes she watched his chest lift as he sucked in a deep breath.

'I'm sorry, you must be—'

'I'm not asking for anything from you,' she interrupted quickly. She saw some emotion, indefinable but strong, flare briefly in his eyes before she ploughed heavily on. 'I appreciate this is my responsibility. Of course, if you want to have some input, that is fine.'

CHAPTER TWELVE

'INPUT…' Luc repeated, looking at Megan as though she had run mad.

She exhaled a small gusty sigh of relief as she managed to wrench her fascinated eyes from the muscle in his lean cheek that was clenching and unclenching. 'And if you don't that's equally fine,' she told him with an upbeat smile. 'There's no pressure.'

'Are you trying to be funny?'

'I'm trying to be positive,' she rebutted. Considering she was attempting to make this easy for him, he didn't seem wildly appreciative.

His narrowed eyes scanned her face. 'So you've decided to have this baby.'

'You sound surprised?'

His brows lifted. 'Well, what about your career?'

'What about my career?' Angrily, she pretended not to see where he was going with this.

'I thought that was the most important thing in your life. The thing you're prepared to sacrifice a personal life for.'

'It is part of my life, and it is important, but my priorities have changed…' Her expression grew defensive. 'I'm allowed to change my mind.'

'It could change again…?'

Megan's heart gave a sickening thud. This was what she had been dreading him suggesting. She shook her head and ran her tongue over her dry lips. 'No, I've thought this thing through quite carefully,' she insisted. 'I'm sorry,' she said, feeling the prickle of hot tears behind her eyelids. 'I can see how you'd like this to go away, but I want this baby.'

An expression of revulsion crossed his face. 'Are you suggesting I would pressure you into having a termination?'

As this was exactly what she had assumed he was talking about, she just stared back at him mutely. His white-lipped fury gave lie to her assumption that he was taking this reasonably calmly under the circumstances.

Luc wasn't calm, unless you considered volcanoes about to erupt calm!

'I misunderstood,' she admitted with a shrug. Misunderstanding or not, there was a point that needed making here. 'Accidental or not, you're the baby's father... I can't prove it, of course—'

'For God's sake, woman, of course it's my baby. Do you think I imagine you make a habit of having unprotected sex any more than I do?' he demanded impatiently. The furrow between his brows deepened as their eyes locked. 'My God,' he breathed. 'You did think that, didn't you?'

Megan shook her head, then nodded, then grabbed two handfuls of hair and grimaced as she rocked forward and back again. 'I don't know what I thought,' she admitted huskily.

The anger faded from Luc's face as he looked at the dejected, dispirited set of her hunched shoulders. 'It must have been a confusing few weeks for you. It might make things a little easier to have someone to talk this out with...?'

The soft suggestion brought her head up with a snap. 'Get any idea I came here to ask your advice right out of your head. I already know what I'm going to do,' she ground out.

'So basically what you're saying is you're going to do exactly what you want to, no matter what I say.' His eyes, like molten silver, locked onto hers.

'In a nutshell.'

Luc took a deep sustaining breath and told himself he didn't have the right to be angry. What else could she have said? He'd backed her into a corner.

He even agreed with her, in the abstract, *her* body...*her* baby…*her* decision, but this wasn't an abstract baby. This wasn't just *any* baby. It was *his* baby… A few minutes ago he'd been aghast to hear what she had come to tell him, with bewildering speed his attitude had undergone a dramatic change. It amazed Luc how the idea of having a child could grow on a man.

'So if you've thought this out, tell me, how are you going to cope with a baby and a demanding job?'

'As luck would have it the firm I work for is relocating to a site nine miles from home so I'm going back,' she explained. 'It's a good place to bring up a child. I should know; I was brought up there.'

'And you're expecting your mother to bring up your child for you… Have you considered that having a young baby foisted on her at her age might not be what she wants? What's so funny?' he wanted to know when her lips twitched.

Megan shook her head, she judged that he had had enough shocks for one day. Besides, this wasn't her news to share. 'Actually,' she explained, 'Mum is moving to Paris.'

The quiver of laughter in her voice made his strong features clench in disapproval. 'Planning to give birth at your desk and be back at it the next day?'

'I'm planning on taking maternity leave,' she contradicted, 'and afterwards…' her shoulders lifted '…the firm has no problem with job-sharing.' She'd been thinking on the way down that this might be the way to go. The balance between work and home was going to be hard to get right, but she was determined to strike a balance that she could live with.

Luc gave a thin smile, he didn't bother to hide his scepticism as he snorted, '*Job-sharing!* Is the real Megan in there—?' He stretched his hand out, intending to touch the side of her head.

Megan, who knew exactly what the casual contact would

do to her, flinched away before he made contact. She saw his jaw tighten and repressed a groan. Well, she told herself, if he thought she couldn't bear to have him touch her, so much the better. If he knew how much she craved his touch it would only complicate things even more—it wouldn't do her pride much good either.

'What do you mean?' As if she didn't know.

'Well, you have to admit job-sharing doesn't sound like you.'

'You don't know me.' *Neither do I, these days.* 'And why do you assume that I'm going to be a disaster as a mother?' she asked sharply. She might not have felt this angry if his dig hadn't magnified her own fear that she would be inadequate for the daunting task of parenting.

'Why do you assume that I'd be relieved to offload my responsibilities to this baby?' he countered.

Protesting that it wasn't the same thing at all would have laid her open to a legitimate accusation of sexism. Instead Megan shook her head and insisted, 'I didn't.' Then added weakly, 'Not exactly.'

'I just don't believe you sometimes. You think I'd let my child grow up not knowing who the hell I was!'

He shook his dark head and she thought, *God, he's furious.*

'As for all that rubbish about you being responsible, like they say it takes two...and I was most *definitely* there. Or had you forgotten?'

His response was the first indication she had had so far that he wanted anything to do with the baby and Megan wasn't sure how she felt about it. What was he talking about anyway? Gifts and cards on birthdays and Christmas? Every other weekend and alternate summer holidays?

The image of a future where Luc turned up with his latest girlfriend in tow to take their child to the zoo filled her with horror.

'I wish I could forget!'

A raw silence fell between them.

A cautious light entered her eyes as she looked across at him from under the protective shade of her lashes. She was almost sure he didn't even know that he was grinding one clenched fist into the other open palm. It was very much the action of someone who was struggling to suppress strong emotions. She could see every sinew, every taut muscle of his lean body screaming with tension.

'I'm going to be a father.' He said it as it had just begun to sink in.

There was a blank look of incomprehension on his lean, devastatingly handsome features in the moment before he leapt to his feet in one lithe motion.

'Luc…?' He appeared not to hear her tentative voice as, with one fist clenched to his forehead in an attitude of deep thought, the other thrust in the pocket of his snug-fitting trousers, he began to pace from one end of the room to the other.

It was impossible, even in her present distraught frame of mind, not to look at him and experience a shivery frisson of sensation in the pit of her stomach while hearing the words *lithe* and *luscious* in her head.

'If you need time to think about this, I understand…' Coming here had been a mistake, a major mistake.

'Shut up, I'm thinking.'

Megan's eyes narrowed at his tone. 'I'm being understanding,' she told him wrathfully.

He looked over his shoulder and for a moment the intensity of his expression melted into a delicious grin. 'Be understanding quietly, *chérie*,' he instructed, pressing a finger to his lips.

Even without the grin the endearment would have got to her; with it she melted like butter on a hot knife.

He continued to pace for a few more minutes before moving back to the sofa. He sat on the edge, his body curving towards her so that their knees were almost touching. His body language created an illusion of intimacy that made it difficult for Megan to think straight. She had a horrible notion that her feelings were written in letters a mile high across her forehead as she gazed back at him, but she couldn't do a thing about it.

'I want...' he studied her face for a moment before his sensual lips slowly curled upwards into a self-derisive smile while she tensed her body, almost quivering with anticipation '...*Input.*'

Colour flooded Megan's pale face; the embarrassment and anticlimax was intense.

'Megan...?'

Megan blinked before arranging her features into something approaching composure. Just what made you think he was going to say I want you? That was the last time she went into fantasy mode. The fact was if Luc had wanted her, he could have had her.

'Fine.'

His eyes narrowed warily. 'You don't sound fine.'

'Are you going to dissect every inflection in my voice?' she demanded spikily.

He shrugged, and *almost* grinned. 'Point taken.' He leaned back into the squashy cushions of the sofa and, hands linked behind his head, looked at the ceiling.

What's he thinking? she wondered. No more wild guesses for her. She didn't have to wait long to find out.

'Do you actually think it is such a good idea?'

He rubbed his scalp vigorously with his long fingers, causing his dark hair to stick up in sexy tufts on the crown. Megan, her expression abstracted, was watching as he smoothed down the dark strands of glossy hair. She remembered sinking her fingers into that silky dark thatch and drawing his head down to hers.

'Do I think what is a good idea?'

'You moving back home...'

This casual comment focused her attention.

She smiled narrowly and sucked in her breath. 'Naturally

your opinion means just so much to me…' Luc grimaced, rolled his eyes towards the ceiling, before folding his arms across his chest in an attitude of long-suffering patience. The action incensed her further. 'But I find myself thinking just what the hell has it got to do with you? I'm having a baby—that doesn't mean I'm going to have anyone treating me like one!'

'*Finished?*'

Megan sniffed and refused to let him see how close to tears she was.

'I have absolutely no desire to pull your strings…' *Just pick you up and carry you to my bed.* 'Besides, I'd have to be mad to even try—you're about as malleable as a steel bar.' *But very much softer to hold.*

Not the most flattering comparison she had ever heard, but she was glad he realised she wasn't a pushover.

'Can I finish saying something without you jumping down my throat?'

Megan gave a curt nod of her head. 'I'll listen.'

'I can see why you might want to move back home at the moment, familiar surroundings…people willing to wait on you hand and foot…'

'I'll forget the people-willing-to-wait stuff.' He obviously had no idea about the staffing levels on the estate. 'But what's wrong about wanting to be in familiar surroundings?' she challenged.

'They're not *your* surroundings.'

She frowned and he looked exasperated. 'I know it will be yours one day, but right now it's your mother's home, and she doesn't look like she's going to vacate the position of lady of the manor any time soon to me. You can't run back to Mummy every time the going gets tough, Megan.'

'She won't be there.'

'You know what I mean. You need your own home, Megan. You need to start as you mean to go on.'

'The estate is my home.'

'It's your mother's home.

She shook her head. 'Underwood doesn't belong to my mum.'

Luc looked puzzled. 'Then who does it belong to?'

'It's mine. I thought you knew.'

She saw the shock register on his face. '*You* own the estate?'

Megan nodded.

She watched him as the information sank in. 'Does that mean you're filthy rich?'

'Why, Luc? Wishing you hadn't chucked me out of your bed?' she taunted.

Luc inhaled sharply. 'I didn't do that, Megan, and you know it. I couldn't have even if I wanted to,' he commented with a self-derisive grimace. 'For the simple reason I don't have that sort of will power, Megan, not where you're concerned.'

'You don't?' she whispered in blank amazement.

'You can ask that?' His incredulous glance moved across her face.

Ask it? She was tempted to ask for it in writing.

'Considering,' he continued heavily, 'that your condition is due to the fact I don't think with my brain around you, I'd have thought you'd have realised that.'

Megan tried to temper the hot thrill she got from his blunt admission by reminding herself that he was talking sex, not love. The wild, raw sex he was discussing was a temporary condition. She was pretty certain he would consider it a temporary insanity.

'Well, anyway, I'm not filthy rich…not in the way you mean.'

His brows arched sardonically. 'There's more than one way?'

She flashed him an unamused grin. 'Dad left Mum well provided for, but the bulk of his estate went to me,' she admitted. 'But I don't take any money out of the estate,' she went on to assure him. 'I went over things with John, and he explained that Dad ploughed the money back into the estate. He managed to do a lot over the years but when he bought the place it was really run down; there's still a lot of work to be done.'

'I thought your family had lived in the place since for ever?'

'They have, but Dad's grandfather had to sell the place to pay off death duties. Dad bought it back years later when he'd made his money. I suppose he wanted to make sure that history didn't repeat itself—that's why he handed the place over to me years before he died. Up until now it hasn't really been feasible for me to live there on a permanent basis. John will be pleased that I'm moving back,' she reflected thoughtfully.

That name again. 'Just who the hell is John?' he demanded.

A perplexed frown pleated Megan's brow. 'John...?' The overt hostility Luc was radiating bewildered her. 'John is the estate manager. To be honest I don't know how we'd cope without him,' she confided. 'He's been totally marvellous—a tower of strength.'

More muscle than brain, Luc translated. Why did women go for men like that? 'I'm sure he is,' he agreed pleasantly. He probably thought marrying the owner would be a good career move.

Megan warmed to her theme. 'The hours he puts in are unbelievable; I sometimes feel quite guilty,' she admitted.

'So your mother's been running the estate for you...with the help of John?'

'Gracious, no, she'd *hate* that. When Dad died, John just carried on running things. He's very committed. He runs things by me but I trust him implicitly.' The hints he'd been making recently about retiring were a source of concern. There were not many like John out there—plenty of people with impressive paper credentials but not many with a genuine love of the land.

'And how did your mother feel about all this?'

'How do you mean?'

'Being effectively disinherited. Being out of the loop?'

'Relieved,' Megan said immediately.

Luc looked sceptical and, annoyed by his response, she pushed home her message.

'You can take the girl out of the city...' Her slender shoulders lifted expressively before she went on to explain. 'Mum got married and moved into the place with Dad when she was eighteen. She *tried* to love it because he did. Dad,' she recalled with a reminiscent smile, 'almost threw a fit when she suggested moving into a vacant cottage on the estate.'

'That must have put a lot of pressure on their marriage,' Luc observed.

'Not really, they were both prepared to compromise. Dad bought the house in town and spent time there even though he hated it. He said if Mum could spend time in a drafty old pile with bad plumbing, he could put up with London traffic and fashionable dinner parties.'

She knew she'd lost him before she'd reached the end of her explanation. Luc had tuned her out.

She watched as he ran his fingers along his jaw. His expression indicated his thoughts were not just elsewhere...but another solar system.

'This changes things.'

'It *does*...?' she said, expectant. *What?*

He flicked her an impatient look. '*Obviously.* If we're not going to get our own place together, I suppose the logical alternative would be for me to move in with you.'

Mouth open, she looked at him in disbelief. Had he really said *logical*...?

'Did I miss something...? Get a place together? Since

when were we getting a place together?' Had he planned on mentioning this at some point? she wondered...

'Ah.' His speculative gaze skimmed her face. 'You were thinking of marriage?'

She gasped. 'No, I was *not* thinking of marriage!' she denied, turning prettily pink.

'Most women are,' he observed, 'no matter what they say to the contrary. Are you telling me it hasn't even crossed your mind?'

She directed a narrow-eyed look at the tall, lean figure sprawled on the sofa; his contemptuous attitude made her want to hit him. 'No, it damn well hasn't! I can't think of anything more stupid than marrying someone you have not the slightest thing in common with.'

'Outside the bedroom...' Megan froze at this soft addition, her eyes sealed with his brilliant cynical gaze...and beyond the cynicism was a primitive hunger that made the core of heat in her stomach tighten.

His sensual mouth twisted. 'Not that we made it to the bedroom.'

By sheer force of will she made herself smile back as though the subject were one that amused her. Inside her head she could feel every inch of his hard, vital body pressed up against her. She had perfect recall of every insane, intoxicating moment up to and including the moment of shattering climax. If he asked, she'd do it again in a heartbeat. This insight really shook her.

'I didn't come here to ask you to make an honest woman of me,' she croaked contemptuously.

'Why did you come here, Megan?'

'Do you need to ask?' she exclaimed indignantly. 'Fine! I came because I thought you had a right to know about the baby, and I'm not cold enough to send news like this via an email. The fact is I wouldn't marry you if you came gift-wrapped!'

'That makes you my sort of woman. *The fact is,* Megan, I've been married once and I'm not very good at it.'

She widened her eyes and, not wanting to drop Uncle Malcolm in it, feigned ignorance. 'You were married...?' *My sort of woman...* If only that were true, she thought sadly. How different this would feel if she were carrying the baby of the man who loved her.

He nodded. 'For ten years.'

This time her surprise was genuine. Ten years was a long time! 'You must have been very young,' she observed.

'I was twenty, Grace, my wife, was a couple of years older.'

'Were you unfaithful?

There was a startled silence during which Megan wished herself anywhere but here and now. *Me and my wretched tongue!*

'No, I was never unfaithful,' he said, scanning her flushed face, his glance lingering longest on the full soft contours of her mouth. He pressed back harder into the seat; it was getting increasingly difficult to ignore the voice that urged him to part those delicious rosy lips and slide his tongue inside her mouth.

'But I was a lousy husband,' he framed matter-of-factly, 'who wasn't there when my wife needed me.'

A comment like that and you'd have to be not human not to be curious, but from the closed expression on Luc's face and his body language as he picked up his mug of tea it was obvious that, as far as he was concerned, the subject was closed.

I'll respect his privacy, she decided.

Almost as soon as she had made this resolve, a sudden thought came to her that made it impossible for her to honour it. 'Did you and your wife...did you...have you got any children?'

Why hadn't she thought of this earlier? She had been assuming parenthood was as new an experience for him as it was for her, when for all she knew Luc might have a brood of children already!

'Grace was pregnant once,' he told her without any discernible expression in his voice, 'but she lost the baby.'

He'd come to realise that by that point in their marriage they had drifted so far apart that the prospect of the baby had been the only thing holding them together. Perhaps if he'd spent more time with Grace and less trying to make money to buy her the pretty things she loved things might have turned out differently. The irony was he had hated the job that he had put before his wife.

Megan felt the deep, abiding pain behind his pragmatic words as if it were her own. She wanted to hold him so badly it hurt.

'I'm so sorry.' The trite response was wildly inadequate, but she couldn't think of anything else to say.

His bleak eyes narrowed on her face. 'She had a fall,' he supplied without her asking.

It had been at the height of the scandal and the press pack, who had been after blood—specifically his—had latched onto the personal tragedy. Without anyone printing anything libelous, they had managed to intimate that there was a question mark over the accident.

Had the wife fallen or had she been pushed? Grim statistics about domestic violence would coincidentally appear on the same page. The fact he had been in Spain trying to locate his treacherous partner at the time had been no obstacle to a good rumour.

'That must have been terrible for you both.'

'Maybe it wasn't meant to be,' he reflected. 'The baby had a congenital abnormality; they picked it up on a scan. Nothing life-threatening or anything—a cleft palate.'

Megan nodded. She had a friend who had been born with the condition, not that you could tell—the surgery she had had as a child had been very successful.

'Grace,' he recalled in a voice wiped clean of all emotion,

'wanted to have the pregnancy terminated when they told us. She couldn't stand the idea of having a baby that wasn't perfect,' he explained.

Megan tried not to let her natural repugnance to the idea show on her face. You couldn't judge another person's actions without standing in their shoes, her father had always said, and he was right. Who knew what pressures the other woman had been under?

'But she changed her mind.'

'I changed it for her,' Luc admitted. 'And in the end she lost him anyway. If I hadn't pressured her she wouldn't have had to go through the pain and trauma of a miscarriage.'

'It wasn't your fault!' Megan protested, horrified by this insight into the burden of guilt he carried with him. 'It was an accident, a terrible accident,' she added, her voice thick with emotion.

Her spontaneous outburst brought his eyes to her face. The tears trembling on the end of her dark lashes made his jaw clench. 'Please don't go all soft and understanding on me, Megan.'

His sardonic sneer, the sudden cold hostility in his manner, made Megan tense.

'I can see you're just aching to be a shoulder for me to cry on. Frankly I don't have any use for your pity. And before you suggest therapy, I'm totally in touch with my feelings,' he pronounced caustically. 'And I don't believe in living in the past or pointlessly dwelling on things I have no ability to change.'

To have her sympathy thrown back in her face was incredibly hurtful. Megan instinctively hit back. 'If you're so *over it*…' she gave a derisive snort and sketched invisible inverted commas in the air '…tell me how is it you got writer's block when your wife wanted a divorce?'

His eyes narrowed to suspicious slits. 'How would you know that?'

Oh, God! She felt as if guilt were written all over her face. 'Never mind how—'

'Oh, but I do mind,' he cut in silkily. 'I'm assuming you've had a heart-to-heart with Malcolm…' An icy note of menace entered his voice as he added softly, 'Just exactly what did Malcolm tell you?' His expression was so savage that Megan began to feel concerned for her uncle.

'Malcolm didn't tell me anything…well, he might have mentioned in passing that you had got divorced.'

'So you already knew I'd been married?'

She nodded. 'And don't blame Uncle Malcolm; he didn't want to tell me where you were. In fact he refused point-blank until I told him about the baby. He was pretty shocked.'

'And exactly who else knew about the baby before me…?'

CHAPTER THIRTEEN

MEGAN stuck her chin out. She was getting pretty cheesed off with Luc's attitude. 'I told my mother,' she announced. 'Do you have a problem with that? Actually, I don't care if you do because what I do or don't do is none of your damned business. You may prefer to grit your teeth and be a *man* when your life falls apart, and I'd be the first to defend your right to behave like a total prat.' She paused briefly for breath; she was so mad that she was shaking.

At any other time the gobsmacked expression on Luc's face might have made her laugh, but right now she was too angry to see any humour in this situation.

'But when I'm upset,' she continued, '*I* talk to people, the people who care about me!' She swallowed as her voice developed a wobble. 'They'd be hurt if I didn't.'

For a moment Luc sat there watching her struggling not to cry. 'That's some temper you have.'

She sniffed and found a tissue placed in her hand.

'Thank you. I'm generally considered to be a pretty placid sort of person.'

He grinned. 'Sure you are.'

'It's not me,' she protested. 'It's you! You just…' The tissue between her clenched fingers mangled as she struggled to come up with a suitable definition for what he did to her. 'You're hopeless,' she pronounced irritably.

'And you're delicious.'

Her mouth fell open at the unexpected tribute. *Delicious…?* For God's sake, don't start reading too much into it, she cautioned herself.

'I'm glad you had people to share this with over the past few weeks, Megan,' he continued as though he'd not said anything out of the ordinary. 'You're lucky you have people who care about you.'

'People care about you...or they would do if you let them!' She was going to have to stop blurting out the first thing that popped into her head. 'That is...'

Without warning he leaned across and brushed a strand of soft honey hair from her brow. This time he made contact, his touch was brief, but enough to send a shiver of intense longing through her body...

'Don't worry too much—there are still one or two people who are prepared to put up with me.' It had been a brutal method of learning who your real friends were, but he did have a group of loyal friends who had stood by him during the scandal.

Megan flushed. She felt a total idiot—of course he had friends!

'And would you be one of those people who cared if I let you, Megan?'

Megan stiffened and felt her heightened colour intensify until she felt as though she were burning up. She was going to have to learn to guard her tongue in the future.

'Well, you're my baby's father; it would be better if we learnt how to get on.'

'That's a reply but not to the question I asked.'

'It's the only reply you're getting.'

Her grim retort drew a reluctant bark of laughter from Luc. Then his expression hardened. 'Grace and I separated not long after she lost the baby, but we wouldn't have if the baby had survived.'

'Can you be so sure?' Megan wanted to know.

Luc responded without hesitation with a firm nod of his dark head. It would have taken compromises but he would have made it work. 'A child needs two parents, whether they are married or not is irrelevant,' Luc announced, nursing the hot drink between his big hands. 'What matters is that they operate as a single unit where that child is concerned.'

'I think they call that a family. Hardly a new concept, Luc.'

While she respected his views, and even shared them, there was no way she would countenance going along with what he planned. Her smooth brow creased, she searched his lean face. It was weird—while she felt emotionally and physically drained by this difficult scene, now that it had sunk in that he was going to be a father Luc appeared incredibly energised. Never an easy man to say no to, he looked so charged up and resolute at the moment that she knew it was going to be difficult to make him recognise that his idea was a non-starter.

'Like they say, if it ain't broke don't fix it,' he quoted. 'Families work.'

'Not all families are nice or safe places to grow up in,' Megan pointed out gently.

His eyes narrowed on her face. 'But yours was?'

She nodded. 'I was very lucky,' she agreed.

'Would you deny your child what you enjoyed?'

She gave a sigh of frustration, he was trying to tie her in knots and mostly succeeding. 'It isn't the same thing,' she gritted.

'Why?'

Her eyes slid evasively from his. 'My parents loved one another.'

'I loved my wife...' Or thought he had. Lately he had begun to appreciate that what he and Grace had shared had been an infatuation, strong, but not long-lasting.

His honesty had inflicted more pain than she would have believed mere words could.

'But *love* isn't a magic formula for happy ever after,' he continued. 'My father brought me up alone. He didn't have any option—my mother died when I was ten.' His dark lashes swept downwards, making it impossible for her to read his expression. 'I don't want that for my child.'

This explained his determination to make sacrifices for

his unborn child. The image of Luc as a small boy without a mother flashed across her vision and immediately Megan felt the sting of tears behind her eyelids. Maybe it was her newly awakened maternal instincts that made her empathise so strongly with the motherless child? Then again, she had grown to accept that all her emotional responses seemed to be heightened where Luc was concerned.

'Are you all right?' His deep voice held a rough note of concern.

She blinked to clear her blurred vision. Her throat ached as she shook her head and tried to get a grip. 'God, yes, I'm fine. Totally fine,' she assured him, smiling to illustrate the point.

'When did you last have anything to eat?' He gave a self-condemnatory grimace. 'I should have thought.'

Megan pushed her hair behind her ears. 'I had something on the motorway.' The *something* had been a sandwich, which had tasted like plastic; she had left most of it untouched on her plate.

'That was hours ago.'

'Was it?' The last twenty-four hours had been such a blur that she had lost all sense of time.

His searching scrutiny took in the dark shadows beneath her big china-blue eyes. 'You're running on pure adrenaline, aren't you?' he accused.

'Please don't fuss—I hate being fussed.'

Her frown deepened ominously as he talked right across her petulant complaint. 'You've got to look after yourself now,' he reproved.

'I do…I am…'

'How about an omelette? You sit there…better still, lie there, and I'll…'

As he began to rise Megan reached out and caught him by the wrist. She lifted her eyes to his and thought she saw something move at the back of Luc's eyes as he stared fixedly at the pale, slim fingers curved over his much darker skin.

Self-consciously she let her hand fall away and struggled to regain her composure.

The muscles in Luc's brown throat rippled as he swallowed hard, but still he didn't meet her eyes.

'I couldn't eat now…not with things the way they are.'

He turned his head and their eyes locked, smoky grey on shimmering blue. Megan's breathing slowed, everything slowed as she registered the build-up of tension in the air around them.

Even in the privacy of her own thoughts Megan was reluctant to use the only adjective that could begin to describe this dangerous tension—*sexual*. It had a tactile quality and like an invisible envelope it enclosed them in a highly charged bubble.

'The way they are…?'

The throaty rasp of his voice vibrated through her. 'I'm sorry that you didn't have the sort of upbringing every single child deserves, but proposing that we set up home together is no solution. You can't realistically expect us to pretend that we are a couple…?' She shook her head. 'It's a crazy idea. I can't even believe you're suggesting it.'

'I don't want my child growing up with a father he sees every other weekend. I want to be an integral part of his life.'

'I appreciate that,' she said softly. 'But you have to see that living under the same roof, but leading separate lives, is a non-starter even in a house as big as Underwood.'

He frowned. 'Who said anything about leading separate lives?'

Megan went pale. 'Well, naturally I just assumed…' She swallowed and directed a questioning look at his chiselled features. 'You're not serious…?'

'I'm deadly serious,' he assured her grimly. 'Actually I've never been more serious in my life.'

Megan lifted a hand to her spinning head. 'You want us to *live* together...? Live together like...share the same...?' She gulped and began to shake her head vigorously.

'Isn't that what I've been saying? It's the practical solution.'

'I don't want to be practical,' she wailed. 'I want...' Her eyes lifted to his and she stopped dead just before she blurted out the forbidden, *I want you to love me!*

Luc wasn't sympathetic. 'You don't want to be pregnant but you are; people do things they don't want to all the time.'

Megan found this contention deeply depressing, she had to assume that living with her came under the heading of *Things he didn't want to do*. His what's-your-problem attitude stemmed from the fact he was willing to do anything for the sake of his unborn child.

There were any number of flaws in his reasoning, which Megan suspected had more to do with emotion than common sense, but she had to admit he made his case pretty effectively. If she said no she would be putting her own selfish needs before those of their unborn child. She took a couple of deep breaths to calm herself.

'What about love?'

Luc studied her in silence for a moment before responding, 'You want me to say I love you?'

'I want you to consider the very real possibility that one or both of us will fall in love for real at some point. What's that going to do to our child?'

'I'm not going to fall in love with anyone.'

'It's not something you plan.' She could attest to this personally. Had she planned to walk into that flat and find a man who would change her life totally? 'And you may have given up hope of finding a soulmate, but I haven't.'

Luc's regard became cold as stone as his eyes narrowed on her flushed defiant face. 'Did you have anyone in particular in mind?'

Megan frowned; his soft query confused her. 'I don't know what you mean.'

'He wouldn't happen to be called John, would he?'

'John? I don't know any—' She broke off, a bubble of laughter forming in her throat. 'John…you mean John Saxon, my estate manager?'

How many *Johns* did she want? he wondered sourly. 'The John who runs the estate single-handed, the one who is waiting your return with bated breath.'

'John is very attractive, but he celebrated his sixtieth birthday last year. It was a great night—his wife, three sons and eight grandchildren were all there,' she said, taking malicious pleasure from the bands of dark colour that appeared across the angles of his cheekbones.

'Were you jealous? My God!' She gaped, studying his face. 'You were, weren't you?'

Luc's mouth thinned. 'I don't want another man bringing up my child.'

'Well, there's not much chance of that happening in the near future,' she admitted.

'So you're not planning on falling in love?'

'That's an extremely stupid question.'

'Humour me and answer it.'

'Like I already told you, it's not the sort of thing you plan,' she retorted, studying her feet. 'But as I can't rule it out totally at some future date,' she lied, 'you'd better get used to the idea.'

His eyes narrowed to slits. 'I don't damn well want to get used to the idea!'

'That's not a very sensible attitude.'

'*Sensible!*' His sensual upper lip curled in derision. 'Sense doesn't come into any of this. No buts,' he added before she had even opened her mouth. 'Just sit there and be quiet while I make you some food.' He scanned her face with an unnerving laser-like intensity before pronouncing, 'You look absolutely awful.'

Luc was efficient in the kitchen, but then, she thought, he did everything efficiently. The omelette, which he filled with mushrooms and chives from a pot on the window ledge, was delicious. The crusty bread he spread with butter was equally tasty.

Luc brought the food to her on a tray, which she balanced on her lap. He didn't eat; he just sat and watched her, which ought to have put her off, but once she started eating Megan discovered she was so ravenous that nothing could stop her enjoying her impromptu meal.

'Thank you, that was delicious,' she said primly when her plate was clean.

'I feed all the women I get pregnant.'

The self-recrimination in his voice made her frown. 'I don't blame you you know.'

He removed the tray and shot her a strange look. 'I know you don't.'

Megan puzzled over his somewhat enigmatic response as she listened to him banging things in the kitchen area. After a long, exhausting drive and all the days tension, a full stomach and the warm fire had a predictable effect.

She'd just close her eyes for a few moments.

The next thing she knew the room was in darkness. Her fingers touched an unfamiliar throw that was laid over her. Totally disorientated, Megan sat bolt upright with a start.

'Don't panic,' a voice in the darkness soothed.

It all came flooding back. 'I fell asleep.'

'That you did.' Luc flicked the switch of a table lamp and a gentle glow illuminated the big room.

'Why didn't you wake me up?'

She ran a hand over her hair and found one side was sticking up. She tried to pat it down. Luc was the sort of person who didn't get sticky-up hair; he was the sort of person who managed to look perfect no matter the situation.

Now was no exception to this rule. Looking at him, she was engulfed by a wave of longing so intense it hurt.

He looked amused by the question. 'For what reason?'

'Well, I can't drive back home tonight...' Her glance drifted towards a darkened window. 'What time is it anyway?' she wanted to know.

'Ten.'

'What?' she groaned, pushing aside the throw. 'I'll never find a hotel room now.'

'There's a perfectly good bed upstairs.' He saw her expression and he gave a cynical smile. 'And a perfectly good sofa here, which I will take, and,' he added, 'there are clean sheets on the bed.'

Megan was not happy with the arrangement but she accepted the inevitable with as much good grace as possible under the circumstances.

There were no blinds on the roof windows in Luc's big bedroom so she could lie in bed and see the stars above. She could also see the time on the dial of her watch.

She consulted it now and found that it was three-thirty, five minutes later than the last time she had looked! Perhaps a drink of milk might help...?

The getting of the milk involved going downstairs where Luc was sleeping. But, she reminded herself, Luc sleeping wasn't a problem—it was Luc awake that she had to worry about.

Without switching on the lights she slipped quietly downstairs. She winced and froze warily when the electric light from the fridge spilled out into the dark room. Tensely she waited...but no voice in the dark demanded to know who was there...

Clearly Luc was a deep sleeper.

Obviously she was relieved. She didn't *want* him to wake up and find her there; that would be *really* stupid.

Her foot on the bottom step, she stopped and turned back... *Impulse...?* Isn't this what you planned to do all along? Her heart was beating so fast she was sure it would wake the sleeping man. Isn't that what you want…?

With a frown she dismissed the intrusive voice in her head and stood looking down at the shadowy sleeping figure. She couldn't see his face, but the blanket spread over him had fallen down to waist level as he slept, revealing that he was naked at least from the waist up. Below…? Do not go there, Megan!

She looked with longing that made her throat ache at the smooth, supple line of his strong back and the deliciously defined musculature of his broad shoulders. The muscles low in her belly cramped.

What am I doing? She pressed a hand across her tight, aching breasts. If he woke up now what would she say? I couldn't resist a quick peek…? In the darkness a flush of mortification spread over her skin.

She was literally about to turn away when a deep voice enquired, 'Well, are you going to stand there all night, or are you going to get in?'

Megan froze like a startled animal caught in the beam of a strong headlight as Luc flipped over onto his back.

'You're awake,' she gasped stupidly.

'Of course I'm awake.' The scathing derision in his voice was mingling with a distinguishable note of strain.

In the semi-darkness their eyes locked.

Still holding her gaze, he flung back the thin blanket and Megan saw that his naked state extended below the waist. Her entire body started to shake; even in this light there was no mistaking his state of arousal.

'There's no room,' she protested weakly.

'Underneath me…on top of me…'

Megan gave a low moan of sheer lustful longing. She pulled the tee shirt he had given her over her head in one smooth motion. She stood poised, her pale body gleaming translucently and heard his sharp intake of breath.

'Your feet are cold and you're shaking!' he said as she slid in beside him.

'So are you,' she discovered. 'You have no idea how much I have wanted to touch you,' she admitted, running her hands over the lean, smooth contours of his body and making him shake a lot more.

'Tell me about it,' he invited.

Megan did.

At some point in the night he carried her upstairs to the big bed.

When she complained that the bed had gone cold Luc laughed throatily and said that there was a tried and tested method of warming up a bed.

As he pulled her beneath him and touched her in her most secret places with a skill that was simply devastating she wondered if he had utilised his bed-warming skills with anyone else in this particular bed.

She pushed aside the intrusive question and let the tension flow from her body. Why spoil what was perfect by wanting more? What Luc was giving her was more than she had ever imagined experiencing.

CHAPTER FOURTEEN

LUC, behind the wheel of Megan's car, stopped in the village to fill the car with petrol. Megan took the opportunity to nip to the village shop, which was next door. The place, which smelt of newly baked bread, was amazingly well stocked. Megan peered at the amazing selection of cheese and cooked meats in the cold cabinet and the attractively displayed local organic vegetables, commenting on the fact to the woman behind the counter.

'If we want to encourage people to shop locally and not go to the big supermarkets in town we have to give them what they want.'

This sounded like good business sense to Megan, who left with some locally produced cheese, which the woman had personally recommended, as well as the two fat Sunday newspapers she had come in for.

Luc was sitting in the car waiting for her when she got back, drumming his fingers on the steering wheel. She slid in beside him. They had agreed to drive in shifts—at least, she had agreed and he had said nothing at all, which to save argument she had decided to believe equalled assent.

'Where have you been?'

'Like there's so much choice? Though you can get pretty much what you want in the shop. I bought some blue smelly cheese.' Luc laughed when she attempted to read the Welsh label on it.

'I know the one and it is delicious, but you can't have any.'

Megan's chin went up. 'Because you say so.' If he thought he could go around issuing autocratic decrees left

138

and right and she would meekly sit there and take it, he was in for a disappointment.

'Because you're pregnant and pregnant women should not eat, amongst other things, soft cheeses.'

'Really…?'

His sensual lips curved upwards. 'Really.'

Megan shook her head; this being pregnant was a mine-field. 'How on earth did you know?'

He inserted the ignition key. 'I'm well read, talking of which…' His pained glance touched the pile of newspapers on her knee. 'What do you intend to do with those?'

'Don't worry, I'm not going to eat them. What do you think I'm going to do with them? I'm going to read them.'

'While I'm driving?'

'Well, not while I'm driving.' What was his problem?

'Broadsheet newspapers?'

'You prefer tabloids?'

His lips moved in a spasm of fastidious distaste as she selected a paper and cheerfully tossed the other one over her shoulder. The pages scattered over the back seat. His thoughts were diverted from the unreadable quality of crumpled papers when Megan then crossed her legs, long, sexy, go-on-for-ever legs. She proceeded to balance one edge of the paper precariously on one knee, leaving the other to flap against the driving mirror.

'I'd *prefer* you didn't distract me while I'm driving.' Luc, whose eyes were riveted to the expanse of smooth, rounded thigh her knee-crossing action had exposed, fully appreciated the irony of his comment.

Tight-lipped, she folded the paper with a lot of loud sighs. 'Am I allowed to *talk*?' she enquired spikily when she had disposed of the newspaper in the back seat. She had seen him look at her legs and was excited and trying desperately not to show it.

'I'm a captive audience.'

Megan looked at his hands on the wheel, and a freeze-frame image flashed across her retina—an image straight from a fantasy, only it hadn't been, had it…? She really had sat astride him and pinioned his hands above his head? Not that he had seemed to mind very much.

The memory of her depravity and how much she had enjoyed it sent her body temperature soaring by what felt like several hundred degrees in the space of a single heart-beat.

'I don't feel like talking,' Megan grunted, turning her face away from him. She looked out the window and tried really hard to concentrate on the scenery. In direct contradiction of her earlier comment she almost immediately added, 'About last night…' Did she imagine that his hands tight-ened on the wheel?

Up to that point neither of them had commented on the sleepless night they had shared. Megan, exhausted, had drifted off to sleep near dawn. When she had woken up she had been alone, a holdall sitting in the middle of the bed-room. Then Luc had walked into the room minus clothes and modesty!

Megan, who had been taking a sly peek into the bag, almost fell over. Her eyes had moved in helpless approval of the sleek, muscular lines of his incredible body. His skin, still dusted with water droplets had gleamed the colour of old gold.

A disturbing half-smile had played about his fascinating lips as he'd continued to towel his dark hair dry.

'I can think of better uses for that towel,' she croaked, tearing her hungry eyes from his body.

'It's not like you've not seen it all before, and I think you're wearing enough for both of us,' he commented, turn-ing his amused attention to the blanket she had arranged sarong-wise to cover herself. 'Nice outfit, but not really suit-able for the journey. You'd better get a move on,' he added casually, flicking the towel in her direction. 'There's a se-vere gale warning out for later. I don't fancy getting caught in the middle of a storm. You do remember agreeing to me moving in on a trial basis?'

Last night, she would have agreed to anything he'd suggested. The way she remembered it she pretty much had. Once Luc had got over his concern about sex not harming the baby, he had been pretty inventive.

'I remember everything.'

She still did, which made bringing up the subject now hard, but she had to know.

Luc slowed at a crossroads and squinted up at the signpost partially hidden by a hedge. 'What part of last night specifically did you have in mind?'

'It was all pretty incredible,' she responded with a husky catch in her voice. Beside her she was aware of Luc inhaling sharply. 'At least I thought so...' She took a deep breath. 'I have to know...'

He slid a teasing look at her flushed face and turned left onto a quiet country road. 'If it was good for me?'

She shook her head, then, aware that his attention was on the winding road, explained. 'I have to know if you slept with me because you wanted to get me to agree to you moving in.'

There was a long silence. Megan risked a peek at his profile, it was totally unreadable as he concentrated on the road ahead.

'In a kind of look-what-you'd-be-missing sort of way?'

Megan's heart sank. There was no anger in his voice, his manner was almost indolent, but the deliberate pauses in between his words just screamed with it.

'If that had been my motivation, would it have worked?'

Megan heaved a massive sigh. 'Oh, God, yes...*totally*,' she admitted. 'I have absolutely no will power where you're concerned,' she revealed rashly.

A long sibilant hiss escaped through his clenched teeth, as if this piece of devastating honesty was the last thing Luc had been expecting to hear.

'I had no ulterior motive last night beyond the fact I haven't thought of anything else but having you in my bed since that first time. Does that make you feel better?'

Megan didn't reply, she couldn't, her vocal cords simply didn't function—for that matter nothing else did either. *Better*, he had said! Catatonic might be more apt.

'You've gone awfully quiet.'

'I'm thinking,' she croaked.

'Thinking what?'

'Thinking great sex isn't a sound basis for a long-lasting relationship, but we might as well enjoy it while it lasts.' Megan was pleased that she'd managed to inject the right light-hearted note into her response.

Luc's jaw tightened as he gazed grimly ahead. 'It's going to last a hell of a long time.'

He was wrong, of course; it didn't. Though for a while there she had started believing him, they were the best three months of her life. They were also some of the busiest.

The first month she was still commuting up to London and then the next two months there were the inevitable teething problems that came about from the upheaval of the transfer. She had to work late frequently and arrived home depressed and tired.

Luc didn't complain about the hour or demand to know where she had been. He would take one look at her pale, exhausted face and tell her she looked like hell, then he'd kiss her until the colour returned to her cheeks.

Luc knew a lot about kissing; even thinking about his mouth made her insides melt.

On a typical evening, while she soaked in a scented bath with her non-alcoholic drink he would sit on the edge and sip his wine while he coaxed the details of her days from her. He had a unique ability to make her see the funny side of things that had seemed like major disasters. Then he would tell her about his day, things that had happened in the estate or the entire chapter that had been consigned to the bin.

Like their love making, no two evenings together were the same, but they were all magical to Megan who had never experienced this sort of sharing with anyone before.

The magic was short-lived. At the beginning of November she was searching for a piece of paper that she had scribbled down a friend's change of address on when she saw THE LETTER. She always thought of THE LETTER in capital letters. She had only needed to read one line and the signature: 'I will always love you. Grace.' This had been enough to send her little world crashing around her ears.

Had she imagined that Luc was happy because she was? The irony was she had begun to think lately that he really might actually share her feelings…that he really might be in love with her. On one or two occasions she had even imagined that he had been on the brink of saying something; now she knew for sure that this had been wishful thinking.

Humiliated and hurting, she had taken immediate and drastic action. The result was that she now slept alone in the big bed that they had once shared.

CHAPTER FIFTEEN

'DON'T worry, the boss has already been down,' the man who had been given the roofing contract had said when she'd appeared on site.

Megan's chin lifted at the patronising tone. 'I am the boss,' she told him before she asked exhaustive questions about every detail of the project.

As she made her way back up to the house using the short cut through the wood she turned the interchange over in her head, getting madder and madder. Of course she was glad Luc had fitted into estate life so easily. It was just he fitted in *so* well that there were occasions when she felt as though she was surplus to requirements.

It would have been nice to be needed, she reflected with a self-pitying sigh. As she reached the kitchen door John saw her and came across.

'How are you feeling?' He addressed the question to her bump, not her, but Megan didn't mind this. She had got used to being the uninteresting part of a joint package.

'Fine, thank you.' She patted her stomach with a smile. 'But I'm looking forward to meeting this little one.'

'If you're looking for Luc, he's over at the old stables.'

'Is there a problem, John?' Megan had been as excited as everyone else when a Sunday supplement had expressed an interest in doing a piece on the old stable workshops—work on the extension was due to be finished the next month and this opportunity to publicise the place was heaven-sent.

The newspaper people were due this morning and the last thing they needed was any last-minute hitch.

The older man shook his head. 'Not now. There was a power problem,' he admitted. 'That looked like really

144

throwing a spanner in the works, but that man of yours,' he conceded, 'can turn his hand to most things. He's still got a lot to learn, but he's willing, and he doesn't mind admitting when he's wrong.'

Megan stared at him. Were they both talking about the same man…? The Luc she knew had an inability to even realise when he was wrong, let alone admit it!

'I admit,' John admitted, 'that I had my doubts when he first arrived, but I was wrong. No, I'd say you've got a first-rate man there, Megan, lass.'

Megan just restrained herself from denying ownership.

His comments echoed almost exactly the words her mother had used when they'd spoken on the phone the previous evening—'I hate not being able to see you, but I can relax knowing that Luc is there to look after you, Megan. He really is one in a million.'

'He's driving me mad; he won't let me lift a finger!' Megan complained.

'Isn't that a good thing? I really don't see what your problem is, dear,' Laura responded in a bewildered voice. 'From what you say, he's thrown himself into the place and, quite frankly, supplied what it's been lacking since your father died. I think you've fallen on your feet there.'

Everyone loves Luc, she thought…*including me*. But Luc loves Grace, who loves him right back.

'Oh, yes, he's so busy making himself indispensable around here that we barely see one another. That,' she added bitterly, 'is probably the idea.' Megan listened to the loud silence on the other end of the line and covered her mouth to stifle the groan that rose to her lips.

Her waistline might be a distant memory, she might waddle and not walk, but some things didn't change—such as her unerring ability to say the wrong thing at the even *wronger* time.

'Don't talk nonsense, Megan, the man is obviously deeply in love with you.'

If she hadn't felt so miserable she might have laughed.

'Are you and Luc having problems…?' her mother wanted to know.

'No, we are not having problems,' her daughter gritted. How could you have problems when you never saw one another? When Luc wasn't writing he was busy inspiring admiration and devotion with his enthusiasm. Before she had started her maternity leave it had been easier. Now she saw him all the time and it hurt.

'Because if you are you should talk. It's not good bottling things up.'

On this subject at least her mum was right—things surely couldn't go on like this for much longer. She was pretty certain that Luc was feeling the strain too. Why else did he avoid being alone with her? He was thoughtful, kind, concerned for her welfare, but all this tender loving care was inspired, she was sure, from a strong sense of duty, not love.

At her last appointment with her obstetrician Megan had listened to one heavily pregnant woman confiding to another that her husband expected a medal if he whisked a duster around the living room *and*, she'd complained, barely able to restrain her smugness, '…he can't get enough of me. We've had more early nights than you would believe!'

Megan would have welcomed some slackness with the household chores if Luc had suggested a few early nights, but Luc kept late nights; sometimes it was two or three in the morning when she heard him coming up. She heard him because she was listening out for his tread as he walked past her door. Sometimes as she lay there in the dark, her breath coming fast, she thought she heard his footsteps stop outside her door, but they never did.

Pretending never had been Megan's strong suit. It was ironic really—she had secretly hoped that Luc would fall in love with her and he had actually fallen in love with the damned estate. She had to be realistic: things were not going to change and she would be a fool to pretend otherwise.

Well, he could stay, she'd probably have to contend with a workers' revolt if she asked him to leave, but she couldn't keep up the illusion they were a couple. Luc would probably prefer to stop pretending too, she realised. It couldn't be much fun for him either. If he agreed, he could move into the newly renovated farmhouse by the river next month.

It wasn't ideal, but this situation required some compromise…mostly on her part, admittedly. As far as she could see her plan provided the best of both worlds for Luc; he would be on hand for the baby, but he would be a free agent.

Of course there were drawbacks to this arrangement, especially as his freedom would no doubt involve the reappearance of Grace. So long as he didn't flaunt her under her nose she could cope. After all, they were both adults…

'Is anything wrong, lass?'

Megan pushed aside the nagging concern that her coping mechanisms might not be up to dealing with the reality of Luc having sex with another woman five minutes' walk from where she was sleeping and shook her head.

'I'm fine. The stables, you say…?'

'I suppose you know that this is bribery?'

'So long as it's not extortion.'

Megan, who had taken the shortcut, was halfway through the ivy-covered door when she identified the owner of the ironic tone. She came to a halt and glanced at her wristwatch. How typical—she had finally made a decision and worked up the courage to carry it through and Luc had company. If she hadn't already done the entire I'll-definitely-speak-to-him-later thing and known for a fact that when later came she wouldn't, Megan would have gone back to the house.

'You can laugh about it.' The stranger's voice was lifted in wonder. 'Does this mean we're quits?'

'Let me see,' she heard Luc muse. 'A double-paged feature for a reputation ruined…?' There was a pause and he added in a voice that was chill and contemptuous, 'I don't think so, Malone.'

Megan stepped back into the shadows, feeling guilty as hell for eavesdropping, but unable not to. She had never heard Luc sound like that; she hardly recognised his hard voice. She knew she ought to reveal herself, but 'reputation ruined'—*what was that about?*

'It was nothing personal, Lucas,' she heard the other man placate.

'Strange that it felt pretty personal from where I was standing.'

'Yeah, well…it's a tough old world, and we did print an apology.'

'Two lines on an inside page?'

'All right, I still owe you,' came the reluctant admission. 'But just don't let on I've got a conscience or my career will be over.'

The men must have begun to walk away, because she could hear the deep, distinctive sound of Luc's voice, but, frustratingly, not what he was saying. She stood there for a couple of minutes waiting to be sure that they had gone before she emerged.

Her head was in a whirl. One thing was pretty clear— this newspaper article hadn't been the marvellous piece of unsolicited good fortune they had all imagined. Luc had arranged it. Clearly he felt that this journalist owed him for his *ruined reputation* and he was calling in that favour.

Now she owed *Luc* and she couldn't even let on she knew, let alone thank him—not without giving away the fact that she had dragged the story from Uncle Malcolm.

Her mind bent to this new dilemma, she walked through the arch into the courtyard and straight into the solid chest of a tall figure. Even with her eyes closed she would have recognised that very individual scent, a mingling of soap and the warm male and totally unique fragrance of his skin.

Megan's eyes weren't closed. At the moment of collision

she had automatically tilted her face up to him and found herself looking straight into those scarily penetrating eyes of his...eyes that had as many moods as the stormy sea they reminded her of at that moment.

Luc's hands came up to steady her. She was very conscious of them lying heavily on her shoulders.

'Where are you going in such a hurry?'

Megan fought her way out of the soft fog of desire that misted her vision and made her thought processes slow and sluggish. This was physically the closest they had been in several weeks and the desire to lean into his warm, gloriously hard body threatened to overwhelm her.

She was afraid that if she started leaning she might not be able to stop—*ever*! *I miss you,* she wanted to say, which, considering they saw one another every day, was a comment he might find strange.

'Nowhere...that is here...' Oh, God, if I look as guilty as I sound, I'm in *big* trouble.

Luc, apparently satisfied she wasn't going to fall over, allowed his hands to slide down her shoulders.

The feeling of loss as his hands fell away was quite irrational and totally devastating.

'Oh, they've arrived,' she cried, affecting surprise as she observed the signs of activity in the courtyard. 'How are things going?'

'Did you miss that bit?'

Megan gave a panic-stricken gulp and, playing for time, shook her head. 'Pardon...?' Had he known she was there or was her guilt making her imagine things...?

'Did you miss the part of our conversation from your little hiding place?' he enquired politely.

To be caught listening like a naughty child by Luc, of all people, brought a mortified flush to her cheeks.

'Oh, in that case, let me bring you up to date. Malone, the reporter, says it's going well, but he thinks it would go better if our bronzed blacksmith would take his shirt off.'

'Sam!' she exclaimed, momentarily diverted. 'You're kidding.'

Luc shook his head. 'I'm not and neither,' he added drily, 'was Sam when he told them where to go.'

'I can imagine.'

'After ten minutes of negotiation he has agreed to roll up his sleeves. You know, Megan,' he added seamlessly, 'you don't lie very well.'

This wasn't true. She had told him some big fat lies and he had swallowed them hook, line and sinker! But maybe, she thought despondently, that was because he had wanted to believe them.

'Do you suggest I start to take instruction from an expert...?'

'I don't lie to you.'

'No, you just don't tell me anything. And I wasn't hiding,' she added with a defiant sniff.

One satirical brow lifted. 'No...?'

'No. I came here looking for you.'

'Now that's unusual enough to merit my attention,' he observed sardonically.

She angled a wary look at his lean face. It was hard to gauge his mood, but then it always was. Not only did Luc have mercurial changes of mood, he was very good at hiding what he was feeling. 'I've had an idea that could solve all our problems.'

'It must be quite an *idea*.' he drawled.

So he wasn't trying to pretend they *didn't* have problems. This was good, she told herself firmly. They were being grown up about this.

Megan repressed a very un-grown-up urge to stamp her feet and yell, *It isn't fair!* 'I've just been to see the farm; the roof's almost finished.'

Luc released an exasperated hiss through clenched teeth. 'I *know* it's almost finished; I went down earlier. There was no need for you to go.'

'I wanted to.'

'I don't suppose it occurred to you to take the Land Rover...? Or better still ask someone to drive you.'

'Don't be silly.' The impatient recommendation brought a glint to his deep-set eyes. 'People have better things to do than ferry me around, and it's only a five-minute walk.' To drive that distance seemed to Megan the height of indolence.

'A five-minute walk down a track that has a two-in-one incline and is at the moment slick with several inches of mud.'

'The doctor says exercise is good for me.'

'I hardly think that's what he had in mind.'

'So now you're a doctor too, are you?'

An amused expression settled on his lean, dark features as he took the brunt of her angry glare. 'I've noticed you always get shrill when you're in the wrong.'

'I am not shrill...or,' she added belatedly, 'in the wrong.'

'Yeah,' he agreed, 'I'd noticed that too.' His expression hardened as he went on. 'Since last week's rain that path is lethal. If you slip there's a nasty...what would you say— twenty-foot drop...? Why,' he demanded, drawing a frustrated hand through his collar-length ebony hair, 'do you insist on taking unnecessary risks?

'Risk...what risk?' she scoffed.

His furious glance was drawn to the pale, slender column of her neck. 'It's only a matter of time before you break your damned neck,' he forecast huskily.

Megan, recalling the path, had to admit he did have a point. 'I didn't fall,' she placated. *Nearly* didn't count, did it...? And there was no point winding him up. 'It'll be lovely when it's finished, don't you think?'

'The only lovely thing he could think about at that moment was her neck. A muscle in his lean cheek clenched as his eyes were compulsively drawn to the blue veined delicate hollow at the base of her throat.

'The renovations are a good quality.' His eyes narrowed

suspiciously. 'What's this about, Megan?' he wanted to know.

'So you like the farmhouse?' she persisted, in a doggedly upbeat manner. 'The lovely views,' she enthused. 'And the attic conversion is a very useful space, very versatile. It would make a great studio don't you think?'

'Have you decided to become an estate agent? Is that your grand idea?'

Megan gave an exasperated sigh. Subtlety, she reflected, was wasted on Luc. 'As us living together is not working out I thought it would be a good idea if you moved into the farmhouse when it's finished. That way you'd have your freedom and be near enough to be involved with the baby as much as you liked.'

The fact he hadn't interrupted and had heard her out in attentive silence was, she decided, slanting an enquiring look at his lean, enigmatic face, encouraging. So encouraging she felt like curling up in a foetal ball of misery and crying her eyes out.

Can't live with him can't live without him. The words popped into her head—a cliché maybe, but it was a cliché that was particularly appropriate to her unenviable situation.

'What do you think?' she asked brightly.

His long lashes lowered in a concealing dark mesh over his eyes but he barely skipped a beat before replying, 'I think…no.'

'No what?' Her shoulders lifted and tried to hide her growing desperation. 'Which bit of my idea doesn't work for you?' If he didn't like the farmhouse there were other options—there had to be because she simply couldn't go on this way!

'No as in no, none of it works for me.'

She opened her mouth to protest at his uncompromising response, but Luc got in before her.

'How long were you standing in your little niche eavesdropping?'

The abrupt change of subject threw Megan. When it came to mental gymnastics she had learnt that she couldn't keep up with Luc. It was a waste of time hoping he'd drop it. Once he got his teeth into a subject that was it—he just didn't let go. She shrugged evasively and tried not to look guilty.

'I just happened to be standing there.' This explanation sounded lame even to her. 'You can't just say no like that.' There was more than a hint of desperation in her hoarse addition.

'I just did,' he reminded her.

Megan gritted her teeth. He had to be the *most* infuriating man ever born. 'We have to discuss—'

'So how long did you *just happen* to be standing there?'

His sarcastic enquiry deepened the flush that already stained her smooth cheeks. 'I didn't want to disturb you. It seemed like a private conversation. Now, about the arrangements for your move—'

'No move, no arrangements. The only place I'll be moving is into your bedroom. I'm sick of being stuck out in Siberia in more ways than one.' While she was still digesting this extraordinary statement he seamlessly picked up the previous topic. 'So you decided to listen in—don't feel too bad about it. It's a perfectly normal response. I just want to know how much you heard.'

'So you can fill in the blanks...?' Her lips twisted in a self-derisive grimace.

It was so unfair, she reflected despondently. She obsessively craved details about his life, but, with very few exceptions, the things she had picked up about him she had gained second-hand. Even during the time when they had been close he had held back.

Luc shared nothing of himself with her and she wanted to know everything there was to know! Some of her thirst for knowledge bordered on the masochistic, especially in matters concerning his marriage and his wife. Did he still talk to her? Did he keep all her letters?

But she would have settled for the silly little things like how old had he been when he learnt to ride a bike? What was his favourite flavour ice cream? What did he think about when he went on his long, solitary walks?

She wanted to know so much, but she knew so little, and yet it seemed to her that Luc knew all her secrets…all except one. And if he refused to move out of the house, she suspected it was only a matter of time before he found that out too! Well, one place he wasn't going to move was her bedroom—pretty obvious she had misheard that casual insertion, but she had to check it out…

'Did you just get all Alpha male and announce you were moving back into my bedroom?' Her mildly amused tone invited him to correct her.

Luc, his expression stony didn't respond to her smile. 'You can move into mine if you prefer.'

'Why would you want to share a room with me?'

One darkly delineated brow rose to a satirical angle. 'Why does a man normally want to share a room with a woman?'

Was he trying to be deliberately cruel? 'The normal hardly applies in this instance.'

Luc's face darkened with displeasure as he noted the resigned expression on her face as she scanned her own ripe body.

'Or are you worried about what Uncle Malcolm will think when he comes to stay next week?' The probability that this was all about keeping up appearances brought a despondent slump to her shoulders.

The same potentially awkward situation had arisen at Christmas when her mother and Jean Paul had come to stay. It had been Megan who had come up with a solution. Luc's response when she had assured him she would sleep on the camp-bed in the dressing-room had been scathing.

'Why not go the whole hog and sleep on the floor?' he'd suggested. 'It makes about as much damned sense.'

Megan had talked him round eventually, though he'd insisted on being the one to sleep on the camp-bed, and he hadn't pretended to like it—but then what man of six four was going to like the idea of sleeping on a narrow put-you-up bed. She hadn't liked it either, but it had been better than the alternative. It had been bad enough with her mother dropping broad hints abut weddings without having to field awkward enquiries about their sleeping arrangements.

'Uncle Malcolm really isn't going to notice,' she reassured him. 'Besides, I think he already knows you only moved in because of the baby. And you can't possibly sleep on that camp-bed again.'

Luc's long lashes came down over a gleam of anger. 'I wasn't intending to sleep on the camp-bed.'

'Well, normally I'd take my turn but it would probably collapse under my weight.'

'You're not sleeping on it either.'

'But—'

'And Mal's not coming,' he revealed casually.

'Of course he's coming.'

Luc shook his head. 'No, I explained to him that you're not up to visitors.'

For a moment Megan stared at him in open-mouthed incredulity. '*You what…?*' She expelled a wrathful pent-up breath in one long, sibilant hiss. 'How dare you tell him that!? She pressed her fingers to her temples where she felt the blood throbbing. 'I'm absolutely sick of being treated like a child. You,' she declared, stamping her foot, 'have absolutely no right whatsoever. You're not my husband.'

Luc's glance lifted. A look she couldn't quite pin down flickered briefly across his face. 'If I was, would that mean you'd do what I suggested?'

She released a scornful laugh. '*In your dreams!*'

'I thought as much.'

'And you don't suggest, you issue proclamations and expect everyone else to meekly follow them.' Most people, as far as she could tell, did just that. His orders might have been concealed behind a smile and a laid-back attitude but, as far as Megan was concerned, they were still orders. 'I don't respond well to authority.'

'Why, you little rebel, you.' His thin-lipped taunt drew a gurgle of rage from her clamped lips. His brows lifted in enquiry. His phoney smile faded as he added, 'Look, I'm not going to apologise for looking after your best interests, Megan. You need plenty of rest; remember what the doctor said.'

The occasion a couple of months earlier when she had turned up at his bedroom door in the middle of the night had borne no resemblance to the fantasy he had polished and nurtured over the weeks since they had shared a bed. The fear in her eyes when she had sobbed she was losing the baby would stay with him for ever.

'Among other things, I remember he said it would be advisable for me to refrain from sex,' she reminded him, flushing.

It had seemed pretty ironic at the time. Luc had been suitably supportive, dismissing the burden of celibacy with a shrug of his magnificent shoulders. But he had grilled the unfortunate medic on every possible aspect of her condition and treatment.

She didn't have a condition, the doctor had said, her blood pressure was slightly raised and she was, quite simply, exhausted. The treatment he had recommended was rest and plenty of it. The slight blood loss that had alarmed her, he went on to explain, was most probably not significant. It happened to a lot of women and he was merely erring on the side of caution.

'Most probably' was not a phrase that Luc had been happy with, and he'd had no qualms about sharing this with the doctor. The GP, who usually had an air of reassuring calm, had looked in need of some rest himself by the time he had finally managed to get rid of Luc.

'Do you think I'm going to leap on you Megan? You've made your feelings on that subject perfectly plain and I'm not in the habit of forcing myself on women who find my touch repulsive.'

'Of course I don't think you'd do that,' she retorted flushing.

'Haven't you ever wanted to hold someone?' He broke off and turned away.

'You don't want to hold me; you want to hold…'

Luc swung back and the expression of ferocious anger in his taut face shocked her.

'What are you talking about?' He heard the breathy whisper of her forlorn sigh and his anger slipped away.

CHAPTER SIXTEEN

THERE was an unusual air of indecision about the habitually assured Luc as he ran a hand down his jaw. The frown line between his darkly defined brows deepened as he met her wary eyes.

'Megan, you're beautiful and you are carrying my child! But I have never felt my child move,' he continued in a thickened, impassioned voice. 'I have never held you in my arms at night, and felt my baby kick.' His glance lowered to her belly.

Just as Megan felt she could not take that long, dragging silence for another second without screaming, Luc's long lashes lifted from the curve of his razor-sharp cheekbones. The raw expression glittering in his deep-set eyes made the breath catch painfully in her throat.

'You have erected a wall—a damned ten-feet-high three-feet-thick wall—between us.' He spread his expressive hands to illustrate the dimensions under discussion. 'And I've no idea why. One minute we were happy together, the next you act as though I've got the plague.'

This grim accusation startled Megan, who opened her mouth to deliver a horrified denial. She paused; could she deny it? Was there not a grain of truth in his accusation? For the first time she looked at things from his point of view; the things she saw brought a worried frown to her brow. It had been her desire to retain a little dignity that had prevented her from telling him she knew about the letter and about Grace. Now she wasn't so sure it had been the right call.

'Hell!' he yelled into the silence. 'You're not just content to push me out of your bed, now you want me out of the damned house. What is it, Megan—out of sight, out of mind?'

If only it were that simple, Megan thought, shaking her head despondently. Suddenly she couldn't hold her frustration in another second. 'That's the problem—you never are.'

He gave an impatient frown. 'I'm never what?'

'Out of my mind…I think about you constantly.'

Luc froze and took a deep shuddering breath. His hard, probing stare pinned her to the spot and he seemed to be able to see straight into her head. 'You think about me…?'

Megan who was already regretting like crazy her candour, flushed and replied icily, 'Didn't I just say so?'

'Then why the big sell…lovely farmhouse, views-to-die-for thing?'

'I said you're constantly in my head, not that I want you to be there or that I like it!' She bit down viciously on her quivering lower lip.

Luc watched a single tear slide silently down her cheek and cursed softly under his breath. 'For God's sake, don't cry!' he pleaded in a husky voice. 'I just can't bear to see you cry—it kills me!' he confessed, swallowing hard.

She gave a sniff. 'S…sorry.'

Luc swore again and took her hand. Megan's eyes widened. She could literally feel the tension and urgency in his lean body.

His eyes swept across her face. Something in his look made her heart pound. 'We need to talk, but not here.'

Overwhelmingly conscious of the warm fingers curled around her own, Megan walked at his side without protest as he led her along the path to a group of buildings that housed amongst other things, the estate manager's office.

'This should be private enough.'

'Hardly private—what if John comes in?' Apparently whatever Luc had to say was so urgent he couldn't wait to get back to the house? Suddenly she wasn't so sure she wanted to know.

Luc dismissed her complaint with an off-hand shrug. 'John has gone home early,' he said, closing the door of the manager's office behind them. 'I told him to take the rest of the day off. He's picking his daughter up from the station.'

'He didn't tell me.'

'I expect he thought I'd tell you.'

'He probably didn't realise that you don't talk to me any more.'

Luc was in the act of pulling forward a leather-padded swivel chair; at her bitter comment his dark head whipped up. 'What the hell are you talking about? We talk...at least I do.'

'*Don't make me laugh!*' Megan, closer to tears than laughter, pleaded. 'You can't bear to be in the same room as me!' She heard her voice rise to a shrill, accusing shriek and winced.

A look of blank astonishment settled on Luc's lean, expressive face.

'Did you think I hadn't realised, Luc? *Please.* I may not be as clever as you, but I'm not *stupid*. You're not exactly subtle,' she told him. 'I walk in a room and you remember you need to be some place else. I know that the baby was all you wanted. But I need to be wanted.'

Luc shook his head and released a hoarse laugh of incredulity. 'That's what you think—that's actually what you think...?' Like his voice, the hand he dragged down his jaw was not quite steady.

'I don't *think*, I *know*,' she retorted fiercely.

Muttering darkly under his breath, Luc wheeled the chair towards her and, ignoring her complaints, pressed her firmly down into the leather seat.

'I don't want to sit down.'

Luc, his hands on the armrests, leaned down towards her. The intimate sensation of his warm breath brushing against her cheek made all the downy hairs on Megan's ultrasensitive skin stand on end. A sigh shivered through her body.

'Tough.'

Her eyes widened in indignation. 'I'm pregnant!'

'So I have to be nice to you?' One dark brow arched. 'Even,' he added grimly, 'if you go out of your way to be unpleasant to me. *You're* the one who wanted not to have any special treatment just because you're pregnant,' he reminded her.

'You're a bully!'

Her tremulous contention drew a harsh laugh from Luc, who, with a stern warning to, 'Stay put, and shut up,' settled himself down on the desk opposite. He pressed his hands against his thighs and stretched his long legs in front of him.

Megan did as he asked, not from any desire to be co-operative, but because the sheer shock at being addressed this way had literally robbed her of speech. She was just rediscovering her vocal cords when he said something that struck her dumb all over again.

'Are you surprised I can't be in the same room as you under the circumstances?' he wanted to know.

Megan turned the colour of her white shirt and tried not to let him see how much his words had hurt her. 'I suppose not,' she agreed unhappily.

She knew it wasn't uncommon for men to be turned off when their partners were pregnant, but Luc's revulsion seemed to go further. Was it all pregnant women he didn't like being around or just her?

Luc was a very sensual man. It was not logical to expect a man like him to survive without sex. Her dreams were plagued with jealous nightmares of slim, eager women throwing themselves at him and him not ducking! Did Grace still enjoy his bedroom skills? Had they ever stopped being lovers? The not knowing, and the not knowing whether she *wanted* to know, was killing her.

'It's not my fault.' It was, though—she was the one who had chucked him out of her bed.

A spasm of irritation crossed his dark, devastatingly handsome features. 'It's your fault I can't be in the same room as you, you stupid, infuriating, *gorgeous* woman!' he yelled.

Gorgeous? Am I hearing things, or did he just call me…? Her glance dropped to the bulky mass of her body and she shook her head; she had *definitely* misheard.

'*My fault…?*' she said cautiously while noting the dark bands of colour that stained the high contours of his chiselled cheekbones.

'You set the damned rules: separate bedrooms, no sex, just good friends…this ringing any bells?' He broke off, breathing hard, and lifted his hands to his head, sinking his fingers into the dark strands of thick glossy hair.

'The doctor said it wasn't safe…'

'You had already asked me to leave, Megan.'

The man who prided himself on his self-control, his ability to view situations with objectivity, made a visible effort to control himself, but his hardly fought composure slipped again when he encountered her wide shocked intensely blue gaze.

'Dear God, don't look at me like that,' he pleaded hoarsely. 'I respect how you feel at the moment…it's just damn hard.'

'How would you know how I feel?' Please let him not know.

'You told me.'

Megan shook her head. If she had confided her feelings she thought she might have remembered. It occurred to her that they might be talking at cross purposes.

'Did you or did you not say the idea of sex while you're pregnant makes you feel ill?'

Of course she recalled the words slung in the heat of an argument. '*You believed me…?*' She gasped, unable to disguise her amazement.

'There's absolutely no way I'm going to force myself on you; it's just difficult for me to be around you when I want…' He stopped, his vibrant colour fading dramatically as his narrowed eyes darted over the contours of her face. 'You *lied*…?'

Megan barely registered his hoarse question. An extraordinary idea was forming in her head. Dear God, now wouldn't *that* be ironic? I'm sitting one end of the enormous house lusting after him and he's sitting the other…!

The baby chose that moment to remind her of its presence, launching a kick at her ribs so strong that she scrunched up her eyes and cried out softly. It also reminded her that the idea of anyone being driven mad with frustrated lust for her in her present condition was remote, to put it mildly.

The moment the cry left her lips Luc was on his feet. 'Are you all right?'

She opened her eyes and found Luc sitting on his heels at her feet. His lean, strong face was chalk-white, the skin drawn taut with anxiety across his magnificent cheekbones. Megan rubbed a hand across her big belly and smiled reassuringly.

'This one packs quite a punch.'

He visibly relaxed. 'Is he kicking you now?'

She nodded and his fascinated eyes returned to her stomach. 'He could be a she,' she reminded him.

'I'd settle for either.' He stretched out his hand towards her. 'Can I…?'

Megan's eyes dropped to his hand. The tentative quality of his request brought a lump to her throat. By way of reply she caught hold of his wrist and laid his hand against her belly.

'I can't feel anything,' he said, disappointed.

'You will,' she promised just before, on cue, the baby launched a kick, less vigorous than the previous one, but strong enough to make Luc cry out in wonder.

'Does that happen a lot?'

The awe in his voice made her smile mistily. 'All the time.'

'Good God…!'

Megan, who found sitting in one position for long made her back ache, shifted her position. Immediately Luc's hand fell away from her stomach.

Instead of straightening up, Luc sat back on his heels and looked at her.

Their faces were almost on a level and there was a quality in his silent, unblinking regard that made Megan deeply uneasy.

'What…?'

He responded to her querulous enquiry with an enigmatic smile. Then, after a suitably nerve-racking silence, he revealed the reason for his odd behaviour. 'You said you lied.' She began to shake her head and he added in a voice that brooked no opposition. 'You lied about being off sex.'

Megan's eyes dropped from his. The perceptive clarity of those opaque depths made her ashamed and defensive at one and the same time. 'I might have stretched the truth,' she admitted gruffly.

'Then your skin didn't crawl at the thought of me touching you?'

Her head lifted. 'Did I *really*…?'

He nodded. 'You did. For God's sake, Megan, *why*…? It's been a total nightmare wanting to touch you, hold you…' He released an unsteady groan. 'Of course I couldn't bear to be in the same room as you; I didn't trust myself!' Pure silver, his molten eyes moved hungrily over her features, which pregnancy had made softer and rounder. 'When I think what you have put me through these months I could strangle you!' He took her chin and tilted her face up to his.

The expression stamped on his lean features took her breath away.

'So,' he said, scanning her face with a heart-stopping

blend of fierce hunger and devastating tenderness. 'You fancy me…'

He sounded so unbelievably smug that she grinned. 'Pity,' she said with a rueful glance down at her body. 'It's too late now to do much about it.'

'*Who says…?*'

'Don't be silly,' she retorted. 'Look at me,' she invited.

'You're beautiful, ripe and luscious.'

This husky fulsome praise sent a tidal wave of warmth through her body. 'That's nice to know,' she admitted, blushing rosily. 'But I'm…well…' *Burning up with lust…?*

Luc looked puzzled. 'You're what?' he prompted, sliding his fingers into her hair. With a sigh Megan let her head fall back as he massaged her scalp.

'It isn't just about sex,' he said.

'It isn't?'

'You think I'm that shallow?' he ground out, looking exasperated at her response.

'Not shallow, but you can't tell me it's not important to you.'

'And it's not to you?

Watching the honey strands fall through his fingers, a handful of her rich, plentiful hair in his hand, he lowered his mouth to hers.

The kiss was so tender, so sweetly passionate that the tears sprang to her eyes as she melted into him.

'Why did you say it, Megan?' he demanded as they drew apart. 'Why did you lie to get me out of your bed?'

It was the question she had hoped he wouldn't ask. Megan shook her head mutely and would have turned away had he not taken hold of her chin firmly between his thumb and forefinger.

'*Why…?*'

'I saw the letter; it was lying there,' she admitted huskily. Luc looked at her blankly. 'What letter?'

'It was an accident. I was looking for my address book,'

she explained stiltedly. 'And…I didn't read it,' she added with an urgent shake of her head. 'But it was open and I saw…I read…' She swallowed and lowered her gaze, too ashamed to look at him.

'I will always love you.' The words had leapt from the page as had the name scrawled at the bottom of the page— *Grace*.

She had not known until that moment that jealousy could be like that, be like a physical pain, a constant gnawing ache that invaded every cell of your body.

Would Luc have got back with his wife if it hadn't been for the child she was carrying? When he'd made love to her at night had he thought abut his ex-wife, had he seen her face when he'd closed his eyes in the moment of release…?

The thought that she'd been a substitute, that while he'd been with her he'd dreamed of being with someone else, was something she just couldn't bear.

Luc was looking mystified. 'What letter?'

'From your…from Grace,' she whispered.

'I get a lot of letters from Grace.'

This was something she could have lived without knowing. Did she declare her undying love in all of them? Megan wondered.

'Considering you're divorced, isn't that a little unusual.'

'She likes to keep in touch, even though she's remarried,' he admitted.

His guarded manner was confirming all her worst fears. 'She's married to someone else now?'

'For the time being.'

Of course, Grace was getting a divorce and she wanted to get back with Luc…who wouldn't? she thought, sliding a covetous look over his long, lean, supremely gorgeous frame. The idea took hold and she felt physically sick. You could be prepared for the worst but when it finally came it still hurt like hell.

'Does that mean that things are not working out for her?'

She was amazed that she could feel so totally wretched and still appear normal.

She realised that she must be faking it really well because Luc didn't appear to have a clue that she was ready to fall apart. He was probably blind to everything else when he thought about his marvellous Grace.

'I told her at the time that...' His shoulders lifted in one of his expressive shrugs. 'But that's Gracie for you.' The rueful tone of his voice increased the icy grip of the fingers that were squeezing her heart.

'She's impetuous?'

He nodded and said with feeling, 'And then some.'

And Megan wanted to head for the nearest dark corner to lick her wounds. Instead she rubbed salt in them by imagining all the outlets for her impetuosity that *Gracie* might have found in the bedroom; or, being impetuous, she probably didn't limit her surprises to one room. They had probably made love in every room of the house.

'The guy's years older than her; he's got children older than she is.'

'A lot of women are attracted to older men. I suppose they offer stability...?'

'It helps if they've got a lot of money stashed away.'

Was he saying his ex-wife had married for money—?

'Don't look so shocked, *chérie*, not everyone is the hopeless romantic you are. Grace is one of ten children; she had a tough life as a kid and just when she had started to get used to having the flashy cars and the big houses it was snatched away from her. She was honest—she couldn't be the wife of a poor man.'

Megan, who had always considered herself the most pragmatic of people, shook her head in protest. 'I'm not a romantic.' A romantic she might not be, but the idea of walking away from your man at a moment when he most needed a wife's support filled her with disgust.

'You haven't asked me how I lost my money...?'

Well, he had plenty of money now, Megan thought. Which meant his avaricious ex was grasping and greedy.

'It's not my business.'

For a long moment Luc scanned her face, then with the deliberation of someone who had come to a decision he pulled out a chair and, spinning it around, straddled it. 'Five years ago I had a successful business and a partner.'

'Yes, you told me.' She gave a quick uninterested smile. 'You hated it, but you made a lot of money...and then lost it.' This moment, the moment when Luc felt able to confide in her, could have meant something very special if she didn't already know what he was going to say. If she hadn't gone behind his back, to Uncle Malcolm.

'Aren't you curious?'

Feeling guilty as sin, she shook her head. 'Not especially.'

'Amazing! You really are the most incredible woman.'

His admiration made her feel worse than ever. 'I'm not incredible at all; I'm terrible!' she wailed, covering her eyes with a hand as she gave a self-condemnatory groan. 'I already know about your partner running off with all the money and the man who committed suicide and how the press were hateful to you.' Megan couldn't look at him.

A short static silence followed her emotional confession. *'Malcolm...?'*

The question had a resigned ring to it and Megan, who had expected him to go ballistic, opened her fingers and peeked cautiously through them.

'It wasn't his fault.'

'No, that I can believe. I have noticed,' he continued drily, 'that when you make up your mind you can be difficult to divert. In fact you can be difficult full stop.'

'Aren't you angry?'

One corner of his fascinating mouth lifted. 'Do you want me to be?'

'No, of course not, it's just I know how you value your

privacy and I know I should have waited until you wanted to tell me.' She bit her lip. 'I wish I had,' she confided huskily.

'If it makes you feel any better, Malcolm supplied me with some information...reluctantly supplied,' he added with a reminiscent grin.

Megan's smooth brow puckered. 'I don't understand.'

'I wanted to know a few things about the creep you almost married.'

'Brian!' she exclaimed, astonished by this revelation. 'Whatever for?'

Megan watched as his white teeth bared in a smile that did not touch his eyes. 'I was kind of curious about what you saw in him in the first place. Now I know. The man is a total creep, but a *pretty* total creep.'

Pretty...? Megan mentally compared Brian's weak chin and average features with the man she was looking at and she laughed; she couldn't help it.

'What's so funny?' he growled.

Megan didn't respond. 'How do you know what Brian looks like?'

'I happened to swing by a bar and he was there.'

Megan's eyes widened. 'You wanted to see him...why?'

Luc passed a hand across his forehead. 'Why the hell do you think...?' His attitude suggested she ought to have found the explanation obvious—she didn't.

'I've not the faintest idea,' she told him.

'I wanted to kick the slime ball's teeth down his throat...' His nostrils flared as he inhaled deeply. 'He hit you,' he gritted.

'And you intended to do what? Hit him?'

'It did cross my mind,' he admitted, rubbing a hand over the stubble on his jaw.

'But you didn't...?' She felt she had to check.

'I got a case of better judgement,' he admitted with the air of someone who regretted the decision. 'I blame it on my dad—he always told me I couldn't pick on anyone smaller than me. The creep only came to my shoulder.'

Megan's eyes dropped from his. 'I'm glad you didn't hit him,' she admitted.

Luc's expression hardened to granite.

'Aside from the fact I really don't need anyone to fight my battles. No big feminist statement,' she promised, 'just plain fact. When I said he hit me, I might have missed out the part where I hit him back…?'

Luc stared at her for a moment, then started to grin. 'You did?'

Shamefaced, she nodded. 'I'm not actually a violent person; it was a reflex action.'

'Did you cause much damage?' he asked with a hopeful expression.

'None that I could see, but apparently the bridge work that needed repairing cost him a packet. He threatened to sue me.'

Luc threw back his head and laughed. 'God, what a prat! You,' he added with an approving warmth that brought a glow to her cheeks, 'are incredible.'

'I know…I mean,' she added hastily, 'I know he's a prat. Landing the punch was more luck than good judgement,' she admitted.

'So now that we have both invaded each others' privacy I think you could say we're quits?'

'I suppose so.' She looked at the hand he stretched out towards her and after a moment placed her hand in it. The contact sent a neat electric thrill through her body, which she endured with a fixed smile. As soon as it was possible—without causing offence—she removed her hand.

'Now tell me what you read or didn't read in Gracie' letter that made you chuck me out of bed.'

'I know she loves you and you love her.'

'I don't love her.'

'Well, you would say that, wouldn't you?' she countered sadly.

The phone in Luc's pocket began to ring.

Megan, grateful for the reprieve, watched him pull it from his pocket.

'Don't switch it off. It might be important.'

'More important than my infidelity…?' His anger made her wince. '*Patrick,*' he snarled into the mouthpiece.

Megan tapped her toe on the floor as he began to listen. When he responded it was in rapid French. Megan tuned it out; she was quite proud of her grasp of the language, but there was no way she could follow what Luc was saying.

It was only when she heard her stepfather's name that she began to actually listen. She caught Luc's eye and, mouthing, Let me speak to him, held out her hand. Luc shook his head and turned his back on her.

When Luc finally hung up his expression was preoccupied.

'Why didn't you put me on? I wanted to talk to Jean Paul.'

Without replying he caught her hands in his and drew her towards him. His grave expression made her stomach lurch in fear.

CHAPTER SEVENTEEN

'Now don't panic.'

An instruction, Megan reflected, that was guaranteed to make her do exactly that.

'Is it Mum?' Unconsciously her hands went flat to her own belly.

Luc nodded. The compassion in his eyes made her spirits plummet; people didn't look like that when they were about to give you good news.

'The baby…?'

'Your mother is in hospital. They're performing an emergency Caesarean.'

The blood seeped out of her face leaving her skin marble-pale. 'How is she? This is my fault…I should have told her that she was too old to have a baby, but I encouraged her.'

'Cut that out right now!'

His bracing tone made her blink. Dazed, Megan looked from the hands encircling her wrists to his stern dark face.

'This isn't anyone's *fault* and certainly not yours. Laura had every test going; she was given a clean bill.' Megan reluctantly nodded. 'And even if her age was a factor, which we don't know, this was not your call; it was hers and Jean Paul's. You did what you had to; you supported her decision.'

Megan's eyes remained on his face, then after a few tense moments she nodded.

'So you're not going to go all hair-shirty on me?'

Megan exhaled deeply and shook her head again. 'No, what…what happened? Did Jean Paul say?'

'Something to do with the placenta. Jean Paul was…unclear.' The Frenchman had actually sounded as though he was in shock. 'She began to bleed, apparently.' He didn't mention the pain that the distraught Jean Paul had graphically described.

Luc wished he hadn't said as much as he had when Megan literally swayed.

'Come on, now, you shouldn't upset yourself.'

'Don't upset myself? My mother is bleeding to death!' Her voice rose to a shrill, scornful crescendo.

'She isn't…she'll be fine,' he said, hoping like hell he was telling the truth. 'And Jean Paul will ring the moment she gets out of surgery…or they know something. In the meantime we should be positive.'

'*Know something…?*' With a distrustful frown she homed in on his comment. 'What do you mean, *know something*?' Her eyes narrowed into suspicious, accusing slits on his face. 'You mean if she dies, don't you?' She pulled her hands from his clasp and let out a wail that made the hairs on his nape stand on end. 'They think Mum's going to die and you're not telling me everything. I know you're not.'

'I swear I am.'

'Then why didn't you let me speak to Jean Paul?'

Her breath coming in short, frantic gasps, her eyes darted around the room. She reminded Luc of a cornered wild animal.

'He doesn't know any more than I'm telling you, Megan.'

In the midst of her heart-wrenching anguish Megan experienced a sudden icy calm and sense of purpose. She knew exactly what she had to do. She explained it to Luc.

'I have to go to Paris.'

'Megan, you're thirty-seven weeks pregnant; you can't travel.' Luc's expression was compassionate, but his tone was inflexible.

'I'm not asking your permission; I'm telling you what's going to happen.'

'Calm down, Megan, you're not thinking straight.'

'You don't understand,' she accused, backing away from

him. 'I *have* to. She needs me.' Her shoulder blades made contact with the wall and she leaned back against it, glad of the support.

'How do you intend getting to Paris?'

She looked at him blankly.

'You're not thinking straight, Megan.'

'If I catch the next flight…I could be there by…'

He shook his head slowly from side to side. 'They won't let you fly.'

Megan glared at him, leaking self-control from every pore. Why was he making this difficult? 'I'll *make* them. I'll say I'm only twenty…' how pregnant could you be before they wouldn't let you fly? '…something weeks.'

'And even if they would permit it, I wouldn't let you go.'

She looked at him for a moment with real loathing. At some level she was aware that she was being totally irrational but she couldn't stop. 'God, but I hate you!'

Luc flinched as though she had struck him, but not a muscle in his face moved.

'We can discuss your feelings for me at a later date.'

'I don't want to discuss anything with you. I want to see my mother.'

'Listen, I know you're scared and you want to be with your mother, but she has Jean Paul. He's her husband; it's his job to be with her. Your first concern has to be your own health and that of our baby.'

God, he was right! She knew he was *right*. Megan caught her trembling lower lip between her teeth. The antagonism in her eyes faded as their eyes meshed.

'She's so far away…' She closed her eyes, silent tears sliding down her cheeks.

Luc was at her side in a heartbeat. He stroked her hair; his expression was so tender that the trickle of tears became a flood. 'I know,' he crooned, drawing her close.

With a cry Megan collapsed weakly against him, her body shaking with sobs.

Luc had never felt more helpless in his life.

Long after her tears had abated Megan remained where she was in the protective circle of his arms seeking comfort from his strength, the warmth of his hard body, the familiarity of his scent.

It was the sound of the phone ringing that made her break away. She looked at the phone in his hand, her eyes wide and fearful.

'You all right?'

She nodded and even managed a watery smile. 'Go ahead, answer it,' she said, brushing the hair from her damp face with the back of her hand. 'I'll be fine, promise.'

Luc nodded and lifted the phone. After a moment he covered the receiver. 'She's out of surgery and she's fine,' he told her, grinning from ear to ear.

Megan experienced a rush of relief so intense it made her head spin. Weakly she leaned against the wall. 'Thank God!'

'Are you all right?' Luc asked, half listening to the relieved husband's emotional and extremely loud outpouring in his ear.

Megan dug deep into her reserves to give him the ghost of a smile, oblivious to the fact that, far from reassuring him, it scared the hell out of him. When she closed her eyes tight and began to shake, visibly shake, he shoved the phone back into his pocket and crossed the floor to her side in two strides.

He fell onto his knees beside her chair and framed her face in his hands.

'I th...thought...' Her eyes, so big and so intensely blue that he still got a shock every time he looked into them, flickered open.

Luc smoothed the hair from her eyes and pulled her head onto his shoulder. 'I know what you thought,' he said quietly. 'Don't try and talk, just give yourself a minute; you've had a terrible shock.'

For once Megan didn't resent his fussing. 'I'm sorry I yelled at you.'

'Forget it.'

'And I'm really glad you're here.' Her eyes lifted to his. 'I don't know what I'd have done if you hadn't been here.'

Something flickered at the back of Luc's eyes. 'I'll always be here for you, Megan.'

He'll always be here for the baby, she sadly translated. 'I know you will.'

Her eyes suddenly snapped open. Arms pressed against his chest, she pulled upright. 'The baby…?' she asked fearfully.

'The baby…?' he repeated blankly. Then his eyes widened. 'Oh, the *baby*. Fine, a little small so they're keeping it in an incubator.'

'*It?* Is it a boy or girl?' Because of her age her mum had had an amnio, but she hadn't wanted to know the baby's sex. Megan didn't think she could have shown the same restraint if she had been offered the same opportunity.

'Almost definitely.'

'No, seriously.'

'I'm not sure…Jean Paul might have said before I hung up on him.'

The outrageous admission made her stare. 'You hung up on Jean Paul!' she gasped. 'How could you? I have to know if I've got a brother or sister.'

'What's the hurry? It'll be the same sex in the morning.'

'Only a man would say anything that stupid,' she told him. 'I'll ring. Give me your phone….' Without waiting for him to comply she reached inside the breast pocket of his shirt where she could see the outline of his mobile.

'It won't do you any good ringing. Jean Paul's phone will be switched off now…it is a hospital.'

'You're probably right.' Megan, who in the last few seconds had realised that the niggly back pain she had had all

morning was actually something more, gave a distracted
smile.

Everything she had learnt in antenatal class had gone! Her
mind was a total blank.

'I was simply prioritising.'

'What could possibly be more important?'

He stilled. What the hell was important to him? Not long
ago he wouldn't have had to think about it. It had been
doing what he wanted when he wanted.

'Are you all right?' she asked, concerned by the dazed
expression that had settled on his lean features.

His eyes focused on her face. His life if he had never met
Megan—no drama, no epic battles of will, no spending frustrated nights reading his way through the library.

Megan who had strained to catch his soft reply, shook
her head. 'Sorry, what did you say?'

'You.' This time Luc's voice was not soft, it was firm and
resonant.

He had experienced one of those rare moments in life
when all the pieces slotted into place. It wasn't a gentle
voyage of self-discovery, more a kick in the pants.

A kick that Luc thought he deserved for taking this long
to see something that would have been so obvious! He loved
Megan, and loving her wasn't going to change because they
got old or were separated. Megan wasn't Grace and he
wasn't the kid he had been when he had got married. He
needed this woman, without her his life was empty.

He exhaled, then said it again and said with more confidence, 'You, you're the most important thing in my life.'

He means the baby, she told herself, so don't say anything
stupid. Their eyes met and she said it anyway.

'If this is your way of saying you have feelings for me,
you have very bad timing...' she told him huskily. 'In fact,'
she added grimly, 'it's probably the worst timing possible.'

'It feels like a good time to me,' Luc rasped. Unable to
resist the temptation of her white smooth neck, he pressed

his lips to the pulse spot at the base of her throat. Megan felt his tongue and mouth move up her throat and sank her fingers into his dark hair.

'Luc…?'

'Uh-huh,' he said, not stopping the lovely things he was doing.

'I think we should stop.'

His head lifted. 'If you're worried about making love don't be. There's more to making love and giving pleasure than penetrative sex. There's touching and tasting and…'

She shook her head. At any other time his frank explanation would have given her a case of terminal embarrassment, or more likely pleasure, but she was beyond that now.

She leaned backwards. 'No, Luc, I'm serious. We have to go.'

Her urgency finally seemed to register with him. 'Go where?'

'To the hospital.'

It took several seconds for her meaning to sink in; when it did he froze. 'Are you saying…?'

She nodded. 'I think…actually,' she confided, 'I'm pretty sure I'm in labour. I've had this funny feeling all day and a backache and just now I…' She took a deep breath. 'Yes I'm definitely in labour.'

'You're going to have the baby?' Despite his flat level tone there was an undercurrent of panic in his voice that irrationally made Megan feel much calmer.

'Well not here and now…I hope.' The last vestige of colour fled his face and Megan added hastily. 'Only joking.'

'Don't,' he pleaded with feeling.

'I think a sense of humour is going to be essential.'

'Let me think,' Luc said, pressing his hands to his head as if to speed up the process. 'I'll call an ambulance. Don't worry, everything's going to be fine.'

'Or you could drive me…?' she inserted gently.

'God, yes, of course!' he exclaimed. 'Right, let's go. Can you walk?'

'In a minute,' Megan said, grabbing onto the nearest object, which happened to be Luc, to wait for the contraction to pass.

'Breathe.'

'I am breathing,' Megan panted.

He had absolutely no recall of driving to the hospital, but he must have because they had got there.

'Don't they realise that this is an emergency?' he seethed. 'This is a hospital—you'd think they'd be able to find a damn wheelchair.'

Megan laid a hand on his sleeve and begged him to sit down and not shout.

'I wasn't shouting. I just don't want our baby to be born in a damned hospital waiting room.'

'Neither do I. They know what they're doing, Luc, and I'm not the first woman to have a baby,' Megan pointed out, looking amused.

Luc subsided into the chair beside her looking frustrated. 'How can you be so calm?'

He asked the same question several times during the next few hours. She was so focused and so brave that he got choked up just thinking about it.

'I'll never call women the weaker sex again,' Luc said as he stroked the hair from Megan's damp forehead.

Megan lifted her eyes from the face of their sleeping daughter—a tiny, perfect miracle and she was theirs. The sense of awe she felt was overwhelming.

'I want lots of babies!' she announced suddenly. 'Lots and lots.'

Luc lost his colour and looked at her as though she had lost her mind. 'How can you say that after what you've just been through?' he asked her.

'Yes, but look what I got at the end of it,' Megan, who seemed to have miraculously forgotten the pushing and pain, gloated joyously.

'Your wife actually had a very easy labour considering this was her first,' the midwife told him.

'*Easy!*' Luc exclaimed. 'She was incredible,' he retorted indignantly.

The midwife smiled indulgently. 'Of course she was.'

'I couldn't have done it without you.'

Luc glanced down and saw Megan was looking at him. 'Me!' he exclaimed. 'I didn't do anything.' It had been the inability to help that had been the worst aspect of the entire experience.

Megan looked astonished. 'You were incredible,' she retorted. 'I definitely couldn't have done it without you,' she added firmly. 'You kept me focused.'

'Really?'

'Absolutely,' she told him with complete conviction. 'Look at her fingers, Luc, and she's got so much hair.' She tentatively touched the abundant silky dark hair that covered their daughter's tiny head. 'I've never seen a baby with so much hair…*she's* so perfect.'

The tiny bundle opened her eyes.

'She knows we're talking about her,' Luc said.

'Do you think her eyes will stay blue?' Megan wanted to know.

'Of course, she looks exactly like you.'

'Oh, no, she looks like you…well, I hope she does anyway.'

'Why on earth would you hope she looks like me?'

'Because, Luc, you're very much prettier than I am.' She laughed when Luc looked deeply embarrassed by her observation.

'Would Dad like to hold the baby while I help you to freshen up and put you in your own nightgown?'

Dad looked shocked at the suggestion. 'Thanks. I'm…
actually…'

'Go on, Luc,' Megan urged. 'You might as well get used
to it if you're going to be a hands-on dad. She won't break,
you know.'

For a long time Luc just looked at the sleeping baby in
his arms. When his eyes lifted Megan saw there was a gleam
of moisture in those fantastic silvery depths.

'I think we should get married.'

Megan froze.

'You don't have to answer now…think about it.'

CHAPTER EIGHTEEN

THERE wasn't much time to think about anything. The first six weeks were the worst, Megan had read somewhere. That meant they were halfway through. She would never have believed that one small creature could demand so much attention. They hadn't had the time or energy to continue the conversation they had started just before the dash to the hospital.

Their personal life had gone on hold. Everything revolved around Rachel, as they had named their daughter. Megan and Luc were both suffering from sleep deprivation big time, although the mirrors told her it showed more on her face than his!

Megan hadn't actually been keen on the spa idea, but Luc had insisted she needed some time to herself and rather to her surprise she had actually enjoyed being pampered. Despite this she was glad that the pedicure was her last treatment; she wanted to go home.

'I wish someone had treated me to a day at a spa after I had my baby.' The girl who was painting her toenails a pretty pearly shade sighed enviously. 'How old is your baby?'

Megan's face softened. 'She's three weeks now. This is the first time I've been away from her.' She glanced at the silent mobile phone—she had made Luc promise to ring if anything went wrong.

'Three weeks and you have your waist back...you lucky thing. It was six months before I could get into my jeans.' She patted her midriff with a sigh. 'I'm still a good ten pounds heavier than I was before I got pregnant.'

Megan smiled. She knew the girl was being kind—she

had lost some of her pregnancy weight but she still had a long way to go.

Driving back home, she decided it was time she gave Luc the answer he had been so patiently waiting for. She would marry him. Her heart beat faster in anticipation as she got closer to home.

Luc was in the library; so was the small, delicate-looking brunette. She was talking and Luc was listening. From where she was standing Megan could not see his expression, but the woman looked emotional. The tear stains on her cheeks suggested she had recently been crying.

'I've been such a fool, Luc. Can you ever forgive me? It's not too late, is it?'

Megan felt as though she had walked into one of her own nightmares as Luc said, 'Gracie, I wish—'

Megan was as startled as the couple standing there appeared to be by her shockingly loud, 'No!'

'Megan, you're home.'

'Sorry, am I back too early?'

Luc's jaw tightened as he absorbed the hostility and pain shining in her eyes.

'Don't be angry with her, Luc,' the other woman said quickly, laying a restraining hand on his arm. 'Megan, I'm Grace,' she added.

'I know who you are.'

'Megan, this is—'

'This must be very difficult for you,' his ex-wife interjected softly.

Megan's chin went up. 'In what way difficult?'

'You do know who I am?'

'You're the woman that Luc used to be married to.' She ignored the other woman totally and turned to Luc. 'Did you plan this, Luc?'

'No, I swear—I know how this looks, but I didn't know she was coming.'

Megan exhaled and nodded. 'Have you had a cup of tea, Grace? I'm sorry, I don't know your surname.'

The older woman was looking a little confused. 'No, I'm afraid you don't understand—'

'Oh, yes, I understand perfectly,' Megan contradicted with a smile.

Luc, who had been poised to intervene, leaned back against the wall, his arms folded across his chest.

'I still love Luc.'

'I don't think so,' Megan said, still smiling. 'A woman who loves a man doesn't walk out on him when he needs her most.' Her glance flickered briefly in the direction of the tall, silent figure whose eyes hadn't left her face for a second since she'd begun to speak. She stopped smiling. 'A woman who loves a man doesn't kick him when he's down.'

'It wasn't that way at all,' Luc's ex-wife protested flushing to the roots of her hair. 'I never stopped loving him. He never stopped loving me!' she declared in a voice that throbbed with emotion.

The brunette looked so beautiful and sounded so convincing that for a moment Megan's resolve faltered. This was the woman whose very existence had threatened her but now she almost felt sorry for her.

'He doesn't love you anymore.' She tempered her announcement by adding gently, 'I'm sure he'll always have a special fondness for you, but what you and Luc had ended a long time ago.' Her eyes turned towards the tall, silent presence and almost imperceptibly he nodded. Megan exhaled. 'You can't turn to him every time something goes wrong in your life.'

'You have no idea what you're talking about. Luc loves me.' Her voice rose to a shrill crescendo as she added, 'He always has and he always will. He's only with you because of the baby.'

'Rachel.' Luc's voice made both women turn to look at him. 'Our daughter's name is Rachel.'

Grace gave an uninterested shrug. 'Oh, it's a girl, is it?'

'Did she sleep?' Megan asked.

'She was fine—at least she was when I wheeled her pram around the garden. Every time I stopped she woke up.'

'This is all very interesting,' began Grace, who had listened to this interchange with a bemused expression, 'but—'

Luc's ex was obviously a woman who didn't enjoy being ignored. 'The fact is, Grace, Luc and I are going to be married, not because of Rachel, but because we love one another.' The eyes she turned to the tall man who was walking towards her sparkled with unshed tears.

Luc crossed the room to her in two impetuous strides. 'You're sure, Megan?' His anxious eyes scanned her face. Whatever he saw in the shimmering blue depths made the tension drain from his body.

'Totally,' she tried to say, but he was already kissing her.

Grace stood rooted to the spot as a passionate embrace was exchanged.

'Right, well, let me be the first to congratulate you both.' She gave a brittle laugh. 'Luc always wanted a family. I just hope this domestic scene doesn't turn out to be a case of the grass is always greener.'

The formal leave-taking was predictably awkward, but when Grace had driven away in her bright red Porsche Megan came down with a case of delayed guilt.

'I wasn't very nice to her.'

'Yeah, I noticed that,' her husband-to-be murmured.

'But she did come here to steal you,' she added in her own defence. 'And I couldn't let her do that, could I?'

Luc framed her face in his hands. 'You were totally magnificent!' he declared. 'You blew me away. When you walked in I thought you'd think…'

'I did for a split second,' she admitted.

'What changed your mind?'

'I just knew that even though you've never said you love me that you do. You show your love a hundred times a day,

Luc.' He was showing it now with his eyes as he looked into her face.

'I know I've never said it, Megan,' Luc responded in a suspiciously thickened voice. 'I said it once before and I didn't mean it…I thought I did. With you it was different, but I was afraid that if I gave what I felt for you a name I would jinx it. But…'

Tears welling in her yes, Megan pressed a finger to his lips. 'You don't have to say it for me, Luc.'

'But I do for me. I didn't know what real love felt like,' he interjected. 'I do now, Megan. I love you with all my heart. My life would be empty without you in it.'

She ran a hand lovingly down the strong curve of his cheek and he turned his head and kissed her palm. Megan's tummy muscles quivered receptively. 'And mine without you,' she told him simply.

Unable to resist the temptation of her lips any longer, Luc sealed his mouth to hers. 'You know,' he teased as they drew apart breathing hard, 'I think I fell in love with your mouth about five seconds before I fell in love with the rest of you. Or maybe it was your voice…did I ever mention it flows…?'

'You did and you knew exactly what you were doing to me,' she accused.

Luc laughed.

'Talking of voices…?'

They both stopped and listened to the fretful murmurs emerging from the baby alarm Luc carried in his pocket. They both knew that if ignored those hungry baby sounds could and would get a lot louder.

'Sorry,' Megan said ruefully.

'Not to worry—we'll steal a moment or two to seal our engagement with a bit more than a kiss. But for now…'

Emerging from the long, lingering kiss with a smile on her face, Megan pulled his dark head towards her and whispered in his ear. 'It's going to take a lot more than a moment or even two.'

'Sounds good to me,' Luc murmured, as, hand in hand, they went to attend to the demands of their new daughter.

THE PREGNANCY SECRET

BY
MAGGIE COX

The day **Maggie Cox** saw the film version of *Wuthering Heights*, with a beautiful Merle Oberon and a very handsome Laurence Olivier, was the day she became hooked on romance. From that day onwards she spent a lot of time dreaming up her own romances, secretly hoping that one day she might become published and get paid for doing what she loved most! Now that her dream is being realised, she wakes up every morning and counts her blessings. She is married to a gorgeous man and is the mother of two wonderful sons. Her two other great passions in life – besides her family and reading/writing – are music and films.

Don't miss Maggie Cox's exciting new novel, *Secretary by Day, Mistress by Night*, **available in May 2010 from Mills & Boon® Modern™.**

To Gary
with all my love

CHAPTER ONE

ALL DAY long the ocean had called to her. At a minute past five-thirty in the afternoon Caroline closed the shop, mounted her bicycle and pedalled with all the urgency of a prisoner making a jailbreak down to the beach. When she got there she left her bicycle in the usual place and all but ran down to the water's edge, breathing in the sharp, salty air with increasing need—as if she had indeed been imprisoned in a dank, dark cell and deprived of clean fresh air for too long.

That was why she knew she could never live far from the sea. On some unexplored, mysterious level it had become part of her. It didn't matter what type of day she'd had, it was the only sure-fire thing that seemed to have the power to rejuvenate her and somehow help put her world to rights.

Caroline didn't know why she'd woken up feeling so intensely restless that morning. There seemed to be no good reason for her sudden strange inability to concentrate or even conduct a simple exchange with any of the customers who came into her little shop for art supplies. Yet she couldn't deny that there was a niggling disquiet deep within her that wouldn't go away—a disquiet that would act like a cattle prod until she relented and gave it the attention it deserved.

There had been plenty of work for her to do in between customer visits too, but because of her state of mind Caroline had barely applied herself to any of it. All she'd done all day was glance longingly at the clock, torn between displaying the 'Closed' sign on the front door and escaping down to her favourite little cove or painting out her agitation onto canvas.

In the end she had acceded to neither of those options.

Now, studying the white-capped waves breaking over the rocks, inching further and further onto the sand like an encroaching colossal army of silver-backed ants, she was taken aback by the intolerable ache that climbed into her throat. If she was honest, she'd been trying to suppress that ache all day, but now—in the one place where she could freely give vent to her feelings—she no longer tried to fight it. It was an old, familiar ache that had its inception in events that had occurred seventeen years ago, and sometimes she wondered at its power to still affect her with such savage intensity.

But Caroline didn't want to start any emotional excavating right now. She would simply allow the feelings to temporarily deluge her, then slowly ebb away again. Just like the tide that so fascinated her. She had escaped to the sandy cove which she had come to secretly regard as her own private oasis hopefully to derive some peace from her unwelcome discontent of spirit, and diving into the past too deeply would surely only visit on her the very *opposite* to that.

All she could do was plant her feet as firmly as she could on the shifting sand, gaze out to sea and *breathe*. This same technique had anchored her so many times in the past, when despair had almost driven her out of her skin, and it would anchor her again today…

Jack hadn't been back to this place for *years…seventeen* years, to be exact. Now he saw that the small coastal town that had haunted his dreams at night had more or less stayed doggedly the same. Summer was long gone, and it was coming on to winter. Thankfully there were no noisy arcades or stands selling sugar candy, as he'd feared—no burger bars polluting the pure sea air with unsavoury aromas, and the population hadn't discernibly increased. *Not to his eyes, anyway.* It still appeared to be the same unassuming and quiet, almost nondescript seaside town that it had always been. The march of time had not rolled over it and left it unrecognisable.

The knowledge made Jack feel so hollow inside that for a moment anyone close enough to study his face would have seen the hard glitter of tears sheen his riveting blue eyes. Perhaps it would have been better if it *had* changed? At least then he wouldn't be so relentlessly attacked by memories that he'd sooner bury for good and forget. Now, the sight of a familiar row of buildings facing the beach, in much the same weathered state that they had been seventeen years ago, and a bend in the road that led to the small cul-de-sac where he had lived with his mother, brought it all back in an unforgiving tide of recollection.

One memory in particular stood out like a beacon in the dark amongst all the rest. *Jack's first ever sighting of Caroline Tremayne.* She'd been walking home from school with her friends, and his youthful attention had been immediately dazzled, entrapped, enchanted by her beautiful smiling face, her long, curling blonde hair, and the most sensational pair of legs that ever graced a pair of school regulation black tights. *He had been under a spell from the moment he'd seen her, and not once since had his heart beat so hard and furious at the sight of a pretty girl...*

Shoving his hands further down into the deep pockets of his Burberry raincoat, Jack walked on, suddenly glad of the soft steady rain that wet his lashes and made his dark hair sleek as a pelt. He told himself she must be long gone from the small town where he had grown up, having moved there with her family the year that she'd turned sixteen. Most likely she had got married to some ambitious young doctor with the blessing of her father, who had been a local GP, and had probably gone to live either in the Home Counties or some gentrified borough in London.

Continuing his speculation on how her life had unfolded without him, Jack wondered if she'd ever done anything about her interest in art, as she'd intended, or whether instead she'd been content to stay home and raise a family while her husband concentrated on *his* career.

The thought automatically slowed Jack's brisk stride right down and with impotent rage he scraped his fingers through his sodden dark hair. He *despised* the fact that the thought of her being with somebody else still had the power to unglue him—to make his heart beat as fast as a rally driver taking a dangerous bend way too fast. Having to make billion-dollar decisions for his companies was a walk in the park compared to the tormenting, blood-stirring and heartrending memories he had of Caroline Tremayne. And the brutal truth of the matter was that she didn't *deserve* him devoting even one second of the time he stupidly spent thinking about her. Not when she had blighted his capacity to trust for ever by what she had done to him seventeen years ago…

Telling himself to snap out of his dark mood and concentrate instead on the main reason he had come back to this place, Jack started to walk on again, his pace determinedly resolute as he headed for the bend in the road that would take him back to the once dilapidated Victorian semi-detached dwelling that he had grown up in…the house that he now *owned* outright and could do with what he damn well pleased…

The driving rain had cut short Caroline's emotionally charged but somehow vital trip down to the sea. Negotiating the roads home on her bicycle, she blinked rapidly into the ensuing downpour, clenching her teeth as wind and rain stung her cheeks and cursing her luck that she should forget to bring her waterproof. Her light cotton jacket was no protection against such an on-slaught from the elements.

Startled by a car driving too fast, coming down the street towards her, she jumped off the saddle and steered her bicycle onto the pavement instead. She wasn't far from where she lived and would simply walk the rest of the way. She began to increase her pace—head down, her freezing hands gripping the bicycle handlebars—and didn't see the man walking just as rapidly in the opposite direction towards her until it was too late and they unceremoniously collided.

His hands immediately shot out to steady himself, gripping her upper arms with a hint of steel in his hold as Caroline careened right into him—the front wheel of her bicycle catching him hard against the shin. He swore out loud, not sparing her blushes, and Caroline began to apol-ogise profusely, blinking up at him in alarm and regret.

But as her dark, fair-lashed eyes locked onto the as-tonishingly vivid blue of the stranger's unrelenting waves of shock hit her like a high-pressure fire-hose—the ferocity of it almost knocking her over. *Oh, my God...*

'Jack?'

Her throat almost locked as she let the name out. She'd forbidden herself the use of it all these years, and now, in one blinding, devastating second, it was out there...just as if it had been waiting to be let loose for the longest time...

'Caroline.' He blinked the rain from his eyes, staring back at her with neither warmth nor pleasure, his hard jaw visibly tightening, as though having been dealt the most unwelcome of surprises.

His frigid, glacial glance cut her to the quick, and Caroline wanted to weep for all eternity at the sheer hostility she saw directed towards her. Instead she grazed her teeth anxiously across her bottom lip, immobilised by shock and distress, wanting to walk quickly away from this cruel encounter fate had dealt her, but somehow unable to make the necessary move to do so.

He abruptly let go of her arms. 'You've hardly changed at all' he ground out, almost as though resenting the observation.

Inside, Jack's senses were spinning and wheeling, his body protesting in silent agony, as though he'd fallen from a great height onto broken glass. What was she doing here? Surely she didn't still live here after all these years? If he had suspected for even one second that of all the people he might possibly bump into from his past Caroline Tremayne would be the first he would *never* have set foot in the place again...never mind returned to buy the house he had grown up in!

He had loved and then *hated* her, with equally voracious passion, and now all he felt for her was ice-cold disdain. But as Jack held remorselessly onto his low opinion he couldn't deny the unsettling evidence of her disarming beauty—a beauty that hadn't faded in the slightest in all the time that had passed…that had in fact blossomed into even more *heartbreak.*

Her skin was still as fine as the most expensive silk, her dark caramel eyes bewitching as an eastern princess, and her mouth…devoid of lipstick and tempting as sin, with that delicately plump lower lip glistening damply with rain… Apparently it still wielded the power to make Jack burn to taste it again.

'What are you doing here?' she asked him now, her hands curving tightly round the handlebars of her bicycle, the knuckles paler than pale.

'That's *my* business.'

'I'm sorry, I—'

'You remember I never *was* one for small talk?' he said, raising an openly scathing dark brow.

Caroline stared. Hot, embarrassed colour surged into her face at his mocking remark.

Jack nodded, one corner of his hard mouth lifting with what might well have been satisfaction at her visibly acute discomfort. 'Well…nothing's changed.'

Digging his hands deep into the pockets of his raincoat, he started to walk on.

'Goodbye, Caroline.'

'Is Dr Brandon finished for the day?'

'His last patient's just left, Miss Tremayne. Why don't you go on in?'

Not giving herself a moment's opportunity to change her mind, Caroline swept past the obliging receptionist to knock briefly at Nicholas's door, and at his automatic 'Come in' let herself inside.

The man who had been her father's best friend and closest confidante right up until his death was now hers, and as her agitated gaze fell upon his calm, smiling and familiar face she only just about held onto the last vestiges of composure that had so irrevocably unravelled at the sight of Jack Fitzgerald.

'Caroline!'

He walked round the large oak desk that occupied a fair portion of the room space and, pulling her towards him for a hug, kissed her fondly on the cheek as well.

'What a lovely surprise! I was just thinking about you.'

'You haven't any brandy, have you? Purely for medicinal purposes, you understand.'

She laughed a little harshly, blinking back the scalding sheen of tears that surged helplessly into her eyes.

Nicholas frowned, his steady, concerned gaze locking immediately onto her clear distress. 'What's happened? You're wet, and shivering too…blasted weather! Come and sit down and talk to me.'

Hurriedly pulling out the chair in front of his desk— the one reserved for his patients—Nicholas saw Caroline settled into it before pulling open one of the capacious drawers and extracting a bottle of best malt.

'No brandy, I'm afraid, darling, but whisky should do the trick just as well.'

Pouring her a generous measure into a small tumbler—also retrieved from the desk drawer—he handed it to her, the grooves at each side of his mouth deepening as he watched her tip the glass towards her lips and drink.

'This is so unlike you. You have me quite worried,' he confessed, briefly squeezing her shoulder.

Feeling the whisky burn inside her, Caroline winced. After just a couple of seconds the uncomfortable burning sensation became surprisingly pleasurable and warm, providing a welcome if brief respite from the intense anguish she'd suffered since literally bumping into Jack just half an hour ago.

Turning her troubled dark eyes towards Nicholas, she offered him a shaky smile. 'You must think I've completely gone off the rails, or something. I'm sorry to land myself unannounced on you like this.'

'Caroline…we've been friends for a long time now…*good* friends since I lost Meg last year. You know if you're in any sort of trouble I'm always here for you, don't you?'

She knew that he meant it. Nicholas Brandon had been a rock for her since she'd lost her father. She had never seen him as a substitute parent, but her relationship with him and his wife Meg had helped her foster a sense of security that for a long time she'd lacked. When her father had died, Caroline had sorely grieved for the affection she had never had and had always longed for. Her friends had all been in London, and Nicholas and his wife had been unstinting with comfort and support when she'd decided to move back to her old home. But Caroline had never spoken about Jack Fitzgerald to the kindly couple before. Had never told them how, at sixteen years of age, she had fallen deeply and passionately in love with the man and would have willingly followed him to the ends of the earth if only he'd given her the chance…

But Jack had had a burning desire to rise above his family's troubled and debt-ridden daily existence and make a fortune for himself. And after events that had changed the course of both of their lives for ever he had followed that desire to America. *But what had brought him back here?*

At their very last meeting, when he'd all but torn out Caroline's heart with the vitriolic tirade he'd lambasted her with, telling her that he would never set foot in England again, she'd been convinced that he truly meant every word he had uttered. He *hated* her for what she had done, and was never, *ever* going to forgive her. And if his reaction at their unexpected meeting today was any indication, he clearly still saw no reason to rescind his promise… Her throat tightened with agonising hurt at the memory.

'I appreciate—I appreciate that, Nicholas, but I'm not in any trouble…really. I've just had a bit of shock, that's all.'

Nursing her glass between her hands, Caroline stared down at her lap.

'What kind of a shock?'

'A ghost from the past…only he's not really a ghost. He's flesh and blood and bone.' *And once upon a time*

I loved him so much my days were consumed with thoughts of nothing but him…

'Are we talking about an old boyfriend, perhaps?'

Lowering himself onto the desk next to her, Nicholas put his hand thoughtfully up to his jaw, a subtle draught of the classic cedarwood-scented aftershave he wore briefly stirring the air.

'I can see that you really are shaken up, darling, so it must have been someone who meant something important to you once upon a time.'

'He wasn't a boyfriend.' Caroline shrugged, the dampness from her thin cotton jacket making her shiver. But she also silently acknowledged that shame factored somewhere in there too. 'At least…not in public.'

By necessity she'd had to keep her relationship with Jack as secret as possible, because her father had issued dire warnings to her when he'd inadvertently found out she'd been seeing him. He wasn't from their world, he'd told her and when it came to prospective boyfriends he expected someone much, much better for his only daughter—not the son of a junkie and a drunk.

Three months later, when she'd just turned seventeen and found herself pregnant with Jack's baby, Caroline had had to confess to her father the truth that she'd been seeing him in secret.

Terrified, because Jack had already told her of his plans to make some 'big money' in the City, which would naturally necessitate him moving to London, and that nothing was going to stop him, Caroline had seen all her options dwindling before her eyes. *She hadn't wanted to hold her boyfriend back in any way. She knew what he'd endured and she'd only wanted the best for his future.* So, buckling under brutal pressure from her enraged father, Caroline had brokenly agreed to have an abortion.

When she had told Jack what she had done his love for her had immediately turned to *hatred. He'd never forgive her,* he'd promised and then he had sworn that he would never see her again.

Until today, he had kept that vow.

'Are we talking about Jack Fitzgerald?'

Caroline glanced up in shock, the colour leaching from her face at Nicholas's painfully astute question. 'You *know* about him?'

'Your father was my closest friend, my dear. Of course I knew about your infatuation for that boy.'

That 'boy' was now a man of thirty-seven—three years older than Caroline.

A startlingly vivid picture of his disdainful handsome face less than an hour ago, now etched with distinct grooves in his forehead, and with bitter lines bracketing a mouth that once upon a time had been devastatingly sensual and charming instead of frighteningly forbidding, flashed up in her mind. A jolt of deep, bruising sorrow almost made her moan out loud.

'Then you…you know what happened?'

'That you were expecting his child and had to have an abortion? Yes, my dear…I know about that.'

Thankfully, there was no criticism evident in Nicholas's

voice, and he left Caroline to her own preoccupied thoughts for several seconds, before following up his quiet matter-of-fact statement with a deeply thoughtful sigh.

'Your father thought it was the best thing to do at the time—and he was right. You were only just seventeen, Caroline, with your whole future ahead of you. He wanted you to go on to university and study, find a career you would love. He knew that a boy like Jack Fitzgerald would never have stood by you. You would have been a single mother, raising a child on your own, while your friends were doing the very things your father wanted for you. He really loved you, you know.'

'Did he?' Tears were like a thick net curtain, blurring her vision, as Caroline stared up at the man beside her. 'If he had really loved me, Nicholas, would he have put me through an abortion at seventeen years of age? Wouldn't he have stood by me and helped me when I found out I was pregnant, instead of condemning me and helping the man I loved to despise me for ever?'

'He tried to make amends by leaving you the house, and enough money to set up in business,' Nicholas asserted, quietly yet firmly—his steadfast loyalty to Caroline's father was unwavering.

Rising disconsolately to her feet, Caroline delivered her glass to the small leather coaster on the desk. Tossing back her mane of curling blonde hair, she sniffed, regarding the man beside her with distinct hurt in her eyes.

'He hardly ever told me that he loved me,' she told

him. 'I could count the number of times on one hand! Do you really think that leaving me a house and money could come anywhere *close* to making amends for such a grim lack of affection, as well as helping me to lose my baby and driving Jack away?'

When Nicholas said nothing in reply, Caroline inclined her head briefly in sorrow.

'I should go home now. I shouldn't have come here and burdened you with all of this.'

'Your troubles are not a burden to me, Caroline, and they never *could* be. I would do anything I could to alleviate your pain…you know that.' Taking her small cold hand in his own, Nicholas squeezed it tight with genuine fondness. 'But, whatever the reason Jack Fitzgerald has returned here, I really think it best if you don't get involved with him again.'

Extracting her hand as though it had glanced against burning blue flame, Caroline immediately backed away and walked stiffly to the door.

'I know you mean well, Nicholas, but you can save your advice. If I lay unconscious on the ground Jack Fitzgerald would step over me…never mind get involved! He despises me for what I did. When I saw him again today I could see it in his eyes.'

CHAPTER TWO

AFTER thrashing out some of the finer details with the contractor he'd hired to oversee the renovation work, Jack left the house that had once been his childhood home, jumped into his car, and drove along the coast for several miles without really paying much attention to where he was going.

Emotionally he was under seige. Seeing Caroline again after seventeen long years had made the blood stampede through his veins like escaping wild horses.

But after almost an hour of aimless driving, and feeling no less overwhelmed, Jack pulled in to the side of the road, switched off the voice of the DJ on the radio that had been droning monotonously in the background and, staring out through the windscreen, vocalised his mounting frustration out loud.

She had no right to look so gut-wrenchingly beautiful...to taunt him with the fact that clearly life had been kind to her since they had broken up. Jack couldn't bear to imagine that her undimmed radiance was the result of a happy marriage with a man who *adored* her—who would have *died* for her as once upon a time Jack willingly would have.

He had fallen so hard for the blonde dark-eyed beauty that her unexpected act of treachery had all but *killed* him. Since then relationships had come and gone, and although his life had by no means been devoid of sexual passion there hadn't been the love that Jack had instantly felt in his heart for Caroline. And now, since his divorce from Anna last year, he was alone again.

Rubbing his chest beneath his shirt, he sucked in a harsh breath to steady himself.

Despising the pulse of fear that jolted through him, an aggravating thing that seemed to happen a lot these days since his heart attack, he continued to stare out through the windscreen.

The surrounding countryside, with its timeless and arresting beauty, should have helped instil some calm inside him—but no such luck. Jack was a million miles away from calm today, and expecting it to suddenly arise was a fruitless undertaking…no matter *how* long he sat there. *All he felt was empty.*

He'd come back here to set right a wrong. To prove to himself and the town that despite his poor beginnings, and the mostly negative perceptions people there had had about him, he had achieved success beyond their wildest dreams. He was a multi-millionaire entrepreneur, with several thriving companies to his name and a much-admired reputation for proving that there was still a place for integrity and not just flair and daring in business. That admiration had massively highlighted Jack's profile in the international business community, and had won him the cover of the *New Yorker* just one year ago.

It was the kind of dreamed-for reputation that should have long ago rubbed out the taint of his boyhood shame—of having an alcoholic father who had abandoned his family and a mother who had heavily relied on prescription drugs to sedate her from the hurt she'd known was waiting if she should try and face her days without them. But Jack had to silently acknowledge that seeing Caroline again—the sight of her cruelly reminding him that she had not thought him good enough to be the father of her baby, and had preferred to have an abortion rather than raise their child together—had frankly robbed him of the sense of triumph at returning home that he'd been hoping for.

But he had laboured too hard and too long for success to let this unexpected, glitch completely quash his satisfaction at buying the house that had once belonged to his parents but had been repossessed for non-payment of the mortgage. That unhappy and shameful fact had forced Jack and his mother to be housed in run-down council flat accommodation on the outskirts of town, and had no doubt helped contribute to her growing despair and eventual demise. Now that the place was his again, Jack's plans were to have it converted into a stunning showpiece of a home that would elevate it into one of the most desirable properties in the area—*in any area*—and would obliterate every bruising, shameful memory that might still be lurking there from his past.

His mother might no longer be alive to witness his achievement—but he wasn't going to let that stop him from seeing through the burning desire that had gripped him with a vengeance while he was recovering from surgery in hospital six months ago, after suffering his heart attack. But how was he going to deal with the startling discovery that the girl who had broken his heart when he was just twenty was still living in the area? It was definitely a complication he hadn't foreseen.

'Goddamn!'

Colouring the confined space with his invective, Jack impatiently switched on the ignition and roared out of the lay-by, as if by putting his foot down hard on the gas he could outrun the threatening cloud of his own troubled past…

'My idea was to make a collage of butterflies…'

'I'm sorry, what did you say?'

Guiltily, Caroline brushed back her hair with her hand and deliberately focused her attention on the pale young teenager in front of her, a swift upsurge of concern galvanising her attention. A shy, unconfident girl, Sadie Martin had latched onto Caroline at the school where she taught arts and crafts once a week and now regularly visited her shop—often with no other aim in mind than to chat.

'I said I wanted to make a collage of butterflies.

They're so beautiful, don't you think? I got some books from the library to study them.'

A soft, self-conscious tinge of pink seeping into her naturally milk-pale complexion, Sadie sighed wistfully—as though her dream of creating something beautiful out of butterfly imagery was somehow just out of reach.

Caroline empathised. She knew what it was to have a dream that was out of reach. Once she had dreamt that she and Jack would be together for ever, but it had all ended in a dreadful nightmare. Now that he was back she found herself dreaming about him again…only this time there was no prospect of a happy resolution, or even the *remotest* possibility of one. He had clearly hardened his heart so emphatically where she was concerned that he found it difficult to even look at her, let alone converse.

All morning Caroline had speculated feverishly about why he had come home. Would he be staying long? *Would he ignore her every time their paths accidentally crossed?* It was only a small town—it was inevitable that they would. She didn't think she could bear to see that despising glance he had swept her with for a second time.

'Well…' Diverting her own unhappy thoughts, she levelled a tender smile at Sadie instead. 'Books are a good place to start if you want to study butterflies. But if you want to start work on a collage why don't you look through some magazines for pictures you can cut out? I have a pile of them at home I could bring to class on Friday for you, if you like?'

Sadie's pale lips edged upwards. 'Would you? Oh, that would be great! My mum doesn't read magazines, and I can't afford to buy them myself.'

'I tell you what…I'll help you get started, if you like. I've got loads of material scraps out at the back of the shop that you can have. You'll be able to create something really amazing.'

'That's very kind of you, Miss Treymayne.'

'I told you…call me Caroline.'

'All right. I'll see you on Friday, then…at school?'

'I'll look forward to it…and, Sadie?'

'Yes, Miss?'

Smiling at the automatic barrier of formality that the girl could not so easily relinquish, Caroline reached out to tenderly smooth away a stray auburn hair from her earnest young face.

'Any time you need to talk…I'm here for you, okay?'

She knew it wasn't the 'done thing' to encourage pupil/teacher relationships outside of school. But, remembering her own sense of abandonment and isolation living with her father, Caroline believed that everyone deserved a helping hand now and then, as well as emotional support—and there was something about Sadie Martin that indisputably tugged at her heartstrings.

'Thanks, Miss.'

The bell over the door briefly jangled, and Caroline stood alone in the ensuing silence and reflected how hard it was to teach someone how to have self-confidence at the tender age of sixteen. God knew it was enough of a challenge sometimes even at thirty-four!

Jack had been walking with no particular aim in mind other than to reacquaint himself with his home town. When he left the main street and turned into a series of charming connecting lanes—the chocolate-box imagery of typically pretty English country villages springing immediately to mind—his pulse accelerated sharply as he came upon a small shop with a bright blue, painted frontage and a swinging sign that declared 'Caroline's Paintbox'. He knew before he even glanced in the window and saw her serving a customer, amid picture frames and paintings decorating the walls, that the purveyor of the business was none other than the woman who had been haunting his dreams all these years...

He hadn't intended to go inside, but before he knew it Jack's hand was gripping the brass handle on the front door and he was stepping into a colourful treasure-trove of paints and paintings, pencils and stencils, racks of handmade occasion cards, artists sketchbooks and much more besides.

The customer Caroline had been serving—a middle-aged woman, immaculately dressed in a smart pearl-grey trouser suit—smiled almost girlishly at him from beneath her heavily mascaraed lashes as she passed him. A waft of Chanel No 5 impinged strongly on his senses. But the woman's smile glanced off Jack like water sliding down glass, hardly registering with him at all. All his attention—all his focus—was intently on Caroline.

'Just a minute and I'll be with you.'

She was bundling up some unwanted paper and depositing it in the bin with her back to him as she spoke, clearly unaware of who her next customer was. She straightened again, a ready welcoming smile on her it had to be said radiant face. The smile vanished almost instantly when she saw that it was Jack.

'Was there something you forgot to be rude to me about?' she asked stiffly, her arms folded defensively across her chest in her chocolate-brown wool sweater.

'I was passing and saw the sign with your name on it. I wondered if this might be your place.'

Deliberately avoiding looking directly into her wary brown eyes, Jack instead took inventory of his surroundings, minutely interested in every detail—every corner and every crevice overflowing with artistic implements of one kind or another—simply because this venture belonged to Caroline. *Was this what she had done with her love of art?* Somehow he told himself it didn't sit right. The Caroline Tremayne he remembered hadn't been a facilitator of other people's artwork—she'd created her *own.*

Back then, she'd been bursting with excitement and ideas about what she was going to do when she finished art college. Her aim had been to eventually have a fantastic studio overlooking one of the London parks 'to inspire her' she'd said. Where she would create the most wonderful paintings that she would exhibit in galleries and that the great and the good would admire and hopefully buy.

'Eat your heart out, Leonardo!' she'd used to say with great delight and not a little self-mockery.

Jack had truly believed she'd be a roaring success. Her ravishing beauty and the utter passion she'd exuded for life had swept him off his feet like a sensual cyclone…how could it not have? His mother—during some of her more lucid bouts with reality—had used to tell him that Caroline would break his heart. *Well, she'd been right on the money with that one.*

'Take your time, why don't you?' Her voice was tinged with sarcasm. 'But you'll have to excuse me. I've got work to do.'

When she would have turned away from him again, Jack's next words kept Caroline rooted to the spot.

'Any of the stuff on the walls yours?' he asked, nodding his head towards the three rows of paintings behind him. Her chin came up and her dark eyes glittered, as if she was offended by the question, and Jack knew that if he had been an artist himself he would have been spoiled for choice of which angle to paint her from, because she looked so damn good from whatever perspective you gazed. A sizzle of molten heat carved a direct path south in his anatomy and made him feel momentarily dizzy.

'No. These days I paint purely for my own satisfaction, but not for public viewing.'

'Why not?'

Characteristically blunt, Jack levelled his clear

blue gaze on Caroline's startled face with no remorse whatsoever.

'I can be freer if I only have myself to please. I make art because I take pleasure in it…not because I want other people's opinions about it.'

'You used to want to make it your full-time career'

'Well, now I have this shop—and I teach too. That's quite enough to be going on with.'

She was prickly and defensive, yet she still painted—even if it was just for her own satisfaction—and apparently did lots of other things as well. Clearly what had happened had not quelled her drive in any way…neither had the fact that their romance had so abruptly come to an end. The thought did not sit easy in Jack's already disturbed gut.

'What do you teach?' he asked reluctantly.

'Arts and crafts. Are there any more questions? I have to get on.'

Jack frowned at the distinct coolness in her voice. 'I didn't expect to find you still living here,' he commented, changing tack.

'I moved to London for a while, but then my father died and left me the house. When I came home to sort things out I decided to stay here. I love the sea…it's always had a pull for me.'

Caroline hadn't meant to tell him so much. It had just sort of come out, due to nerves. Because here she was, having not seen this man in what felt like a lifetime, and there he stood, frighteningly mature and handsome in his casually expensive clothes, the body inside them clearly having had the benefit of not just good genes but good nutrition and exercise too, judging by the strongly athletic build of him. His appearance was a far cry from the lean and hungry energetic youth she had fallen in love with, who'd had a burning desire to break the bonds of his less than advantageous background and make both his fortune and a name for himself. But, with his disturbing blue eyes searing her like living flame, it seemed to Caroline that his dangerous attraction was even more potent than ever. Why else would she be standing in front of him privately shivering hard with longing?

'So…is there a husband somewhere on the scene?' he asked, looking as though he couldn't care *less* if there was.

She could ask him the same question. Are you married Jack? And if you are…why have you come back here to haunt me? Once the question entered her mind Caroline found it hard to let it go. She had a dangerous fascination in knowing the answer.

'No… How about you? Did you ever marry?'

Her voice shook with nerves as she gave in to her own helpless curiosity.

'I'm divorced. So…neither of us is a success in the marriage stakes…surprise, surprise.'

A knot of unbearable misery twisted inside Caroline's stomach.

'Why are you doing this, Jack? You already told me that you hate making small talk. You don't need to come in here and rake over old coals when the past is better left alone…don't you think?'

His face grew briefly dark, and the bitter tension that rolled towards her hit Caroline like an icy wave. She knew immediately what he was thinking. He'd made a bad mistake coming into her shop and making contact again, and now he was sorely regretting it. There was not one thing he'd missed about her…not *one*. Watching him walk to the door, she saw Jack shrug, and before pulling it open he considered her with a supercilious and definitely mocking smile.

'Your father died, then? Forgive me if I can't bring myself to offer my condolences.'

Without another word, he left her alone.

The large Victorian house that her father had left to her in his will, which for the past five years had been Caroline's permanent home, failed to inspire her usual pleasure as she entered the airy hallway with its chequered floor and polished chiffonier. All of a sudden it didn't feel like home, because her normal ability to experience delight in things had been severely suppressed by Jack's cruel parting remark when he'd left her shop.

Not that she could entirely blame him for not being sorry to hear of her father's death.

Charles Tremayne had disliked Jack on sight, calling him a 'sly little upstart' who only wanted to elevate himself by association with Caroline because she was a doctor's daughter and came from a different class. For different read *better.*

Her father's unapologetic snobbery and prejudice

had made Caroline feel intensely ashamed. They might have been more comfortably off than Jack and his mother, but that hadn't given them the right to feel superior in any way. Right from the start Caroline had quickly seen that Jack was smart and industrious, as well as devastatingly good-looking. And he might have appeared as a bit of a cocky, brash youth to outsiders, but to her he had displayed a tenderness that had sometimes made her weep for joy. Having grown up with a father whose affection towards his only child had been sparing, Caroline had found Jack's loving like a salve to her starved-for-love soul. *Once experienced...nothing else would do.*

Sighing with deep unhappiness, Caroline dragged herself into the kitchen. With her mind constantly drifting back to the past, like a wary onlooker positioned on the edge of a dormant volcano, she prepared a baked potato and a small salad for her dinner. Eating it in the large, formal dining room a little while later, she stared at the dark emerald drapes at the imposing Victorian windows and asked herself what she was doing, still rattling around in this big old house on her own after five years? Why had she rebuffed every bit of interested male attention that had come her way, as if she didn't deserve to find happiness with a man who loved her? *She knew the answer to that one.*

After he'd found out about the termination, Jack's fury at her had known no bounds. His passionate, enraged words, eloquently expressing what he thought of her, had slashed deep wounds in her heart that would probably *never* heal. He had made her feel like a murderer…as if she had made the decision to terminate her pregnancy on a mere casual whim. He had had no idea of the guilt, shame, or total devastation Caroline had felt when, at her father's bullying instigation, she had gone through with the deed. He had had no notion of the terrible scene her father had caused when he'd found out about the pregnancy, *or* the dreadful names he'd called her for sleeping with Jack. Events like that left an indelible imprint on a person that was hard to relinquish. Caroline had found it almost impossible to forgive herself for what had happened, and because of her guilt had subconsciously put up barriers where other men were concerned.

'Oh, Jack' she said out loud as her fork clattered back down to her plate, her meal still left largely untouched. 'Why did you have to come back? I've made a life for myself since you went away… Maybe I'm not the successful artist that once upon a time I thought I could be, but I've been happy in my own way with the shop and my teaching. Why did you have to come back and spoil that? Why couldn't you just let the memory of you die in me for good?'

CHAPTER THREE

HAVING had negotiations with the architect who was overseeing the renovation and redesign of the house, Jack left the hotel where he was staying the next morning and went for a long walk along the seafront. Dressed in black sweats with a matching fleece, he tried to quash the need to run that arose inside him—to pound the pavements as he was used to doing every day back in Manhattan, where he lived and worked—because since his heart attack the doctors had advised him to 'kick back a little' and not push so hard with the exercise regime he'd devised for himself.

Resenting their advice like hell, Jack nevertheless had to satisfy himself with a brisk walk rather than a run, and as the surprisingly cold autumnal air bit into his hollowed-out cheekbones he found himself recalling his parting words to Caroline yesterday. *It had been a stupid and childish response to have a cruel dig at her about her father's death,* he decided. No matter how vehement his dislike for Charles Tremayne and the appalling way he'd treated Jack back then—as if he was nothing less than *pond-scum*—Caroline had no doubt loved her father, and missed him not being around.

It surprised him that he should seriously be considering giving her an apology. If he had an ounce of sense he'd leave things be and not try to see her again. *But Jack never had been able to do the sensible thing around Caroline.* How else had she wound up pregnant with his baby at just seventeen? The pavement seemed to loom dizzyingly closer for a second as he remembered how much he had loved her, how *crazy* for her he had been from the moment he'd seen her. She should have been off-limits to him right from the start—and *would* have been if her dark eyes hadn't gazed at him with equally desperate longing at their very first meeting.

Increasing his stride without thinking—his heart maintaining a steady, reassuring rhythm as he did so—Jack made himself concentrate on the exercise. He knew he was getting fitter by the day. The heart attack—though disturbing and a cause for concern—had thankfully not been life-threatening. It had, though, been a *warning* that he couldn't afford to treat his body's innate need for rest and relaxation with the near *contempt* with which he'd treated it previously.

'You're not some battery-powered *machine,* Jack Fitzgerald…a battery runs out and you replace it with another one. The body doesn't work like that. You can't work flat out seven days a week, getting by with the minimum of sleep indefinitely, without it exacting some kind of price on your health.'

His doctor had been right, of course. But after Jack's marriage had started to come apart at the seams—and Anna had naturally sought solace elsewhere—Jack had preferred to spend his time at work and take his chances with the toll on his health. To his mind it had been infinitely easier than going home to a luxurious penthouse apartment and having the empty rooms that were mockingly bereft of his wife's presence chillingly remind him that this was one arena in which he patently *didn't* excel…

Slowing to a stop, he ran a hand across the thin film of sweat clinging to his brow and returned to the knowingly dangerous idea of making contact with Caroline to apologise for his rudeness of yesterday. She might not have wanted to have his baby all those years ago, and he could never forgive her for what she'd done, but there was no need to stoop to the condescending level of her father and treat her with anything less than civility. After all…she was *nothing* to him now. What could it hurt to merely drop by her shop and say sorry for his ill-mannered passing quip?

She didn't have a head for heights at the best of times. Now, on a ladder reaching up to the topmost shelf in the back room where she kept her stock, searching for that box of material odds and ends that she'd promised to Sadie, Caroline sighed with relief when she found it, only too eager to get back down the ladder and onto *terra firma* again.

But as she drew the large box towards her chest to balance it her foot missed the next rung it had been groping for and she felt herself literally crash to the floor. Releasing a shocked yelp, she landed unceremoniously on her backside at the foot of the ladder, the box of material scraps spilling out everywhere. Cursing her bad luck, Caroline groaned out loud in pain and frustration—because she could already feel the bruises forming on her most tender spot.

Hearing the jangle of the bell above the shop door at that exact moment, she rolled her eyes heavenwards. 'Great timing, Caroline,' she muttered. Pushing away the colourful kaleidoscope of debris that covered her, she attempted to rise to her feet. *Everything hurt.* The place on her body that *didn't* hadn't been invented.

Hobbling to the door, and at the same time trying to smooth back her dishevelled hair as she went out into the shop, she was totally unprepared for the sight of Jack, leaning against the counter examining a box of crayons as though they were the most fascinating thing on earth. He straightened when he saw her, and Caroline saw the grooves on his handsome forehead crease in a frown that was unexpectedly concerned.

'What have you done to yourself?'

It wasn't fair that he of all people should walk in the door and catch her at her most vulnerable. *Someone up there in the cosmos was having a big joke at her expense.* If that wasn't bad enough, Caroline knew she must look dreadful too. Apart from nearly doing herself some serious damage falling off the ladder, she was wearing a pair of jeans that were just on the uncomfortable side of tight, and a smock-type Indian print blouse she was convinced she looked fat in but that she'd worn anyway because it was roomy.

She'd been in the middle of cleaning the stockroom when she'd remembered the box of material scraps she'd promised Sadie for her butterfly collage. Knowing it was dusty work, she'd thought it best to change into clothing that she didn't care about. Now, with her hair shaken loose from the bold pink scrunchie that had kept it on top of her head, and practically every bone in her body screaming in silent protest from her undignified tumble, all Caroline wanted to do was to be left alone to entertain her humiliation in private. What she expressly *didn't* want was to be under the despising scrutiny of a man who clearly thought she wasn't fit to be in the same room as him—never mind be spoken to.

'I'm all right. I accidentally fell off a ladder, that's all.'

With her hand shaking, Caroline tried in vain to push her hair back from her face, but the stubborn silky strands spilled heedlessly back across her cheeks again.

'You *fell* off a ladder?'

Before she could do anything to stop him, Jack had walked commandingly over to her and clamped his hand down firmly on her shoulder. His blue eyes were as intense as she'd ever seen them as they blazed down at her.

'Are you hurt? You look like you're in shock… What the hell were you doing up a ladder on your own?'

The question was so surprising that Caroline's lips couldn't help twitching into a perverse grin. 'What do you mean? Since when does a person need an escort to go up a ladder? That's taking it *too* far, if you ask me!'

'I don't think this is any time for joking,' he said seriously, wiping the smile off her face with his chilly reprimand. 'You'd better come and sit down. Do you have anything for shock?'

A double vodka might do the trick if she had any, Caroline reflected in sudden panic. Still holding onto her shoulder—the heat from his hand was making her feel almost delirious—Jack guided her to a nearby straight-backed chair with a floral seat-pad and gently but commandingly pushed her down into it. Just when she didn't think she could cope with his painful concern for her welfare one second longer, without it making her dissolve into sorrowful, angry tears, he stood in front of her with his arms folded, regarding her with all the forceful presence of a commander in the SAS towards a member of his team who had badly let him down.

The thought would almost have made Caroline smile if it hadn't been for the sober reminder to herself that he would *never* in a million years want her on his team.

Glancing tentatively up at the harsh jaw—that was distinctly unshaven this morning and made him look almost dangerously unpredictable—and seeing his expression of searing inscrutability made Caroline literally squirm in her seat.

'I asked you if you had anything for shock?' he repeated.

She shook her head, knowing that it wasn't just because he was standing and she was sitting that he had a distinct psychological advantage.

'I don't believe in taking medicine unless I really have to. I've got some Rescue Remedy in my bag, but that's about all.'

'Rescue remedy?'

'It's a flower remedy…very good when you've been upset.' Caroline's stomach lurched as Jack surveyed her with an almost tangible sceptical air.

'You'd rather take some dubious alternative remedy over an orthodox one and your father was a doctor?'

'I *do* have a mind of my own, you know.'

As soon as the words were out of her mouth, Caroline painfully recalled caving in to the pressure from her dictatorial father to have the termination she'd had…*despite* her vehement protest that she didn't want to, that she *loved* her baby and she loved her baby's father. It hadn't helped her having a mind of her own then—not when her father had crushed her insistence with all the rough and pitiless force of a sledgehammer.

Painfully, she swallowed down the inevitable, almost unbearable twist of loss and grief inside her and attempted to rise up from the chair. *She had to make Jack leave, and leave now!* What was he doing here anyway? Surely he had better things to do than visit a woman who aroused nothing but *contempt* in him?

It bothered Jack greatly that he'd witnessed such disturbing vulnerability in her soft dark eyes. Let her show him indifference, or even tell him to go to hell, but dear God don't let her look as though she was suffering the torments of the damned.

It frankly astounded him that the idea of Caroline being in pain still had the power to bring out the protector in him…even after what she'd done. He told himself to take a swift reality check and get the hell out of her shop and her life for good. Just because the sight of her still had the power to stir explicit male fantasies in him—her snug, faded jeans emphasised that her figure had lost none of its charms and had inevitably become even more womanly and alluring than ever—it didn't mean that he should stay around any longer than was sensible. *He'd already been burned by her.* He didn't intend to be burned again.

'You need a little more reliable help than a flower remedy, in my opinion. Don't you have the common sense to keep a first aid kit here?' Jack asked impatiently, irked because he felt more affected by her presence than he wanted to be.

'I do, but it's only got bandages and plasters in it. Please don't give it another thought. I'm fine, really.'

'You could have broken your damned neck!'

The tension in him suddenly too extreme to stay contained, Jack threw Caroline a fierce look. He heard her shocked intake of breath at his vehement outburst.

'Well, how inconvenient for you that I didn't!' she

came back at him, a distinct catch in her voice despite her seeming bravado.

'I don't deny that I wanted you to suffer after what you did, but I'm hardly likely to want you to kill yourself.'

Deeply affected by the grating quality in his voice, Caroline felt her anxious gaze stare up at him, mesmerised.

'One day you were telling me that you were pregnant with my baby, and the next that you'd had the pregnancy terminated. Talk about a kick in the head, Caroline!'

Her whole body protesting in pain, Caroline dug her nails into her palms, as if deserving of even more. She wanted to tell Jack about her father…how he had *forced* her into having the abortion…but what would telling him such a thing achieve? Jack's reaction would probably be to despise her father even more—and maybe even her too, for being too weak to resist his coercion. She could hardly bear any more of his contempt.

She sucked in a deep breath. 'You were planning on going away… I knew how desperately you wanted to change your life for the better, to make some money and free yourself, and I—I was only seventeen, Jack.' She shook her head in an agony of searing emotion, feelings surfacing that for seventeen years she'd had to lock away deep inside her, in a cast-iron trunk with chains and a padlock, in order to stay sane. 'I—I was afraid.'

'You should have talked to me…not just gone ahead and done what you did.'

Jack couldn't even bring himself to say the words *You*

killed our baby…the miracle that they had created out
of their passion and love. He just about managed to rein
in the fury and pain that was surging through his blood
like a fiery contagion. She might have been afraid, and
just seventeen years old, but still he couldn't help but
feel cruelly betrayed that she hadn't come to him and
asked his help to work things out.

It didn't matter that he'd had that feverish desire to
escape the small, going-nowhere town where he'd
grown up… He'd been in deep shock when she'd told
him she was pregnant. He would have definitely delayed
his desire for flight if Caroline had only asked him to—
if she had not made such an irreversible decision on her
own. In any case, he had planned for her to move in with
him just as soon as he'd got himself established and
she'd finished her education… They'd *talked* about it
enough times, for God's sake! She'd known he wasn't
playing a game with her—she'd known that his feelings
for her were all-consuming and completely genuine…

'Can we stop this? Can we stop this right now? I really
don't want to talk about the past any more. I have to get
back to work… And although it might look hunky-dory
from the outside, you shouldn't be so quick to assume
that my life has been nothing but a breeze since you left.'

Determinedly Caroline got to her feet, despite feeling
dizzy and sick and close to wanting to die right then.
There wasn't one emotion Jack could display that she
didn't feel acutely. *She hated it that she'd hurt him so
badly.* If she could somehow turn back time she

would—just to undo that one heartrending deed. But she couldn't. And she'd clearly received the message that Jack was still no more *near* to forgiving her for what she'd done than he had been all those years ago, when they had both been so young.

The agony of that realisation seemed even more raw than it ever had been…like a blister that would never heal. All Caroline could do was live with it as best as she could—just as she'd been living with it all this time, until his shocking reappearance.

'Why did you come back here to see me, Jack? There's nothing for you here.'

She was absolutely right, of course. There was nothing he wanted from Caroline Tremayne ever again.

Trying to clear his head, Jack forced himself to remember why he'd sought her out.

'That comment I made yesterday about your father…I'm sorry. It was uncalled-for.'

'You came to apologise about that?' She looked dumbfounded.

'How did he die?'

'In his sleep…he had a brain aneurysm.'

'Did he suffer?'

He saw her wrestle with the answer, suspicious of his interest, probably wondering if he was only trying to be malicious. *Damn!* He had no business being concerned one iota at how she was perceiving him! All he needed to do was close the conversation and get the hell out of there as quickly as he was able—not prolong the undoubted agony of their meeting one moment longer.

Brushing back her tumbled hair, Caroline briefly surrendered her defences and met Jack's gaze head-on. 'Thankfully, it must have been very quick and very sudden. Nicholas—a friend of ours who's also a GP— told me he wouldn't have suffered at all.'

'Good.'

Turning on his heel, Jack started to walk away. He told himself the only reason that he stopped halfway to the door was that she'd suffered a fall and he had to be sure she was properly okay. He utterly refused to entertain the renegade idea that the sight of her was stirring up that old dangerous attraction he'd harboured for her so long ago, and knew that if he had the remotest instinct for self-preservation he'd better keep a good distance between him and her for the remainder of his stay—for *however* long that might be.

'You ought to get yourself checked over by the doctor after having that fall off the ladder. Sometimes there can be internal injuries you can't see.'

Oh, God, did she know about those! Unable to handle his rough-voiced concern for her well-being another moment, Caroline smoothed her hands down her jeans, fiddled with her hair and cleared her throat determinedly to give her the courage to stay strong.

'Really, I'm fine. I don't need to see a doctor. I'm disgustingly resilient. Rubber bones, don't you know? I bounce right back when I get hurt.'

A curious expression she couldn't read crept into Jack's inscrutable blue eyes at her flippant words.

'How fortunate for you,' he remarked, his lean jaw tightening with a visible jerk. In less than half a minute he'd exited the shop, leaving the mocking tinkle of the little bell above the door sounding more like a cacophony of gunshot behind him than gentle, wistful chimes…

'No bones broken, thank goodness, but you should have come to see me straight away after it happened. You've got some nasty bruising and stiffness, that's all, and that will heal in a few days.'

Walking round his desk, Nicholas strode over to Caroline, where she stood after her examination, pulling on her jacket.

'Let me take you out to dinner…you look as though you could do with a little TLC.' He touched his palm to her cheek, his hazel eyes crinkling at the corners with both concern and humour.

With her own doctor away, Caroline had reluctantly asked Nicholas to check her over. Jack's words about seeing a doctor had been ringing in her ears when she'd woken this morning—barely able to get around with the bruising on her hip and thigh that she'd suffered from her fall. But, truth to tell, most of her misery had been more to do with the fact that Jack still blamed her for having the termination than any physical bumps and bruises she'd suffered. She'd woken in the night wishing with all her might that she had stood up to her domineering father more and refused the abortion he'd insisted on.

Now, her thoughts returned irrevocably to Jack. His appearance had created all kinds of mayhem inside her. There was no question that whatever he'd done and achieved it had been a resounding success. His clothes were of the very best quality—Caroline had seen that straight away—and he had the accomplished, confident air of a man who had diligently shaped his own destiny. *But there was also an edgy desolation in his eyes…as if all he'd achieved wasn't nearly enough to quell the deep unhappiness he harboured within himself.*

'Dinner?' she repeated, her mind reluctantly breaking away from thoughts of Jack.

'I'll pick you up at around eight. Try not to look so unhappy, darling…a few bruises won't do you any lasting harm.'

Forcing a reluctant smile to her frozen lips, Caroline nodded in agreement. 'I know. I'm just annoyed at myself for being so stupidly clumsy, that's all. I'd love to go out to dinner tonight. Thanks, Nicholas.'

'You're not still fretting about Jack Fitzgerald being back on the scene?'

Unable to keep the disapproval from his voice, Nicholas returned to his desk.

Feeling her stomach plummet to her shoes at the mention of the man who had been dominating her mind for the past three days, since his return, Caroline's reply was vehemently dismissive.

'Of course not! It's all in the past, and I got over him a long time ago. I was only upset when I saw you because it was such a shock to see him again like that. Like I said…I'm over it now.'

But as Caroline said her goodbyes to Nicholas and went to the door, she thought, with a little sigh of despair, *You're such a hopeless liar, Caroline Tremayne.*

CHAPTER FOUR

IT WAS one of those seaside hotels steeped in the elegance of a bygone Victorian era, yet brought unobtrusively up to date with all the trappings and conveniences of contemporary life. It had a fabulous Michelin-star-winning restaurant much beloved by both local visitors and those who travelled from further afield. Caroline liked to have afternoon tea there sometimes—not so much for the delicious cucumber sandwiches and mouthwatering selection of cakes, but more for the ambience. She would sit in the lovely drawing room, with its proud antiques and unapologeticially faded English grandeur, and dream the time away until it was time to leave.

She rarely had dinner there, so—in deference to dining out with Nicholas—Caroline had raided her wardrobe for something a little more dressy. Her red and white chiffon dress, with its sequin-inlaid scooped neckline, lent elegance and grace to her curves, and in defiance of the anxiety she'd suffered over the past few days she'd painted her lips with vibrant scarlet lipstick. Nicholas had told her she looked lovely, and the genuinely kind compliment had given Caroline a much needed boost. She definitely needed her friend's more positive response after her dealings with Jack yesterday afternoon.

'Some wine, darling?' Perusing the leather-bound list at their table, Nicholas lowered it for a moment and smiled.

'You choose.'

Caroline knew it was the reply he was expecting. Nicholas Brandon epitomised 'old-school' chivalry—his undoubted good manners underscored with an unapologetic dose of masculine chauvinism. It was the background and era he came from, and Caroline knew she shouldn't be offended in any way. On the other hand, when her father had employed similar attitudes—often to demonstrate his power over her—it had completely rubbed her up the wrong way.

She glanced unhappily down at her menu, the writing seeming to swim and blur in front of her eyes at the unwanted memory. It was when she lifted her head up again, glancing round the room in a bid to bring her spiralling mood back into more positive check, that she spied Jack, sitting alone at one of the tables on the far side of the room from them. A tall sash window with oyster-coloured drapes provided an elegant backdrop to his clearly preoccupied appearance as he glanced straight ahead of him absently nursing his wine glass—apparently regarding nothing in particular.

Sucking in her breath deeply with shock, Caroline promptly sent her menu flying off the table, taking her own empty wine glass with it before she could prevent it. The glass tumbled to the thickly carpeted floor but thankfully did not shatter into pieces—as her composure was busy doing. Automatically she dropped to her haunches to retrieve it, along with the menu, her hand trembling as her fingers circled round the stem, all the blood roaring inside her ears at the realisation that Jack was dining there too.

On the other side of the room Jack's attention was diverted by a beautiful blonde in an eye-catching red and white chiffon dress, crouching down by her table to retrieve a fallen glass. When she glanced up, and Jack's gaze fell helplessly into her dark-eyed caught-in-the-headlights stare, his insides tensed in astonished surprise.

Caroline!

It was as though the concentration of all his thoughts for the past hour—which had been about her—had miraculously summoned her physical appearance, and Jack was genuinely stunned. As she sat down again, deliberately averting her gaze, he saw to his chagrin, he glanced across the table at her companion. The man was clearly much older than Caroline. At a guess Jack would have said late fifties at least. *Who was he? Surely not her current boyfriend?*

Jealousy seared his blood like the excruciating slash of a whip across his bare flesh. The man was old enough to be her father, and Jack didn't like the proprietorial air he had about him as he leant over and reassuringly squeezed her hand after she'd picked up the glass. Acting purely on instinct, Jack was on his feet and striding across the richly furnished dining room towards them before he even realised that that was what he intended.

'Hello, Caroline.'

To Jack, it was as though her companion didn't even exist. When she glanced up, startled, into his face, her cheeks pinkening in obvious embarrassment at his direct address, he was transported back to their first proper meeting—when he'd asked her what her name was and then told her that she was the most beautiful girl he'd ever seen. She'd blushed in the same unknowingly sexy way then, and he had been gripped by a fever of wild longing so profound that he had known meeting her would make an impact upon his life for ever. *He hadn't been wrong about that.*

'Jack.'

Pulling her glance away, she delivered what seemed to Jack to be an apologetic frown at the man on the other side of the table, and it made his blood boil. It reminded him of the condescending, superior way her father had once regarded him…as if he was the dirt beneath his feet.

'Aren't you going to introduce me to your friend?'

For now, he refused to assume that the man was involved with Caroline in any meaningful way. It simply did not bear thinking about.

'Of course.' She tried for a smile, but the gesture barely touched her scarlet-painted lips for a scant second.

Jack could see that he had put her immediately on edge. *Good. He wanted to put her on the defensive. He wanted her to suffer the way he had suffered when her father had humiliated him by telling him he wasn't good enough to go out with his daughter.*

'This is Dr Nicholas Brandon. He was a good friend of my father's.'

Jack smiled easily at the other man's clear and instantaneous dislike, feeling somehow gratified that Caroline had introduced him as her father's friend but *not* specifically *hers*…

'Nicholas…this is Jack Fitzgerald.'

'Indeed.'

Even though Nicholas rose to his feet, to briefly and reluctantly shake Jack's hand, Caroline could tell straight away that his view of Jack had been indelibly corrupted by her father's opinion from way back. It made her furious. Nicholas had no right to treat Jack with anything but courtesy and respect. He didn't even know the man, for goodness' sake!

'Pleased to make your acquaintance,' Jack responded, smooth as silk—the slight drawl in his otherwise English accent denoting he'd spent a long time on the other side of the Atlantic. But, no sooner had he mouthed the insincere platitude, he diverted his attention straight back to Caroline. 'You're looking pretty as a peach,' he remarked, shocking her rigid with the unexpected compliment. 'What's the occasion?'

'There is no special occasion, as such,' Nicholas interceded with irritation, his hazel-eyed glance seeming to issue Caroline with a silent reprimand for even deigning to introduce him to her one-time boyfriend. 'We are merely two friends having dinner together. Now, if you don't mind excusing us...'

Caroline could hardly believe that Nicholas was dismissing Jack so rudely. Her sense of justice and fair play would not allow it—no matter how contemptibly Jack might treat her for past misdemeanours.

'Have you had your meal yet?' she asked him, silently terrified at what she was about to propose. 'You're welcome to join us if you'd like.'

To say that Jack was surprised by the invitation that issued from her very distracting lips was putting it mildly. Uncaring that the other man might register his definitely over-familiar and possessive glance as he let it travel from her face down to her shoulders, then lower, he felt bold, naked lust rip into him like a sword. The scooped neckline of her alluring red dress couldn't help but call attention to the firm ripe breasts that were contained within it, and the ruby-red pendant she wore nestled tantalisingly in the shadowy valley between them.

No wonder Dr Nicholas Brandon wanted her all to himself! Caroline might fool herself that her relationship with this man was platonic, but Jack could see from a mile away that the man lusted after the sexy brown-eyed blonde as much as *he* did. The fact that Jack didn't even pause to question the wisdom of desiring Caroline's body again after all these years, and after the damage she'd done, didn't even impinge upon his consciousness right then. All he knew was that he had to have the chance to get her back into his bed again…*even if it was a one-time only deal.*

'I'll have to pass,' he replied in answer to her question, and briefly but deliberately smiled knowingly at the visible relief in her companion's eyes. 'I'm going to have my coffee, then go up to my room to do some work. Another time, perhaps? No doubt we'll be bumping into each other again.'

'You're staying here at the hotel?' Caroline asked in surprise.

'I am. Oh, by the way…how are the bruises from yesterday?'

Knowing that he was acting as if he'd been intimately acquainted with the sight of them, Jack played up to Nicholas Brandon's evident annoyance with relish.

'You *know* that Caroline had a fall?' the other man demanded, his expression accusing.

'I was there just after it happened. She always *did* have a tendency to be a little accident-prone…didn't you, Caroline?'

His voice grew deliberately husky on that last statement, and his blue eyes burned into Caroline's panicked dark gaze with the kind of hot sparks that started forest fires. *She turned boneless and hot in an instant.* Jack had always had the disturbing ability to look at her and make her feel as though she were practically having sex with him at just a glance. *But why should he regard her like that, when he'd already made his dislike of her crystal-clear?*

In spite of her confusion, Caroline could barely tear her gaze away from him as he leant towards her and provocatively brushed the side of her cheek with his lips. The stubble on his jaw lightly scratched the delicate tenderness of her own soft skin, and the smell of his cologne acted like a flame-lit arrow fired straight into her womb. Inside her dress, Caroline's breasts grew exquisitely tender and achy.

'Did I?' she answered nervously, embarrassed to recall a tendency to be clumsy in front of both men. But, that aside, she couldn't believe that Jack had kissed her. It had been seventeen interminably long years since she had known his touch, and now that the drought had ended she couldn't help but feverishly crave *more.* She felt an intense surge of joy rush into her blood, despite knowing that her craving was probably doomed to remain unsatisfied.

'Well...I'd better be going.' Sending her another maddeningly provoking glance—that made Caroline's breath catch and seemed to suggest that he had a lot more on his mind than coffee and work—Jack turned and left her alone with her clearly disgruntled dinner companion.

Had he meant it when he'd commented so casually that they would be bound to bump into each other again? Or had he simply said it to annoy Nicholas? Caroline suspected that Jack had taken an immediate and intense dislike to the man who was a family friend and wondered why. Maybe it was the association with her father that irked him? Maybe he'd intuited that he must have been the subject of some discussion between them at some point in the past, and of course strongly resented it. Certainly Nicholas had made no effort to hide either his negative judgement *or* his disdain for Jack.

When Jack had walked away from them, Nicholas wasted no time in warning her for a second time about seeing him again.

'If you know what's good for you, Caroline, you'll steer clear of that man,' he said disapprovingly across the table. 'I'm rarely wrong about people, and I confess I don't particularly trust him. To my mind he can bring you nothing but trouble.'

She resisted the urge to hotly disagree, because underneath the profound agony of need that was burning anew for Jack in her blood Caroline silently conceded that her friend was probably *right*. What if Jack was up to something? What if seeing her again had prompted the idea of some kind of *revenge* in his heart for what she'd done?

Wondering how she was going to eat when she'd completely lost her appetite, Caroline merely toyed with her delicious meal when it came, until it was time to go…

The following day, having finished teaching her Friday arts and crafts class, Caroline hurried to catch up with a distracted-looking Sadie Martin as she headed out of the school gates, feeling a stab of concern that needed answering. In fact, the girl had been dreamy-looking all through the afternoon's lesson, and had not given her work her usually eager attention.

Thoughts of Jack suddenly banished, Caroline released her brightest smile as she drew level with the schoolgirl. 'Hey, there! You're in a big hurry…going somewhere nice?'

Slowing down her stride, Sadie guiltily dipped her head and blushed furiously.

Caroline's undoubted curiosity as to what might be the matter was piqued even more. 'Is everything all right, Sadie?'

The girl waited until the sea of girls behind them surged through the gates ahead of them, then continued a little way up the road with Caroline before gradually slowing to a stop.

'Everything's fine, Miss…really.'

It was the *really* that spoke volumes to Caroline. Her dark eyes narrowed in concern. 'Do you want to talk? We can go to the park, if you like? I'm not in any hurry.'

'Thanks, Miss…I'd like that.'

There was a flash of gratitude in the girl's surprised glance, and Caroline intuited she'd done the right thing in catching up with her.

In the park, after finding a suitable bench situated beneath a large sheltering oak that was liberally shedding its golden and brown leaves on the grass beneath it, Caroline surveyed the younger girl with another undeniable throb of concern as she sat down beside her.

'I've met a boy…a boy I—I like very much.'

Her concern expanded into a disturbing lightning bolt, and Caroline stared in astonished surprise. It was the *last* thing she would have expected Sadie to say, and for a long moment she just sat there, bereft of words.

'Miss?'

'So…' Caroline cleared her throat, then took a deep breath to calm the wild fluttering in her stomach. *Sadie was sixteen*…the same age Caroline had been when she'd lost her heart to Jack. 'When did all this happen and how did you meet?'

Again, Sadie's pale complexion was suffused with visible heat. 'I've been seeing him for about a month now. His name is Ben and he goes to the local art college. A friend of mine has an older sister who goes there, and she got us tickets for a dance they were having. That's when we met.'

'He's obviously older than you if he's at college?'

'Only by three years, Miss…that's not much of an age difference, is it?'

'No.' Quickly gathering her scattered wits, Caroline combed her fingers through her mane of blonde hair. 'That's not much of an age difference at all. So now I know why you've seemed particularly distracted lately. Is everything going all right? Have your parents met him?'

'Yes, they have. I wouldn't see him behind their backs, Miss! Besides…I'm not one for going out much usually, and lately…well…I've been going out quite a lot, so they'd immediately know that something was going on if I didn't tell them. My dad likes him very much, as it happens…and my mum's slowly coming round to the idea that I've got a boyfriend…I *think*.' Sadie shrugged self-consciously. 'She's a bit of a worrier, my mum. I think she's afraid that I might get into trouble.'

'What kind of trouble?' Even as the words left her mouth Caroline knew that Sadie meant becoming pregnant. For a moment anxiety made it hard to breathe. *Oh, God, don't let history repeat itself,* she thought in anguish. Sadie *deserved* her bright future, untarnished by the pain of a romance that had gone wrong or a man who'd rejected her before she had really even grown into a woman…

She took another deep, steadying breath. At least Sadie had parents who loved her…who would in all likelihood stand by her should things go wrong. It was a very *different* scenario from her own cautionary story.

'You know…I meant getting pregnant, Miss.' Her pale hands tightening around her dark blue school bag, Sadie grimaced a little. 'But even though I'm only young, I'm much more sensible than my parents give me credit for. Ben and I are just really getting to know each other still. We haven't slept together, and when and if we do I'll go to the doctor and get protection. I won't jeopardise either of our futures.'

'That sounds…extremely sensible, Sadie.'

Swallowing hard, Caroline forced a smile to her lips. *If only she and Jack had been nearly so sensible…* But unassailable passion had made them its willing slave, and they'd been like pieces of driftwood afloat on a stormy ocean of insatiable lust. The word 'sensible' hadn't even been in their vocabulary. Her stomach flipped over at the bittersweet memory.

'But even when you're trying to be sensible, sometimes things can get a little out of hand. You know that the Head of Sociology at school—Glynis Hopkins—does relationship counselling for teenagers? Why don't you go and have a word about things with her? She's very kind, and anything you tell her will be in the strictest confidence, I promise.'

Sadie's face lit up with touching beauty. 'Thanks, Miss…it's been great to have you to talk to. I knew you'd understand.'

If only I didn't understand half so well, Caroline reflected painfully as she reached out to squeeze Sadie's hand. 'As your teacher and your friend I only want you to be happy,' she replied softly.

Later that evening, although on edge, and once more consumed by thoughts of Jack after Sadie's revelation that she was seeing a boy, Caroline did not have the heart to visit the little cove in search of some calm. Instead she opted to go for a drive—anything to try and distract herself for a while.

Usually the ocean would call to her whenever she was remotely upset, but not *tonight*. She was simply feeling too anxious about the parallels she'd drawn with Sadie to even summon up the energy to walk on a deserted beach. Instead she drove by it, barely even glancing over at the waves that were splashing onto the shoreline.

The evening was drawing in, and the air had the sting of frost in it when she finally returned home and parked the car on the drive. Retrieving her bag from the passenger seat beside her, she locked up, then proceeded to walk wearily up to her front door.

'Do you usually stay behind this late at school?'

Her heart in her mouth at the sound of that voice, Caroline felt her knees react as though they might fold like paper beneath her—just like a marionette when the puppet-master stopped working the strings. Spinning round in shock, she found Jack just a scant foot behind her, his face unsmiling, his blue eyes seeming to drill into her like lasers.

'Jack! What are you—? How did you know I was teaching today?'

Feeling a hot shiver go right through her, Caroline helplessly focused on his mouth—on the little diagonal scar just above his top lip that he'd acquired when he was seventeen, after a fight with another boy who'd had a flick-knife. The way Jack had told it, the boy with the knife had come off far worse than he had, and had never bothered him again after that night. Looking at him now, Caroline could *easily* believe it. To her, he had always been like *electricity*…utterly necessary, but at the same time *dangerous* and unpredictable too… No doubt that teenage boy had completely underestimated what Jack was capable of.

'I knocked next door and asked your neighbour.' He smiled, but the gesture lacked warmth. Instead it was the lethal, purposeful smile of a man who knew he had the upper hand where she was concerned...would *always* have the upper hand as long as she couldn't resist him. 'She was most obliging too.'

Nicolette was an attractive forty-something divorcee who regularly combed the lonely hearts ads in the local paper with steely-eyed determination, in search of 'husband number three'. Caroline didn't doubt she had been only too happy to tell Jack practically *anything* he wanted to know. But—as much as she was overwhelmed by his presence—she wasn't up to raking over old coals tonight, if that was what he had in mind. *Like the boy who had attacked Jack with the knife, she knew she would come off the loser.*

Clutching her bag to her chest, Caroline frowned, secretly longing to get out of the biting wind and into the warmth of her centrally heated house. 'What is it you want? It's—it's cold out here.'

'Then why don't you invite me in?'

Stepping towards her, Jack shrugged beneath the expensive leather of his dark brown jacket, the material making a soft creaking sound as he raised his arm and pushed back his hair.

Confusion, then resignation crept into her expressive eyes. Jack couldn't deny his moment of triumph. He'd had a very brief moment of doubt, when he'd thought she might refuse him, but the tension between them was palpable and he knew immediately how to manipulate it in his favour. *She was as jumpy as a newborn kitten around him,* he realised, *and he had no compunction…none…in taking the utmost advantage of the fact.*

'All right, then…just for a minute.'

The house was warm and inviting, and Caroline's perfume—a mixture of jasmine and roses, if Jack wasn't mistaken—lingered enticingly in the air. It was the kind of home that Jack had dreamed of living in growing up. There was a real sense of permanence and beauty about it, which no doubt Caroline's artistic soul had liberally contributed to over the years.

Following her into the spacious hallway, he watched her hang up her jacket and bag on the coatstand and free her long curling hair from the back of her knitted cardigan, where it had become trapped. The perfectly blonde curls unravelled down her back with a jaunty bounce, and Jack had to slip his hand urgently into his jacket pocket to prevent himself from acting on the almost irrepressible urge to grab a handful of those luscious curls and twine them possessively round his fingers…

Turning to face him, she clearly had no inkling of the impulse that had gripped him so hard. 'Would you like a cup of tea or something?'

He had a mind to tease her… to ask her what she meant by 'or something' and insinuate a very *different* agenda to the one on offer. But when Jack studied that beautiful and, it had to be said, *guileless* face of hers, he was suddenly filled with the memory of how devotedly and ardently he'd loved her, and how she had taken that pure, passionate love he'd offered and destroyed it in one shocking, irretrievable act…

'Jack?'

He shouldn't have come. But he'd been as unable to resist seeking Caroline out again as a drug addict was unable to turn down a free fix. He was playing a dangerous game that could only end in unqualified disaster, but he asked himself what he had got to lose when he'd already lost everything that truly meant anything in his life a long time ago.

'Tea will do fine,' he said, combing his fingers through his dark hair. But he said it without a smile, and he knew that she knew too that the past had suddenly bitterly intruded into his thoughts.

Crestfallen, she lowered her liquid dark gaze and turned determinedly away. 'I hope you don't mind drinking it in the kitchen,' she threw over her shoulder, her voice falsely bright as she hurried ahead of him down the long, echoing hall…

CHAPTER FIVE

'YOU'VE obviously got a good reason for being here, Jack, so why don't you tell me what it is?'

Cupping her hands around her hot mug of tea at the kitchen table, Caroline decided there was nothing for it but to face head-on whatever was on his mind. She'd spent seventeen years racked with an inordinate amount of guilt about what she'd done…guilt and *fear*…so much so that she had been unable to form a lasting relationship with anyone. Every time she'd tried…every time she'd met someone she'd started to feel herself attracted to and who had been attracted to her…it hadn't been long before that dreadful burden of guilt and terror had submerged any growing feelings of pleasure or hope in the relationship continuing, and eventually—*inevitably*—it had come to an end.

Hadn't she carried that debilitating burden for long enough? Her heart *longed* to be able to love again, to give itself wholeheartedly to the right man without fearing that she might fall pregnant and be forced to terminate again. But, looking into Jack's stare—Caroline was convinced it was contemptuous—it was obvious he didn't think that she'd suffered *nearly* enough.

'You live here alone?' he asked, ignoring the question.

'Yes.'

'I always wondered what this place looked like on the inside,' he commented, glancing around him, his gaze alighting on the beautiful Irish dresser with its eye-catching display of highly collectible blue and white china. 'Your father would never let me over the threshold.'

Feeling shame at the memory, Caroline dipped her head.

'So…you're not in a relationship?'

Her head shot up.

'No.'

She could have said more, but she didn't. Whatever she said, Jack would no doubt draw his own conclusion as to the reason for her still single status anyway, and she didn't need to hear his self-righteous judgements against her.

'So…you and the disapproving doctor aren't an item?' His lip curled slightly as he put his emphasis on the word 'doctor', and Caroline knew he was only looking for an opportunity to 'put her in her place' and keep her there.

Suddenly resentment welled up in her heart, for all the pain he had caused but clearly took no responsibility for, and she could barely speak over the abominable tightness that locked her throat.

'That's totally irrelevant. What interest can it possibly be to you who I'm seeing or not seeing? Let's have this out for once and for all, shall we? You must have looked me up again for a reason and if that reason, is merely to drive home your point that you can't ever forgive me for what happened between us, then save your breath! I already *got* that point—loud and clear. We were both so young when it happened, and we've both moved on a long way since then. You clearly got everything you wanted in life, so why come back here simply to dig up old unhappy memories?'

Leaving her mug on the table, her tea untouched, Caroline pushed to her feet and, hugging her arms across her chest in her dark green sweater, walked unseeingly over to the darkened kitchen window that only reflected back her own unhappy solitary reflection.

She tensed when she heard Jack rise from the table, sensing immediately that he had moved up behind her.

'How do *you* know that I got everything I wanted, huh?'

His voice was hoarse with accusation and Caroline hardly dared breathe. Instead, his rage wrapped itself around her and held her prisoner in an icy vice, so that it was impossible to move out of its powerful sphere.

'All I meant was that you look like you've made a success of your life, Jack… I didn't mean that I—'

'You think because I've got money now, and I'm clearly not the poor boy from the wrong side of town any more, that I'm a *success*?'

Turning towards him, everything in her taut with

trepidation, Caroline was utterly dismayed by the desolate and savagely bleak expression she saw written across his remarkably striking features.

'I—I don't know who you are any more, Jack. I don't know enough about you to assume anything.'

The intoxicating scent of leather from his jacket— an expensive, almost *earthy* smell—mingled with the palpable heat from his body and made a devastating ambush on Caroline's already acutely charged senses. The clock on the kitchen wall ticked with hypnotic precision, lulling her into a kind of frozen suspended animation, and outside somewhere a car door slammed.

When Jack's hands locked fiercely onto her upper arms she dizzily registered the unmitigating *bite* of them with a soft, surprised groan. Then his mouth descended upon hers in a hot, punishing kiss that seemed to be governed by equal parts rage and desire, and Caroline was shockingly reminded that pain and pleasure could be as intimately and destroyingly intertwined as love and hate.

Her heart was thumping so crazily inside her chest that all the blood seemed to drain from her body, leaving her like a limp rag doll in his arms. That was until she came to her senses, felt the tenor of the kiss change into something even more dangerous, something even more potentially explosive, and became terrifyingly aware that every honed-to-perfection muscle and granite-like inch of his devastating body was pressed as intimately close to hers as a body could be, making them virtually inseparable.

Grappling with the urgent need to set herself free, as well as to stay right where she was and accept the earth-shattering consequences that contact with him wrought throughout her body, Caroline shoved against the implacable hardness of his chest and abruptly disengaged from his tormenting embrace.

'No!'

The terror in her voice was unrecognisable to her.

Having no choice but to let her go, Jack smiled tauntingly against the back of his hand. He had started to wipe away her taste, as though it was somehow beneath him to bear it. Her eyes stinging with outraged, furious tears, and her mouth quivering defencelessly as she fought the frighteningly potent seductive allure of him, Caroline was shocked at how powerfully and treacherously the old magnetic attraction had asserted itself between them.

'What the hell do you think you're doing?' she demanded, moving nervously across the room to the door. 'Get out of my house and don't come back! Do you hear me? I want you to go! I want you to go right now and never come back!'

'Still think you're too good for me...don't you, baby?'

The smirk on his lips and the derision in his eyes made Caroline feel quite wretched. But beneath the drowning sensation of despair that washed over her she couldn't believe that he could even *utter* such a calumny with the smallest *grain* of conviction. She had never, *ever* felt that Jack wasn't good enough for her, and she had certainly never treated him like that either. He was quite unfairly getting her mixed up with her father—his fury towards Charles Tremayne blinding him to the truth of her own feelings towards him.

'I've *never* thought I was too good for you! You're twisting things around so that you can heap more blame on me…so that you can make me the brunt of all your old bad feeling towards my dad!' Catching the corner of the door, Caroline pushed it deliberately wide. 'I only invited you in because of plain good manners, but I should have listened to my better instincts and left you standing there! I've had a long day, and now I just want to be on my own and have some peace. Please go, Jack. Just go.'

It was hard to get his feet to move. In those melting, feverish seconds when once again Jack had tasted the irresistible soft satin of the most lustfully sweet pair of lips he had ever kissed all his passion, all his urgent, re-lentless, *destroying* need for the woman in his arms, had been furiously and frighteningly rekindled. So much so that Jack really didn't know what to do next. To incite some urgently needed self-preservation he ruthlessly reminded himself of what she had so callously de-stroyed, and as that old hatred towards her helpfully re-surfaced, and made another painful score across his heart, he was finally able to move.

'I'm going, Caroline, don't worry.'

Unable to resist stopping in front of her before going out through the door, Jack deliberately took his time ex-amining the wild rose colour that had flared so arrestingly in her cheeks. 'Living alone must be quite a challenge for you. I'd say that you've definitely been without a man too long, sweetheart. I'd certainly put my last dollar on it that that superior doctor friend of yours can't effect the same shamelessly undone expression you're wearing right now with *his* kisses. Am I right?'

When she didn't reply, but glanced away from him instead with a resentful, hurt look in her eyes, Jack laughed softly.

'Don't fret…I'm certain we'll be seeing each other around again quite soon…of that I've no doubt.'

'Why? I should have thought that you'd want to go out of your way to avoid me.'

'What? And deprive you of the beautiful memory of me and our happy times together for ever?'

'You don't have to be so cruel'

'Yes, sweetheart…I do.' Smiling arrogantly, Jack scathingly angled his jaw. 'It helps remind me of your own cruelty towards me.'

As he turned to go, Caroline couldn't resist asking one final question. 'You still didn't tell me why you came back here. I think you could at least have the decency to tell me that much.'

His mocking expression unchanging, Jack shrugged. 'I bought my parents' old house—the one that got repossessed…remember?'

Caroline experienced a heartfelt jolt. 'I remember.' *He'd been enraged about that. She remembered the savage look on his face when he'd told her about it the same night it happened...unhappily recollected that there had been tears in his dazzling blue eyes as he'd told her and how it had shocked her to witness them.* It was then that he'd asserted his intention of leaving this 'Godforsaken place' to make his name and fortune. When he came back, his mother would never be afraid to hold her head up in this 'ignorant, small-minded town' again.

'What are you going to do with it? You're not going to move back there, are you?' Her voice almost dropped to a crushed whisper at the very idea, and she thought wildly that she'd have to move away, or even go abroad herself...*anything* but live in the same small town as Jack Fitzgerald again!

As if sensing her panic, Jack studied her with a deliberate taunt in his fierce blue gaze. 'You're just going to have to wait and see, Caroline...just like everybody else in this town.'

It was when he got back to his hotel suite, his body as restless as someone high on amphetamines from their charged encounter, unable to do anything but pace the floor for several minutes until he'd calmed himself down, that Jack reluctantly recalled the fear and panic he had witnessed on Caroline's beautiful face.

He didn't want to feel the slightest grain of compassion for her obvious distress. He didn't want to remember that she'd trembled like a leaf in his arms when he'd kissed her so savagely—probably scaring her half out of her wits as well as making him almost crazy with desire. But she'd looked so *good*…more than he'd been able to bear…and smelled so divine. She was a fully matured woman now, not a young, innocent schoolgirl, and she was even *lovelier* than ever.

Briefly touching his fingers beneath the bridge of his nose, Jack sucked in a deep ragged breath at the taunting waft of her perfume that clung to his skin. *Dear God! Why did this have to happen to him after all these years, when he'd spent a lifetime trying to forget her?* Why now, when he'd established himself as a man of means, when he could go anywhere, do anything, be with practically any woman he wanted? Why was it that the *only* woman he craved beyond any good reason was Caroline Tremayne? *It was like having an addiction to dynamite. And he didn't doubt that pursuing her in any way would cause his whole life to blow up in his face.*

Dropping down onto the bed and shrugging off his leather jacket, Jack impatiently undid the first three buttons on his black shirt, as if their being closed was choking him, and sat for long minutes just staring off into space, his hand against his chest, beyond furious that he should have to consider the effect of the stress he was suffering on his heart.

Why was it that she hadn't married? Impatiently considering the possible reasons, Jack could have crawled out of his own skin at not knowing the answer. Why was it that she wasn't even living with someone, didn't have a man in her life on a regular basis? Of course she might well have been married and it just hadn't worked out. Whatever. The mere idea that she was single now was enough to conjure up all kinds of impossible dangerous fantasies in his head.

It would have been so much easier for both of them if they'd been involved with someone else, he realised. Jack had a strict code of conduct about fidelity. Even when Anna had been playing around he hadn't retaliated by taking a lover outside of their marriage himself, and he wouldn't have persuaded Caroline to cheat on her husband if she had had one...*no matter how badly he yearned to have her in his bed again...* His father had destroyed his mother with his heartless philandering. His cheating and drinking and lying had driven her to resort to 'medication' to numb her pain. Even as a young boy, Jack had realised that.

'For God's sake! The past is dead and buried...just leave it alone, why can't you?'

Pushing to his feet, he walked across the room and, moving the velvet drape at the window aside, stared out at the quiet empty street below—the silence only broken by the sound of the ocean in the distance. Why *had* he been so compelled to return to this place? There was no salvation for him here...no one except the seller of the house he had bought for too high a price because he wanted it so badly to be glad that he'd returned to the town he was born in.

No...his coming home was *nothing* like he'd once envisaged it would be. The sooner he finished overseeing the renovations on the house the sooner he could leave, return to the life and work that had brought him an undoubted measure of success in the world…an undoubted measure of the *respect* he'd so badly craved as a young man. He should think about that and stop driving himself mad with thoughts of what he *couldn't* have and definitely *shouldn't* want if he knew what was good for him. *And he was damn sure that when he did leave Caroline Tremayne would mourn his going about as much as she'd grieve over some unknown stranger leaving town…*

Like a naughty child who'd been warned about staying away from a place that might potentially bring her harm, Caroline walked surreptitiously down the little cul-de-sac where Jack and his mother had lived all those years ago, glancing guiltily from side to side as if Jack might appear at any second and demand to know what she was doing there. *Truth to tell, she didn't really know what she was doing there herself.* But Jack's telling her that he was having his old home renovated had feverishly sparked Caroline's curiosity, and instead of driving to open up the shop—as she should have been doing—here she was, creeping about like some kind of private detective hoping to get an illicit compromising picture of somebody's wife or husband cheating on their spouse.

Automatically she touched her chilled fingers to her mouth and imagined she could still feel the lingering aftermath from his blisteringly hot kiss of yesterday. *The fevered recollection of that kiss in every detail had dominated Caroline's dreams last night.* Even though she knew all Jack had wanted to do was punish her in some way for what had happened in the past, it hadn't relegated her near-erotic dream to a nightmare, as it should have done. *No—her body had thrashed around in bed, tormented by the memory of his touch as though it would never know peace or rest again.*

Work had begun on the old Victorian semi-detached dwelling with a vengeance, she saw. Besides the huge digger outside, and the crew of workmen going in and out of the front door with wheelbarrows full of bricks and mortar, or busily occupied up scaffolding, a well-dressed man in a beige raincoat and with a bright yellow hard-hat on his head consulted drawings with another man dressed in jeans and sweatshirt with a well-known sports logo on it.

It looked like a huge and pretty serious undertaking, and Caroline could only stand there in wonderment that Jack had made his passionate promise come true... made his fortune and been able to come home and buy the old place where he and his mother had lived their sometimes hand-to-mouth existence.

It hurt her deeply to remember his despair over their lack of money, but even then Caroline had known that Jack would turn his family's fortunes around. He'd always had a Herculean determination to rise above any adversity and turn a disaster into a triumph. It was just too bad and too tragic that his mother had not lived to enjoy the fruits of her son's labour…

But why? Why had he wanted to buy the house and do it up? As far as Caroline knew, he didn't have any family left around there to keep in touch with, and most of his memories of their little town were hardly the kind he would look back on with fondness—so what had driven him to commit to such a strange undertaking?

Telling herself that her curiosity was bound to be left unsatisfied, because relations between them were hardly conducive to exchanging secrets, Caroline turned to walk back the way she'd come. Right now she should just be getting on with her life and enjoying the results of her own personal success. Jack might imagine she'd failed somehow by not making art her full-time career, and he might see her working in the shop and teaching as a poor substitute—but Caroline knew better. She had the best of both worlds. She could still enjoy her painting without earning her living by it, and working in the shop and teaching arts and crafts at the school helped her enthuse and assist others in making their own art.

There was nothing in that arena she should feel remotely ashamed or regretful about. She should certainly not allow her hostile ex-boyfriend to make her feel bad about the way her life had turned out.

Jack was just walking round from what was now a flattened and decimated garden, in preparation for the spectacular transformation that he and his designer had in mind for it, when he stopped, his stomach jolting at the sight of Caroline, walking away down the street on the opposite side of the house. *What the…?* Before he could check his own rash decision, he removed the hard hat the foreman of the site had given him, threw it down amongst some rubble, and ran to catch up with the rain-coat-clad figure down the street.

'Were you looking for me?' he asked huskily, planting himself in front of her so that she was forced to stop.

Digging her hands into her coat pockets, Caroline felt her astonished glance trapped as thoroughly as a rabbit in a snare. She was wearing her hair loose today, and it flowed over her shoulders in healthy and shiny golden curls that, coupled with her shapely figure were already attracting the inevitable wolf-whistles from some of the men on the site.

Glancing round at the direction they came from with a frown, Jack soon had them silenced with an icy ad-monishment from a reproving blue glare.

'No… I mean, I was—I was just…'

It was no use. *How could she act nonchalant when last night's combustible kiss was clearly in their minds as their heated glances locked?*

She had been *drawn* here as inevitably as moths drew near bright light.

Struggling to maintain her rapidly diminishing com-posure, Caroline tried to move around him, but Jack touched her coat-sleeve to waylay her.

'I suppose you came to take a look at the house? I'm having some major work done, as you can see.'

Caroline found it near impossible to tear her too-starving gaze from Jack's compelling and mesmerising visage, but she gave the house a cursory once-over anyway—thoroughly embarrassed and ashamed at being caught out showing an interest in his project. An interest that might lead him to believe she still felt something for him after all these years.

The thought electrified her. She should know well enough by now to give him a wide berth—not deliberately put herself in the vicinity of wherever he happened to be! *Hadn't they hurt each other enough without coming back for more?*

'It always was a beautiful old building,' she commented, her face flushing hotly when he continued to examine her with the kind of searing intensity reserved for objects of impossible fascination.

'Beautiful, but dilapidated. There never *was* any money to maintain it back then.'

'Well, I'm sure you'll more than restore it to its former glory.' About to smile, Caroline nervously withdrew the gesture and told herself it was time to go. 'I'm on my way to work and I'm already late,' she explained lifting her shoulders in an apologetic shrug.

Jack helplessly focused in on her lips. She had a mouth that teased and provoked even when she didn't mean it to. A throb of languorous heat radiated straight to his groin. Apart from idle curiosity he had no idea what had prompted her to come and look at the house this morning—*especially* after their passionate clash yesterday—but her appearance told him that she was finding it as difficult to remain immune from him as he was to her.

Amid Jack's undeniable flare of satisfaction at the idea, he knew deep down that their dangerous attraction for one another could only lead to the kind of trouble he should be hell-bent on avoiding...

CHAPTER SIX

'DO YOU take a lunch-break?' he found himself asking, before the thought had even fully formed in his brain. Her brown eyes visibly widening in surprise, he heard her release a long slow breath.

'If I can spare the time…why?'

Why, indeed? Jack was asking himself as he listened in on his own suggestion with increasing incredulity at the lack of wisdom it contained. *Just what in God's name did he think he was doing by making it clear that he wanted to see her again?* He scrubbed his hand round his jaw, as if he was all but contemplating flying a plane and then turning off the engine mid-flight and letting himself plummet to the ground, to crash, burn and die.

'I don't think I have an answer for that right now… do *you?*'

Trapped in a hypnotic spell that suddenly seemed to make the world stand still, Caroline stared back at him with equal confusion…equal knowledge that in the world of right-thinking decisions this one wouldn't even get its *toe* in the door.

'No…no, I don't.'

'One o'clock okay with you?'

A little shudder of heat rippled through her. 'That's fine.'

'See you then.'

Before either of them could come to their senses and fully realise the sheer stupidity of such an arrangement Jack quickly walked away in the opposite direction, and didn't once glance back…

Nicholas rang. He told her he had something important that he wanted to discuss. Fearful that he might be going to reiterate his warning to her about Jack, Caroline found she wasn't looking forward to the prospect.

Having agreed that he could drop round that evening to see her, she tried to focus on work. But—between serving customers and trying to put her piling paperwork into some kind of helpful order—her thoughts inevitably returned to Jack, and that promise of his to stop by at lunchtime…

The shop was empty, and there was a sign on the door that read 'Closed for Lunch'. Not entirely certain that Caroline hadn't decided to go out for lunch and stand him up, Jack hesitated for a long moment before pressing the bell at the side of the door. If she was out, he told himself, she would be doing them *both* a huge favour. One of them should come to their senses and put an end to this…this *suicide* mission.

But, even though he prayed she *would* be out, so he could walk away from her relatively *unscathed*, Jack knew that it was already too late. From the moment he'd bumped into her the other day, and they had stood face to face after a lapse of time that should have permanently erased all want, need, or desire for ever, Jack had known that trying to resist Caroline Tremayne was like trying to resist a life-saving drink of water when you'd been stumbling through the desert for days without one. He was fatally infatuated by her…always had been and probably always *would* be. *It was an infatuation that was surely destined to bring them both nothing but further agony of spirit.*

He pressed the bell.

'Come in.'

Jack both cursed and thanked God at the same time for her almost immediate appearance.

Watching him warily from beneath her dark blonde lashes, worrying that she had answered the bell too quickly and might appear over eager to see him, Caroline stood back to let Jack enter. Once inside the colourful interior of the shop, she carefully shut the door again, and turned the latch. Glancing up guiltily as he watched her perform this action, she witnessed the merest glimmer of a mocking smile touch the corners of his mouth.

'If I don't lock the door we won't get any peace

while we're eating,' she remarked nervously, endeavouring to keep her voice light.

Pulling the knitted edges of her long dove-grey cardigan closer together, so that they overlapped the plain black sweatshirt and jeans she wore underneath, Caroline was glad she had donned these nondescript items of clothing, because they lent her psychological protection against the man who was currently putting her so helplessly on edge. She would not have him imagine for even a second that she was hoping to appear alluring or appealing in any way, to resurrect potentially hazardous long-dead feelings between them. All she planned for them to do was eat the sandwiches she had bought from the bakers, have a cup of tea, and keep the conversation as neutral as possible—because they were both mature adults…and then Jack would leave.

But when she glanced across the room, and her anxious searching gaze fell beneath the spell of his dangerously irresistible blue eyes, Caroline knew with devastating certainty that the supposedly 'long-dead' feelings they had once passionately felt for each other still simmered perilously close to the surface, and weren't going to go away any time soon. *Surely she'd been mad to think that they might do something as ordinarily mundane as share some sandwiches and tea together, as though they were two old friends catching up on old times?* Especially when the Jack Fitzgerald who stood before her today had the kind of imposing presence that was hardly conducive to relaxation of any sort. Everything about his expensively groomed appearance quite frankly put him completely out of Caroline's league. He was a far cry from the wild passionate boy who'd willingly shared his dreams with her, who she had fallen in love with so long ago…

'We'll go into the back room, if you like,' she said breezily, sweeping past him. 'I usually eat my lunch there. I've got the kettle on and I—'

Before she got any further Jack swung her round, captured her head between his hands and kissed her ruthlessly on the mouth. When she drew back, stunned, his hands slid down from her face onto her shoulders, and Caroline was immediately aware that he intended to keep her right where she was until he decided different. His nostrils flared a little as he swept her with a heated, ardent stare, and such a feeling of hunger raged through her blood that she wondered how she didn't immediately succumb to it—completely abandon all common sense and caution and simply let the most basic of primal longings have its way.

'What is this…this *hold* you seem to have on me, Caroline?' he asked gruffly, the palpable tension he exuded holding her spellbound.

Her mouth aching from his avidly voracious assault on her lips, Caroline barely knew how to answer him. His words had astonished her, because the very *idea* of her having any kind of hold on such a man seemed completely *preposterous*. He was angry with her, that was all. Still furious because she'd had an abortion instead of going through with the pregnancy. Anger could easily spill over into passion, and Caroline knew with certainty that that was *all* this was about. There'd been no mellowing towards her over the years, and certainly no forgiveness now that Jack had seen her again. *Did she dislike herself so much that she'd willingly let him walk in here and treat her with such demoralising disrespect?*

'I don't have any kind of "hold" over you, Jack. It's all in your imagination. I didn't *ask* you to come back here. I've just been minding my own business and getting on with my life, never once looking to contact you or see you again. Do you know how upsetting it is for me to have you walk in here and kiss me like you just kissed me? As if—as if I still *owe* you something? I think it's probably best if you just go. Having lunch together was an *insane* idea.'

Hearing her words, Jack didn't dispute the sense in them. Yet still he lingered, still his fingers bit possessively into her slender shoulders, as if waiting for some kind of divine inspiration that would tell him what to do about this—this *compulsion* he had for this woman.

Thinking about her accusation, he couldn't deny that he *did* have a sense of Caroline 'owing' him. She'd dispensed with their unborn child as though the decision were hers and hers alone…as if he'd had *no rights and no say* in the matter whatsoever. According to her father, only people from *their* class had those kind of rights. That thought alone had kept his animosity towards her simmering beneath the outward show of his material and professional success all this time.

Releasing his grip, he stood back and breathed in deeply through his nostrils. He thought about all that had happened in those intervening years since he'd left Caroline. First travelling to the States, working and studying at the same time, to gain an understanding of the world of finance, putting his cast-iron determination to good use in helping him rise above his difficult beginnings and make money…a *lot* of money…so that he would never be poor again, *never* be shown the door by anyone who imagined themselves better than he was ever again.

And, besides the money that had started to rain down on him in ever-increasing abundance, there had been *other* compensations too. There had been the undoubted admiration from the financial world in which he worked—the 'movers and shakers' in that world often holding their breath as they watched him accomplish success after success, until eventually he usurped theirs. And there had been the accumulation of beautiful homes—in New York, California and Connecticut, and lately Paris. He'd just signed the lease on a fantastic penthouse apartment in the heart of that lovely city.

Then, of course, there had also been the *women*. Over the years Jack had dated models, actresses, socialites, and women who were as ambitious in their careers as he was. He'd had some good times, some reasonably exciting sex, and led the life of a highly ambitious, successful and *rich* man about town. *But no woman had really touched his heart since his youthful passion for Caroline Tremayne.* Not even Anna—the stunning ballerina from the Russian ballet whom he had met and married after a surprisingly swift courtship just three years ago, and to whom he had vowed he would stay faithful even if he didn't—*couldn't*—love her as she deserved. When he'd discovered that she was having an affair with the interior designer he'd hired to redesign their Manhattan apartment Jack had felt deflated, resigned, but *not* devastated by her betrayal. How could he when he had known where the fault *really* lay? It wasn't necessary now, at Jack's level of success, to put in the working hours that he did, and he *certainly* didn't need any more money than he had already, but any woman would eventually become frustrated by a husband who was never home.

And then had come the heart attack. Thinking of it now, Jack automatically laid his hand against his chest and winced, wishing he could demolish the fear that gripped him for good. Seeing the slight drawing together of Caroline's dark brows—a frown that might spell concern—he quickly moved his hand away and shrugged.

'Why didn't you ever marry?' he found himself asking.

Snapping out of the spell she had fallen under, Caroline felt her fingers clench a little round the edges of her wool cardigan. 'I wasn't aware that getting married was on the statute books,' she answered a little coolly.

'It must have disappointed your father that you didn't

wed,' Jack remarked. 'No high-powered and ambitious son-in-law from the right class to welcome into the fold?'

Hearing the undoubted bitterness in his tone, Caroline shivered. 'Did you ask that question just so that you could have another pop at my father? What's the point, Jack? He's long dead.'

Turning away from him, Caroline moved towards the door she'd just locked and unlocked it. Clearly upset, she opened it and carelessly brushed back a pale frond of golden hair from the side of her cheek.

The gesture made her appear far too vulnerable for Jack's liking, and he deliberately stayed where he was…*almost* but not quite despising himself for his next question. A question that had troubled him often over the years and caused him many a 'dark night of the soul'.

'Did it make your life any *easier*, going through with the abortion?'

Witnessing the convulsive swallow in her throat, and the immediate sheen of tears covering her liquid dark eyes, Jack decided he *did* despise himself after all…

'Get out.'

There was no fury in her voice, just a quiet dignity and a deep, abiding sense of heartbreak that cut Jack to the quick and made him feel like an utter bastard. Unable to do anything but regard her with equal parts longing, regret and rage swirling inside him, Jack nodded his head—as if in complete agreement with her decision for him to go—and swept past her without saying another word…

* * *

'What happened to your lip?'

Before she could duck away, Nicholas had tilted Caroline's chin towards him and examined the slight swelling at the right-hand corner of her lip with a concerned and at the same time professional eye.

'I—I must have inadvertently bit it, or something…I don't know. It's hardly important.'

Pulling away, Caroline tempered her irritable response to Nicholas's concern with an apologetic smile. She too had been slightly shocked to see the damning evidence of Jack's furious kiss when she'd seen it reflected back at her in the bathroom mirror. She certainly didn't want to tell her friend the truth about the cause of her tender abrasion. He'd already warned her against seeing Jack again, and she had ignored his advice and visited nothing but heartache on herself once more.

How could Jack believe for one moment that her life could possibly have been made easier because she'd had an abortion? Caroline wanted to die every time she recalled him asking that wickedly cruel question. But she expressly didn't want to discuss Jack Fitzgerald this evening and make herself feel even more blue. She really hoped that that particular subject was *not* on Nicholas's agenda.

Shaking off the gloom that kept clutching at her heart, she decided to try and keep the conversation as light as possible. 'Will you have a glass of wine?'

Moving across the room, Caroline lifted the bottle of

Châteauneuf-du-Pape she'd left on the tray next to two sparkling wine glasses.

Settling himself into the studded Chesterfield-style armchair by the fire, Nicholas smiled warmly in agreement. 'That would be lovely, darling…thank you.'

Thinking how at home he appeared, sitting there by the crackling open fire on this chilly almost winter evening, in what had been her father's favourite chair, Caroline wondered why, for the first time ever, she wished he *didn't* make himself look so at home there. Telling herself it was because she was still feeling on edge and unhappy from yet another upsetting encounter with Jack, she dismissed her slight feeling of unease and poured out the wine.

Handing a glass to Nicholas, she lowered herself into the fawn-coloured chair opposite and took a sip of her own drink. The alcohol immediately warming her, Caroline told herself that everything was going to be all right…that there was no need for her to be worried about anything.

'So…what was it you wanted to talk to me about?' she asked, leaning forward in her chair.

Nicholas took a sip of his wine, savoured it for a moment, then regarded Caroline with a deepening of the kindly smile she had long grown used to.

'I suppose I may as well get straight to the point.' Still smiling, Nicholas leant back in his chair with a relaxed sigh. 'I wanted to talk to you about something that has been on my mind for quite some time now.'

'Oh? What's that?' Caroline gulped a little too much wine and felt the alcohol hurtle through her veins with fierce heat.

'It's a *personal* matter, actually,' Nicholas replied.

When she didn't immediately comment, he frowned.

'Shall I go on?' he asked.

Caroline wanted to say no. She was all of a sudden very tired, as well as feeling emotionally bruised, and she wanted to say she had a headache and didn't feel up to spending the evening with him after all. But good manners and gratitude for the man's friendship to both her father *and* herself prevented her from going with her natural instincts.

'Of course…please, do go on.'

'We've known each other for a long time, haven't we?' Briefly tapping his wine glass with his fingernails, Nicholas stopped the action almost immediately he realised he was doing it—as if inadvertently revealing a displeasing character trait he'd much rather keep hidden.

Watching him, Caroline was surprised by the tension in him that she'd immediately picked up. For some inexplicable reason a sense of acute alarm arose inside her. His question not really requiring a reply, she nodded her assent instead.

'It was hard losing Meg after being married for so many years…I can't begin to tell you how hard. I've discovered that I'm not a man who likes being alone, Caroline. I need conversation, stimulus, after a long day's work, and Meg was always there for me…come rain or shine. A man gets used to that kind of care from the woman in his life. Anyway, at the risk of making myself sound too foolish…I have decided that I would rather not be on my own any longer.'

CHAPTER SEVEN

He wasn't… He couldn't be going to ask her to—

Sitting straight-backed in her chair, Caroline stared hard at Nicholas, almost willing him to change his mind and not say another word on the topic that was clearly presenting him *and now her* with such unease. Besides…it was too ridiculous, too preposterous to even—

'I'd like us to become engaged to be married—if that's acceptable to you, Caroline?' Nicholas pressed on, reaching up to his shirt collar to pull it slightly away from his neck, where it had suddenly clearly become uncomfortably tight.

Oh God… He was… Leaving her wine glass on the coffee table between them, Caroline got up from her chair and put her hands together, almost as though unconsciously praying. The heat from the fire feeling suddenly more akin to the heat from a roaring bonfire, she tried to smile at the man waiting patiently in her father's old chair for her reaction.

'Engaged Nicholas? You and I? Are you serious?'

'Perfectly!'

'But it's—this is such a shock!'

'A pleasant one, I hope?'

He didn't rise from the chair, as Caroline had half expected him to. Instead he regarded her from it, as though his greater age and experience, his profession, dictated he had the right.

She tried to imagine being married to this man she had long regarded as a family friend. Apart from the age difference, which wouldn't have been an issue at all if she had been in love with him, she knew no matter how desperately alone she felt at times she could not, *would* not, simply marry a man to fill the void left by the death of his wife—*or* because she might end up on her own if she didn't. Nicholas didn't love her either. He might genuinely be fond of her, Caroline mused, but all he really wanted was a companion and housekeeper—someone to be there to listen to the events of his day, someone to cook for him and clean his house, and, yes…someone to pour him a glass of good red wine while he sat by the fire on a cold winter's evening.

And when she thought about going to bed with him… Caroline felt herself grow alternately hot then cold with embarrassment. She'd known this man since she was a teenager. At her father's behest she had looked upon him as a kind of 'uncle'. But—more pertinent than that—how could she even contemplate sharing the intimacies of marriage with a man she neither loved *nor* desired? And especially after becoming so shockingly reacquainted with the *one* man she'd given her heart to so long ago?

Without really meaning to, she found herself touching the slightly raised area on her lip where Jack had kissed her so bitterly and yet with such undeniable need earlier today, and was taken aback by the inescapable rush of pleasure that suddenly throbbed like molten lava through her veins. Immediately Caroline dropped her hand, silently scolding herself for dwelling on the memory of his lustfully hot kiss instead of that cruel question he'd asked, which had wounded her almost too deeply for tears.

'I—I know how much you loved Meg…how much she meant to you. How can I be anything but tremendously flattered that you would even consider asking me to get engaged to you, Nicholas?'

Hugging her arms across her chest, Caroline knew her awkward smile was concerned, but regretful. She didn't want to hurt Nicholas, or make him feel bad in any way, and she certainly didn't want to lose his very dear and valuable friendship but she had to make him see that a more personal relationship, was definitely *not* on the agenda.

'But the truth is,' she continued, 'I'd much rather keep our friendship than potentially spoil what we have by trying to turn our relationship into something it *isn't*.'

This time Nicholas *did* get to his feet. Putting his wine aside, he captured the ends of Caroline's fingers in his own and brushed over them with the pads of his thumbs. It was true that there was tenderness in his expression as he gazed at her, but against the fiery, electrically-charged glances that Jack cast her it was like comparing ice-cubes to burning hot coals…

'Why assume our getting engaged and then married would spoil our friendship…hmm?' Releasing one of her hands, he brushed aside a radiant curl of shining gold that had glanced against her smooth forehead. 'The strongest unions are *always* the ones that start out with friendship. It was certainly that way for Meg and me. We have a great *bond*, Caroline. I admire you and like you more than I could begin to say. I can't think of anyone I would like more to be my wife than you. At least think about it, will you? I wasn't expecting a decision straight away…'

'I'm sorry, Nicholas, but I don't really need any time to think about it. I know it can't have been easy for you to broach the subject…and it's a terrific compliment to be asked…but I'm afraid my answer *has* to be no.'

Not liking the sudden sense of intimacy he was forcing upon her that was so at odds with all these years of steady platonic friendship, Caroline drew away from his near embrace and moved across the room to the door that stood ajar.

'I think I'm going to make a cup of tea…would you like one?'

Genuinely perplexed, Nicholas shook his head. 'No, thank you. I don't think I *would* like a cup of tea right now. If I've offended you in any way, Caroline, let me be the first to assure you that I——'

Suddenly wishing that he would go, Caroline felt as

though she might explode with the tension that had gathered force inside her. So many emotions were charging through her all at once that she scarcely knew what to do with them. *She didn't want to marry Nicholas—her father's closest friend.* She didn't want to sacrifice herself for *any* man—no matter what the reason—*ever* again. And she certainly didn't want to spend another seventeen years heartsore and racked with too much guilt over a man who barely even accorded her the *right* to possess hurt feelings because he was so certain that *he* was the one who had been so cruelly wronged. She would not be pushed into a corner again by anybody!

'You haven't offended me at all, Nicholas, but I really don't want to discuss this any further. I just—I'm sorry, but I really need to be by myself right now. Please try and understand.'

Straightening the cuffs on his shirtsleeves beneath his very conservative tweed sports jacket, Nicholas patted down his pockets distractedly as he walked towards her, clearly both embarrassed and confused by Caroline's rejection of his proposal—a response he obviously had not been expecting.

'I certainly wouldn't dream of outstaying my welcome, Caroline. We'd best just leave things as they stand for a day or two, under the circumstances, and then I'll ring you. That all right with you?'

Unable to bring herself to look at him directly, Caroline nodded mutely.

* * *

Feeling the need to escape for a while, Jack had driven to London, booked into a small chic hotel in Chelsea owned by an American friend, then called up that same friend's sister, whom he'd briefly dated before meeting Anna and who was now based in the UK, working for an insurance company in the city.

Amanda Morton was a woman of the world—she'd understand that Jack wasn't calling her to renew their relationship but was simply looking for a little female company while he was in town. They'd parted on amicable terms, remained friends, and Jack was merely fulfilling a promise that if he was ever in London he'd look her up.

Now, as he sat next to her in the low-lit bar area in the luxurious lounge of a famous hotel, her slender thigh pressed up close to his as she regaled him with gossip from her office as though any higher concerns—such as life, death and the universe—never even entered her brain, Jack remembered why his relationship with Amanda had not progressed much beyond two or three dates. Certainly her looks couldn't be faulted, with her elegantly styled blonde hair, slender figure and sparkly blue eyes, but Jack couldn't help thinking of another blonde—one with delectable *brown* eyes—who he'd last seen wearing an expression of inconsolable sadness and hurt…*put there by him.*

About to take a deep slug of the bourbon on the rocks that he had ordered, Jack shifted in his seat, put down his glass, and came to a decision that surprised even himself.

Amanda immediately stopped talking and cast him

a highly flirtatious glance from beneath her heavily mascaraed lashes.

'What's up, sweetie? Don't you like it here? We can go someplace else if you'd like?'

'I'm sorry, Amanda, but I have to go.'

'Go?'

She blinked up at him in bewilderment as he rose to his full six feet two inches. His handsome face was preoccupied and his mouth drawn—immediately alerting even the oblivious Amanda to the fact that his mind had not been as attentive to her conversation as she might have liked.

'What do you mean, you have to go? We've barely just got here!' she declared in dismay. 'I know you're not interested in seeing me on a regular basis, Jack, but I'd at least hoped we'd wind up in bed together before the night was through!'

Why had he done it? Jack asked himself. Why had he called up a woman he'd barely been able to muster the most fleeting interest in when he'd first stupidly dated her and expected her to help distract him from the unpalatable turmoil that had assailed him since he'd left Caroline back home with that stricken look in her eyes? All he knew right then was that his need to see the girl the youthful Jack Fitzgerald had fallen in love with was impossible to ignore, and his thoughts and feelings would give him no peace—even if he jumped on a plane to Alaska to escape them—if he didn't drive straight back to her right now. It didn't matter that his inexplicable desire had no rhyme or reason, or that the outcome of it would probably result in even *more*, unwelcome turmoil than he was enduring already, he simply had to go back and see her.

'I'm sorry, Amanda.'

Employing full mercenary use of his undoubted charisma, Jack tipped up Amanda's chin and smiled beguilingly into her eyes as she stood up and seductively leaned towards him. Her perfume was a little on the overpowering side, and Jack fleetingly wondered why some women never understood the power of subtlety, no matter if they came from money or not. Money couldn't buy class, and that was a fact.

The thought immediately made Jack think of Caroline, and he couldn't help but silently admit that she had always had that commodity in abundance...*even* when she was only seventeen. And it wasn't just social class he was thinking about either. Her grace, beauty and innocence had made Jack feel like a much better man than he knew himself to be whenever he'd been around her.

'I don't mean any insult, but it was wrong of me to call you when I had other things on my mind that need taking care of. Things that I now realise I simply *can't* leave unattended. Can you forgive me?'

'It depends what "other things" are on your mind, Jack,' Amanda crooned softly, winding his silk tie round her fingers and tugging on it a little. 'If it's work...well, being ambitious for my own career, I can totally understand such a preoccupation. But on the other hand...if

it's another *woman* that's been distracting your mind…
then I might, just *might*, be a teensy-weensy bit upset
about that.'

Feeling his patience getting a little strained, Jack
abruptly rescued his tie and kissed the pouting Amanda
as briefly as possible on her forehead. Pressing some
notes from his wallet into her hand, he smiled. 'Get
yourself a cab home. I won't forget I owe you dinner,'
he declared as he turned to walk across the hotel lounge.

And tomorrow he would send her the biggest
bouquet he could order from the florists to make up for
the disappointment of his desertion tonight. But even as
he ventured one last glance round, as he reached the
twin doors that led into the lobby, he smiled wryly to
himself as he saw Amanda walk confidently up to the
bar and start avidly chatting to the young, good-looking Spanish bartender behind it…

Caroline had driven to the beach after Nicholas had left,
and walked the length of the sandy cove with the rain
and wind lashing at her clothing and stinging her face.
She'd cried, secure in the knowledge that nobody else
would witness her descent into misery, that only someone desperate of spirit would be out walking along a
deserted beach in the dark with the rain bucketing down
as though God was emptying out a heavenly reservoir
upon her head.

She'd desperately needed the release of tears, and
after Nicholas's unexpected and, it had to be said, un-

welcome proposal she knew the tide of change that was rolling towards her was both inevitable and unstoppable. After this, she could rely on nothing to stay the same. Even her good memories of Jack would be tainted by his reappearance, and the churning-up of emotions that his presence had cruelly revisited upon her. Caroline had sobbed desperately for the predicament she found herself in—for the unimaginably traumatic sense of loss and grief that she had suffered through having the abortion and then being shunned by her baby's father, the man she had loved *beyond* imagining, the man who was never, *ever* going to either understand or forgive her for what she had done…

By the time she got back to the house she was thoroughly drenched, and shivering with cold, and she immediately went upstairs, stripped off, donned her warm dressing-gown and ran a hot bath. Half an hour later, once again ensconced in the old-fashioned comfort of her dressing-gown, her feet up on her armchair's matching footstool as she sipped a mug of hot cinnamon-flavoured milk in front of the fire, Caroline silently and thankfully acknowledged that her misery had ebbed a little and the heat and comfort of her home were helping subdue some of the tremendous hurt that had deluged her.

The only way forward, she concluded, thinking hard as she stared into the flames flickering in the grate, was to somehow learn to forgive herself for what she'd done…*and also forgive Jack for blaming her.* That was the only way she could really put the past behind her and look forward to a happier future. Maybe she should re-examine the possibility of earning her living as an artist? It wasn't too late. And she could still teach part-time, as she was doing, and give encouragement and the benefit of her experience to young girls like Sadie Martin. Change shouldn't be feared.

If Nicholas couldn't remain the friend he'd always been she still had other friends she could count on…and she would make new ones too. But at the same time she couldn't keep looking *outside* for the source of her happiness…it simply *had* to come from within, or else she'd for ever be at the mercy of external forces. When she next saw Jack…*if* she saw him again…and her pulse raced a little at the idea she might not…Caroline was determined to tell him about the decision she had reached. He could continue to blame her for as long as he liked, but he would have to understand that she was no longer going to be a willing victim of that blame. She was steering the ship of her own life and would not let anyone knock her off course again, no matter *who* they were.

Having finished her drink, Caroline put down her mug and snuggled up into the chair with her feet drawn up beneath her. Continuing to stare into the hypnotic flames that danced across the coals in the grate, before she knew it sleep had seductively beckoned.

Into her dreams intruded the incongruous chimes of the doorbell. Jolting upright with shock, Caroline opened her eyes wide and glanced frantically up at the clock on the mantel. It was almost half-past one in the morning…hardly a sensible time for callers of any description…so who could it be?

Uncurling her legs from beneath her, and rising anxiously, she yelped in pain when the arch of her foot almost bent double with cramp. Falling back into the chair, she quickly rubbed at the offending area, praying that the doorbell would not chime again—hoping that whoever it was who had rung it had mistakenly stopped outside the wrong door and had now realised his or her mistake and moved on. *No such luck.* As the echo of the ringing chimes demonstrated her caller's persistence, Caroline got slowly to her feet, her cramp now gone and her skin clammily cold with fright.

Glancing at the iron poker in the brass stand beside the grate, she did seriously wonder about taking it with her—but then an obstinate refusal to believe that she wasn't safe in her own home suddenly collared her fear by the throat and sent her striding confidently out to the front door…*without* the poker.

When she saw the definite shadow of a man's figure outside the stained glass panels in the door, Caroline almost breathed a sigh of relief, thinking it must be Nicholas. He'd probably been called out to see a patient and, driving home again, had seen some of her house lights on because she had fallen asleep in the chair and hadn't turned them out yet. Hoping that he didn't hold a grudge against her because she'd earlier refused his request to get engaged, Caroline undid the locks and pulled open the door.

'Jack!'

Her legs trembled hard at the sight of her ex-lover. Grasping the fleece lapels of her robe together in her hand across her chest, Caroline simply stared at him as he shrugged inside his raincoat, his dark hair sheened by the rain and the starkly defined planes and angles of his amazing face disturbingly highlighted by the illumination from inside the house.

'What is it? Has something happened?'

She had the most unnatural feeling that she was speaking in slow motion. But, even though Jack's appearance was a total mystery and a shock to her, something inside Caroline couldn't help but foolishly grasp at the most impossible hope.

'I needed to see you. I realise it's very late, but can I come in?'

As logic briefly superseded her impossible hope, she wanted to say no. This man was like a broken arrow embedded in her heart. Inviting him over her threshold would be like inviting him to deepen that wound even more. Already her throat was constricting with anguish at the sight of him.

In the end, because words simply deserted her, Caroline just watched with a mounting sense of unreality as Jack came inside, shucked off his raincoat, hung it on the coatstand, then came back to her—his ardent gaze studying her in a way that made her bones turn to liquid silk. Without saying a word he cupped the side of her face with his hand, the startling touch of his cool skin acquainting her with the chill of the rainy night outside. He kept his palm there with a gentleness that ripped the breath from Caroline's lungs. As her wary and captivated gaze examined the arresting features and sharply drawn jawline before her—that jawline denoted he was wilful as well as meeting life on his own terms, with little regard for anyone else's *modus operandi*— she found herself wondering if they would still be together now if she hadn't fallen pregnant and her father hadn't made her have a termination. God knew she'd been crazy about him…crazy enough to jump ship and elope with him to the States or anywhere else he suggested if he had but asked. *He never had.*

She knew this was dangerous thinking. What Jack was doing here in the middle of the night she had no idea, but one thing Caroline *was* certain of—she wasn't going to let him make her feel bad about herself ever again.

She broke free of his touch, unconsciously pursing her dry lips to moisten them as he watched her, his brooding gaze still cleaving to her face as though he couldn't bear to look anywhere else but at *her*.

'What do you want, Jack?'

'Isn't that obvious?'

'I wouldn't have asked if I didn't—'

'You,' he came back, before she'd even finished the sentence, his lips unsmiling and for once without mockery.

A high-voltage charge of heat bolted through

Caroline's middle, making her hips soft and the rest of her body feel as if she could climb out of her very skin with the seductive promise his disturbing reply created.

'That's a very bad joke, under the circumstances,' she returned huskily, feeling as if she really was losing her hold on reality. 'I think you'd better just go.'

'What if I don't want to?' Jack asked, moving purposefully towards her even as he registered the distress on her face. 'What if…deep down…you don't *want* me to go either, Caroline?'

CHAPTER EIGHT

'YOU must be delusional!' Her dark eyes flashed her indignant denial even as, terrifyingly, she registered his
hand sliding expertly behind her neck beneath the soft
tousled fall of her hair, and his mouth moving threaten-
ingly closer to hers. 'I don't want you to stay…I want you
to go! Do you think I *enjoy* being hurt by you? When I
saw you last you left me under no illusion as to what you
thought of me and your words cut me in two! What we
had was finished a long time ago, Jack. Why not just
accept that and walk away now? Just forget me and go!'

Jack was struck by the ragged truth of Caroline's impassioned words. He *should* just walk away and forget
her, as she'd advised, and spare them both further agony.
But even as his lips stilled, scant inches from hers, he
knew that trying to curtail his increasing desire for her
was like hoping to douse an inferno with a mere thim-
bleful of water. His senses were held in thrall by her.

In the gently dimmed light that flooded out into the
hall from the living room, she looked like the impossi-

bly beautiful heroine from a fairy tale. Her dark gaze was
sleepily soft, even though her eyes danced with anger,
and her hair felt like gossamer as it glanced against the
back of his hand. God help him, but Jack had dreamed
of holding her like this so many times over the years!
But then usually, after he'd surrendered to the impulse
to think about Caroline, he'd be infused with agonising
hurt about her having the abortion and betraying both
him *and* their unborn child. He'd *hate* her then, and the
impulse—the tormenting, feverish longing to recall how
she had felt in his arms—would abruptly leave him.

But right now it wasn't hatred that was dominating
Jack's senses but a ravenous, almost obsessive compulsion to know her again in the most libidinous and
intimate way. Everything about her put him under a
spell of longing.

'I know what we had is long over,' he intonated
throatily, his compelling blue irises darkening as he
stared into Caroline's startled gaze. 'But what if—what
if I asked you to share just one more night with me?
What then, Caroline? Would you turn me away out into
the rain again when right now I need to hold you more
than anything else I need in this entire world?'

*He didn't play fair. He found her most vulnerable
spot and ruthlessly exploited it.* Right from that very first
moment, when he'd arrested her curious, aroused gaze
with his lazy and bold examination of her when she was
with her schoolfriends, Jack had assumed an early and
definitely *powerful* advantage over Caroline's capti-

vated senses. Now she was once again besieged by his
blatantly sensual masculinity, and the incessant throbbing yearning that surged through her heart at his seductive words made her realise that she was too weak to
deny him…to deny *herself.*

Feeling herself sway, all the strength in her legs
seemed to treacherously desert her as Jack caught her
feverishly in his arms and with devastating thorough-
ness laid voracious claim to her lips. Drenching heat
and exquisitely male flavours burst over her mouth,
and Caroline heard herself making small betraying
sounds of shameless longing. Jack swept her mouth
with his tongue, stroking and teasing hers with unbelievably erotic torment as he gathered a fistful of her
soft silken hair in his hand and massaged her scalp
with his fingers. His lean hips increased the torment
he was delivering as he pressed them demandingly
into hers, hinting at a wild white-water ride of incal-
culable pleasure and rediscovery that made Caroline
breathless.

'Jack…'

*Every ounce of longing she had in her entire being was
in the soft, heartfelt whisper of his name.* She had lost so
much…her baby *and* Jack… How could she pass up the
chance for them to be together again for even a short
while, she asked herself desperately, when she ached so
hard for him that it was *unthinkable* to ask him to leave?

'Have mercy,' he replied, his warm breath caressing
the side of her neck, closely followed by his lips. 'Please

don't tell me you've changed your mind… I want you so badly I'm shaking. Can you feel it?'

She could. Although there was humour in his wry remark, there was an underlying fear and desperation there too. Extricating herself firmly from his ardent embrace, Caroline swept back her dishevelled golden hair with her fingers and glanced nervously towards the open door that led into the living room.

'There's a fire…it needs—it needs building up, but the embers are still burning.' *She could have been talking about their relationship and the irony was not lost on her.*

Jack's piercing gaze examined her for so long that Caroline momentarily feared that *he* was the one who had changed his mind about making love to *her*. Glancing anxiously away, she felt her breath catch in her throat when he suddenly moved closer and slipped his arm possessively around her waist, bestowing a smile so dangerously beguiling that she was reminded of the eager, devil-may-care, youthful Jack—who had so determinedly and doggedly pursued her in spite of the dire warnings and threats from Caroline's father. There was a big part of her that still grieved for the innocent passion they had lost so cruelly…

He made up the fire again while Caroline watched, silently begging him to finish quickly and join her again. When he did, he drew her down to the patterned colourful rug, with its tones of burnished copper and warm reds, that adorned the space in front of the fire. Then, lifting his dark green lambswool sweater over his head, he carelessly discarded it before slowly undoing the tie-belt of Caroline's dressing-gown that was fastened around her small hourglass waist.

She couldn't stop shivering as his hands first touched her clothing, then her skin—his intensely blue eyes making her a slave to his increasingly heated glance. When she did manage to tear her gaze free, it was only for it to linger on the taut, well-formed display of muscle at the tops of his arms, so temptingly revealed by his fitted T-shirt.

A hot, melting flurry of acute awareness dispersed through Caroline's insides when she saw the dark tattoo of a raven carved into his left bicep. He must have acquired it after he had left her, she realized, curious as to what it was supposed to symbolise. *And there was no doubt in her mind that it meant something.* Something that very few people would know outright. That was one of the things about Jack that had been such a magnet for Caroline. *He'd always been almost frighteningly inscrutable and unpredictable—had always left her with the sense that he knew things about life that no one else knew...*

'Let's take this off, shall we?'

Relieving her of her dressing-gown, Jack directed his attention to the perfectly beautiful delineation of her slender shoulders in the flimsily strapped white cotton nightgown, to the temptingly bountiful swell of her full breasts and the noticeable imprint of her puckered nipples behind the pristine cotton. With her hair tumbling and curling like golden flame down her back, highlighted by the vivid colours reflected from the fire, her expression was focused totally on him and entirely serious. *Jack guessed how King Solomon must have felt when the Queen of Sheba had revealed herself to him from a rolled-up carpet.* Her incandescent beauty stunned him.

A powerful memory surfaced inside Jack from long ago, when they had made love for the very first time. Her loveliness had left him dry-mouthed in awe then too.

The venue for the occasion had been a cheap hotel on the outskirts of town where no one would know them, and when Jack had eagerly helped Caroline undress he had finally seen her the way he'd been hungering to see her since the day they'd met. She'd been the most breathtakingly beautiful girl he'd ever set eyes on, and she had wanted to be with him—not some 'upper class aspiring doctor' that her father picked out for her. That very gratifying realisation alone had helped cement Jack's already strong feelings for her. His spirits had soared to the sky at the knowledge that she wanted to share her beautiful body with *him…that he was going to be her very first lover and, if Jack had his way, her only lover.*

Now the denial of that fervent wish twisted his heart with unbelievable hurt. To imagine her giving herself in that way to somebody else… *Caroline was his.*

Faced with the extraordinarily jealous urge that swept him, Jack could no longer pretend even to himself that his possessive feelings towards her had grown less passionate or intense throughout all the years of separation.

'What's this?' With a shy smile that caught him completely off guard, Caroline gently touched the outline of his tattoo.

Capturing her slender, fine-boned wrist between his fingers, Jack made a gruff noise in his throat, then smiled. 'It's a raven. The Native Americans believe that it has the power to shape-shift—to move from one dimension to another. It can also symbolise visiting the darker parts of your soul.'

She detected the minutest flicker of a shadow in his fascinating blue eyes that left her in no doubt that he was well acquainted with the darker parts of his own soul.

Shivering as he raised her hand to his lips and gently kissed it, Caroline longed to be able to convey to him how desperately she regretted perpetrating the act that had finally forced them apart. In that moment she realised that Jack was still harbouring a wealth of animosity and pain in his soul because of her. And, although she definitely intended to let him know that she was no longer going to be a willing victim of that animosity and pain—no matter *how* regretful she was— Caroline also experienced an overwhelming urge to demonstrate to him her intense sadness that their love had been dashed to the rocks and splintered for ever…

'I've done that too, Jack,' she whispered, studying him intently. 'Visited the darker part of my soul. But despising what I found there didn't help me. We have to learn to forgive, don't we? I mean…even ourselves. Then we can move on and hopefully make something of our lives. I'm so sorry about what happened between us. If I could turn back time and undo all the dreadful hurt I would.'

Learn to forgive? For a moment his jaw tightened with overwhelming emotion. Jack didn't know if he would *ever* be able to do that. Because of what Caroline had done, he had not sought to father another child with a woman. He had been far too fearful of a repetition of the past. But—deep in the far reaches of his soul—Jack still *longed* to experience fatherhood. Else what had all his hard work and driving ambition been *for?* Having a child of his own would help make up for every excruciating splinter of hurt that his own disastrous family life had driven into his heart…

'I think you've grown even more lovely over the years.' Deliberately diverting the conversation from things that were too painful to reflect upon, Jack kissed Caroline softly on the mouth, contact with her moist, sultry lips fuelling his desire once more into restless burning flame.

How could she do anything *other* than dissolve in his arms at such a heartwarming statement? Even though she was crushingly disappointed that he hadn't responded positively to her suggestion of forgiveness, Caroline nonetheless couldn't deny the increasingly restless need that was building inexorably inside her body at Jack's closeness.

His kiss deepened devastatingly. The pleasure it wrought inside her took Caroline to such heights of unimaginable joy that she knew that when Jack was long gone she would remember the intensity of those feelings for the rest of her life.

Feeling his hands drop to her shoulders to guide her gently onto the rug beneath them, she watched him undress—her mind registering his undoubted masculine perfection with growing anticipation, seeing for herself that her girlhood lover had definitely turned into the most awesome man. Yanking his T-shirt over his dark head, Jack let it drop where it fell. Then, kneeling down, he joined Caroline on the rug.

As he bent towards her, she was taken aback by the slender ridged scar she saw on his chest. Glancing up into his unfathomable blue eyes, she felt her stomach tighten as a bump of fear pulsed through it. If he saw that she was curious, Jack chose to ignore it. Instead his warm breath fanned across her mouth as he lowered his head to kiss her again.

'What happened? How did you get this?'

Her words interrupted his all too clear intention. As the firelight flickered across her illuminated and concerned features, Jack silently cursed. 'It's nothing,' he answered dismissively.

When he would have touched his lips to hers, Caroline put her fingers haltingly across his mouth. 'Tell me. I know it's not nothing,' she said astutely.

Sighing, and unable to conceal his frustration, Jack

felt his own expression harden a little as he scanned her anxious, expressive eyes. To admit his heart attack to *Caroline,* of all people, would be tantamount to admitting that he wasn't the great success he'd gone out of his way to prove himself to be. Having always striven to keep himself in A1 physical condition, he would expose the kind of vulnerability that he deliberately guarded against, and it would drag him right back to being the boy her father had so despised from the wrong side of the tracks who in other people's eyes, was 'destined to fail'.

'Do you mind if we *don't* discuss my physical defects right now?' he replied somewhat bitterly, and he watched surprise and hurt infiltrate her lovely face.

'A scar isn't a defect,' Caroline protested softly, her fingers curling into her palm to stop herself from reaching out and gently inspecting the so-called 'defect' that clearly engendered such strong emotion in him. Of course she wanted to know how he had acquired it—was frightened at the idea that it had been caused by something serious—but right now all she could do...all she *longed* to do...was bring him comfort in whatever way she could.

Underneath the outward show of undoubted success, elements of the angry young man Caroline had met and fallen in love with still existed, and it still clearly haunted him. *She sensed it deep down in her very bones.*

'Besides...you look amazing,' she breathed softly, venturing a smile up into that suddenly sombre face of his.

'Are you telling me that you like what you see, sweetheart?'

A smile broke free from his lips that was like a precious glimpse of the sun glimmering through a dark raincloud and, as he ran his palm up the side of her bare leg until it reached the curve of her hip and bottom, she felt his electrifying touch induce a stunning shower of hot little shivers inside her that made her urgently reach towards him, to bring his head down to hers.

Their mouths clashed heatedly, greedily tasting each other as if the world was running out of time, and all thoughts were suspended while pure, uninhibited sensation assumed powerful command.

Pulling down the front of Caroline's nightgown with sudden impatience, Jack fastened his mouth to one tight velvet nipple, then the other, finally surrendering to the insistent demanding need to touch her in the way he had long dreamed of—that tonight had caused him to put his foot down on the accelerator as if his life depended on it all the way back from London, just to be with her.

As his tongue swirled over and hotly dampened the softly quivering flesh, a thunderclap of heat exploded straight into his groin and his swiftly unashamed arousal caused him to emit a hoarse and ragged groan. Exploring her body beneath her thin gown, Jack impatiently pushed the material out of the way before purposefully directing his hand between her thighs, and gently but firmly coaxing them apart.

Her eyes closed of their own volition, to experience

the full devastating wave of erotic pleasure that washed over her as Jack's fingers entered her body—unashamedly stoking the searingly provocative damp heat that flooded into her centre. Caroline silently rejoiced that her most secret heartfelt wish to know the magic of his touch again had come true. But her body tensed as he pressed deeper, her hand instantly grabbing onto his to still it, her heart pumping hard against her ribcage at the realisation that she was still maybe a little too tight for his erection to follow.

Jack wouldn't know that no other man had ever been invited to enjoy the intimacy of touching her as he was doing now, since he had left her seventeen years ago. Her most feminine muscles were not used to being aroused the way he was arousing them at this moment. *And then there was Caroline's deep abiding fear that the termination she had had could have somehow damaged her in some way—even though she'd been given the all-clear by her doctors.*

She didn't doubt that the tremendous guilt she had suffered over the years had played its part in fuelling this fear. It was one reason why she had never allowed herself to get really close to a man in all this time. Besides…there was only *one* man she had ever loved. And even though Jack was here now, doing all the things she yearned for him to do…he didn't love *her.*

'What's the matter?' His deep voice thick with arousal, Jack withdrew his hand and softly touched her face. 'Nothing's wrong, is it?'

Feeling like a terrible fool, Caroline stared up at him, her soft brown eyes unable to contain their fear.

'It's…it's just that it's been such a long time since—' She broke off, feeling her cheeks burn with heat and her throat tighten.

'I *know* how long it's been, Caroline…*seventeen* years.'

Jack's searing glance didn't leave her face for even a moment. But just when Caroline was about to express her relief that he understood, he went on…

'But I'm sure you must have had plenty of practice in between, sweetheart.'

Unable to keep the inevitable derision from his tone, Jack felt half crazy that their lovemaking had been temporarily thwarted, as well as furious that he had been inadvertently forced into thinking about the inevitable fact that Caroline had known other lovers since they had parted. *Why shouldn't she?* She was a stunningly attractive *single* woman. Now, as he regarded her with undeniable frustration, he saw her throat convulse with obvious distress, but he hardened his heart against the sight.

'You—you think I've had other lovers? I know this might be hard for you to believe, Jack…but the truth is I haven't been this intimate with another man since you left.'

The heat from the fire gathered noticeable force and ejected a glowing burning coal that sizzled on the tiled surround.

The impact of her words finally computing in his stunned brain, Jack's gaze narrowed with disbelief.

'You're trying to tell me that I'm the only man you've ever had sex with?'

Hurting abominably that he'd referred to their intimacies so crudely as 'having sex', and not 'making love', Caroline despondently pushed her nightgown back down over her hips and sat up. Threading her trembling fingers through the tumbled golden strands of her long blonde hair, she adjusted the straps of her gown back onto her shoulders and looked suddenly pale.

'Yes, Jack…that's what I'm telling you.'

'I don't believe it.'

'I have no reason to lie.' She shrugged, and her mouth quivered a little.

'If you *are* telling me the truth, Caroline, I want to know why? Why haven't you been with anybody else since we broke up?'

Staring at her as if she was someone he'd never seen before, Jack furrowed his handsome brow.

'I've had boyfriends…of course I have. But I just haven't wanted to sleep with any of them. Is that a crime?'

Feeling chilled to her very bones at the way their passionate reunion was turning out, Caroline stared down at her hands as if they belonged to a stranger. Resting in her lap, they looked too pale…too *unloved,* somehow. If only she had been able to relax a bit more, she anguished miserably. *If only she hadn't worried so much that she wouldn't be able to love him as she yearned to because of her fear…*

But what was the use in condemning herself for her

feelings? She wasn't deliberately trying to be obstructive. She wanted Jack's loving more than she wanted to see daylight after enduring a nightmare alone in the dark! But she was also beginning to think that their brief reunion was utterly doomed.

Looking as if he didn't know whether to believe her or not, Jack sighed heavily.

'And just now…when you stopped me? It was because you were—'

'Like you said, Jack.' Caroline's eyes and her voice were similarly flat. 'Seventeen years is a long time. Can you wonder that I was a little *tense*?'

Before he could say anything, tears were spilling down her cheeks in a steady, agonising flow.

CHAPTER NINE

HE WAS the only man she'd ever properly made love with? Faced with such a momentous revelation, Jack found himself examining Caroline's crestfallen face with an increasing sense of shock. As the pinnacle of that shock ebbed away, he was unable to resist the sudden great need to hold her. Taking her into his arms, Jack cradled her head protectively against his chest.

The last time he'd seen Caroline break her heart in front of him was when she had confessed to having the termination. and he had been so outraged and so destroyed by the news that he had been *stone* to her tears. Now, as well as needing to make love to her more than ever, Jack found her distress the one chink in his armour that he hadn't expected. Emotions were coming to the fore inside him that he'd sworn to keep under lock and key for *good*, and the realisation disturbed him deeply.

'Shh…don't cry…please don't cry.'

Kissing her gently dishevelled blonde head, Jack became a willing slave to the exquisite sensuality of her subtle yet pervasive scent. It was nothing to do with the shampoo or perfume or bath oil she used. It was *everything* to do with Caroline herself. Jack was *undone* by her, and he knew it.

What if he had been too *hasty* in relinquishing her to her fate all those years ago? Coming out of nowhere, it was a stunning, disconcerting thought, and one he wouldn't be at all wise to pursue. Instead, Jack moved Caroline a little way away from him, so that he could glean for himself how she was feeling. Holding onto her arms, he started to seductively massage her skin.

'Explain to me,' he instructed quietly, 'why there hasn't been anyone else?'

Not liking the growing sense of vulnerability that was descending upon her, Caroline realised then that Jack had not been aware of the sheer magnitude and scope of her love for him. Hadn't she shown him enough? Hadn't she *proved* it by giving him her virginity when she was just seventeen? *Maybe he'd thought what she felt for him was just infatuation*? What if that was why he had been able to believe that she had relented 'too easily' to an abortion? If he'd realised how much she had loved him, with all her heart, Jack would have known it could have been nothing less than *torture* to make the decision about their baby. The guilt she'd suffered over that whole distressing episode had tainted almost everything. *Especially* the possibility of ever enjoying an intimate relationship with someone new, or trusting that she wouldn't ever be pressured into terminating a pregnancy again…

'I just—' With the heels of her hands Caroline harshly dismissed the evidence of her tears, suddenly furious that Jack was putting her in such an untenable position. She didn't want to reveal her deepest secrets to him any more. He probably wouldn't believe her anyway, so what was the point? His mind was already made up about her and *nothing* was going to change it. 'Meeting someone and falling in love isn't automatic, you know. I suppose it simply wasn't on the cards…'

Jack didn't know what to think about that. The truth—if he was honest—was that he didn't *want* to speculate too hard about why Caroline had resisted intimacy with other men. Somewhere not too deep inside him he had to admit he was *glad* that she had… and doubly glad that she hadn't fallen in love again…no matter how selfish that might sound. Yet here she was, living in this large old house all by herself, supposedly content with a single life and seeing no one but a man who was old enough to be her father. Jack didn't care how strenuously he denied it—Caroline's doctor friend's interest in her was definitely *not* platonic.

Feeling another jealous wave settle over him, he moved his hands up Caroline's graceful and slender arms to her shoulders and slowly—with a deeply possessive glint in his eye—pulled her flimsy straps back down again. Her soft flesh quivered delightfully, sending another spear of scalding need straight to his groin. He heard her emit a soft, startled breath, and before she could utter a word Jack was kissing her with

a stark, ravishing hunger that must have been simmering inside him for *years*.

When he reluctantly slowed things down, to obviously search for protection in his discarded clothing,
Caroline's heightened senses descended briefly back
down to earth again. *What if they didn't use protection?*
If they could make another baby together… If Caroline
could only get pregnant again… She would be able to
show Jack that her most heartfelt wish was to be the
mother of his baby. *A wish she had been cruelly robbed
of at her father's shameful and brutal instigation.*

Distressed at the impossible and dangerous direction
her thoughts were taking her, Caroline let her gaze cling
heatedly to Jack's as with breathtaking expertise he
stripped her of her nightgown. Naked in front of him,
there was nowhere to hide, and she shivered almost violently as the heat in his eyes licked over her with barely
contained lust.

Taking her cue from him, Caroline dipped her gaze
to examine the fine display of tight, trained muscle that
was so evident in his lean but awesome physique, her
stomach jolting in reaction when she saw how aroused
he was. Raising her glance level with his again, Caroline
was even less able to stop from violently trembling.

'God must have created you just to drive me out of
my mind,' he ground out, his voice hoarse with longing.
'But you're in my blood and I can't get you out.'

With a just barely civilised groan, Jack pushed her
down onto the rug. In even less time than it had taken

to accomplish that, he had settled her beneath him, turning the attention of his expert kisses to her breasts, her ribcage, her sexy tucked-in navel and her hips—skimming over her bones and skin, his mouth and tongue doing things to her body that made Caroline clutch at the rug beneath her to try and stay on the planet.

When he slid his hand between her trembling thighs to part them, his fingers sliding in and out of her wetness with destroying ease, Caroline shut her eyes and no longer *cared* about staying earth-bound. She almost leapt out of her skin when Jack replaced his fingers with his mouth, and nothing could have prepared her for the sheer dazzling violence of the climax his erotic torment finally and inevitably elicited.

All the tension and doubt about whether everything would be okay vanished in a blaze of sensation so strong that Caroline didn't have a prayer when it came to keeping her feelings silent. Crying out with pleasure, she blinked dazedly up at Jack as his firm, muscular thighs straddled her hips. Then he laid passionate siege to her mouth once more.

Her already reeling senses stayed in the ascendant somewhere, circling the heavens. But even as she registered their languid descent Jack had sheathed himself and thrust into her with destroying deliberation. Inevitably Caroline tensed a little at his masculine invasion—for a moment her fears that it might hurt returning—but Jack cleverly seduced her into relaxing, melting any resistance away with amazingly addictive and sublime kisses that left her whimpering for more. Contracting her hot silky muscles around his hard satin length, she felt any trace of lingering anxiety vanish, quickly turning to feelings of pleasure and relief instead. Caroline prayed that Jack now knew with indisputable certainty that he was still her first and only lover.

As he loved her with an intensity that snatched her breath from her lungs—reuniting their bodies even more passionately, it seemed, than he had done all those years ago, when they were both so young— Caroline had to keep reminding herself that she wasn't going to wake up from a dream any time soon—that this blood-stirring erotic encounter was really part of her present and *not* her past.

Sometimes her powerful longing to see Jack again had been so all-consuming that she'd almost believed she could *will* him to come back to her. Now, Caroline wouldn't swear that she'd been able to accomplish any such feat, but even so…she would not discount the possibility of magic. Taking unimaginable delight in simply touching him—in reacquainting her love-starved hands with his powerfully strong body once more—she told herself that even if it all went horribly wrong again she *couldn't* regret this uninhibited loving. In seventeen years she hadn't met *one* other man who had come anywhere *near* making her feel like Jack did.

Knowing that her adoration must be beaming from her gaze like a beacon, Caroline wondered how she was supposed to contain it under these most intimate of circumstances. Whether Jack knew or cared about her feelings or not, she was not adept enough to completely hide them from him. Anchoring her hands around his tautly flexed biceps as he thrust deeply inside her, Caroline watched the passion and purpose intensify on her lover's indisputably charismatic face—every masterfully etched muscle straining to delay the gratification of his desire until her own peak had sent her spinning off into the heavens once more.

Jack was suggesting with gravel-voiced ease that she wrap her long legs around his back—to 'better enjoy the ride, beautiful'—and Caroline didn't hesitate to comply, gasping out loud as desire rose to a whole new level…loving the way the strength in him was brought home to her as she gripped him hungrily with her thighs. Driving himself even deeper, Jack smiled wickedly down at her, giving Caroline no quarter whatsoever. When want, need, and bone-deep desperation to reach the stars found its ultimate reward she cried out again, with every atom of love and longing in her soul, tears slipping helplessly down her face as Jack looked down at her…revealing for just the tiniest moment something like regret or sorrow in his eyes.

Then he bent his head and commandeered Caroline's lips harshly with his own as he ardently surrendered to the need that had been multiplying inside him with ever-increasing command—emptying himself inside her with an echoing shout that wouldn't be contained.

Clearly overcome by the raw, unfettered emotion of

the moment, he laid his head on Caroline's breast and groaned again—his dark silky hair tickling her chin and his strong heartbeat matching hers beat for rhythmic beat. Fear as well as joy swirled inside her chest, and although part of her felt buoyed-up by happiness—at the same time Caroline experienced pain that was like a thousand razor-cuts bleeding into her very soul.

'You always were intoxicating,' Jack whispered husky-voiced against her breast, his warm breath skimming her sensitised skin, 'but you've become even more so.'

'Have I?'

The brief tormented smile that he hadn't witnessed melted away. Staring up in silence at the shadows from the fire, moving like dancing silhouettes on the ceiling, Caroline felt the tears she had cried dry on her cheeks. She would be very 'adult' about what happened, she decided resignedly. She wouldn't make demands or sound 'needy', as he might already be anticipating she would. Fear settled more profoundly in her bones, like a brooding storm deep in her vitals. *He wouldn't stay. She knew that.* So how *did* a person go about forgetting the love of their life, not once but *twice* in a lifetime, without losing their mind?

She'd fallen asleep in his embrace, right there on the rug in front of the fire, giving Jack ample opportunity to study her peaceful sleeping features and to conclude once again that she was *still* the most beautiful girl he'd ever seen. He tried to recall how enraged he had been when she had confessed to having the termination, but right then—sated with the passion they had expended with such uninhibited fervour—Jack found that his anger had somehow diminished.

He didn't doubt that his long-held rage towards Caroline for making the decision that had shaped the course of his life for ever would no doubt resurrect itself once he was away from her sphere of intoxicating influence. In the cold light of day he would remember in detail how she had betrayed him, how she had committed the most unforgivable of actions. But right now…for the first time in a long time…a *lifetime* perhaps?…Jack peacefully surrendered his embittered defences.

For a while he lay there alone with his thoughts, listening to the flurry of wind and rain slam against the windowpanes and inside the soporific 'womb-like' hiss and crackle of the fire burning comfortingly beside them. Then, getting to his feet and being careful not to disturb the woman he'd lain beside, he recovered her fleecy dressing-gown and draped it gently across her sleeping form, so that she wouldn't get cold when the fire went out.

Lord knew it was so *tempting* for Jack to stay right where he was and spend the night there in Caroline's house…the house he had been *barred* from as a youth. If he'd still been immersed in his usual fury towards her and her dead father he would have taken a perverse kind of pleasure in staying there, only to disdainfully leave in the morning. But just what was Jack supposed to say to Caroline when she woke? His store of words was wor-

ryingly *empty*. He was, instead, swamped with all kinds
of feelings that were taking him by storm. Feelings that
he hadn't expected. In the light of this confusion, any
words he *did* utter would be like the sound of scraping
fingernails down a blackboard. They would be harsh
and unpalatable, because his familiar, automatically
employed barriers were already slamming into place
and Jack knew he would defend his position to the hilt.

Concluding that all he could do was leave Caroline
to sleep on undisturbed, he quickly gathered his strewn
clothes together, dressed with regretful ease as he
watched the soft rise and fall of her breath and glimpsed
the smooth alabaster perfection of her breasts beneath
her robe, then left the house with the stealth of a thief
in the night, to return to his hotel…

Caroline had *known* she was alone, that Jack had left,
as soon as she'd opened her eyes. The heat from the fire
had noticeably died to barely warm embers that threw
off scant comfort, and even though she found herself
covered by her dressing-gown she shivered hard as she
quickly pushed her arms into its fleecy sleeves and got
shakily to her feet. Inside, a silent keening rose up from
the emptiness of her heart. Desolation and confusion hit
hard. She felt like the only child in a wintry playground
being pelted by a bombardment of icy snowballs from
her uncaring classmates.

*Jack had left her even sooner than she'd thought he
would.* He hadn't even had the decency to wait until the

morning to demonstrate his contempt. Caroline could hardly believe that even *he* could be so heartless. She hadn't been foolish enough to imagine that they might be going to take up where they had left off seventeen years ago, but even so... Jack had seduced her into loving him again one more time, allowed her to let down her defences long enough to fall asleep in his arms, and then—cool as you like—left her there to wake up alone.

Was this particularly cruel behaviour something he had devised on the day that he'd bumped into her? Was it his abominable way of getting back at Caroline for the deep grudge he obviously still bore her? She must have been out of her mind to let him into her house like that in the middle of the night. Now she only had herself to blame for the fall-out. It had been obvious from the start that Jack's reappearance would bring her nothing but more trouble and heartache, but Caroline hadn't been able to resist the compulsion to get burnt by him again. She should have just told him to get the hell out of her life and stay out! Not invite him to make things worse! Why had she done that? *Why?*

'Because I'm a sad, stupid idiot—that's why!' she shouted out loud, kicking the rug. 'He only wanted to get back at me...to hurt me all over again because of what I did...what I was practically *forced* to do! Jack Fitzgerald doesn't possess a forgiving bone in his entire body!'

Giving vent to her frustration and fury, and at the same time making an Olympian effort to suppress the anguished sob that arose inside her throat, Caroline briefly stooped to pick up her crumpled nightdress, then resignedly left the room to go upstairs to bed…

Out of the chaos of scaffolding, cement and mud, the improvements that Jack had devised with his architect for the undeniably neglected Victorian house were slowly but surely taking place. Having just inspected the downstairs area, where a major extension was being built onto the back of the building to utilise some of the space of the three-hundred-foot garden, Jack allowed himself a momentary burst of pleasure and anticipation.

For the last week, being actively involved on site—overseeing building work and having long, productive discussions with the architect and the contractor he'd hired to undertake the renovations—Jack had welcomed long, busy days that started at around seven in the morning and continued long into the evening, when spotlights were rigged up all over the site to replace the fading winter daylight. It had helped him to push the thought of Caroline and what he was going to do about the confusion of feelings he felt towards her out of his mind at least temporarily.

One thing was crystal-clear. She must think him a contemptuous bastard for leaving before she woke the other night, and not even saying goodbye. But, as he'd silently admitted to himself at the time, he wouldn't have known what to say to her after what had transpired between them…what should *never* have transpired between them if it hadn't been for the fact that Jack had allowed his *lust* for her to tow him round by the nose…

He'd needed time to assimilate everything that had happened. By now, she must *hate* his guts…

Stepping out of the luxurious hotel room shower and winding a generous white bathtowel around his spare, taut midsection, Jack paused to examine his sombre reflection as he passed the large bathroom mirror. To say he didn't like what he saw would be massive understatement.

When he looked into his own glacial blue eyes in the harshly delineated planes and angles of his sculpted, lean face, Jack despised the fear and control he saw reflected there. *Fear* that had been generated by driving his body almost into the ground, with his ruthless ambition to rise above his poor beginnings, and that had shockingly culminated in a heart attack. A 'warning shot', if you like, that had told him he had to either lessen that suicidal drive of his to a more reasonable degree or pay the consequences. And a rigid *control* that meant he hardly ever allowed himself to experience tender or loving feelings towards anybody. A control that had dictated he walk away from the one woman who *did* stir strong feelings inside him because he still believed she couldn't be trusted.

Giving vent to a ripe expletive as he reached for the can of shaving foam on the marble ledge beside the mirror, Jack glanced up and frowned as he heard a knock at the door. Crossing the thickly carpeted bed-room in his bare feet, and walking out into the luxuri-ous sitting room that made up his suite of rooms, Jack pulled open the door with hardly any curiosity at all. He'd ordered coffee and brandy to be brought up to his suite in about half an hour but obviously his order had arrived a little early. However, the way he was feeling, Jack could do with a strong drink *sooner* rather than later, to help dull the pain of unwanted thoughts that were right now driving him crazy. He wasn't supposed to drink, given what had happened to him, but *hell…* he'd never been attracted to alcohol the way some of his equally driven business associates were. A little brandy wouldn't hurt.

'Caroline!'

He was honestly stunned to see her there.

'Hello, Jack…this is for the other night.'

Before he could glean what she meant, Caroline had raised her hand and delivered a stinging, resounding slap hard across his face…

CHAPTER TEN

SHE HADN'T gone to Jack's hotel with the express intention of slapping his face. But the minute that Caroline had been confronted by his disturbing presence, and the expression that was far too relaxed for her liking crossing his handsome features, she'd realised how powerfully close her emotions were to the surface.

She'd soared to the highest of heights in the past week, just thinking about their lovemaking, and sunk to the lowest of lows as well, when she'd continued not to hear from him. Finally, unable to wait a minute longer to set the record straight once and for all, and tell Jack exactly what she thought of him, Caroline had decided she wasn't going to waste another *second*…let alone another *day* on thoughts of the callous, unforgiving man who was causing her such grief. The man who had walked out on her when she was at her most scared and vulnerable seventeen years ago and had then exhibited the same despicable behaviour again just days ago! And what was more…Caroline was going to spare him nothing when she told him so to his face!

Rubbing his stinging jaw with a wry smirk, Jack stepped back from the door.

'I guess you could say that I deserved that. Well… why don't you come on in, Caroline? My guess is that you have a lot more that you want to say to me than that… Am I right?'

'No.' The blood rushed to her head with such emotive force that Caroline's balance was momentarily at risk. 'You're wrong. I've suddenly decided that I'm not going to waste another word or even another *breath* on you, Jack! Because you know what? You're not *worth* it!'

About to turn around and leave, she was shocked by the powerful grip that Jack used on her wrist, to practically haul her into the room. 'What do you think you're—?'

'You're not going anywhere until we've talked.'

The door slammed shut. His hard jaw like immovable granite, he glared at her, openly daring her to defy him.

Shaking off his hold on her wrist, Caroline pushed her hair behind her ears and scowled. 'Bit late in the day for talking, isn't it, Jack?' she remarked scathingly. 'As I recall…it's not exactly your forte, is it? Either talking about feelings *or* doing the decent thing!'

Wishing that she had found him a little more *clothed* than he was currently so that they would be more on an equal footing, as it were, Caroline felt her legs treacherously shaking as he trained his cynical glance upon her hot, indignant face.

'And who are *you* to talk about doing the "decent thing", Caroline?'

As soon as the words were out of his mouth, Jack wished that his seemingly innate ability to wound her was not quite so lethally accurate. The colour seemed to seep away from her face before his very eyes, and she actually swayed a little. Her hand moved shakily down over her hip, and Jack's gaze was helplessly ensnared by the way the black velvet material of her trouser suit so sexily encased her gorgeous figure. The brightness of her hair glowed like living sunshine, and was an arresting contrast to the dramatic severity of the black. Even in the middle of the most excruciating tension between them he couldn't help but be aroused by her beauty.

'You are such a bastard.'

Her words…so softly yet devastatingly spoken… were like hammer-blows to Jack's soul. To counteract his escalating misery, he deliberately let loose a slow but savage smile.

'What? You think you're the first person to label me with that tag? So sorry to have to disappoint you.'

'And you're proud of that?' Caroline swallowed across the stinging pain inside her throat as though it were a landscape filled with cacti. 'I feel sorry for you… always having to appear so hard, so tough. You may have achieved everything you've ever wanted, but I'd stake my house on it that it hasn't made you happy. Bit-terness can eat you up, you know. You have a cold, unforgiving heart, Jack, and the way I see it now…I've probably had a lucky escape, haven't I?'

Hands on his hips, Jack briefly glanced down at the carpet, as if trying to restrain the temper she seemed hell-bent on rousing. When he regarded Caroline again, the steely blue eyes that couldn't help but command attention reminded her of a hard frost that hadn't thawed all winter, and her blood actually ran cold.

'Why didn't you come and tell me you'd decided on having a termination, Caroline? Why didn't you talk it over with me instead of just going ahead and doing it? I was the baby's father…didn't you think I should have any say in the matter at all?'

For a long, distraught moment everything inside Caroline seemed to shudder violently. Staring at him with undeniable agony in her dark gaze, she was forced to remember the distressing and frightening circumstances that had led her to check in to that soulless, aloof private hospital in London, where they had removed the growing foetus inside her as coldly and dispassionately as if she'd been having a mole or adhesion taken away.

'Of *course* I believed you had the right to have a say! And, contrary to what you might think, I *wanted* to keep the baby…that's why I told my father that I was pregnant. If there had been a way to keep it don't you think I would have? But he—he just went crazy when I told him.'

She smiled nervously, to try and calm her quivering

lips, but the smile slid off her face as easily as a raindrop sliding down a windowpane. Checking behind her, Caroline saw a Queen-Anne-style armchair covered in a pattern of cream and pink rosebuds and gratefully sank down into it. Her legs were shaking so hard that she felt as if she'd been ploughed into by a rhinoceros. Knowing that she had Jack's full undivided attention, as she'd never had it before, she took a painful swallow and tried desperately to pluck out a coherent strand of thought from the black cloud of hurtful memory that was pressing in on her with such unforgiving force.

'People thought he was marvelous, you know…how kind, how *understanding*. Well…he *was* like that with his patients and his friends…but *not* me. My mother died giving birth to me…did I ever tell you that?' Her dark eyes glistening, Caroline looked straight at Jack.

'No.' He folded his arms across his chest—the movement drawing her attention to the tight, mouth-watering curve of his biceps—and his dispassionate expression contained neither warmth or understanding.

Ignoring his blatant lack of encouragement or support, Caroline pressed determinedly on. 'I think he blamed me because he lost her. In fact I *know* he did. It was no secret. She was so beautiful, and they were so in love. Then *I* came along and put an end to their happiness together… Anyway, when I told Dad that I was pregnant he completely lost his reason. Actually…' She grimaced and linked her hands nervously together in her lap. 'That's a bit of an understatement, if you want to

know the truth. His anger just escalated into something—something quite *ugly*. He hit me hard, and
knocked me to the ground.'

'He *what*?'

'He *made* me have the abortion, Jack. He couldn't
stand the shame of it, he said.'

Jack's stomach plummeted violently, as though he'd
just been pushed off the top of a skyscraper. *This wasn't
happening…she wasn't saying what she was saying…it
couldn't be real…* He didn't doubt that her father had
gone crazy when he'd heard that his seventeen-year-old
daughter was pregnant…and by a boy whose very existence he *despised*…but if Jack had thought for one
second that the man—a *doctor*, for God's sake!—would
coerce his own flesh and blood into having an abortion,
then he wouldn't have been so quick to judge the woman
he loved and punish her even further by walking away
for good. Now Jack realised that they should have faced
her father together. It was *unthinkable* that he'd let her
confront him alone.

'Maybe he hoped that the shock of his attack might
make me lose the baby…or—or maybe he didn't think
at all. He was simply too furious with me. I'd shamed
him, he said. I'd let him down and made him look like a
fool. He said didn't I *know* that boys like you didn't stick
around after they'd had their fun? I was no better than
a—than a whore and a slut and I'd throw away every
chance of a decent marriage if I didn't get rid of the baby.
He told me I had no choice but to do what he said. He

left me alone then, and went to make a phone call. The next morning he drove me to London and it was done.'

When her haltingly voiced explanation was over, Caroline leaned back in the chair—the beautiful and elegant piece of furniture that lent such a contrasting civility to her painfully sordid revelation—and briefly shut her eyes. There were no words to describe either the psychological pain of having her own father assault her *or* the physical hurt that she'd endured—both from the attack and afterwards the abortion. Now, having told Jack the truth behind her actions all those years ago, Caroline was emotionally and physically drained of everything. She just prayed he wouldn't be expecting her to get up and go anywhere for the next ten minutes at least, because it was doubtful whether her legs would have the strength required to enable her to stand, let alone walk.

'Sweet heaven, Caroline! Why didn't you tell me all this before?'

His senses reeling in protest at what he had just heard, Jack made his feet stay rooted to the floor as he watched her wearily close her eyes again—as if she didn't know what else to do after such a revelation. Everything that was decent and good inside him clamoured for him to go to her…haul her into his arms, keep her safe and never let her go. But now that he realised for the first time in seventeen years that it was *he* who had betrayed Caroline—by not staying around to find out the truth before packing his bags and heading off to

a completely different continent never to look back—
Jack couldn't do it.

He'd condemned her. He'd relinquished all right to
comfort her when he'd walked out on her to ruthlessly
pursue his dream of wealth and status—to fight his own
demons of poverty and shame and command respect
from the world instead of disdain. Well, he'd achieved
his ambition in spades, and it still hadn't filled the
yawning chasm inside him that craved something much
less tangible yet *infinitely* more valuable. Something
that he'd allowed his single-minded ambition to over-
ride…*no doubt to his detriment.* Caroline's house was
safe. She could easily stake it on her bet that his wealth
hadn't made him happy and she'd be absolutely right.

Jack remembered the night she had come to him and
told him that she'd had the abortion. He hadn't seen her
for two days—her father had slammed the door in his
face when he'd gone to their house to ask after her
whereabouts, and Jack had been beside himself with
worry. His stomach muscles gripped with a vengeance
as he suddenly recalled the pain and sorrow in her beautiful dark eyes when he'd finally seen her…but more
than that…the vivid purple bruise on the side of her
delicate jaw. Caroline had told him that it was nothing,
that she'd accidentally walked into a door when she'd
been hurrying and not looking where she was going. For
that read…*running away from her father to avoid
further mistreatment*?

The thought was akin to a nuclear meltdown inside

Jack. Automatically, his hands clenched into fists at his side. *That cruel bastard.* If he was here now Jack would willingly do time in prison for what he would do to him in recompense…

Opening her eyes, Caroline pushed her fingers through her hair and softly sighed.

'You weren't ready to listen,' she told him in answer to his impassioned question. 'You were always so sure you were right about everything, and you were so hungry to get away from here and make your mark on the world. I told myself after you'd left that it was probably for the best. Me having a baby would only have made you feel obliged to stay, and I know you'd never wanted that. But you know what, Jack? Just for the record…my father didn't just look down on *you.* Until a few years before his death I was a great disappointment to him too. I wouldn't let him mould me like he wanted to. I wouldn't aspire to the things he thought I should aspire to. But we reached a kind of unspoken accord after a while, and he didn't try to interfere in my life any more. He left me the house and some money in his will—to try and make amends, I'm sure.'

'It's a wonder you can even bear to live in it!' Jack remarked with bitterness, a wealth of regret and a soul-deep sorrow crowding his chest so strongly that he barely knew how to ease it. All he could think was that he'd possibly made the worst decision of his life when he'd walked out so callously on Caroline. He believed her father to have been a cruel bastard, but perhaps the truth in Jack's case was that it *took* one to know one?

'I told myself that if my mother had lived *she* would have wanted me to have the house too. Anyway…every child loves their parents, don't they? All a child really wants is their love and approval, and they'll forgive even violence against them to get it. I forgave my father everything the day he died. He acted like he did because he was hurting…because he'd lost my mother. Only hurt people hit out at others.'

'Your compassion is a credit to you, Caroline…but I'll tell you for the life of me I can't understand it.'

'Well…'

Feeling as if he'd judged her again, and found her completely lacking in any universally accepted common sense, Caroline forced herself to think about leaving. She couldn't sit here in this chair for ever, and she couldn't make the wrong between her and Jack right again just because her heart ached to do just that. Now she really had to show her quality, and demonstrate just how strong she really was. Strong enough to make her life a success without him. Strong enough to put what they had once so joyfully shared down to experience and move on. Undoubtedly she was a talented, capable woman, and she would show the world that no matter what happened—no one else would ever knock her down, or *put* her down again.

'We all have our own ways of looking at things, don't we? Even though it might seem skewed to others. I won't keep you any longer. I'd best just get going.'

'No…wait!'

Panic made Jack's blue eyes glitter and his hard jaw tighten even more. She couldn't just walk in here, deliver such a gut-wrenching bombshell and then go. He wouldn't *let* her. He'd been a fool, an idiot, selfish and self-seeking even… But what Caroline had revealed to him had rocked his world harder than an earthquake.

'Why, Jack? What for?' She pushed to her feet, her pale cheeks reddening a little. 'Five days ago you knocked at my house in the middle of the night, asked me not to turn you out into the cold, made love to me…then left while I was asleep. I woke up to a dying fire and an empty space beside me. There was no hint *why*. When I examined all the possible reasons, I concluded that you were getting your own back on me, and no doubt you *were*. You amply illustrated that I wasn't even deserving of the most *basic* respect. I only came here to tell you that I *refuse* to be blamed for what happened any longer. And I refuse to spend the rest of my days carrying the burden of that blame and letting it spoil my life! I have plans, Jack…plans that might take me only God knows where…and now I just want to go home and get on with them. I'll see myself out.'

As she reached the door Jack stared at her stiff back and tried desperately to command the words that were rapidly backing up in his brain, practically tripping over each other. He knew what he *should* say…what he *longed* to be able to say… But he already sensed her moving away from him in more ways than one, and he wouldn't expose his needs to possible derision…even though he no doubt richly *deserved* it.

'What do you mean, you've got "plans"?' he demanded, his frustration peppering the words with anger. 'Do they include that doctor friend of yours? The one who's old enough to be your father?'

Slowly Caroline turned around, for once her expression unreadable. 'You mean Nicholas?' She sighed.

Even the man's name had the power to practically unhinge Jack. He'd seen the way he'd looked at Caroline that night when they'd been having dinner together at his hotel. The man's glance had been nothing less than *predatory*... 'platonic', indeed!

'I believe that is his name.'

'I honestly don't think it's any of your business...do you?'

Caroline opened the door and went out, shutting it behind her.

Cursing the fact that he wasn't dressed—hardly fit to chase after her when he was wearing nothing but a towel—Jack forced his fevered brain to work overtime and think what to do next...

The winter sun, shining powerfully through the back window of Caroline's store room, illuminated the vivid display of colour that she'd been painting onto a canvas. Taking a moment to consider her handiwork, she allowed herself a triumphant pleased smile. She'd been finding out a lot about butterflies in the past couple of days, and the more she discovered about their symbolism and meaning—as well as their biological make-up—the more intrigued Caroline had become by them.

It was the symbolism of *transformation* that had captured her interest the most. The caterpillar spun a cocoon in which to birth a new aspect of itself—then, when the time was right…after a time of what some might call spiritual waiting, it emerged into the light and a new beginning as a beautiful butterfly.

Caroline had undertaken the painting as a gift she might give to Sadie. The shy, unconfident schoolgirl was blossoming into a woman…she was on the brink of falling in love, perhaps, and the future seemed bright. For a moment Caroline remembered that feeling of infinite possibilities in the world and felt her breath catch. But a strange thing was happening. Because the more she stroked paint onto the canvas, the more the bright colours inspired her imagination and made her hopes for her *own* future soar…and the more Caroline saw that the painting was also a gift to herself.

She'd already decided that in the spring she would put both the house and the shop up for sale. 'Infinite possibilities' awaited her too, and she would use some of the money she made from the sales of her property to maybe explore some of them. She might even buy herself a round-the-world ticket…who knew?

But what about Jack? The smile on her face faded slowly away as her thoughts turned to the one topic that put a hitch in her excited plans. When she'd left his hotel room yesterday she'd dragged her feet as she'd walked away, hoping…*praying*…that he might say something that would make her stop walking away from him… something that might herald even the *tiniest* ray of hope for them both. *It hadn't happened*, and finally… *finally*…Caroline had had to tell herself that their relationship was irretrievably over. All she could hope was that Jack could go back to wherever he lived now and perhaps think of her with a little more forgiveness in his heart than he had previously extended to his memory of her. She didn't think she could bear it if all his thoughts of her were negative ones.

With her paintbrush hovering over a dazzlingly brilliant blue section of a butterfly, Caroline was taken aback by the jolt of fear that suddenly assaulted her. *That scar on Jack's chest was over his heart…* Why hadn't she realised that before? With a trembling hand she laid the sable-haired brush she was using down on the easel's shelf and walked like someone in a trance out of the store room and back into the shop to find the telephone…

CHAPTER ELEVEN

'SOMEONE to see you, Mr Fitzgerald.'

Frank Ryan, the site foreman, ambled over to Jack where he stood by the side of the house, examining some plans with his architect.

'Who is it?' Barely glancing up from the drawings that were occupying him, Jack frowned at having his train of thought interrupted.

'Didn't ask, guv'nor.' Frank shrugged, as if to indicate it was none of his business. 'He's waiting for you over there.'

He pointed to where the cement mixer chugged, on the paving stones leading up to the house, and Jack did a surprised double-take when he recognised Nicholas Brandon…Caroline's doctor friend. Wearing an expensive-looking double-breasted pin-striped suit, he appeared both uncomfortable and on edge as he paced up and down, looking about as out of place in what was in effect a building site as a diamond brooch pinned to the shirt of a vagrant.

'Give me a couple of minutes will you, Justin?'

Handing over the plans to his architect—Jack made his way past the general melee of rubble and sand to greet his unexpected visitor.

'What can I do for you?'

It was a terse demand rather than a civil greeting. He snapped out the words as though barely able to spare the time to talk, even while his blue eyes weighed and assessed and weighed again. *What did Caroline see in him?* Jack thought resentfully. The man had a weak chin and shifty eyes. The thought of him even fantasising about Caroline—let alone *touching* her—was apt to make Jack feel ready to knock his head from his shoulders.

'I've come to talk to you about Caroline,' Nicholas began, clearly taken aback by Jack's less than polite acknowledgement.

Wrong answer, Jack concluded in silence, his resentment escalating.

'What about Caroline?'

'You should stay away from her. She was perfectly happy until you showed up again.' Fingering the knot of his tie, Nicholas jerked his chin a little, as if to add emphasis to his advice. 'You've caused her enough trouble as it is. Why did you come back here, Fitzgerald? Why didn't you just stay wherever it is the devil took you? You made a bloody nuisance of yourself seventeen years ago when you were here, and caused her and her family untold grief!'

'I have a suggestion for you, Dr Brandon. Why don't you mind your own damn business and stay out of mine?'

Feeling his spine tense, as though a steel rod had been jammed down his back to replace it, Jack knew his ire was well and truly provoked. He took exceeding umbrage at the fact that this man standing before him should even *dare* to raise the subject of Jack's relationship with Caroline and what had happened in the past. His mercurial eyes directed a deliberately menacing glint.

'Caroline *is* my business,' Nicholas insisted. 'She's a good friend, and so was her father.'

'If her father was a good friend of yours then I *pity* you.'

'What do you mean by that? Charles Tremayne was a good, decent man, and I remember what you put him through,' Nicholas responded, with self-righteous indignation.

'Is that right?'

Edging closer, Jack was satisfied that his superior height, breadth of shoulder and comparative youth were enough to intimidate the other man, even if his words didn't help the message filter through. It gave him untold satisfaction to see Nicholas Brandon flinch.

'Well…did your "good, decent" friend happen to tell you about the "untold grief" and hurt he caused his own daughter? No…I didn't think so.'

'What are you talking about?' the other man replied defensively, turning a little red in the face. 'Charles loved Caroline! He would never have deliberately caused her pain. If you're referring to her having the pregnancy terminated…it was for the best. When he told me what he'd decided I totally supported his decision. A pregnancy would have ruined her life at that point, and Charles knew you weren't the sort of chap to stand by his daughter. You already had a bit of a reputation and it wasn't an admirable one, Fitzgerald!'

So this friend of Caroline's…this pompous little weasel…had colluded with her father to make her have the abortion? A red mist was starting to come down over Jack's furious eyes.

'What the hell did you know about me that you thought you had the right to judge me…hmm? You, with your comfortable upper-crust existence, who probably never got your hands dirty or went hungry in your whole life! But that aside…you have the bloody bare-faced audacity to stand in front of me and tell me that you colluded with Caroline's father to make her have that abortion? You *both* had the temerity to make that decision over our heads?'

'Don't try and tell me that you welcomed the idea of becoming a father!' Nicholas's tone was scornful. 'You were probably *grateful* that we'd got you off the hook, so that you could disappear into the wide blue yonder, untroubled by your conscience, leaving Caroline to shoulder all the blame!'

Jack went cold as the grave. His eyes narrowing to burning blue chips of glittering glass, he stared the other man down as though his glance alone could render him dead.

'Do you know how lucky you are to be still standing there in one piece? If it wasn't for the fact that I really don't think you're even worth the trouble, I'd leave you in need of medical services for the rest of your natural life, Brandon. But then I guess if I descended to that I'd be as bad as Caroline's father, wouldn't I? At least my one redeeming quality is that I don't get my kicks out of beating up defenceless women, like he did!'

'Beating up defenceless wom—? What on earth are you talking about?' Nicholas was looking about as nervous as a man could get, and there was genuine alarm in his gaze. 'Charles didn't hit women!'

'The night Caroline went to him to tell him that she was pregnant, he hit her so hard he knocked her to the floor!'

'Who told you such a despicable lie?'

'Caroline told me herself. Do you really think that she would make something like that up? If you know her at all, then you know she doesn't find it easy to lie…except maybe to protect those she loves. She had a bruise the size of a small country on her pretty face when she came to tell me she'd had the abortion. She told me she'd accidentally walked into a door. You know what the truth is, Brandon? We *all* let her down… her father, you, me… We make a fine bunch, don't we?'

The backs of his eyes burning with unshed tears, Jack threw the man a last pitying glance before striding back towards the house.

* * *

She'd agreed to have dinner with Nicholas at a new Mexican restaurant that had recently opened in the high street. She hadn't wanted to make a big deal of her request to see him, but when she'd rung and told him she needed to talk to him he'd insisted that he take her out to dinner, and he had been the one to suggest the venue. Quite honestly Caroline had been totally surprised by his choice. Nicholas was conservative with a capital 'C', and generally didn't express interest in so-called 'foreign' cuisine.

When Caroline had asked him the reason for his preference, he'd said lightly, 'Perhaps I've become a little too set in my ways...maybe I should try new things more often? They do say it helps keep you young.'

It hadn't been hard to detect that he wanted to please her. Glad that he was being warm and friendly, and not bearing any grudge towards her for turning down his request to get engaged, Caroline was relieved that their friendship could continue without any undercurrent of difficulty or resentment. Feeling determined to present a much more positive and upbeat image than of late, to emphasise her newfound determination to recreate her life, she wore a long, tiered ethnic-style skirt in warm browns and reds, with a black velvet top and boots, and finished off the ensemble with a pair of jet earrings shaped like teardrops.

'You look very lovely tonight, if you don't mind my saying so.'

A brief flare of peculiar intensity in his glance,

Nicholas took a long sip of his Margarita—another choice that had surprised Caroline. Generally he always selected wine when they went out to eat, and didn't really touch spirits as a rule—except for an occasional snifter of the good malt he kept in his surgery drawer. She'd certainly never seen him imbibe a cocktail before. Somehow a drink like that seemed far too frivolous for someone like him.

Flushing a little at the unexpected compliment, Caroline surveyed her companion across the dinner table with slight unease, and for the first time realised that he appeared uncharacteristically nervous.

'Thank you.'

A lively salsa tune filled the small, rather intimate restaurant from hidden speakers, and Caroline mused that it was another thing that somehow seemed totally at odds around someone like her companion—a man who was a bit of a self-confessed snob about music, who believed there was no music worth listening to other than classical.

Nicholas considered the beautiful vivacious girl seated opposite him and couldn't help but feel his blood quicken. Over the years, he'd watched her blossom from a pretty, engaging teenager into a stunning and graceful woman. There had been many times when he and Meg had yearned to have a daughter just like Caroline, but sadly they had not been blessed with children of their own. Then, after Meg had died, Nicholas had slowly started to see Caroline in a completely different light.

His feelings of friendship had deepened into something much more meaningful…something that had quite taken him by surprise. He'd always felt protective of her, and when she'd had that sordid little affair with Fitzgerald Nicholas had been as concerned and furious as Charles, and had breathed a deep sigh of relief when he'd heard that the young tearaway had left home for good and that Caroline would likely never see him again.

It had honestly shaken him to discover that Jack Fitzgerald was back and that he was apparently renovating the old run-down house he'd used to live in with his mother. Having seen the project for himself earlier today, Nicholas saw that the man was clearly pouring plenty of money into the rebuild. He'd easily recognised the name of the contractors he was employing from the livery emblazoned on their vans, and they were about the best in the country. Wherever Fitzgerald had been for the past seventeen years, he'd clearly achieved some wealth and status, and the realisation burned like bile in the pit of Nicholas's stomach.

He'd been disappointed…yes…that Caroline had turned down his suggestion of an engagement, but his hopes had not been seriously dashed. She clearly just needed time to get used to the idea, and he wasn't going to let a jumped-up, swaggering upstart like Jack Fitzgerald come between them…no matter how threatening the man appeared. It had been a real boost to his ego to have her call him today and ask to see him, and he wouldn't be human if he didn't have hopes that she might have reconsidered his offer.

'Anyway…as delighted as I am to have your company, my dear, you sounded as if you were quite concerned about something on the phone earlier. What was it you wanted to talk to me about?'

'I—I just need a little medical advice, if you don't mind?'

Caroline immediately saw the flare of hope that she'd earlier recognised in Nicholas's hazel eyes suddenly dim. It was obvious to her that he had thought she wanted to reconsider the offer he'd made, and her stomach helplessly flipped. There was something about the man tonight that put her on edge. But she had to find a way of bypassing her uneasiness, because she was desperate for some information. Ever since she'd seen that scar on Jack's chest she had been worried about the reason behind it. He clearly did not want to divulge that reason himself, and so she was being forced to try and make some sort of educated guess. Hence her need to speak with Nicholas.

'I'm only glad to give you any advice I can, my dear…you know that.'

'Well, then…I wondered if you could tell me something about heart attacks?'

'Heart attacks, Caroline?' Frowning, Nicholas considered her anxious face intently. 'Do you know someone who has suffered one?'

She sighed and tucked some of her tantalising golden

curls behind her ear. 'Please, Nicholas…can you just give me some information?'

'Well…they happen when the heart muscle fails because the blood flow to the heart becomes blocked. There are a number of ways we can treat them…medication to increase blood flow, for instance, or surgery to open the arteries to the heart. If the patient is willing and determined to improve their lifestyle—to stop smoking, cut down on stress and eat a more healthy diet with less saturated fats—then there's no reason why they can't continue to live a normal life. Does that answer your question?'

She told herself she should be feeling relieved. People weren't automatically going to die young if they'd suffered a heart attack early on in life. There were lifestyle changes that could be made—Nicholas had just outlined them. *But how could Caroline feel relieved when clearly Jack's lifestyle up until now must have been impossibly stressful to have caused him to need heart surgery at the too young age of thirty-seven in the first place?* She already knew that he was angry and bitter about what had happened between them. If he'd been carrying around that rage inside him all these years and on top of that the stress of a demanding job, then no wonder he had suffered a heart problem!

Caroline had read in a self-help book she'd bought that one of the possible metaphysical causes of a heart attack was when a heart felt deprived of joy due to a person's pursuit of making money over everything else…that, plus long-standing emotional problems that eventually helped harden the heart. When you added all that up, Jack was a prime candidate for what had happened to him.

What could she do to help? Caroline bit down on her lip, deep in thought. Had he thought about what she'd said to him about forgiveness? Had he really taken on board the fact that she forgave him for blaming her all these years? Had he heard the truth in her voice when she'd related the distressing circumstances behind her seemingly hasty and callous decision to have the abortion, and was he even *halfway* to letting all that bitterness towards her go?

'You seem miles away, my darling.'

Reaching for her hand, Nicholas seemed a little peeved at her lack of attention towards him. Retrieving her hand and subconsciously rubbing it, Caroline smiled a little distractedly. 'I'm sorry, Nicholas…yes, that does answer my question, thank you. You've been very helpful.'

Now Nicholas looked pained. 'That sounds terribly formal, my dear, if you don't mind my saying? I'm delighted to be able to give you any help I can…I'm your *friend*, remember?'

But one day soon I hope to be a lot more than that… He summoned up a smile that he felt would be perfectly reassuring to her, and was slightly taken aback when he saw Caroline frown instead.

'Yes, Nicholas…you *are* my friend…a very dear and important friend. And I would like us to stay that way, if you don't mind?' Keeping her dark gaze steady, she sighed softly. 'I couldn't ever marry you and risk spoiling that special bond we have between us. And besides…I have to tell you that I'm in love with someone else.'

A muscle twitched beneath Nicholas's eye. Caroline could tell he was having some difficulty in keeping his temper in check. Her stomach sank like a stone.

'You mean Fitzgerald, don't you? I can't believe that you'd be so foolish as to pin all your hopes on a happy union with that despicable man! He's already hurt you beyond repair, Caroline…please don't make the same mistake twice!'

Swallowing down her embarrassment and disappointment that her friend should display such vehement emotion towards the idea of her having a relationship with Jack, Caroline resolved to draw a line under the discussion for good.

'I'm sorry you feel so strongly about it, Nicholas, but I know what I'm doing…I know what I want. And it doesn't matter if it should turn out that Jack doesn't want the same thing. I *still* love him.' She flushed pink. 'I'll probably *always* love him, if you want to know the truth. The question is now…do you still want us to be friends, or will my confession make things too awkward on your part for our friendship to continue?'

Examining his menu, her companion looked at it in secret horror. It was not his cup of tea at all! In fact he wished he'd never suggested coming here in the first place. He wished it even more vehemently since things had definitely *not* gone the way he'd privately hoped that they would!

'I would be a liar if I told you I wasn't upset by your admission of love for this man, Caroline… But frankly I'd be completely shooting myself in the foot if I told you I wanted our friendship to come to an end because of it. If I am truly the friend I have always felt myself to be towards you, then all I can really want is your happiness, my dear. So we will leave things at that, shall we? Now I suppose we'd better order some food. What shall we have? I think I might just have to call over the waitress to help us make a choice…'

Jack was pacing…his expensive Italian hand-made shoes all but wearing a chasm in the plush hotel carpet. He wanted to see Caroline, and the need was like a forest fire raging. But when she'd left him yesterday there had been a resolve and determination in her bewitching dark eyes and in her voice that Jack had never witnessed before. *She was clearly hell-bent on making a new life that didn't include him in any way.* When she'd told him she had plans, and then refused to elaborate on what they were, he'd been truly worried that she was going to leave town without telling him. But then, when he'd calmed himself down, he'd thought, *What can she do? She's got a house and a business to take care of…she can't just take off and not tell anyone…can she?*

Continuing to pace, Jack thought about his confrontation earlier in the day with Nicholas Brandon and wanted to throw something. There were plenty of pretty *objets d'art* in his luxurious hotel suite that would double up as missiles, but again Jack remembered his blood pressure. It wouldn't do him any good getting riled up about that pathetic little weasel. He valued his health far too much these days, he realized, to jeopardise it over such an insignificant excuse for a human being as Brandon. Just as long as he kept away from Caroline Jack would be happy.

He let loose a ripe curse at the idea that he might not, then scraped his fingers irritably through dark hair that had already borne the brunt of his impatience. 'Get a grip, Fitzgerald…you know what you have to do.'

For a moment his gut burned at the memory of what Caroline had told him about her father and how he'd treated her that fateful night she'd told him about her pregnancy. *If he could have turned back the clock Jack would have been there for her, protecting her, persuading her to come away with him and start a new life.* Instead Jack had chosen to blame her, instead of supporting her, and then he'd left. *She'd been just seventeen years old, for heaven's sake! A young, innocent girl and everyone around her had let her down…* But Jack had let her down the most.

Impatient to do what he should have done yesterday, when Caroline had walked out of his hotel room—an action he'd hesitated over far too long because of his fears of a destroying and negative outcome—Jack stopped wearing a hole in the carpet, grabbed his leather jacket and headed out of the door into the corridor, and towards the lift.

Driving his car down the high street on his way to Caroline's place, he almost screeched to a halt when he saw her come out of the Mexican restaurant with its newly painted signage swinging from a bracket overhead. She was being followed out by none other than the famous doctor himself, his hand possessively at her back as they started to walk away beneath the illumination of the streetlights.

An indescribable wave of jealousy and rage snatched the breath from Jack's lungs—his immediate instinct was to park the car and chase after them, and give Nicholas Brandon the comeuppance he richly deserved. *What was she doing out with him?* he thought savagely. Caroline was *his*…didn't she know that?

Quashing the urge to follow them as swiftly as the urge had arisen, Jack decided to bide his time instead and follow her home. He didn't allow himself to consider for one moment that she might be going home with the doctor. If that was her intention, then he would simply have to act to prevent it.

Thankfully his instincts turned out to be right. Nicholas dropped Caroline outside her front door, briefly kissed her goodbye on the side of her cheek…*much to Jack's pain*…then got into his car and drove away again.

As she put her key into the lock, Jack left the driver's seat of his own car, slammed the door shut behind him and hurried up the drive.

'Caroline,' he breathed behind her.

'Jack!' Swinging round, her key left in the lock, she knew her dark eyes registered her surprise and confusion. 'What are you doing here?'

'I had to see you.'

'Why?'

'I'm not talking out here. Open the door and let's go inside.'

'But you—'

'Open the damn door, Caroline!'

Turning the key in the lock himself, Jack pushed open the door and dragged Caroline in behind him. Kicking it shut with the heel of his shoe, he let his heated gaze scan her indignant countenance, feeling no small amount of desire scorching through his blood. *God, she was so beautiful!* How could he have walked out on her as he had? Jack hardly *knew* the man who had done that.

'You had to see me about what?'

As she backed up against the wall, a puzzled angry frown appeared between Caroline's smooth dark blonde brows.

'For someone who despises me you seem to be extraordinarily attached to following me around!'

'Never mind that. What were you doing out with that creep Nicholas Brandon?'

They weren't the words that Jack had wanted to say first, but somehow they'd got in the way of his real intent and acted like an incendiary going off in his face.

He saw the splinters from the explosion make her shiver, and clearly registered the hurt and disappointment in her shocked glance.

'You are unbelievable—do you know that? What business is it of yours who I go out to dinner with? My life is my own, and I don't have to answer to you, Jack Fitzgerald!'

'Do you like him?' he demanded. 'Are you in love with him?' He could hardly bear to hear her answer.

Caroline stared at him as if hardly computing the question.

Driven way past any ability to be patient—*and that particular commodity had always been in short supply in his case*—Jack grabbed her by the shoulders and impelled her roughly against his chest. 'Answer me, goddammit!'

Her soft dark eyes focused with extraordinary concentration on his face, and Jack saw her bewitchingly pretty top lip quiver a little before she finally spoke. 'No, Jack… I don't love him. There's only one man I've always loved, and I think you know who that is.'

Her words blew like a warm, gentle wind through his embittered soul and made his heart expand with a joyful lightness the like of which he'd never experienced before. Jack let go of the breath that had tightened so painfully inside his chest and sighed deeply. Tenderly brushing back the ravishing golden hair from her impossibly soft brow, he gazed deeply into the enchanting dark eyes that had haunted his dreams all these years, everything inside him hurting at the sight of the tears that had helplessly misted over them.

'How the hell did I ever live without you?' he grated, just before fastening his hungry, needy mouth to hers.

CHAPTER TWELVE

THERE was such unbounded joy rippling through
Caroline's veins at Jack's possessive embrace that she
suddenly believed it was possible to fly without wings.

*Did he mean the words he had just uttered so passion-
ately?* His ravenous kiss told her that he most certainly
did. The tears that had glazed her eyes trickled softly
down her face and into her mouth as Jack's lips melded
with hers, his hot silky tongue and dark masculinity
tasting like home and heaven at the same time. With his
hands expressively showing her how enamoured he was
with her curves, it became very clear to Caroline that
there was no going back from this point on.

Grinding his hips demandingly into hers, Jack
trapped her body against the wall and she willingly surrendered to the seductive opiate of his invading heat.
The hotly intense sparks that had been simmering
undimmed beneath the hurt and hostility that they had
each succumbed to in their turn burst into irresistible
flame as their need for each other shattered all bounds

of strained politeness. Jack's broad hard chest imprisoned Caroline's breasts as his kiss enraptured her completely, and she worked her hands down between their
bodies and mindlessly, hungrily, unfastened the zip of
his jeans embedded in soft blue denim. There was no
hesitation in the act…no doubt…she simply *had* to…
they *had* to…

Pulling her skirt up around her hips as if of the same
mind, Jack roughly pushed Caroline's rose-coloured
panties down her shivering legs, then inserted himself
smoothly inside her, employing a long upwards stroke
of voracious male possession.

'You make me—oh, God—you make me *crazy,*
Jack…' She moaned into his mouth, stunned by the
ferocity of heat that radiated like a blaze inside her.

Her arms wrapped around his neck as his thrusts
became more concentrated, then deliberately stopped.
He held himself inside her for long, arousing and in-
flammatory seconds, so that their united pleasure in
each other seemed to magnify into an even more
achingly deep bliss. Her breath left her body in another
deeply affected low-voiced groan.

'Say my name again, Caroline,' Jack taunted
against her ravaged lips, his mouth sliding across her
face to her earlobe, then down her neck, finally
latching in turn onto her tightly budded nipples inside
the black velvet top that he so impatiently shoved
aside. 'Say my name so that I can hear it's me you
want and no one else.'

'Oh, Jack…it's only *ever* been you! There never has been anybody else for me…I swear.'

Jack briefly thought about all the *wrong* turns he'd made personally…the women he'd convinced himself he'd enjoyed—including his ex-wife Anna. None of them had ever produced the uncontained feeling of rapture and untrammelled excitement inside him that Caroline did. Even when he'd been busy blaming her for denying him their child Jack had known underneath it all that he'd never *stopped* loving her…that in fact it was *impossible* for him to do such a thing. He was now convinced that there were some relationships that *absolutely* had to be—no matter how far apart the couple concerned had been, or for how long.

Jack knew for sure that he would love Caroline for ever. How else could he explain the almost instantaneous and soaring heartfelt longing that he'd experienced from the very first moment he'd seen her? It had never just been about lust. Jack *believed* in love at first sight because it had happened to him. Even while he'd so hot-headedly and foolishly denied himself her presence in his life these past seventeen years a secret fever had burned inside him daily—for Caroline.

Now Jack waited until she melted in his arms, and he was the passionate, willing recipient of a heat that was like no other—her soft, rasping sighs turning him on almost to the point of pain, the velvet-textured skin brushing so arousingly up against his own a sensation he never wanted to be free of. Then and *only* then did he allow himself to drive home his own insatiable need for her.

Shaken by the depth of his release, Jack kissed Caroline tenderly on her eyelids, her nose, her mouth, holding her face in his hands and examining her flushed beautiful features with a particularly warm, satisfied smile of undisguised male pride.

'You are *everything* a man could want in a woman and more…you know that?'

'It took you long enough to realise it, Jack.' She raised one finely arched blonde eyebrow, and her soft laughter was infectious.

She was so happy. Her elation flowed through her veins like delightful burgundy wine, flooding all the shadowed places inside her with light and love, and waking up her senses to a world of joy again. Safe in the arms of the man she adored, now there was no doubt in her mind that for both of them their togetherness was for all the *right* reasons.

'I know…but I was a stupid, self-righteous fool who got his comeuppance by consigning myself to endure seventeen long years without you. I didn't only punish you, angel…I punished myself too.'

There was a deeply etched furrow between Jack's dark brows that made Caroline want to kiss every frown he'd ever had away, and bring him so much love and laughter that he'd never need to employ that gesture again.

What was she waiting for? She might as well start

now. Gently, she pressed her lips to the place where that remorseful furrow resided.

'I love you, Jack,' she told him, her heart lifting when an uninhibited smile of pleased satisfaction curved his highly kissable lips.

'I hardly deserve you to… But, however long I live,' Jack began huskily, 'it won't be nearly long enough to show you how much I love *you*, Caroline…and that's a fact.'

'Then we have a great deal of loving ahead of us, wouldn't you say? Let's go up to bed, shall we? I'm anxious not to waste any *more* time.'

Her dark eyes only demonstrating the barest *hint* of shyness, Caroline began to rearrange her clothing and, taking his lead from her, Jack did likewise. Then she took him by the hand and went upstairs with him to her bedroom, just as she intended to do every night for the rest of their lives.

Some time later, in the warm, sated afterglow of their lovemaking, Caroline traced the slender scar on Jack's bare chest tentatively with the tips of her fingers.

Aware of the tension that he suddenly transmitted, Caroline couldn't deny her own underlying unease as she prepared herself to confront him about it. But they had shared the most intimate of intimacies, and if they couldn't share this too then what hope for deepening the trust between them? Glancing up into the handsome face that was both sensitive and troubled now that he had let his guard down, Caroline knew that it was definitely time to get bone-crushingly honest about things.

'Tell me about this, Jack,' she urged, her voice deliberately lowered. 'I need to know.'

She didn't want to exert any pressure, but learning the truth was essential. He sighed, but he didn't push her away or get defensive, as she'd secretly feared he might.

'Six months ago I had a heart attack,' he began, and Caroline hardly dared breathe as she listened intently. 'I'd be a fool if I didn't see it as some kind of serious catalyst for change.'

Absently Jack slid his hand down the side of Caroline's slender bare arm.

'It was entirely self-created. I pushed myself way too hard for far too long. I got rich…but truthfully I derived very little pleasure from the money I made. I discovered to my great shock that there isn't enough wealth and public acclaim in the world to wipe the slate clean of a bitter past. That part was down to *me*. I was still that angry, self-righteous youth who baulked at the cards fate had dealt him…who *despised* being poor. I wanted to show the world that I could rise above anything it cared to throw at me, and in some respects you could say I did. I certainly achieved what I set out to achieve financially…but there was still a gaping hole inside of me the size of the Grand Canyon. Now I know that I should have stayed with you after what happened, instead of using it as a bitter excuse to flee the country. I could have made my fortune anywhere, but I suppose I wanted to get as far away as possible from my past as I could. I'm so sorry, my angel.'

Urging her towards him so that she lay across his chest, Jack kissed her gently on the mouth, his blue eyes blazing at her with profound remorse and love.

Swallowing down the lump inside her throat, Caroline caught his hand and kissed it. 'I know you didn't really mean to hurt me, Jack. I told you—I have no more resentment whatever...*none*. Why don't we just let what happened in the past *stay* in the past, hmm? Today is a new day...a *new* future. Now, tell me about your heart. I want to know the truth, Jack. Are you in any danger still? How can I help?'

Staring up into her concerned brown eyes, Jack felt a wave of warmth permeate his entire being. He had to acknowledge it after all this time—*God had been good to him*. He was still alive, still curious about life, and now he was blessed with the love of the woman he'd thought he had lost for good and had miraculously been reunited with.

'The doctors told me that if I ease my workload and take better care of myself, then I have a damn good chance of living to be old. I'm pretty fit, and still young. Who knows how long I might live if I have the love of a good woman too?' He grinned, and was about to bestow a long, loving, much more leisurely kiss on Caroline's too delectable lips when she deliberately held back and considered him intently.

'Why *did* you come back here, Jack?' she asked

thoughtfully. 'What made you buy your mother's old house and decide to do it up?'

The grin banished, Jack's expression became perfectly serious. 'About a year ago I contacted an estate agency in town to express my interest in the house, should it ever come up for sale. I suppose I had some crazy half-baked notion that one day I might come back and fix it up…just for my own satisfaction. It *haunted* me, losing that house…it *definitely* haunted my mother. I just somehow needed to heal my hurt at it being repossessed all those years ago. Anyway, at the time of enquiring the guy who owned it had no intention of selling. But about a month before I had the heart attack the estate agents rang me to tell me that he had put it on the market. He was moving abroad to Spain and was looking for a quick sale. I bought it there and then. After I got sick, I saw my buying it as some kind of sign that I was meant to go home. I can't explain it…it was just a feeling that came over me. I thought you were long gone…married to some frightfully posh ambitious young doctor in the home counties. But secretly I hoped beyond hope that you might still live here. If you hadn't I would have eventually found you anyway. I'm certain of that.'

Jack let his gaze hungrily roam over her at will, his blue eyes darkening to almost the colour of a perfectly clear night sky. 'Now that I'm here I can see that I was *always* coming back to you, Caroline.'

He was speaking the truth. Ever since he'd suffered the heart attack, Jack had been made frighteningly aware of his own mortality, and pure instinct had sent

him back to the woman he loved. The woman he now
intended to stay with until he breathed his last breath.

'And what about your ex-wife?'

Jack's hand possessively circled Caroline's wrist as
for a fleeting moment he saw doubt reflected in her
steady gaze.

'A desperate mistake.' He jerked her a little towards
him, so that the soft feathery tips of her ravishing long
blonde hair brushed his face. 'I wasn't in love with her,
Caroline…I promise you that. Do you believe me?'

She had no reason not to. Even Caroline knew a man
in love when she saw one, and Jack truly *did* adore
her—she could see that. The tension inside her finally
dispersed as she relaxed against his chest.

'I don't blame you for needing the comfort of
someone else, Jack. Seventeen years is a long time to
be alone…I can personally vouch for that.'

There was no blame in her voice, only a little lingering sorrow that they had waited so long to find each
other again.

'You'll never be alone again, sweetheart…not so
long as I live and breathe. And even after I'm gone I'll
come back and be your guardian angel. So you see?
You'll *never* be rid of me.'

Before Caroline could think another melancholy
thought, Jack had captured her lips lovingly beneath his
own and moved his hands down her body to bring her
closer still…

* * *

'You're miles away, Jack…come back to me.'

Smiling up at his serious, preoccupied expression as they walked along the shoreline together, holding hands, Caroline intuitively tried to glean what her husband was thinking about. They had been married for exactly one week and one day, and had wasted no more time in getting to know each other all over again. They had even started finishing each other's sentences, and sometimes accurately guessing each other's thoughts like a long-time married couple.

With every day that passed, Caroline was more and more convinced that destiny had indeed decreed that they were meant to be together. But now, as he stopped on the wet yellow sand and turned to study her, the wind whipping a lock of his thick dark hair across the handsome brow that seemed a lot less troubled and careworn these days Caroline couldn't deny the sudden jolt of anxiety that ran through her blood.

'Jack?'

'I've been meaning to ask…'

'Yes?' For a moment she didn't breathe.

'Did you—did you suffer any *damage* when you had the abortion?' he asked finally.

Feeling shock roll through her, then ebb slowly away, Caroline sighed.

'No…thankfully I didn't. Why are you asking me this now, Jack?'

'I just needed to know. Perhaps it's too early to bring

the subject up… I don't know how you feel about it, but I was thinking…'

'You were thinking that we might try again…for a baby?'

As soon as the words were out, and she saw the look of complete astonishment on his face, Caroline knew she had guessed right. She was so overwhelmed with elation that she could barely speak.

They had been absolutely honest with each other about so many things since they had got together again six weeks ago, and even more so since their marriage, but this was one topic that they had both somehow *avoided*. Caroline knew the reasons why. Past pain had made the subject brittle as glass, and they were still treading carefully around it to avoid being cut. But now they had a God-given opportunity to address it.

'Is it at all possible, do you think?'

Watching her seemingly tussle with the question, Jack tried not to get his hopes up. Now that he was married to Caroline, he couldn't deny his growing desire to be a father, for her to have his baby. But he also knew that she had suffered deep trauma over having been made to have the abortion, and that that trauma had been made worse when Jack had gone away. He could hardly blame her if the idea of becoming pregnant again engendered strong feelings of trepidation and even *fear* inside her.

'I think it's *more* than possible, given the fact that we've been rather lax with birth control,' Caroline replied grinning.

Relieved that she didn't seem too upset about the idea, Jack let his tense shoulders relax.

'So you *like* the idea?'

His arms encircled her waist in her long red wool coat as her bewitching smile grew even wider. 'I *want* us to have a baby, Jack. And this time nobody's going to stop us! In fact…I have a sneaking suspicion that I could be pregnant already. My period's late. I was going to tell you.'

'My God…' His gaze an intensely hopeful gleam, Jack felt something quicken inside him.

'Well, Jack…you've been keeping me pretty busy for the past few weeks. It was *bound* to happen sooner or later, don't you think?'

Examining her shining brown eyes, and seeing the joy that was all but pouring out of them, Jack was suddenly *more* than certain that his wife was carrying their baby inside her.

For a long moment he couldn't speak, he was so moved by the idea that they were to become parents. Then he scooped her up into his arms and swung her round and round right there on the sand, for the world to witness his exultation. It didn't matter that right then there was only an elderly man walking by with his dog. The man smiled at them both indulgently, lifted his cap and walked on, whistling for his dog to follow.

'We'll need a new place to live,' Jack declared when Caroline had laughingly begged him to stop swinging her round because she was getting dizzy.

They had talked about where they would live, of course, but had arrived at no firm decision as yet. Right now Jack was staying at Caroline's place, and work was still in progress on his house. *But they'd agreed they would reside in neither of those places.* They would start afresh somewhere else…somewhere they would both be free from the wounds of the past.

Tomorrow—when the temporary staff that Caroline had hired to look after her shop started work—they were flying out to the Caribbean for their honeymoon. And after that they would fly on to New York, where Jack wanted to introduce his new wife to his friends. He knew already that they would be absolutely captivated by her.

'Could you bear to live by the sea again?' Caroline asked him, her teeth worrying at her soft lower lip.

'I know how much you love the ocean.' Stroking his knuckles gently down the side of her cold windblown cheek, Jack smiled. 'I have a house in California. It's right by the sea. It's rather beautiful, in fact. You would probably fall in love with it, come to think of it. We could always live there.'

Suddenly it didn't matter to Caroline if they lived by the sea or not. As long as she could visit the ocean from time to time, she would be well content.

That settled, she momentarily rested her head against her husband's chest. 'I'm easy,' she said, and smiled.

'Hey,' Jack said jokingly, 'that's not something you should say in front of your husband, *Mrs* Fitzgerald.'

'I love you, Jack.'

'I love you *more*, Caroline.'

'You can't possibly.'

'I'm sorry, but I beg to differ. The love I feel for you can't be measured.'

'Is it deeper than the ocean?' Her lips dimpled teasingly.

'Fathoms deeper.'

'Brighter than the brightest star?'

'More dazzling than Venus herself.'

'That's a whole lot of love, Jack.'

'Isn't that the name of a song?'

He laughed and kissed the top of her head.

'I'll love you for ever, Caroline…that's a promise.'

And, gazing up into her husband's enraptured and loving face, Caroline saw that his impassioned vow was written on his very *soul*…

THEIR PREGNANCY BOMBSHELL

BY
BARBARA McMAHON

Barbara McMahon was born and raised in the South USA, but settled in California after spending a year flying around the world for an international airline. After settling down to raise a family and work for a computer firm, she began writing when her children started school. Now, feeling fortunate in being able to realise a long-held dream of quitting her 'day job' and writing full time, she and her husband have moved to the Sierra Nevada mountains of California, where she finds her desire to write is stronger than ever. With the beauty of the mountains visible from her windows and the pace of life slower than the hectic San Francisco Bay Area where they previously resided, she finds more time than ever to think up stories and characters and share them with others through writing. Barbara loves to hear from readers. You can reach her at PO Box 977, Pioneer, CA 95666-0977, USA. Readers can also contact Barbara at her website: www.barbaramcmahon.com.

Don't miss Barbara McMahon's exciting new novels, *Accidentally the Sheikh's Wife* **and** *Marrying the Scarred Sheikh*, **available in one 2-in-1 collection in April 2010 from Mills & Boon® Romance.**

CHAPTER ONE

"GOODBYE. Be happy," Sara Simpson called after
the festively decorated car as it drove down the curving
driveway from the high-rise hotel, tin cans clanking
behind it. One of their friends had written Just
Married with foam on all the windows. Another had
painted hearts and cupids. Another had tied ribbons
from the door handles and antenna, all gaily fluttering
in the wind.

She watched until the vehicle was out of sight, feeling
a sudden pang. It had happened too fast. Jimmy
had come home on temporary duty after a year and a
half assignment at a base in Europe. He and Amber
had told her only last week they were going to get
married. Now the deed was done. Her baby was married
and off to start her new life with a husband who
only had another month at most in the States before
returning to Europe.

The wedding had been small, only family and a
few close, longtime friends of the bride and groom.
The young men and women who had gathered to celebrate
the event cheered as the newlyweds drove off.
Now they were leaving. One of Amber's friends came
to give Sara a hug.

"Super wedding, wasn't it?" she said.

Sara nodded, wishing it had been so different.

"Seems like they're still kids to me," Virginia
Woodworth said coming to stand beside Sara. The
two women watched the other young people drift

away. The mother of the groom didn't look any happier about things than Sara felt.

"They are still kids. Amber is only nineteen," Sara said, trying not to feel defensive. Amber was a year older than Sara had been when she married. Of course, look where that had gone.

She shivered a little in the cold air. The sun shone from a cloudless sky, but the February temperatures at Lake Tahoe were still below freezing. Snow blanketed the surrounding mountains—a skier's paradise. And a favorite location for weddings.

"Jimmy's twenty-one, and two years already into his enlistment. After he gets out, he'll have the G.I. bill to help with college," Virginia said. She had put her coat on and stood looking a bit lost.

If he would apply himself. Sara knew better than to suggest any criticism of Virginia's only child. He was the apple of her eye. Sara had known the Woodworths for years, ever since Amber and Jimmy had begun dating while in high school. They'd had their spats over the years, but remained loyal to each other over everything. Jimmy, however, had never struck Sara as particularly ambitious.

Amber had bemoaned the fact Jimmy was a year ahead of her in school, wanting to graduate at the same time. She had not liked the fact he'd joined the U.S. Army upon graduation, but she remained loyal and steadfast, even when he'd been posted overseas.

Now this. Sara wasn't sure they were making a mistake. There were many couples who married young and subsequently celebrated fifty years of happy married life.

But she wished they had waited. Amber was in her second year of college, while Jimmy was posted overseas. She hoped Amber wouldn't throw away her chance at finishing college to go live on base in Germany with him. She knew they'd discussed it. The last she heard, Amber planned to finish the school year. They wanted to see where Jimmy would be posted next before making further plans.

She wished they had waited that extra year instead of rushing things along. But they were grown, and none of her comments had them even reconsidering their impetuous decision.

Sara's own experiences colored everything, she knew. She had married young, like Amber. She and her husband had been childhood sweethearts, like Amber and Jimmy. Yet Bill had deserted her and Amber when Amber had been three months old. There had been no college for Sara at age nineteen. No husband with a good job. Not even a support network to help.

Her parents had turned their backs when she'd married against their wishes. Bill's parents had been equally unavailable. Alone, and with a baby to support, Sara had grown up fast. Those first few years had been so hard.

But worth every moment because of Amber. Her daughter was the apple of *her* eye.

She smiled at Virginia. "I wish they were still little kids who listened to us without question, but they are both adults now, and now embarking on life's journey together. Once they have a college education, the world will be at their feet." She crossed her arms over her chest, hugging what warmth she could. She had to get inside or freeze to death.

"They could have waited," Virginia whined.

"I agree, but they didn't. They're young, in love,

and have been dating exclusively for years,'' Sara said. She could say she blamed Jimmy for rushing the wedding through, but she refrained. No sense starting off with bad feelings with her new in-laws.

"Leave it alone, Virginia," James Woodworth said joining them. "The boy knows what he's doing." He looked at Sara. "You heading back to the city now?" He was a heavy-set man who ruled his family with no questions asked. Sara had never been completely comfortable around him, though he'd always been friendly enough. She hoped Jimmy didn't try to rule his family so totally. She had a feeling Amber wouldn't put up with it.

Sara relished her own independence and it seemed to her as if Virginia was always bowing her wishes to her husband's.

"I'm staying on for a couple of days. I took a week off." Since she'd come up two days ago to help with the final touches of the wedding, she still had several days remaining of her vacation. And she wanted to maximize every second. It was already the first of February, tax season had begun. By the time April rolled around, she'd be putting in long hours to get taxes completed for many of the company's clients. The busiest time of year for accountants was about to begin. She had best enjoy the lull before the on-slaught.

Sara bid the Woodworth's goodbye and looked around. The rest of Amber's friends had left. She was alone.

"Better get used to it," she said softly. Empty nest syndrome, wasn't that what they called it? Slowly she began to smile, wanting to do the Snoopy Dance of Joy. Empty nest was exactly what it was called and she was thrilled. For the first time in nineteen years, she was free. She could go where she pleased and do what she wanted. She could pig out on chocolate without worrying if she was setting a good example. Or sleep late and forget about being responsible and industrious.

She could travel, time permitting. Explore the Yucatan Peninsula and old ruins. Cruise the Alaskan waterways and see an iceberg being calved. Take a trip down the Mississippi or even fly to Paris.

''Yippee for empty nests,'' she said softly, turning to enter the large casino which comprised much of the ground floor of the hotel where the wedding had taken place, and where she had a room. Amber and Jimmy had elected to spend their honeymoon on a trip through the gold rush country, but Sara was spending her vacation right here at Lake Tahoe, where Stateline, Nevada, had casinos and extravagant shows and all the amenities of a world-class resort—including gorgeous Lake Tahoe.

Too bad she'd never learned to ski. It seemed as if half the occupants of the hotel were skiers, looking healthy and vibrant as they walked through in their colorful clothes.

Maybe something else she could try. She was thirty-eight years old, and felt as giddy as a schoolgirl. She was going to spread her own wings at last, and she could hardly wait.

But not today. It was early afternoon, she planned to spend the rest of the day at the hotel spa. First a massage, then a facial and a hair cut. She would lap up the luxury before returning to the mundane aspects of her own life.

Hurrying through the casino floor on her way to

the elevators, Sara glanced at the people crowding the expanse. Slot machines sounded to her left. To the right were huge craps tables surrounded by excited players, less crowded tables for blackjack, and discretely tucked in the back a roped off area for the really high rollers.

She watched as one elderly lady pulled the handle on the slot machine with such an avid look of anticipation, Sara could almost feel her excitement. Sara didn't gamble. She had come by her money too hard to waste it when everyone knew the house always—

She bumped into someone. To her dismay, a bucket of coins flew from his hand and spilled onto the carpet. Nickels rolled everywhere.

"Oh, no, I'm so sorry," she said, scrambling to pick up as many of the coins as she could. She barely glanced at the man, intent on recovering his money before other people realized what had happened and tried to scoop up some for their own use.

"No problem," a lazy drawl sounded above her.

He stooped down beside her, and held out the bucket for the coins in her hands. She dumped them in and scooped up some more.

"I'm not usually that clumsy," she said, dropping in more coins into the plastic container. He also skimmed a handful from the carpet. Several other players stopped to help.

"That looks about right," he said a moment later and stood. She saw his hand and took it for assistance rising.

Then she looked at him and almost caught her breath. Wow, she thought, glad to know her hormones hadn't permanently atrophied over the last nineteen years. She could definitely recognize a hunk when she saw one. And respond. Her heart skipped a beat then settled merrily down into double time. She could feel the flush flash through her and knew she had to take a breath. But holding it seemed easier to do.

"You look like you're on your way somewhere," he said, slowly releasing her hand. "All dressed up."

The majority of the people in the casino were wearing ski togs or casual clothes. His own dark cords and white shirt, opened at the throat, looked superbly casual. Of course, Sara thought wildly, everything about him looked superb. Oh where had he been when she'd been available?

"I just came from a wedding," she said.

He quickly glanced at her left hand, then met her eyes and smiled. "Not your own, I see."

"No, my daughter's."

Surprise flickered in his eyes. "You don't look old enough to have a marriageable daughter."

Was he flirting with her? she wondered, struck by the notion. It had been decades since she'd flirted with anyone. Did she remember how?

"I was a child bride," she said with a teasing smile.

"From Kentucky," he nodded.

"Kentucky?" Where had that come from?

"Obviously you married at age twelve, and I hear hillbillies do that sometimes," he said.

She laughed. He was flirting. And it felt wonderful.

"Well, I can't admit to my age, now, can I? But my daughter is very young to be getting married."

"I knew it, another twelve year old," he teased.

"No! She's nineteen."

He shifted the bucket of coins, stepped back and

reached for her hand, pulling her out of the center of the aisle where they were blocking the way.

Sara felt the jolt of his touch to her toes. She hadn't expected that.

His thumb brushed over her ringless fingers and then he slowly let go. "Any other kids?"

"No, just the one."

"And no husband." It was a statement. An obvious one given she wore no rings.

"And no husband."

"Are you free for dinner?"

"What?" He was asking her out? They hadn't even introduced themselves.

"It's the least you could do for spilling my winnings."

She glanced at the bucket, it was about half full—of nickels. "You're one of the high rollers, aren't you?" she asked.

"Damn, you caught me out. But I promise, I can spend more than this on dinner."

She was tempted. Normally she wouldn't dream of letting herself be picked up. Yet, hadn't she just promised herself she would celebrate being on her own without the respectability and duties of a mother?

Still, she had some sense of self-preservation.

"I don't know you," she said slowly.

"That'll be the fun of dinner, we can discover who each other is. I don't know you, either, but I'm willing to take a chance. It's just dinner. Tell you what, come with me while I turn these in and then try my luck on the dime machines. We'll talk and by dinner time you'll know all about me."

"Sorry, I'm on my way to the spa." Enticing though his offer was, the lure of the spa held sway.

"Ah, a woman who enjoys sybaritic pleasures. A hot oil massage, right?"

It sounded intimate coming from him.

She nodded. If he suggested he could give her a better one, she'd turn and leave in a heartbeat.

"Relaxing, which is probably what the mother of the bride needs. I'll meet you here at seven. Don't be late."

"I didn't say I would have dinner with you."

"Have other plans?"

Sara shook her head before she thought. "But that—"

He placed a finger across her lips, pressing slightly. "No excuses. Meet me here at seven."

Sara remained in place after he left. Vanished almost. One moment his finger had her frozen in place by the tingling sensations that coursed through her, the next, he'd melted away between the rows of slots heading for the change booth. She watched him for a moment, he was taller that most of the people in the casino. But when he turned a corner formed by the bank of slots machines, he was lost from sight.

Shaking her head as if to clear her brain, she continued to the elevators, watching carefully lest she bump into someone else.

She still didn't know his name. How could she have dinner with a total stranger?

How could she not, given how he looked and the reaction she felt? For the first time in ages, Sara felt young and full of anticipation. He'd seemed interested in her. Maybe having dinner would be fun. At least it would be daring for her. Live a little.

Matt Tucker walked away without looking back, much as he was tempted. Who was she? Cute as could be, and bemused by the activity in the casino, unless he missed his guess. She obviously wasn't used to the gambling scene. Which only spoke well of her to him. He rarely indulged himself. And then only to while away the time. His cohort, Dex, was skiing. Matt had time on his hands, and didn't mind wasting a few dollars on mindless entertainment. But not at a fast clip—hence the nickel and dime machines.

He handed his bucket to the change woman and waited while the coin machine she dumped them into calculated how many nickels he had.

She hadn't looked old enough to be a mother of a bride, he thought as he waited. Did it matter? He had come to Tahoe to relax after the last trip and get in some serious skiing. Yesterday he and Dex burned up the slopes. Today he'd stayed inside to catch up on some work via the Internet. He'd been gone from the office more than two weeks and it'd be another few days before he returned. Couldn't let too much work pile up.

Would she join him for dinner? She had said she was unattached, but that didn't mean she wasn't seeing someone, or had a significant other in the wings.

He caught himself when he turned around, trying to see over the crowd. She was just a woman he'd met. Nothing special. So what if her dark blue eyes made him think of the Aegean sea after a storm, or her peaches and cream complexion reminded him of an Irish colleen. Her dress had been flowing, enveloping a figure he could dream about. He liked her laugh, her sparkling eyes. Everything.

He reached for the bills the change woman handed him and stepped aside, thrusting them into his pocket.

An evening shared with a pretty woman sure beat listening to Dex talk about how good the ski runs were today. He didn't need an update, he'd be out on them himself again tomorrow.

Did she ski?

Did a mother with a kid indulge in sports like that?

He had never dated a mother before. He didn't interact well with kids, and he definitely wasn't interested in being tied down by some woman who wanted a picket fence and a dog.

Not that he'd class her in that role—especially now that her child was grown and gone. It had to make her older than she looked, anyone could do the math, and their joking aside, he did not believe she had married at age twelve.

Not that age mattered. He would enjoy the evening, no ties implied. It was only dinner.

He headed for the dime slots. Another few hours of mindless entertainment, and he'd see if his mysterious lady would show.

As the afternoon continued, Sara forgot her worry about Amber and Jimmy, all she could think about was the stranger in the casino. He'd been so good looking, tall, with dark hair a shade longer than the accountants she worked with wore theirs. His body was trim and fit, with a hint of muscles she wasn't used to. He seemed relaxed, yet there was a certain air of authority surrounding him.

And he sure had more than his share of sex appeal. That alone put him way out of her league. She had rarely dated over the years. Her flirting skills were nonexistent. And she still harbored the uncertainty around men that had marked her when Bill had taken off after Amber's birth. They'd been high school sweethearts, sure they were destined to be together forever even over the objections of their parents.

It had been a case where her parents had known best. They'd been furious with her and told her she'd made her bed, she was on her own. That had been before Amber. Even her birth had not softened their stance. Consequently they'd missed out on all her childhood.

Five years ago, Sara had learned they moved to a retirement community in Arizona. She hadn't had any contact with them in almost twenty years. Loving her daughter as she did, she could never understand her parents' position. She'd do anything for Amber, even if she made a mistake along the way. Wasn't that what families were for—to support each other when hard times came? To share in the good times and love each other no matter what?

Gradually Sara gave into the pleasurable sensations of the massage. The darkened room and soft music conspired to relax. The warm oil and soothing strokes of the masseuse were heavenly. She enjoyed the sybaritic delights. If she could have afforded it, she'd do this all the time. What would her mysterious man say to that?

By the time six-thirty rolled around, Sara was in a state. She didn't know whether to go to dinner with a stranger or not. How safe was that? On the other hand, if they ate in the hotel, how dangerous could it be? She wouldn't get in a car with someone she didn't know. She wouldn't go anywhere she didn't know. They'd have dinner, chat a while, and that would be that.

It beat staying in her room and ordering room service.

Especially after getting a complete makeover after her massage.

She lifted the flirty sea-green dress from the bed. It would be a shame to waste it. For the first time in longer than she could remember, she felt like someone else. Someone full of life and anticipation. She could wear this nothing of a dress, the super high heels she bought, and flirt like crazy. Then come back safely to her room and dream about a fabulous evening like none she'd ever had.

She'd do it.

Promptly at seven, she stepped from the elevator, feeling as exposed as if she were wearing a bikini. The sales woman at the boutique had assured her she looked terrific in the dress, but it clung like a second skin and didn't even reach her knees. The new, shorter hair felt as if she'd been scalped. She suspected the sultry look she'd tried for with the new makeup probably looked silly.

Before she could dash back into the elevator, however, he appeared looking as sexy as she remembered. Now he wore a dark suit, pristine-white shirt and dark tie. His eyes captured hers as he sauntered across the expanse, letting her know by his quick glance, that encompassed everything from the new hair style to the sexy heels, that he liked what he saw.

"Matthew Tucker," he said, holding out his hand.

"Sara Simpson," she replied, taking his hand. Instead of shaking it, he drew her closer, tucking her hand in the crook of his elbow when he turned. He headed toward the bank of elevators that serviced the rooftop restaurant.

"I made reservations at the Starlight Room," he said. "Dinner and dancing, sound all right?"

"It sounds perfect."

All her worries fled. He wasn't trying to whisk her away somewhere. They would stay right in the hotel and if things got awkward, she could walk back to her room. But if the evening went well, she'd have a wonderful start on her new life.

"So tell me all about Sara Simpson," Matt invited when they were seated beside one of the floor-to-ceiling windows overlooking the lake. It was pitch dark outside, with only the lights from town and scattered homes on the shore offering any break to the stygian night. A cloud cover had drifted in, blotting out the stars. The windows reflected the soft lights of the restaurant.

A combo playing nearby provided excellent background music, and an opportunity to dance.

Sara looked at him, wondering what about her boring life would appeal to such a fascinating man. A look at his expensive clothes convinced her he would know nothing about struggling to earn a living, working her way through college while raising a child. A single man in his early thirties would know nothing about the turmoil at home when said child was a teen and angry she never met her father. Or the difficulties a woman had competing with the old boys network at work. Her life now suited her, but to tell someone else how she spent it sounded boring.

What she wanted was to have Matt consider her exciting and daring. A woman of the world, totally at ease with going out to dinner with a stranger. She wanted to forget she was a mom and have him see her as a woman of mystery. Someone he'd be glad he'd coerced into having dinner with him.

"The brief version?" she asked, stalling as she frantically tried to come up with something exciting.

"We've got all evening, why be brief?"

She leaned closer. "All right, but you have to be discreet."

He raised an eyebrow. "How discreet?"

"I don't want my cover blown."

Amusement danced in his eyes. "You have my promise."

"I am a kind of detective, ferreting out facts people often want secreted down to the tiniest detail. Depending on the consequence, I expose them. Making them come clean on all fronts."

He looked intrigued. Sara sat back, satisfied. She wasn't just some boring accountant who would make his eyes glaze over with talk of debits and credits. Could she expand her mysterious occupation through dinner? She'd never tried it before, but the challenge was proving to be fun. The real key would be to tell only the truth, while giving a different impression.

"That's the short version, I suspect," he said.

She nodded. "So tell me about you."

"Maybe I'm one of the people who assists those who want to guard their information," he said, his eyes holding hers.

"What?"

"Security. Boring, I know, but there it is. My company designs and implements security features for businesses, from basic burglar alarms, to sophisticated fire walls in mainframe computers. I'm in the computer division."

"You work with computers?" She couldn't believe

it. He looked tan, fit, athletic. How could he be stuck behind a computer all day?

"Among other aspects of the firm. Actually I'm one of the partners. Computers are my speciality. Disappointed?"

Oh, no. He thought she was some super detective with a glamorous life and his would disappoint her. That's why she shouldn't tell tall tales.

"Not at all. I find computers fascinating." And frustrating if they didn't work the way they were supposed to. She was never able to troubleshoot problems herself, she always had to call the tech in. "Do you work here at Lake Tahoe?" she asked.

"No. Headquarters are in San Francisco. But I travel a lot. I'm here on a break. Just got back from Moscow."

"Moscow?" Her eyes widened.

"Ever been there?"

She shook her head.

"Your work is local, then?" he asked.

"San Francisco."

"Ah."

"What were you doing in Moscow?" She tucked away the knowledge he was also from San Francisco. Would they ever run into each other once they returned home? Would he ask her out again?

"Helping a firm set up Internet security, so pirates and hackers don't get in. Before that I was in Brussels working on some of the mainframes for the EU."

"And before that?" She was fascinated. Imagine having a job that took him all over the world. That's what she wanted. A chance to travel and see other cultures, visit historic sites, learn to eat Italian food properly in Italy, or see a bullfight in Spain.

''Hong Kong. Crowded as all get out, but exciting.''

Sara could only stare at him. He spoke about traveling as casually as she talked about going to the supermarket. ''You've been all over the world?''

He nodded.

The waiter temporarily halted their conversation as he served dinner, asking if they needed anything else. Once he departed, Sara looked at Matt.

''I would love to travel. In fact, I was just thinking earlier with Amber married, I'm free for the first time in years. No ties to keep me home. I can travel whenever I want. Splurge and indulge my desires.''

''Are those the only desires you wish to indulge?'' he asked, softly.

Heat washed through her at the look in his eyes. She dropped her gaze to her meal and didn't answer. But a mental picture of Matt and her locked in a heated embrace immediately came to mind. Thank God he couldn't read her mind.

''Hey, buddy. I wondered where you disappeared to.'' A tall man with shaggy blond hair stopped by the table, obviously addressing Matt, but with his eyes on Sara. ''I was available for dinner, but you didn't invite me,'' he said.

''As you can see, I had other plans,'' Matt said.

''And you're not sharing?''

''No.''

Sara glanced at Matt who was looking at her with amusement. He inclined his head slightly. ''I might make an introduction if you leave immediately,'' he said to his friend.

''Or I could join you,'' he suggested, making no move to pull out one of the empty chairs at the table.

"Sara, this obnoxious guy is a fellow partner at Aste Technologies. Dexter Braddox. Dex, Sara Simpson. And no, you can't join us."

"We came up for the skiing and the first thing you do is dump me for work, and now I find you with the prettiest woman in the place. Does that seem fair?" Dex asked.

Sara smiled at the compliment, knowing they were kidding each other, but feeling like the center of attention between two very good-looking, successful males. She'd never been in such a situation before.

Dex chatted for another minute, then left. Sara looked at Matt. "Should you have invited him to join us?"

"No. I definitely didn't want him in on our evening. Let him find his own woman."

So Matt considered her his woman—at least for the evening. She smiled at the sheer delight she felt and resumed eating.

They discussed the food, the ambiance of the restaurant, and the activities the area held. Then Matt said,

"Since we both live in the city, maybe I know where you work. Or is that top secret? Do you live near your office? Do you even have offices?"

"I live near Fort Mason, and it's an easy bus ride to work on Montgomery Street where the office is located. Sometimes I walk on really nice summer days. It's good exercise."

"We're practically neighbors, then. I have a place in the Marina district."

She nodded, knowing they might physically be not too distant, but the small apartments near Fort Mason were nothing compared to the lavish homes in the ritzy Marina district. A view of the water seemed to be required of those places. Her view was of the city buses that traveled the street.

"Who watches your place when you're gone?" she asked. She was finished eating. Would he want to extend the evening or suggest they leave?

"The mail I don't have sent to the office friends bring in periodically. My secretary deals with most of it. No plants, no pets, nothing that requires a lot of attention," he said. Glancing at the dance floor, he noted several couples were dancing.

"Care to dance?" he asked, glancing at her empty plate.

Sara had been hoping for some dessert, she'd seen a tray of fancy chocolate concoctions when they'd first entered the restaurant. But dancing sounded almost as decadent. Not that she was a good dancer. She hadn't a lot of practice, but how hard could swaying to the slow tempo be? She was tempted beyond resistance to be held in his arms. She had noticed the glances from other women while they ate. Matt was the best looking man in the place, and Sara felt a wave of gratitude he seemed intent on her.

He escorted her to the small dance floor and swept her into his arms. The music was seductive. Or being held by such a sexy man was. Whatever, Sara felt like she was a princess. They moved together as if they'd been dance partners for years. She rested her forehead against his lower jaw, relishing the touch of skin against skin. His arm encircled her, his hand splayed over her the small of her back. The slightest pressure guided her. His other hand, large and strong, held hers. It made her feel safe.

She'd always been the strong one in their family of two. It felt odd to feel sheltered. Odd, but nice.

''When do you return to San Francisco?'' he asked.

''Not for a few days. I'm on vacation.''

''Spend it with me.''

CHAPTER TWO

SARA pulled back a little so she could see his face. "Spend my vacation with you? Here at the hotel?"

"I'm staying here, so are you. We could spend our time together. You can tell me more about your job. Or where you'd travel if you had no limits. Do you ski? We could go skiing. Or if you'd rather gamble—"

"I'm afraid I don't gamble, and I don't ski. I planned to walk along the lake, catch up on some reading, maybe indulge myself at the spa again."

"Change your plans," he suggested.

Sara didn't hesitate beyond a split second. Wasn't she yearning for adventure? Wanting something different from the last two decades? What better than to share an exciting vacation with an interesting man? No one knew her at Lake Tahoe. No one had expectations about how she should behave. No one could censure her for taking a chance.

Throwing caution to the wind and feeling very adventuresome, she nodded. "I would love that. You can tell me all about where you've been, to help me decide where I should go first. And I'll tell you what I can about my own job." As long as she could figure out a way to make it sound glamorous, she could keep him intrigued. A mysterious woman to share his vacation with. What fun it was to be responsible solely for herself at long last.

An empty nest was a wondrous thing.

* * *

25

Matt settled her against him, relishing the feel of her feminine body against his. She fascinated him. She wasn't pestering him to reveal his intimate most secrets. She wasn't trying to impress him with all her fantastic accomplishments, or all the compliments she received from other men. Consequently he didn't feel the need to try to impress or put the make on her. He wanted her, that was a given. She was beautiful, and fun to be with—unlike the women he'd been seeing most recently, always wanting more of his time, attention, money.

She seemed content with his idea of spending their vacation together. He'd relax and enjoy his time away from work—or as much as he could allow. There would still be time in the early mornings to catch up on things via the Internet.

For a moment cynicism rose. Was she too good to be true? She seemed eager to embrace the exact life he enjoyed. Was it a ploy or was she genuinely excited about traveling?

If so, maybe she could go with him on a trip or two. Visiting some of his favorite spots took on a new meaning when he thought about showing them to Sara. She'd be enchanted with Paris. Fascinated by Rome or Athens. Probably amazed by the bustle and energy of crowded Hong Kong. He could envision her eyes lighting up in delight, the curve of her lips when she smiled.

Suddenly he wondered what she'd look like in bed—a combination of all the above?

Too soon the combo took a break.

''It's getting late,'' Sara said as they returned to their table. ''If we're going to be up early tomorrow, I'd better get some sleep.''

"Are we getting up early?" For a moment he almost suggested they finish the evening in his room. But something held him back. Sara wasn't like the women he generally saw. She was special. He wasn't going to risk ruining what they had together by rushing things. There were several days ahead of them. The conquest would be all the sweeter for waiting.

"I don't want to waste a minute of vacation," she said. "Besides, who knows how long the weather will hold. It could snow again any day."

He paid the check and escorted her to the elevator. They rode down, changed at the lobby and took one of the other elevators to the rooms. She told him which floor she was on. When he walked her to her door he almost invited himself in. But he resisted the impulse. He could wait. Not easily, but he wasn't some randy young teenager. He'd acquired some polish over the last decade or so.

"I'll meet you for breakfast at eight," he suggested.

"Fine. By the elevator?"

He nodded. Raising his hand, he toyed with a short lock of her soft honey-brown hair. She'd had it cut between the first time he'd seen her and dinner. The new style suited her. Had it been highlighted? Or were the strands of gold mixed in natural? Whatever, the style made her look more sophisticated than he suspected she really was. Studying her, he was struck again by how much he wanted her.

He leaned in and kissed her gently. Her lips were soft and warm. She responded with an enthusiasm which surprised him. Maybe he was wrong about waiting.

Then she stepped back, fumbled with the card and opened her door. "Thanks again for tonight." She shut the door in his face.

Matt rocked back on his heels and looked up at the ceiling, drawing in a deep breath. Maybe he'd miscalculated. Maybe she would have been more receptive than he'd thought.

It wasn't even midnight, but he might as well get to bed. He didn't want to be a second late for breakfast.

"Wow. Oh, wow!" Sara said softly, leaning against the door. He'd kissed her! She hadn't been kissed since that sloppy attempt by Jack Renner seven years ago. She couldn't call that a kiss, more like a wet puppy's salutation.

Matt Tucker, on the other hand, could corner the market on kisses. She felt herself tingle all over, and the smile wouldn't stop. Pushing away from the door, she danced around the room, imagining Matt's arms around her. She'd *loved* their evening together.

A week of his company. She couldn't believe it. Would they get bored? Or find they wanted more than a week? They both lived in San Francisco. Maybe he'd ask her out when they returned home.

She got ready for bed, thinking of all the possibilities, feeling almost giddy with happiness. The worry about Amber and Jimmy was long forgotten.

The next day was one of the best Sara ever spent. At breakfast Matt tried to talk her into skiing. But she refused, choosing instead to walk along the water's edge. She suggested he go with his friend and meet her later. She would be disappointed, but that she could handle. She didn't relish making a fool of herself the first day trying to learn to ski with an expert watching.

To her gratification, Matt had dismissed her suggestions and insisted he'd rather spend the day with her.

"I've been skiing for years. And have had two good days here already. The mountains will always be here. Let's get some coffee to keep us warm and tackle that walk."

The snow had melted enough to reveal the sandy beach. They battled the wind that swept across the lake, but with the sunshine and warm jackets, the day felt exhilarating.

Matt bought coffee for them to take, and when they found a sheltered spot, complete with bench, they sat down to sip the warm beverage. The wavelets breaking against the shore, driven by the wind, rendered a soft melodious background. The water sparkled in the sunshine. The snow on the surrounding peaks gleamed like thousands of diamonds with the tall deep green conifers and deep blue sky startling contrasts.

Sara drank in the beauty as she tried to imprint every aspect of the day on her memory. Especially the man beside her.

"Tell me about Moscow," Sara invited, looking at him over the edge of her cup as she took another welcomed sip.

"If we take turns."

"But you know all about San Francisco," she said.

"But not all about you. I want every speck of information I can get," Matt said.

Flattered, she nodded, hugging the compliment to herself. Don't get carried away, she admonished. He's on vacation and making the most of it.

"Okay, but you start with Moscow," she said, yearning to hear about his travels, his work, every scrap of information he'd give. Did he really feel the same about her?

"Tenacious," he commented, then began to describe the events of his last trip.

When he'd finished, she frowned. "If I'd been there, I'd have visited the museums, walked in Red Square, even done some shopping. You went to work, and back to the hotel. Boring."

"It's my fourth visit. Besides, winter in Moscow doesn't exactly lend itself to saunters around town. To say the least, it's cold there. And I had a job to do."

She watched the way his eyes seemed to delve into her. He looked at her a lot, as if he liked what he saw. She felt flustered.

What had they been talking about? Oh, the weather. Somehow in her fantasies about travel, it had always been perpetual summer.

"Tell me how you cope with the language barrier. Or do you speak Russian?" she asked, wishing he'd talk all day. She liked his voice, the expressions on his face, the way his eyes looked at her, into her. She had never felt another's attention so completely.

"I don't speak Russian, but I do speak a few other languages that come in handy in Europe. When in Russia, I hire an interpreter. This trip I had an old guy who loved to wax poetic about the glory days of the empire—which ended about forty years before he was born."

He continued telling her some of the funny things his guide had said. His descriptions of the bleak winters in Moscow gave her shivers.

He had a way with words that painted pictures in her mind of the sights he'd seen. She felt as if she'd been to Moscow, though she sure would have done more. Would he want to do more in his free time if he had someone to share the adventure with?

By the time they finished their coffee, they were ready to walk again. It was too cold to sit for long.

"Now I want to hear about you and your exciting job," Matt said, taking her hand. Sara glanced at their linked hands, then laughed in sheer joy.

"I'm so sorry to disappoint you, Matt, but it's not so exciting." She regretted her attempts to make herself more than she was. Would he be disgusted at her ploy?

"Ferreting out hidden facts? Detection work, right?"

"Some of it. Actually I'm an accountant. I audit books for companies, and work on taxes. Not very exciting, I'm afraid. But I like it."

"You sound defensive. I would assume you'd like your work, or you'd do something else," he said easily.

At least he wasn't annoyed she'd tried to make it sound more glamorous than it was. She nodded, never having thought about it that way. She liked dealing with numbers. They were logical and predictable. They would never let her down like people did. They were safe.

The day flew by as they explored their section of the shoreline. Pleasure boats were tied at a marina, covered and unused in winter. Many of the large homes that fronted the lake were also closed, though here and there smoke came from chimneys of ones occupied. They ventured onto Main Street, wandering around the shops selling crafts and memorabilia.

Lunch had been at an outdoor café, with heaters to keep the patrons warm. In the best of the German tradition, they'd eaten brockworst and sauerkraut. Surrounding them were skiers taking a lunch break and an occasional family with children running around and playing in the snow near the deck.

"I'll meet you here at seven," Matt said when they reached the elevator bank in the hotel in the late afternoon. "Do you want to eat at the Starlight room again, or try another place?" he asked.

"Surprise me," she said, taking her shopping bags from his fingers, her own brushing his at the transfer.

He'd touched her often during the day, holding her hand while they walked along the beach, placing his hands on her shoulders when they had to go single file in some of the crowded shops. She should be getting used to his touch, but she felt flustered every time.

"Till seven, then," he said, leaning over to brush his lips against hers.

It didn't bother him they were in the busy lobby of a major hotel, with dozens of people milling around and slot machines sounding. It was just a brief touch, but Sara felt it to her toes. Stunned, she stepped into the elevator and watched the doors close between them. She needed to watch herself, he was way out of her league. This was only a vacation, a piece of time out of the ordinary.

But as she remembered every moment of the day,

she fantasized about sharing more than a vacation with him. That's what being married should have been like. What building a life together could have been. She'd missed out on so much when Bill left. She should have done something about it years ago but she'd put relationships on hold for Amber's sake.

Or was it about meeting a special man who had her fantasizing about such things?

She quickly dumped the packages on her bed in her room and then headed back down to the lobby shops in search of another dress. The only dresses she had were her mother-of-the-bride dress and the new one she'd bought yesterday. The rest of her wardrobe consisted of the warm pants and thick tops which were all she had anticipated needing for her vacation.

Matt had seen yesterday's purchase, she wanted something new for tonight.

She chose a subdued dress in dark hunter-green and splurged on a gold chain necklace. The two went together perfectly. Dashing back up to her room, she showered, dressed and got ready for the evening. Excitement built as she impatiently waited for seven o'clock. She missed him—and it had only been two hours since she'd seen him.

She couldn't believe how easily the two of them had meshed. Conversation never lagged, yet there were still worlds to share. Dancing, holding hand, kisses—she couldn't wait.

Sara awoke Wednesday morning with a feeling of impeding doom. Today was her last day of vacation. She had to head for home this afternoon, and start back at the office tomorrow.

She didn't want to end their idyllic time.

Lying back she snuggled beneath the covers, remembering every moment she and Matt has spent over the last few days. Every single one had been special. She was afraid she was falling in love. How crazy was that? He was younger than she by several years, though neither had made mention of the fact. He traveled the world while she had never been much farther from San Francisco than Nevada.

And he was so sexy it made her teeth ache. His casual touch set her heart racing. His kisses each night had grown more ardent. Last night she thought for sure he'd push for more than a few hot kisses. But he remained a gentlemen every time.

Or maybe he didn't feel as she did. Perhaps it was no hardship to leave her at her door and saunter away in that sexy male walk of his. It could be she was just someone to spend his vacation with beside Dexter. Somehow being a notch above his shaggy-haired friend wasn't the best comparison.

Speculation was futile. She'd know soon enough. He hadn't asked her for her phone number. Maybe this was just a vacation fling, a special time that would fade into a pleasant memory once she returned to home.

She hoped not!

Once dressed, she began to pack. She'd check out by eleven, but could stay until late afternoon and still make it home before too late. Since it was the middle of the week, the traffic on the interstate wouldn't be heavy.

Maybe Matt would ask to ride down with her. Had he brought a car or come with Dex? It was odd—she knew about his most recent trip to Moscow, but didn't have that current fact.

Matt stood waiting at the elevators when she stepped into the lobby. He had never not been there, even yesterday when she'd come down five minutes early. That had to be a good sign, didn't it?

His smile set her pulses pounding again. She took a deep breath, hoping he'd ask to see her again. What if today was the last time they were together?

"I thought we'd walk over to the pancake house, splurge on a big breakfast we'll then have to spend the day walking off," he said, reaching out for her hand.

"Sounds great." She laced her fingers through his, a standard practice. Everything they had done together had been special—because he'd been a part of it.

"Sure you don't want to try skiing?" he asked.

It might be her last chance. They'd done everything else the area had to offer—why not? She'd still be clumsy and he was probably an expert. But it was something he liked. She could end up loving it.

"Okay, I'll give it a try."

He squeezed her hand in approval as they headed for the pancake house. "You'll love it. And I'm an expert teacher."

No sooner had their breakfasts been served than his cell phone rang.

Sara couldn't help hearing his side of the conversation and her heart dropped. There would be no skiing today. He was being called to some emergency.

"Sorry, Sara, I have to go," Matt said clicking off the phone a few minutes later.

"An emergency, I got that from your side of the conversation," she said evenly, thought she wanted to rail against fate. "Do you have to leave immediately?"

"I can finish breakfast. Let me call the hotel and see if I can catch Dex before he hits the slopes. I need him to get me to Reno. They've already booked me on a flight from there."

Sara could scarcely eat her pecan pancakes. Usually her favorite, the food stuck in her throat every time she tried to swallow. Only a few more minutes before he left. The refrain echoed in her mind.

As soon as she finished, they hurried back to the hotel. She could already feel the distance growing between them. He was focused on the tasks ahead. While not quite forgotten, he was still holding her hand, his attention no longer concentrated on her.

She had known they would say goodbye today. She had just expected it to be later. After he'd asked for her home phone number.

Dex met them in the lobby. "They've confirmed your space on the 12:15 flight to Denver. You change there for Boston, and then have a red-eye to Amsterdam. You have your passport with you, right?"

Matt nodded. "And laptop. I could use some other clothes, but will pick something up in Amsterdam. I'll go up and pack. Can you take my suitcase back with you?"

"Sure enough." Dex looked at his watch. "We need to get going to make that flight from Reno."

"Give us a minute, will you?" Matt asked. He drew Sara to the elevators and punched the button.

"You don't need to walk me to my room, Matt. I know time is short. You have to pack your things. We can say goodbye here. Thanks for such a special vacation.'' She kept her voice level, steady. She would not burst into tears as she wanted. They had never talked about the future, nor made any promises. He was free to go where he had to, as was she.

He turned her toward him, resting his hands on her shoulders. ''You're one special lady, Sara. Next time I take a vacation, I want you to share it with me.'' He kissed her again as if they were the only two people in the world and not a couple in the midst of a bustling lobby.

The elevator arrived.

''Go pack and catch your flight. Do some sightseeing in Amsterdam for me,'' she said when he looked at the opened door. She gently pushed him away and watched the doors close behind him. Her vacation was over.

Damn! Matt thought as he rode to his room. He couldn't believe the timing. Why did the program have to fail at this point? Now it was up to Matt to repair the damage, not only to the computer, but also to the good will of the company. He played hard, but he worked hard, too. He and Dex and Tony had started the company seven years ago. It had expanded beyond their wildest dreams back then. And all of them, and the other employees they'd hired over the years, wanted to keep it on top. He was a major player in keeping them in the forefront. But today he wished someone else could have been sent to Amsterdam.

He wanted to stay with Sara.

Frowning, he entered his room and began to pack. Where had that thought come from? He loved traveling. He had decided long ago when living with Uncle Frank that given the chance, he would travel the world and never look back. He had done just that. And relished every assignment. Going off into the unknown sure beat a routine nine-to-five job that would have bored him in no time. He never wanted to end up bitter and complaining as Uncle Frank had been. Tied down, unhappy in his work, in his life, the old man had never hidden his resentment at the unfairness of his life.

Matt had left Frank's place at eighteen to work his way through college. He'd known an education was the key to getting out of the rat race his uncle complained about. And he had. He'd visited all the major cities of the world. Vacationed in some of the most exotic and exciting locales known to man.

But this time the adrenaline rush was missing. He would have rather stayed with Sara.

She had been the perfect companion. Each day had been special. His only regret was he hadn't pushed harder to spend those nights together as well. Lively, fun, and enchanted by mundane things, she gave a new view to everything. The days had flown by. Now he had to leave before he was ready. A first. Usually he was raring to go to a new city, face new challenges.

They had made no promises.

Damn! He realized he hadn't even gotten her phone number in San Francisco. What if she had an unlisted number? He lunged for the phone and punched in her room number. The phone rang and rang, finally clicking over to voice mail. Wouldn't do any good to leave a message, he wouldn't be here for her to call back.

Maybe she'd stayed downstairs to talk to Dex. If she had, he could ask her then.

If not, he'd get Dex to find out when he returned

from dropping him at the airport. Best he could do. He threw a few things in the carry all, including his laptop. The rest went into the suitcase for Dex. He'd have to buy some clothes in Amsterdam. At least they didn't expect computer experts to dress up.

Forty-five minutes later Dex dropped him at the curb at Reno Airport.

"Don't forget, get her phone number. Tell her I'll call her as soon as I get back to San Francisco," Matt said.

"Hey, old buddy, you've only repeated yourself a dozen times on the ride here. I couldn't possibly forget. I'll have the number for you today. Look at your e-mail when you get to Amsterdam. If I didn't know you better, I'd think you've fallen for the pretty lady," Dex said. He waved and drove off.

Matt stared after him. Fallen for Sara?

Sara saw no reason to stay once Matt had gone. She finished packing, checked out early and headed for home. There were wedding presents in the trunk of her car Amber had asked her to take back for her. The kids would be coming home later this week. She'd want to hear all about the honeymoon.

Would Amber ask about her stay in Tahoe? And if she did, what would Sara say? I met the most wonderful man in the world? We had a fabulous four days, then he left for Amsterdam? If Sara had her way, it would be the first of many days together. But Matt had not said a word about the future.

Better not to say anything. She'd hold the memory of their special days to her heart. But practicality reasserted itself the closer she came to San Francisco. It had been a vacation fling. He had not even asked for her phone number. Never even given her the classic brush-off line of *I'll call you.* Saying he wanted to spend his next vacation with her was even more vague.

Darn it, she had loved every second with Matt. She'd gladly spend all her vacations with him. And he hadn't even asked for her phone number.

By the following Friday Sara had made some changes to her life. She wanted to plunge into sweeping changes, but found work too hectic. She had stopped off twice at the travel agency near the office—to gather packets and brochures of exotic places. She was planning to splurge on her next vacation and take one of the trips she longed for.

The frantic tax season had grabbed hold with a vengeance. Some companies had still not closed their book for the previous year. Others had audits that required readjustments to stated expenses or capital improvements. Others were looking for creative ways to defer some of the money owed until their cash flow improved. Any trips would have to wait until after April, but she could start planning now. When one of the new accountants asked her out, she said yes— once tax season was over. He had never seemed to notice her before, had the makeover at Lake Tahoe caused him to see her differently?

Amber came over Saturday night—alone. Jimmy was on duty. While happy in her new married life, she was a bit miffed things weren't going just as she'd expected.

"He's still living on base. He plans to come over when he can, but it's as if we are still dating. I hate this limbo. We don't even know where we will be living after this tour. And he's returning to Germany in another couple of weeks. If he gets posted to a U.S. base next, we want to see if I can get into a nearby college. But I should apply soon if I want to get in by fall,'' Amber complained.

''You can always apply once you know, and list the extenuating circumstances. The worse case would be wait a semester before enrolling.'' Sara didn't like that idea, but it was the best she could offer to cheer up her daughter. At least she was in school this term and wasn't flying off to Germany.

''What did you do after we left? Did you go to the spa like you talked about?'' Amber asked as she began to make a salad to accompany the spaghetti Sara was preparing.

''I did.'' And on the way met the most fantastic man.

''Was it fun?''

''Yes.'' To both.

''I like what you've done to your hair. You know, Mom, you could start dating again. I know I held you back. You should get married and have your own life now.''

''You never held me back. I have a wonderful life just as it is,'' Sara said quickly, trying not to think about her initial thoughts after the wedding—that she was once again free to do whatever she wanted. She loved her daughter.

But she was a woman and wanted the attention of a special man. Matt. What would it be like to be married to him?

Fantastic, of that she had no doubt. They'd travel, visit exciting cities she'd only been able to dream about. Maybe she could learn some of the languages he spoke, to better fit in when they stayed in Madrid or Rome.

"But it's different now. I'm gone. I have my own apartment, am married. Once Jimmy knows where he'll be next, I'll be moving there. You'll be alone," Amber persisted.

"I have lots of friends." And lots of plans. But she didn't want to share them with anyone just yet. She enjoyed daydreaming about how she was going to change her life.

"I know, but it's not the same," Amber said.

She was right about that. For four glorious days, Sara had been part of a couple. She and Matt had been practically inseparable. She loved being part of a couple. It had been so long since she'd done that, it seemed completely new and different. Of course, Matt made it memorable. She definitely planned to start dating, to seeing if there was someone out there with whom she could share her life. Doing things with another person sure beat doing it all by herself.

But not just yet. She suspected no one could measure up to Matt.

"We'll see. Right now isn't such a good time. Tax season, remember?" Should she tell Amber about Matt? Or the invitation from the man in her office?

"I know. But come the end of April would be a terrific time. Think about it, Mom."

The problem was, Sara couldn't stop thinking about her and Matt. The days at Lake Tahoe seemed like some fairy-tale story. She remembered the walks along the beach, the fun they'd had just talking. She especially remembered the kisses.

But as one week drifted into two and she heard

nothing from him, she knew she had to let that dream go. He would have returned to San Francisco long ago. Did he even remember the time they'd spent together? Or was she only one in a long line of women he dated?

She looked up Aste Technologies in the phone book. It was located on Montgomery Street, not too far from her own office. She had not resorted to seeking him out. He had given her no indications he wanted to see her again. Not that knowing that stopped her from looking closely at every dark-haired man she passed on Montgomery Street. But she drew the line at deliberately walking by his company in the hopes of running into him.

Late Wednesday afternoon Sara asked her secretary to order in a sandwich for her before she left for the day. She had scads more work to do and there was no one waiting at home. If she had something to eat, she'd be good to go for another few hours. She leaned back in her chair, resting her tense shoulders and gazing at the colorful poster she'd hung of Greece. She'd much rather be strolling along the ruins of the Parthenon than doing taxes for Herberty Construction. This weekend, she planned to buy a few things to wear when she went to Greece. Or to take that cruise to Alaska, she thought as she looked at the other poster—this one of deep blue seas, and glorious glaciers.

Her phone rang. She picked it up, sighing as she returned to reality.

"Do you have any idea of how many Simpsons there are in San Francisco?" a familiar voice asked in her ear.

"Matt?" Her heart rate sped up.

"I forgot to get your phone number. You'd checked out by the time Dex got back to the hotel. So I've been making calls ever since I got on the flight home. I tracked down your daughter a little while ago and told her I was a friend. She gave me this number. God, I've missed you."

Sara couldn't say a word. *It was Matt!* She'd given up all hope of hearing from him again.

"I can't believe it," she said softly. "You're back now? I thought you got back days ago."

"Nope. The problem turned out to be bigger than we thought. Then since I was already in The Netherlands, I took an assignment in Antwerp. But now I'm back and wanting to see you. Have dinner with me. I'll be there in ten minutes."

"It's only five-thirty, a bit early for dinner," she stalled. The stack of work on her desk had not magically shrunk while she talked. But for the first time since she had been hired, she didn't care. Dinner with Matt, she couldn't refuse!

"I didn't tell Amber about you," she said, wondering what her daughter thought when a stranger called and asked about her mother.

"So I found out. She's a bit skeptical. I bet she calls you in a minute to make sure it was all right to give me the phone number. But I convinced her it was safe for me to call you at work, rather than trying to get your home phone number. Which I do want, by the way."

Sara gave it to him, and then ran her fingers through her hair. "I'm not dressed for dinner."

"I don't care how you're dressed, or even if you're

dressed. I'll be there in ten minutes.'' The line went dead.

Sara gave a soft laugh of excitement. Matt was back and wanted to see her! She almost danced from the office. She had no other responsibilities to get in the way. Imagine going off on such short notice. She loved this empty nest life!

She told Stacey to cancel the sandwich order, then dashed to the ladies room to repair her makeup. She wished she'd worn something besides black slacks and a primrose silk blouse. Perhaps one of her new dresses, or something sexy to get his attention. Matt said he didn't care. And she didn't dare take time to go home and change. She couldn't wait to see him.

Exactly nine minutes later she stepped out on the sidewalk in front of her building. The traffic moved as it did every day at rush hour, with stops and starts. She heard the toot of a horn and saw the low-slung sports car swerve to the curb. Matt climbed out, his eyes finding hers in an instant.

''Sara.''

''Matt.'' For a moment, she couldn't speak. He looked just as gorgeous as he had in Lake Tahoe. She longed to touch him. Wished he'd kiss her. Giddy with happiness, she smiled. ''I'm so glad to see you.''

Not very sophisticated, but heartfelt. She just wanted to stand and take him all in. She hadn't realized exactly how much she'd missed him, exactly how much she'd been afraid she'd never hear from him again. The intervening days since they'd been together vanished. It was as if they'd just seen each other yesterday.

''I brought you something from Antwerp,'' he said, walking around the rear of the car. He leaned over and kissed her lightly on the lips. "Get in before some cop gives me a ticket for illegal parking."

She slid into the soft leather interior, feeling as shy as a teenager. "You've just stopped, you're not parked."

"Think that'll hold up as a defense?" he asked, going around to climb into the driver's seat.

"Where would you like to go for dinner?" he said when they started moving.

"Wherever."

"London?" he suggested.

She laughed. "Yes! Except I don't think we can get there before I starve to death." No one else she knew would suggest London for dinner. Oh how she wished they could.

"I know a great Italian place in Columbus Square," he said.

"I love Italian," she said, watching as he competently merged the car into the traffic. Dinner with Matt sure beat a takeout sandwich at her desk. Any meal with Matt beat that. For a fleeting second she considered all the work awaiting, then promptly pushed the thought away. She was taking time with Matt, she hadn't seen him in too long! There was a limit to how much she wanted to give to the office.

"Tell me about your trip," she invited, wanting to know how he spent every moment. Had he missed her at all?

"The first emergency was successfully handled, from a business stand point," he replied.

"Is there another point?"

He flicked her a glance. "I didn't used to think so, but this time I found myself wishing you had been in Amsterdam with me. You would love it. We could have sampled a different restaurant every night, taken an excursion boat on the river. The shopping is fabulous. I bet you'd like Antwerp even more—it's charming. Old, old buildings, monuments, fountains. Talk about walking around, you would never come to the hotel.''

She sighed softly. ''Maybe one day.''

He nodded.

Before long they were seated in a small alcove at the restaurant, the heavenly fragrance of oregano and garlic filling the air.

''What did you do while I was gone?'' Matt asked once their order had been taken.

''Worked. I had dinner one night with Amber and Jimmy. Otherwise, we're coming into tax season and the workload increases. Nothing exciting like visiting The Netherlands.'' She wasn't sure if she should tell him about her plans for her next vacation. Would he come with her?

''I wasn't exactly visiting—I was working,'' he protested, the amusement in his eyes letting her know his kind of work in a foreign setting didn't compare to hers.

''So are you back for long?'' she asked.

''I have to reconfirm my next assignment with the office to make sure it's still a go. But I'm home for a few days.''

''When did you get back?'' Had he not been in his office yet?

He looked at his watch. ''About an hour and a half ago. I called you on my way in from the airport. Once I knew my flight number, one of the guys at the office dropped my car for me at the airport. Saved time.''

She couldn't believe her ears. Had he been as anxious to see her as she was to see him? Then another thought struck.

"You must be exhausted."

"I'll last until after dinner at least. I wanted to see you."

"We can eat fast," she offered, touched more than she wanted to admit at his words.

He looked uncomfortable, glanced around then looked back at her. "I brought you something from Antwerp," he said.

She remembered he'd said that earlier. As if excited that she would like his present, to let her know he'd been thinking of her even when apart. She hadn't had a present from anyone but Amber in years.

"A present?" she asked.

"Sort of." He fumbled in his pocket and pulled out a jewelers box.

Sara stared at it, her breath caught in her throat. Most of the time that would be a ring box, but surely he hadn't bought her a ring!

When he flipped open the lid, she blinked at the sparkling diamond ring nestled in velvet.

"Will you marry me, Sara?"

CHAPTER THREE

SARA stared at the ring, then slowly raised her eyes to his. "Marry you?" she whispered.

"I was hoping you missed me as much as I missed you. We had a great time at Lake Tahoe. Think of the life we could have together. We're just perfect for each other. Our lifestyles match. Quit your job, come with me wherever I go. I can arrange to take some extra time with most assignments so it won't be all work. I'm going to London next week, if the assignment still holds. I still need to verify it. If so, let's spend our honeymoon there."

He'd never asked a woman to marry him before. But Sara was different. She was easy to be with, and fun at the same time—not to mention sexy. He didn't have to worry about her wanting to start a family and buying some house in the suburbs, her daughter was already grown. He could support them both. They could travel, maybe make London their home for a few years while he concentrated on European accounts. That would save time flying over every couple of weeks.

Sara was in shock. She'd known him less than a week, all told. He was virtually a stranger. How could she marry a stranger?

Yet she had loved every moment they spent together. She would forever remember the fabulous days at Lake Tahoe. She would also remember the indecision and worry that he wouldn't call. She loved being with him. Her fantasies all centered around Matt. She'd known she'd fallen for him. But marriage? Forever? Would it be possible?

For a moment she let herself dream…

What did she want? To spend her life doing the accounts for businessmen who argued every point with her, or spend it jetting to the far flung corners of the world with the most exciting man she'd ever met? Dare she take such a risk and go for it? She was footloose and fancy free. Amber had her own life now, with Jimmy. Why not grab the happiness that dangled so temptingly in front of her?

As the seconds ticked by, Matt's expression grew more impassive.

"Forget it," he said, flipping shut the box. "Silly idea."

"It's not at all. You caught me by surprise, but I say yes!" She felt young and alive and daring all rolled up into one. She hadn't felt this way since— ever!

He rose and pulled her to her feet, kissing her like she'd never been kissed before. Several of the other patrons of the restaurant clapped, obviously knowing something was going on.

When the waiter hurried over, Matt stepped back and reseated Sara. "Champagne, please, she's agreed to marry me!"

Once he was seated, he reached for her hand, slipping the ring on her finger. It fit perfectly.

"I wasn't sure you'd even call," Sara said, studying the sparkling stone in total disbelief. Had she really just agreed to marry Matt?

"You must have known I'd find you again. You

are too special to let go," he said, taking her fingers in his hand, caressing the backs with his thumb. "This is probably rushing things, but I want you, Sara, and I don't want some other guy honing in on my woman."

"That sounds like a pick up line," she teased, not sure how to handle the emotions that threatened to overwhelm her. Oh, she'd have to cancel her date with Tim, she thought briefly, staring into Matt's eyes. How could she ever have thought she'd enjoy herself with someone else?

"I have never told another woman that. Nor asked another woman to marry me. Actually I never thought I would marry. But you and I will be perfect together. We'll make the entire world ours! We'll travel. Sometime on business, but plenty of time on our own. You can make up a list of all the sights you want to see. The world will be our backyard. There's nothing to tie us down."

"Sounds fabulous. I pick London first. No, wait, maybe Paris. No, how about Sydney?"

"We'll get to them all eventually." He kissed her fingers, squeezing gently in affection.

The comment he made sank in. "You never thought to marry, why not? You're terrific. Any woman would be delighted to share her life with you!" She looked at him, still a bit shocked she'd agreed to marry again. Her brief experience in wedded bliss hadn't been good enough to recommend she try again. With Matt it would be so different.

"Ah, a man never tires of having his future wife think he's fabulous." The champagne arrived and the waiter poured them both a glass, setting them before them with a flourish.

"To my wife-to-be," Matt said, raising his glass to her.

Wife. Ohmygod, Sara thought, as panic suddenly struck. She was going to be a wife again! To trust her future to this man she'd only met a few weeks ago. Had she lost her mind?

"To us," she said, touching her glass to his.

Granted, she hadn't known him for long, but she trusted Matt in a very basic way. And knowing someone for ages didn't guarantee anything, look at her and Bill. They'd known each other for years and he had walked out without a look behind. Some men were steadfast, some weren't.

"Next week London, who knows after that?" Matt said.

"You're serious about next week?" she asked. "And London?"

"Of course, weren't you? You do have a passport, don't you?"

She shook her head. Why would she have needed a passport before now, she never traveled?

"Not to worry, we'll get one through the office. They expedite things all the time with new employees. I'm sure we can get you one in time. Do you want to get married in a church, or at City Hall?"

"My church, please. And I'll have to arrange some time off from work. Good thing I have a lot of vacation time accrued." The enormity of what she'd agreed to began to sink in. And vacation time owed or not, her boss would have a fit with her taking off during tax season. And what would everyone say— no one even knew she'd been seeing anyone.

"Quit your job, cut your ties, let's fly where the mood takes us. After London, we'll sit down and decide what you'd like to see first and then I'll see what assignments I can wrangle for those locations. With the threat of terrorist activities or global viruses, there are more and more assignments each month at the firm. We are expanding almost faster than we can train representatives.''

"I'd love to see all of Europe, then work our way down-under to Australia and New Zealand," she said, as giddy as a child at Christmas. Her lifelong dreams were coming true. And she'd see them all with Matt. How cool was that!

Her heart raced, almost hurting with so much happiness. Who ever would have thought Sara Simpson would one day be married again, and off to see the world?

"Oh, where will we live? My apartment isn't very spacious," she said, reality inserting itself. It was downright small. And Amber still had a lot of her things there. Amber—she'd have to tell her daughter right away. What would Amber think about getting a stepfather at this late date?

"We'll get a place of our own. My apartment is small, too. We'll find something we both like and combine households," Matt said.

"I need to call Amber. She'll want to meet you." Amber was going to be shocked. None of this sounded like the old Sara.

He shook his head. "I never figured myself as father material. Good thing she's grown and married. Maybe we could all have dinner tomorrow night."

"I'll call her as soon as we get home." She hoped Amber liked Matt. What if she didn't? No, that was the wrong attitude. How could she not like him?

Dinner arrived and Sara spend the rest of the time

quizzing Matt on where they'd go in London and how long they'd stay. She came up with a dozen things she'd need to do to get ready for a wedding in a week's time.

"I can't believe we're doing this," she said as they left the restaurant.

"Second thoughts?" he asked.

"Not one!"

When he pulled into the curb at her apartment, she invited him up.

"Much as I'd love to, sweetheart, I'm bushed. I've been up more than twenty-four hours now and need to get some sleep. I'll call you tomorrow afternoon, and we'll decide where to take Amber and Jimmy for dinner," he said.

His kiss belied his fatigue, despite the contortions they had to do in the small car. Sara's entire body was pulsing with desire and delight by the time he ended the embrace. She wished he'd come up more than ever. But she could wait. Their coming together would be all the sweeter with anticipation.

As soon as Matt left, she called Amber.

"Hi, Mom, I've been trying to reach you. Did some guy call you at work? I gave him your number, but then wasn't sure I should have."

"You definitely should have. His name is Matt Tucker."

"I don't remember hearing about him before. Does he work at your office? Of course not, he wouldn't need the number if he did. Who is he?"

"As of this evening, he's my fiancé," Sara said.

The silence at the other end was deafening.

"Amber?" Maybe she should have explained more

before blurting out the news. But she wanted to shout it from the rooftops. Matt Tucker wanted to marry her, Sara Simpson!

"Mom, did you just say fiancé?"

"I did."

"I didn't even know you were dating. When did all this happen?"

"The proposal was tonight. We're planning to be married next week. We're honeymooning in London." *Honeymooning! London!* Sara still couldn't believe the words tripped from her mouth so easily. She wished they were already married. It had only been moments since he'd left, and she missed him.

"Next week? Mom, I haven't even met the guy. How can you get married so soon? And why? You don't have to, do you? I mean, you're not pregnant or anything are you?" Amber sounded worried.

"No, I'm not pregnant. I've had my family, you know that. Matt and I met in Lake Tahoe right after your wedding. We spent some glorious days together and realized when he got home tonight how much we missed each other."

"So you're getting married next week? Couldn't you, um, be engaged for a while?"

"You and Jimmy got married with short notice." Great, now she was comparing herself with her daughter. It was enough that she knew her own mind. She didn't need to justify her decision with anyone, not even Amber.

Maybe there was a hint of uncertainty lurking, but she wouldn't admit it. She wanted to marry Matt, explore the world, live a little. She was only thirty-eight years old, not too old to still have fun.

"I haven't even met the guy," Amber wailed.

"I know. Matt and I want to invite you and Jimmy to dinner tomorrow night. You can meet him then."

"I can't say if Jimmy can make it. He's at the base and has been working late most nights. I'll see. But I'm definitely coming. In fact, maybe I'll come over to your place now—is he there?"

"No, he just got in from Amsterdam. He's been up for twenty-four hours and needed rest. You can meet him tomorrow."

"Fine. Gosh, Mom, this doesn't sound a bit like you."

Sara smiled as she put down the receiver. It didn't sound like the old her. But it was definitely the new!

The week flew by. She and Matt spent as much time together as they could with their work schedules. His kisses left her breathless. His touch sent her senses into overdrive. But he restrained himself every night, leaving her at the door of her apartment as if afraid the temptation for more than kisses would be too strong if he came into her home. She was honored—and frustrated—by the respect he showed. They would be married forever, he said. He could wait a few more days before consummating their love.

Sara wasn't sure she would have been as noble given the choice.

Thursday morning dawned cold and clear. The sky was a deep blue, without clouds. The breeze from the Bay was light, though chilly. The weather was perfect for a wedding.

Sara found a cream-colored dress to wear, complete with wispy hat to give it a bridal touch. She had arranged for time off again from work, though her boss, Mr. Pepovich, was concerned that she be able to get all her clients handled in the time remaining until tax day. She hadn't told him of her intent to quit. She wouldn't leave him in the lurch, but the plans she and Matt had made were important, too. She couldn't wait to be off to explore the world.

The ceremony went without a hitch. Dex was Matt's best man, and Amber stood up with her mother. She hadn't fully accepted the idea, but was cordial to Matt. She kept eyeing Sara as if she was one brick short of a load. She voiced no objections to the wedding, but had constantly questioned Sara on her certainty that it was the right move right up until last night. Seeing her mother was adamant, she gave in with good grace.

Once the formalities were taken care of, there was a small reception. Sara and Matt had invited a dozen or so friends each. The church hall held them all easily. Soft music played in the background. The caterer had prepared a light lunch complete with wedding cake.

At one point during the reception, she and Matt became separated. She spoke with old friends, laughed at the teasing from her coworkers about her whirlwind courtship, and kept an eye on things to make sure everyone was enjoying the event.

Already missing Matt, she spotted him in conversation with Dex and headed their way. Their backs were to her, but she didn't care. She'd just slip to his side and see how long it took him to notice her.

"...believe the playboy of the western world is now a married man," Dex was saying as she drew closer. Sara smiled. So Matt had a playboy reputation, interesting, if not surprising. Look how quickly he'd charmed her at the casino in Reno.

"Why not, Sara is perfect for me. She's had her

family, isn't yearning for a house and white picket fence. She wants to travel, and we all know my job has me on the road three weeks out of four. I tell you, Dex, she's the best thing to happen to me. We can explore every city I'm assigned, take some trips to others when we can. We'll still have a home base here in San Francisco. What's not to like about married life?''

"No kids in the picture?"

Sara hesitated a moment. They had never discussed children. The only reference Matt had made was an offhand comment about how he couldn't picture himself as a father. Would he want children?

"That's the beauty of it, she's had her family. Amber is all grown and doesn't need a stay-at-home mother. And let's face it, can you picture me as a father?'' Matt asked.

"Don't let your past color your future, friend,'' Dex said. "You never pictured yourself as a husband, either, and here you are.''

Past? The comment puzzled Sara. Matt had said he'd grown up under the care of an uncle. Had something happened to put him off having children?

He turned and saw her, his slow smile turning her insides mushy.

"Come here, Mrs. Tucker, Dex was just telling me how envious he is of us.''

Dex raised his glass in silent salute. "I wish for you both a long and happy life together.''

"Thank you, Dex. I suspect I'll see a lot of you over the years, seeing you and Matt are such good friends. You'll always be welcomed in our home,'' Sara said, stepping close to Matt as he put his arm across her shoulder.

"Hey, old friend, you picked a winner," Dex said, clapping Matt on the other shoulder.

"Mom?" Amber joined them. She smiled at Matt and Dex. "It's time to cut the cake you two, and then you have to get going. Your plane leaves in less than four hours."

As she and her new husband went to cut the wedding cake, Sara made a mental note to ask Matt later about Dex's comment. But there was too much going on now to have a discussion they probably should have had before.

When it came time to toss the bride's bouquet, Sara flipped it over her head, right into the arms of her best friend from work. She laughed when MaryEllen looked right at Dex. Maybe Matt's friend would be next to the altar.

A half hour later Matt told her it was time to leave. She found Amber and Jimmy near the edge of the group. She gave her daughter a big hug, then Jimmy.

"Be happy, Mom," she said.

"Take care of her, sir," Jimmy said to Matt.

Sara had to smile, touched Jimmy felt the need to be protective.

"I'm sure we'll be as happy as you," Sara replied.

Amber made a face. "At least you and your husband get to make a home together. Jimmy still thinks of the Army barracks as home, and it's like he's visiting at our place."

"Hey, Amber, I explained. It's not like it's forever," Jimmy protested.

"Honey, once this assignment is finished, he'll be rotated stateside and you'll be able to get a place together. You return to Germany soon, don't you?" Sara asked Jimmy.

"In a couple of weeks. Anyway, I'm with you this weekend, Amber," he said, throwing his arm across her shoulders.

"There is that," she said, smiling at him. Looking back at Sara, she said, "We're fine. You have a great time in London. I know you've always wanted to see Big Ben and Westminster Abbey and the Crown Jewels."

Amidst a flurry of activity, Matt and Sara headed for their car. Their bags had been packed before the ceremony. They were ready to head to the airport— and their new life together.

The vague feeling of uncertainty had fled. Committed to making her marriage the best thing in the world, Sara looked forward to starting her life with Matt. Her rings shone in the light, the diamond and the plain gold circle. They were bound forever. She hoped they'd be as happy forever as they were this day.

It was morning when they landed in London, but Matt wasted no time in sweeping her into their hotel room, and into bed. His expertise in making love enthralled Sara. She had only vague memories of her first husband, but remembered none of the passion and delight she found with Matt. The long, lonely years had been worth the wait, she thought the next morning, relishing every moment of the night they'd shared. Rolling over in the big bed and finding him there was a pleasure she was sure to repeat for the rest of their lives.

He opened his eyes, drew her close and began to kiss her as if they had all the time in the world. Giving herself to the joy of his touch, Sara knew she'd found her soulmate.

The days in London flew by. Sara initially had reservations about a working honeymoon, but Matt made sure he spent as much time as he could with her. When he was tied up with the client, the local firm had a secretary who offered to accompany Sara wherever she wanted to go. Being London-born and bred, Talia Cummings was the perfect guide.

Though she enjoyed seeing the sights with Talia, Sara loved the moments shared with Matt the most. They saw a show in the West End, took a horse ride in Hyde Park, viewed the crown jewels in the Tower of London, and ate cream tea every day.

"I could live here," Sara said one afternoon as they were wandering through Harrods. "I love London."

"There is still more to see. On our next trip, we can extend ourselves beyond the city," he said. "I thought of transferring here—we could make it our home base for a few years."

"I should love to see Stonehenge, and the Cotswolds and Hadrian's Wall. Could we really live here? I'd get to see it all."

"Not to mention Scotland and Wales."

"Ah, no wonder you are the perfect man, you know how to please a woman."

"Not only traveling, I hope," he said, trailing his finger tips down her cheek. His touch had her forgetting the chess set she'd been examining and turn to him. Would he think her silly if she suggested they return to their hotel room in the middle of the afternoon?

"No, not only traveling," she replied, remembering their nights together. Could life be any more perfect? In the past were the worries she had about raising a child single-handedly, about where to live, how to afford basic necessities. The struggle had paid off, and now she was able to enjoy the reward. And what a reward it was. Matt and London.

Might as well be daring.

"Want to take a nap?" she asked provocatively.

He smiled that slow smile of his that set her heart to racing. "Sleepy?"

"Not exactly," she said, her eyes holding his, seeing the spark of desire flare.

"Me, either, but I think returning to our room might be a very good thing."

And so it proved to be.

Sara had never expected life to turn out perfect, yet their week in London seemed to be as perfect as could be.

She wished they could have stayed longer as they boarded the flight back to San Francisco.

"As a honeymoon, this couldn't have been better," she said, snuggling up against Matt as the plane taxied on the runway. "Are you serious about finding a place here?"

"It's something to look into."

What would she do about Amber?

"Actually, if I hadn't had to work, it would have been better," he said.

"A few hours here and there. I shopped which you don't like, so as I said, perfect."

"So I should plan to make myself scarce at suitable points on other trips so you can help the local economy?'' he asked, brushing his lips against her forehead. His hand tightened its grip on hers. ''I wish we were alone on the plane,'' he said, his dark gaze holding hers. ''It's a long flight to San Francisco.''

CHAPTER FOUR

WHEN they landed at San Francisco International Airport, it was raining. They passed through customs with no problem and before long were in Matt's sports car heading toward the city.

Sara was almost asleep. She had not slept on the long flight and now had been up more than twenty hours. How had Matt stood it when he'd returned from Amsterdam a couple of weeks ago? She'd have wanted to go straight to bed.

"Where are we going?" she asked.

He glanced at her. "Home, where else?"

"And that would be your place or mine?" Despite all the time they'd had since he'd proposed, no firm plans had been made on where they would live. First she'd rushed through the wedding, then getting her passport, wrapping up as much as she could at work.

Matt had been equally busy after being gone so long from his office. Then they'd taken off for London. How could they have left such a basic discussion remain in abeyance so long? Now the question had to be answered.

"My place tonight. Unless you'd rather go to yours."

"I have a small bed," she said, feeling a bit surreal. They'd been married a week and neither had seen the other's bedroom. Did he have a huge bed, or a small single like hers?

"I have a king-size. We'll have to squeeze into my

place until we find a place of our own. Unless you'd rather we squeeze into yours.''

Sara considered the prospects, neither a good choice. Her apartment was tiny. At least there were two bedrooms, so it offered a bit more room than Matt's one-bedroom apartment. But she opted for Matt's place. The bed was the selling point. They couldn't both share hers.

Half an hour later he pulled into the parking garage beneath the apartment building. Sara was almost asleep and had to force herself out of the car. How long until she could be in bed?

They rode in silence up to his floor. At the door, Matt dropped the suitcases. He unlocked the door, and pushed it open, surprising Sara by sweeping her off her feet and carrying her across the threshold.

''Wow,'' she said, laughing up at him.

''Welcome to our home, Mrs. Tucker,'' he said, setting her on her feet and kissing her.

Sara's fatigue fled instantly and she relished the kiss. Matt's very touch was like magic to her. Winding her arms around his neck, she kissed him back.

When he ended the kiss, he quickly picked up their bags and closed the door to the world.

The next morning Sara awoke first. She lay snuggled against her husband, marveling at the changes in the last month. She still couldn't believe she was married. That she'd been to London. Unfortunately honeymoons didn't last forever. She had to get into work today. And she knew there'd be a stack of work awaiting. Her assistant didn't have the experience to deal with the more complex client books. And even the ones she could handle, Sara would still have to review and give her approval.

Slowly she gazed around the bedroom. It was spartan and austere. A bed, a dresser and a night table with a lamp. Would Matt mind when they got a place together if she made it a bit more homey? She didn't like the cluttered look, but she did want a few pictures on the wall.

The view from his place was spectacular. Maybe that's why he didn't have pictures. He hadn't put curtains on the windows. The panoramic view of San Francisco Bay and the Golden Gate Bridge was always a sight she'd never tire of seeing. She hoped they could get a similar view in their new apartment.

"Let's pretend we didn't get back last night," Matt said softly.

She looked at him, thrilled at the desire she saw in his eyes.

"And?"

"And stay right here all day." He drew her closer and kissed her, his hand moving over her, touching her as he'd done so many times during the last week. Every cell went on alert as his caresses turned bolder.

She laughed softly. "I'd love nothing more, but there's work to be done."

"I knew you'd say that." He made no move to stop.

"But I don't have to be there until nine," she said suggestively and began to trace patterns against his muscular chest.

"Still too early," he said before his mouth covered hers.

*   *   *

"We need to find a bigger place," Matt said later as they prepared breakfast. Sara was trying to find enough food for a meal with the meager supplies in his cupboard. No eggs, cereal or fresh milk. She found some bagels in the freezer and made do with them and some of the cheese she found.

Matt made the coffee, bumping into her more than once. She couldn't tell if it were deliberate or not, but didn't mind a bit.

"Where do you want to live?" she asked.

"Here, only in a bigger place until we decide about London. I'll check with the manager and see if there is something open on another floor."

"And if not?" While she liked the idea of moving to London, she had asked him to take things slowly. She still had Amber to consider.

"Then we'll have to locate another place. How about you? Suggestions?"

"Can we afford the Marina area?" She'd always loved walking over from her apartment to see the Bay. How terrific to live where she could see the view from her own home. But apartments and houses here were extremely expensive.

He looked at her consideringly. "Sara, I have enough money to assure we can live wherever you want."

"Oh." They hadn't discussed finances. In fact they hadn't discussed a lot of basic things. Time in the years ahead, she thought.

"I'll check with the manager and if there's nothing open in this building, we'll branch out. I'd like to find a place quickly so we can combine households. It's inefficient to have two separate places."

"I know, I feel like I'm camping out, or on a

spend-the-night with a friend,'' she said, reaching for a bagel as it popped up in the toaster.

''And how many spend-the-nights with a friend did you do?'' he growled, stopping her hand and swinging her around to face him.

''None since Amber was born. But Jenny Knight and I used to take turns all the time in high school.''

''Girlfriends?'' he said.

''You thought boyfriends?'' she teased, surprised at the hint of jealousy that showed in his face.

''Why not, you're beautiful, fun to be around, sexy, intriguing. Why wouldn't the men be swarming at your feet?''

She wrinkled her nose. ''Most men don't swarm around a mother with a little child to care for.''

''Ah, then my timing was excellent—another week, what with Amber married off, and the swarm would have begun.''

She laughed and reached up to kiss him. She loved this wildly sexy man and his flattering speech.

A week away was either too much, or not nearly enough, Sara thought as she walked into her office at nine. She had more work than she thought she could ever get through. Maybe she shouldn't have taken off until after the tax deadline. Time away from the office at this point hadn't been such a great idea. Now she had to pay the piper.

''Ah, Sara,'' Mr. Pepovich stepped into the doorway.

Sara smiled at her boss. ''Hello, sir. Managed fine without me, I see,'' she said, placing her purse in the top drawer as normal.

''Not at all, my dear. I've asked your assistant to

bring you up to speed as soon as you are ready. There's probably more than you'll be expecting, but to tell the truth there aren't many accountants with the firm I trust as much as I do you," he said. He glanced at the stack of folders on her desk.

"I hope you realize what a valued employee you are," he said. A small smile touched his lips. "Actually, maybe it's even better that I realize what a valued employee you are. I'm glad you're back!"

"Thank you, it's good to be back."

Sara called her assistant in and they began to review what had transpired during the last week. Occasionally during the day, Sara would think back to the week in London. It already seemed like a dream. Only the stack of financial records in front of her seemed real.

Sara was still working at six that evening when her phone rang directly to her office. The switchboard had closed at five. This was someone who had her personal extension.

"Mom? I didn't know if you were back or not. I left you several messages. Didn't you get them?" Amber's voice came across the line.

"Hi, honey. I haven't been home yet. To our apartment, I mean. We got in last night and stayed at Matt's place." Sara leaned back against her chair, tired enough to call it quits, but with more she wanted to finish before calling it a day.

"Too late to call?" Amber said. "Was your flight late?"

Oops. No they had not gotten in too late to call, but any thought of contacting her daughter had fled when Matt had kissed her. How could a mother explain that?

"Sorry. Don't worry, you can tell we got home safely. How are you?"

"Fine. Did you have fun?" Amber asked.

"Yes. London was magical." She'd enjoyed every moment spent with her new husband.

Thinking of Matt made her warm all over. She pushed aside the folder she'd been working on. It could wait. As soon as she was finished talking with Amber, she was heading home.

"Want to get together for dinner or lunch or something?" Amber asked.

"Is something wrong?" Sara immediately switched back into Mom mode.

Amber laughed. "No, Mom, nothing's wrong. I want to hear all about being married and your honeymoon in London, that's all. Of course, if you can't spare the time, I'd understand."

"Lunch tomorrow," Sara said firmly, marking it on her calendar. She remembered Friday was the day Amber didn't have classes. "Meet me at the Pelican Room on Montgomery Street at eleven-thirty and we'll beat the rush."

"Okay. Tell my new dad hi for me."

Sara smiled at the nonsense. She could just imagine Matt's face if Amber really started calling him Dad. He'd said he couldn't picture himself as a father. She couldn't either. He was too exciting and free a man to be a father who played ball with his kids, or attended school functions.

Matt stood at the window gazing out at the Bay. It was dark, after six, and where the hell was Sara? He'd tried her office number earlier, but it only rang and rang. Obviously the switchboard had closed for the night. But if she was going to work late, she needed a cell phone or something so he could reach her.

And she needed to remember she was married now and had someone worrying about her when she wasn't where he thought she should be.

There would be a period of adjustment for them both. She worked long hours at tax time, she'd told him that. But hearing it and experiencing it were two different things.

He wanted her home with him.

He'd have taken her with him to work if he could have done so.

First thing tonight, he wanted to discuss her giving up her job so they could be together when he was free. No time like the present to quit. There was plenty to do with finding a new apartment and getting settled. He still wanted to make London their base, but she'd asked for time—still watching over her daughter. But Amber was married and he suspected didn't need her mother's watchful eye. It wouldn't be long before Sara would want to move. He could be patient in the meantime.

He heard the key in the lock. His feeling of anticipation soared. Turning, he crossed the room swiftly, flinging wide the door, and looking at her.

She was so beautiful his teeth almost ached. She smiled broadly and stepped into his arms, lifting her mouth for his kiss. Wildly Matt wondered if she'd be willing to postpone dinner while they detoured through the bedroom.

"I thought you were never coming home," he said a few moments later when Sara shrugged out of her coat, dropped a heavy briefcase on the chair.

"I still have tons of work to do. But I wanted to

get home to you,'' she said, brushing his cheek with her fingers.

He caught her hand and kissed her palm, needing some contact with her. He'd never expected to feel this loss when she was absent. Nor feel connected somehow when she was with him.

"I don't have any more food in the house tonight than we did this morning. We'll have to go out to dinner,'' he said, hoping she'd rather order in.

"Is that your normal way, eat out all the time?'' she asked, kicking off her shoes.

"Yeah, works for me.''

"Well, now you have a wife who enjoys cooking, so we don't have to go out all the time. I want to change my clothes before we do anything,'' she said heading for the bedroom.

If she had to get out of those clothes anyway…

He followed her into the bedroom.

Some time later Matt drove to a small Chinese restaurant on Lombard Street.

As they were eating, Sara said, "I have to stop by the apartment and get some more clothes. Amber called today. She'd left some messages on my machine. I need to check and see if anyone else called.''

"Fine.'' As long as she didn't stay at the apartment, they could stop there as often as she wanted. He liked having her in his place. And in his bed.

"We also need to stop at the supermarket for some food,'' she added.

"Tonight?'' he asked.

"Yes. What were you planning to have for breakfast if we don't get something?''

"We could eat out.''

"Are you made of money?" she asked.

Matt went quiet. They'd never discussed finances in any detail. He suspected Sara hadn't a clue how much money he did have. Aste was a huge success. He and Dex and Tony had made millions the first five years in business. And he had not spent much of it. Even if he quit work today, he'd have enough invested to live comfortably for the rest of his life.

He reached for her hand.

"Sara, I have enough money to cover any expenses we come up with. If we want to eat out every meal, we can. If we want to hire a cook for our meals, that'll work. If you want to cook, that's fine by me, but only if you want to."

She stared at him for a long moment, then shook her head.

"I'm not sure I can comprehend that," she said. "For so long I've pinched pennies to make ends meet. It was so hard when Amber was little. We didn't live in a nice neighborhood or have enough money for the toys I wished I could have given her. Sometimes I had to walk to school and then to work because I couldn't even afford bus fare."

"You don't have money worries now," Matt said.

"No, I don't. I make a good income, but I still watch where we spend the money."

"I meant, with me," he said. He certainly couldn't accuse Sara of being a gold digger. She seemed to have a hard time remembering they were married, a couple who shared everything. He didn't need his wife to work. And she need never worry about money again.

"Oh."

''I wanted you to know so you won't worry about quitting your job.''

''Quitting my job?'' she repeated.

He nodded. ''We talked about it, remember? So you can travel with me.''

''I remember.''

''But?'' Matt didn't like the stubborn look that appeared. Nor did he like it when she withdrew her hand.

''But not yet,'' she said, beginning to eat again.

''Not yet? Why not? I'll be getting another assignment soon. Who knows where, but you'll want to go, right?''

She nodded. ''If I can get time off.''

''If you can get time off! Sara, take the time. Quit the blasted job and come with me.''

''You don't know that you'll get an assignment soon. Besides, I can't leave the company in the lurch at this time of year. You know it's the busiest time.'' Her tone was reasonable, but he didn't like what she was saying.

''They'll find another accountant.''

''My boss told me today how valued an employee I am.''

''He's undoubtably right about that. Should have told you long ago.'' And paid her more. Heck, made her a partner. No, not that. A partnership would be hard to leave.

''Maybe my being away helped him realize that,'' she said, smiling. ''Eat up, Matt. We can discuss this later. We still have to visit the supermarket, don't forget.''

Matt ate the remainder of his meal in silence, studying his new wife. That conversation had not gone the way he wanted. He'd thought she'd be thrilled to learn money was not an issue. Be glad to quit her job and plan their next trip together.

Instead she acted as if he was being unreasonable expecting her to give up the work to travel. Which is what she said she wanted.

Women. He knew he'd never understand them. Where was the logic in her thinking?

Sara ate, forcing the food down. It tasted like card-board. She tried to keep a bright smile on her face, but it was an effort. She felt panic at the thought of quitting her job. She'd worked so hard to put herself through college, get her degree and then the job at the firm. How could she just quit?

What would happen to her if Matt left?

The thought stunned her. She looked at her plate, not seeing the egg rolls and sweet and sour pork, but seeing Bill walk out on her and Amber. Seeing the years of struggle with no help to speak of. The fear that had lived with her for so long that she'd be des-titute.

How could she fear Matt would leave? The circum-stances were totally different. He wasn't some young boy just out of high school, but a man who knew his own mind. She wasn't the uneducated mother of an infant struggling to make ends meet.

Still, the need for security proved stronger than she expected. It was one thing for him to say he had money, something else for her to be dependent on his money. *What if he left?*

"I'm finished," she said, pushing away the plate. Her appetite had fled. The happiness that had bubbled around her for weeks evaporated. For the first time she took a long look at where she was and what she'd done.

She'd married a man she hardly knew. So far married life had been perfect. What happened when it didn't go as they wanted? How would they weather hard times—united, or divided?

Dare she risk her security on a man she hardly knew?

She loved Matt, but as she watched him summon the waiter and settle the bill, it struck her—he had never told her he loved her.

Don't be silly, she scolded herself as they walked out of the restaurant. Of course he loved her. Hadn't he proved that a dozen ways? Men were not as free with emotional revelations as women. Just because he hadn't said the words didn't mean anything. Obviously not, since tonight was the first time she'd realized the lack.

"Where to first, your place or the supermarket?" he asked as he held the car door.

"My place. We'll see what I have on hand that we can take to your apartment and then I'll know more what to get at the store."

"*Our* apartment," he growled.

"Oops, sorry," she apologized. Touchy, wasn't he? It would take a while to adjust to being married, she thought. And the sooner they found a place that was theirs, the easier it would be. No matter what he said, the apartment felt like it was his. Just as her place was hers. He didn't even want to stay at her apartment, at least she'd compromised enough to agree to move into his until they found a larger place.

* * *

The next morning Sara was swamped. Her work seemed to have multiplied overnight and she wondered if she slept in her office, she'd find gremlins mass producing new accounts at midnight each night.

Despite the increase in workload, she left in plenty of time to meet Amber for lunch. The week and a day since the wedding was one of the longest stretches she'd been apart from her daughter. She missed her. She had thought it would be cool to live in London, but now she wasn't sure. Amber would be so far away. They didn't have to decide immediately.

Today, she wanted to catch up on all her news, how her classes was going, if she and Jimmy had heard any more about where his next posting would be. To see if she had any questions now as a married woman she hadn't had before.

Sara arrived before Amber and picked a quiet table in the back. Waving when she spotted her daughter, she rose and hugged her.

"It's so good to see you, honey," she said, brushing back Amber's blond hair, windblown from the breeze.

"It's great to see you, Mom. Wow, you look ten years younger. Being married must agree with you."

"With Matt it does," Sara confirmed, sitting at the table.

When Amber slid into the seat across from her, Sara studied her. "You look tired, honey."

"A bit. The quarter will be ending soon and I'm slogging through for finals."

Once their order had been placed, Sara smiled at her daughter.

"How's married life?" Sara asked, expecting a glowing report, like the one she'd give if asked.

"Okay. Not what I thought it would be," Amber said, studying the menu.

"Only okay?" Never in her wildest dreams could Sara quantify her marriage as *okay*. She missed Matt. Even the difference of opinion last night had been a small blip on the great scheme of happiness. As if he were making up for something, their lovemaking had been fantastic.

"Actually, I don't much feel married. Jimmy is on base all the time. He spends the weekends with me, but says it's too much trouble to fight the traffic to get to my place during the week, when he has to be on duty so early the next morning." Amber sipped her water, and looked around the restaurant. Looking back at her mother, she shrugged. "I guess I thought it would be fireworks. Instead I'm still studying and he's still in the Army. He returns to Germany in another week."

"It'll be different when you two live together," Sara said, wondering why Jimmy wasn't pushing to make sure he and Amber spent as much time together as possible before he returned to Germany. They would be six months apart when he departed.

"I know. When he gets rotated Stateside, I hope we are posted somewhere away from California," Amber said.

"What?" Sara had known there was a big possibility they'd be posted outside California. She didn't want to think about not being close to Amber. But to hear her daughter say it surprised her.

"Virginia is driving me crazy. She's forever stopping over and bringing goodies, as if I don't know how to cook or something. 'Jimmy loves my brownies,' or 'Jimmy can't get enough of my lemon me-

ringue pie.' Sheesh, he hardly eats at my place anyway. We go out on the weekends and he's at the base
the rest of the time.''

''He's her only son, she's probably glad he's back
for a while and just wants to do things for him,'' Sara
said gently, remembering how overprotective Virginia
Woodworth could be.

Their food was served and they began to eat.

Amber looked at her mother and smiled. ''So, tell
me about being married to that hunk and how your
honeymoon was.''

''It's terrific. And the honeymoon was wonderful.
We saw Big Ben, heard it chime. Toured Westminster
Abbey, and the Houses of Parliament. Did you know
they bury people right in the walkways of the church?
I rode a double-decker bus and—''

''Mom,'' Amber said, laughing. ''I don't want a
sight-seeing guide, I want to hear detail about you
and Matt.''

''X-rated,'' Sara said with satisfaction.

''Wow,'' Amber's expression picked up. ''Tell all.''

''I hardly think it's appropriate,'' Sara said, then
giggled. ''Oh, my, if I had had any idea what I'd been
missing all those years, I would have started dating
when you were one!''

''I doubt you would have found many men like
Matt Tucker,'' Amber said dryly. ''He seems one of
a kind to me.''

''I believe you're right,'' Sara said, knowing she
had a sappy smile on her face. But just thinking about
the man made her insides tingle and her heart pound.
She glanced at her watch. Another six hours until she
saw him again.

*　　*　　*

It was closer to eight hours later when Matt arrived home. Sara had beat him by more than an hour. She'd changed, and prepared dinner. When he hadn't arrived by seven, she began to worry. When he opened the door, she felt a wave of relief.

"I thought you'd gotten lost," she said, running to meet him.

"Tough day," he said, drawing her into his embrace and kissing her. Then he lifted his head and sniffed.

"Something smells terrific, and it isn't just you."

"Nothing fancy, just spaghetti and meatballs, garlic bread and salad. This weekend we need to stock up on your pantry. Our pantry," she quickly corrected herself. This was their place, until they found another. She needed to remember that.

He took off his jacket and tossed it on the sofa. "Won't be here this weekend. Pack your bags, sweetheart, we're off to Paris!"

"Matt, Paris!" Her favorite dream, visiting that old city, walking along the Seine, riding up the Eiffel Tower and seeing the entire the City of Lights spread before her.

"I can't." The disappointment was tangible.

"What do you mean, you can't? You said you wanted to see Paris."

"I do, but I can't ask for more time off. I've had two weeks in the last month. This is our busy season. I can't expect the others to shoulder my workload."

"Quit the damn job."

She jerked as if she'd been slapped. "It's my career," she said with dignity. "I'm not asking you to give up yours."

"Mine pays a lot more and offers perks you could never dream of. I thought you wanted to be footloose and fancy-free—going where we could when we could."

"I do. But to quit my job…"

"Independence is a fine thing, Sara. I admire you for all you've done with your life. But live a little. Come with me," he coaxed.

She was so tempted. But doubts rose. She knew they'd talked about her leaving her job and going with him when he went on assignments, but somehow she'd thought of it more like daydreaming. Or long vacations from work. She hadn't really thought it through. What if something happened? She would need a way to support herself. She had a good job, with seniority, the respect of her boss and coworkers. She couldn't just chuck it all for a fling in Paris.

"I can't, Matt."

"Can't? Or won't?" he asked.

"Be reasonable, I've worked hard to get where I am. I can't just leave it all behind."

"We planned to travel, to see the world together. That's what you said you wanted." He had a hard edge to his voice.

"I do want that. I can get more time off after April, really."

"So you'll skip Paris for a bunch of tax forms?"

"I'm sure you'll go again before we die," she said, struggling to keep from throwing herself into his arms and agreeing to anything he wanted. "Can't you see my side of it?" she asked.

"No," he said. "I have money, that's not an issue. You said you wanted to travel, so what's the deal? You don't need a career, unless it's professional traveler. Which you'll never be staying home all the time to do other people's taxes.''

The buzzer sounded in the kitchen. Sara whirled around, glad for the distraction. How could she fully explain her need to keep her career going without giving away her greatest fear—that he'd leave her one day just as her first husband had?

CHAPTER FIVE

SARA had to give Matt credit for not belaboring the point. He tried once more at dinner to convince her to come with him to Paris. When she refused, he dropped the subject, saying only he had to leave the next afternoon.

"I'm sorry," she said again.

"Forget it. You're right, Paris will always be there. I had one of the secretaries at the firm run down a list of places for rent in our neighborhood. Want to go over that tonight?"

"Yes." Anything to cover the disappointment she felt. She was so torn, stay and keep her career as a buffer against what might never happen, or splurge and go. What happened to the new woman, daring and adventuresome? She was too cautious.

As soon as their few dinner dishes were washed and put away, Sara joined Matt on the sofa, looking at the listings. They discussed the locations of several apartments. Sara couldn't help noticing the exorbitant rents. She bit her tongue, not saying a word. Matt had made it clear he could afford this, she would not make an issue of it, but she was stunned at how much money they'd be spending each month. She had better keep her job, and maybe lobby for a raise.

"We can take a look at these in the morning," he said a little while later, indicating the ones they'd circled as being the most suitable—on paper at least.

She wanted to see them personally before deciding anything.

"Let's get up early then," she suggested.

"Good idea," he said, drawing her into his arms. "Which means we should get to bed soon, right?" He nuzzled her neck, causing shivers of excitement.

The next morning they ate breakfast at a bakery near the apartment. The warm croissants were huge, light and delicious. Sara could have stayed all morning, but they were on a schedule. Matt was leaving that afternoon for Paris.

Once finished eating, they headed for the first listing on their sheet. The place had a great location, but no view. Sara shook her head at one point and Matt picked up on it quickly. He thanked the manager showing the place and they headed for number two.

By early afternoon, Matt began checking his watch.

"Is time getting short?" Sara asked, noticing. She felt a clutch of panic. She didn't want him to leave. She wished she was going with him.

"This is the last one we have time to check today. I've got to get home and pack. My plane leaves at six."

Sara paused in the lobby of the building. "Then, let's skip this one and go home now. I don't want to see any more today. I didn't realize how hard it would be to find something we both like. I was so glad to get my current apartment when I did that I never considered how lucky it was to get just what I could afford as well as liked. Too bad we couldn't rent the apartment next to yours and knock out a wall."

"We'll find something. This is just the first day.

You can look at these others while I'm gone. If you like one, we'll go together as soon as I get back.''

She nodded, still feeling the pang of disappointment that he was leaving so soon after they returned home from London. She should have expected it, Matt had told her sometimes he barely had time to change clothes before heading out again. She'd seen evidence of that first hand in Tahoe.

He seemed to thrive on the challenges, but she wondered if she could adapt to such uncertainties. She realized she liked the routine of her job, of her daily habits. Maybe she'd been fooling herself that she was a footloose kind of person.

All too soon he was gone. Sara sat in the empty living room and wondered what she was going to do with the rest of the weekend. Shopping held no appeal. Nor did seeing apartments without him. If she were home, there'd be plenty to do.

Maybe she should return to her own place. She could start packing for the move, get rid of things she didn't need. Make sure all perishables were taken care of.

The knock on the door surprised her. She wasn't expecting anyone.

Opening the door, Sara came face-to-face with a young, busty blonde wearing a tight dark blue shirt and painted-on jeans.

''Hi, is Matt here?'' the woman asked.

''No, he's on his way to Paris.''

''That lucky guy. He's always going somewhere fabulous isn't he? Are you his latest?''

''Latest?''

''Girlfriend. I'm Leslie White. He and I were an item a few months ago. I think I left my favorite lipstick here. I can't find it anywhere and remember using it once when I was here.''

Sara stared at her. "I haven't seen it," she said.

Leslie tilted her head slightly. "It might be in the bathroom, or in the bedside table. I could take a quick look.''

"Come in." Sara stepped aside and closed the door behind her unexpected guest. She watched as Leslie walked straight through to the bathroom, and a moment later headed for the bedroom. Sara followed. It was obvious Leslie knew her away around the apartment. Just how close had she and Matt been?

Sara felt a pang of jealousy. This woman was young, trim and pretty. She moved with assurance. For a moment, Sara could picture Matt and Leslie together. She frowned. That was in the past. Matt was married to her now.

"Nope, not either place," Leslie said with a frown. She looked at Sara again. "You staying here? I saw some girly stuff in the bathroom. Matt usually doesn't use pink razors.''

"Matt and I are married." Sara should have told her that at the beginning.

"Married? Matt? No way! I don't believe it." The surprise on Leslie's face was almost comical.

"A week ago Thursday," Sara said, resisting the urge to wave her wedding ring in front of Leslie's nose. The younger woman was stunning, her eyes large and expressive, her long hair a pale blond, nothing like her own honey-brown color.

"I never thought I'd see the day. If I'd ever believed he'd settle down, I'd have tried harder. Good for you catching him.''

"I didn't catch him," Sara said.

Leslie crossed her arms over her rather large chest and looked around. ''I never thought he'd stay still long enough to get married. He's always going somewhere. But we had fun when he was here. Darn, I wish I knew where my lipstick was. They don't make that color anymore and I loved it.''

''If I find it, I'll be sure to let you know,'' Sara said, trying not to picture Matt with this younger woman. He'd chosen *her* to marry, not Leslie or anyone else.

But it was hard not to compare herself and her conservative clothes to this beautiful, trendy, younger woman.

''Sure. Hey, tell Matt congrats for me, will you?'' Leslie headed for the front door. ''He'll know where to find me if you do find the lipstick.''

She left and Sara remained standing where she was. She'd heard Dex call him a playboy, and for a moment, she'd been thrilled someone like that would single her out. Now she wasn't sure how she felt coming face to face with someone from Matt's past.

Rational thought should dictate she let it go. But she couldn't help comparing the other woman to herself, and coming up short. What had Matt seen in her that caused him to offer marriage? Some of it was the spark of attraction, she knew that. And he'd said he'd always wanted someone to travel with him.

She'd let him down on that front, refusing to go to Paris. It was hard letting go of what was familiar and comfortable.

Not liking her thoughts, she grabbed her jacket and headed to the apartment that had been home for the last nine years.

Sara spent the night at her old place surrounded by

familiar things. As she drifted to sleep, she could almost imagine the last month had been a dream and she would wake up in the morning back to her old routine.

The next morning, she began to pack. By noon her bedroom and the living room were denuded of pictures and knickknacks and books, everything packed into some boxes she'd found.

She loaded her car with clothes and headed back to Matt's apartment. She and Amber would have to arrange a time to go through the rest of the apartment together. Amber had left most of her things in her room when she rented her studio apartment near the university.

Sara wanted to get an apartment with a guest room so Amber and Jimmy could visit if he got posted in another location. Matt had seemed agreeable enough when she brought it up. Only shaking his head again when he looked at her, teasingly telling her he was still amazed she could be the mother of a grown child.

She'd teased him back—calling him Dad, and laughed aloud when he'd looked almost hunted.

"Never pictured myself as a father," he'd said gruffly.

"What did you picture yourself when you were a child?" she'd asked.

"A pirate for the most part, or a marshal in an old west town. Until I discovered computers. Then I was set for life."

When Sara arrived at the apartment, the answering machine was blinking. Matt's strong voice came across when she pushed the button.

"Sara?" He'd waited a couple of seconds. "Are

you there? I'm at my hotel.'' He raddled off a string of numbers. Sara quickly found a pad and paper in her purse and wrote them down as he talked for a few minutes longer, obviously hoping she'd pick up.

Darn! She hadn't thought about his calling when he reached Paris. He probably wondered where she was. Calculating the time difference, she realized it was after midnight in Paris, too late to call tonight.

She played the message again, delighting in hearing his voice. She wished she'd been home to talk to him.

Sara tried to reach Matt the next morning, but he had already left the hotel.

''Probably working,'' she said to herself as she sipped her morning coffee. It was late afternoon in Paris. She'd try calling from work a little later.

Despite calling almost every hour, and incurring a huge phone bill on the company's line, Sara didn't reach Matt. By the time she reached home, she was frustrated at not connecting. Where was he? Had he been this annoyed with her when she wasn't home yesterday? She dialed once again. She didn't care about the time difference, she wanted to talk to him!

'''Lo,'' a sleepy voice answered.

''Sorry I missed your call yesterday,'' she said, feeling complete now that she heard him again. She sank into the chair and closed her eyes, imagining him next to her.

''Sara, hi. I got your messages. I tried to call earlier but someone said you were in a meeting.''

''I didn't get that message. How are you? Sorry to wake you up.'' *I miss you,* she thought.

''I'm glad you did. You should have come, the weather is incredible for March. Flowers are blooming all over the place and nothing's crowded as most tourists don't venture forth this early in the year.''

''I wish I had, too,'' she said, wondering how long she could stand to be away from him. ''The weather is nice here, too. In fact, they're predicting an unusual warm spell for the next week. It seems like it's later in the year rather than early spring.''

''I should wrap things up by Thursday and head for home then. How about I see if we can borrow Tony's sailboat. We'll go sailing on Saturday if the weather holds.''

''Sounds like fun.''

''Where were you when I called yesterday?'' he asked.

''I was at my place packing. I need to get Amber over to help go through things, but we can do that once you and I find an apartment and know when we can move.''

''Did you look at any more apartments?''

''No, it didn't seem right without you.''

''If we go sailing on Saturday, we can spend Sunday looking.''

''Okay. I miss you, Matt.'' More than she was willing to say. But she almost ached with a longing that frightened her. He had become such an integral part of her life so quickly. She wasn't used to being so involved with anyone.

''I miss you, too, sweetheart. Next time, plan to come with me. There are so many things I wanted to show you. You'll love Paris.''

''I want to see it all.''

''Just not until taxes are done,'' he said dryly.

She smiled. Maybe he did understand. ''Right. Oh, you had a friend stop by,'' she said, remembering

Leslie. "She was looking for a lipstick she thought she might have left here."

He didn't say anything right away. Sara wished she'd kept her mouth shut. But she'd started this.

"Her name was Leslie White."

"Sorry she bothered you. I don't think she left anything there." His tone was distant, no longer warm and intimate.

"We didn't find it, but I told her I'd contact her if it showed up. She said you knew how to reach her."

"She works at a company we do business with. We dated for a while. She's not someone to worry about," he said.

"Umm." She wished she didn't feel jealous, but couldn't help it. At least he never need know. "Have a great trip, and hurry home," she said wanting to change the subject.

"I'll call you tomorrow night about this time."

"No, it's late where you are."

"But we can't talk while you're at work. And I'm not waiting till Thursday to hear your voice again. I'll call tomorrow."

She hung up. Dammit, she should have gone with him. Matt was nothing like her first husband. The circumstances were totally different. He wasn't going to walk out on her. She had to believe that.

While she was wishing, she wished she hadn't seen the pretty girl he'd once dated. Still, she couldn't shake the nagging worry that one day he'd wake up and be horrified at what he'd done—and leave.

Thursday Sara was on tenterhooks waiting for Matt to get home. She could hardly concentrate on work. Time after time she checked her watch, trying to calculate when his plane would land. She hoped she would beat him home. She couldn't wait!

Suddenly there was a commotion outside her office. She looked up to see her husband come striding through the doorway.

"Matt!" She pushed back from her desk.

"I told Stacey you'd be glad for the interruption," he said, as she reached him. He pulled her into his arms and kissed her long and deep. The office faded, the work vanished, there was only Matt and the feel of him in her arms, his hard body pressed against hers, his mouth doing wonderful things with hers. His hands holding her as if he'd never let her go.

"I don't know how many of these trips I want to take with you here and me across the world," he said a few minutes later when he reluctantly ended the kiss. He rested his forehead against hers.

Sara clung to his shoulders, afraid her knees wouldn't hold her. He had the power to turn her bones into mush. She couldn't say anything to reassure him, not yet. But she'd given the situation a lot of thought over the days he'd been gone. She had decided she would give notice once the tax season ended. Feeling grateful to the firm for giving her her first job and the promotions that had moved her into her current position, she didn't want to leave them at a critical time. But she wanted to share Matt's life, and if that meant traveling the world, then she was all for it.

"It's been endless. I'm so glad to see you."

He brushed his mouth across hers.

"Can you leave now?" he asked.

"Yes. Let me get my purse." She didn't even tidy up her desk, but grabbed her purse and headed for the door.

"I'll be back in the morning," she told Stacey.

"Y'all have fun," her assistant said with a wide grin.

"I took the bus, so I didn't have to worry about parking. I can ride home with you," Sara said as they descended in the elevator.

"Want to eat out tonight?" Matt asked, linking his hand with hers, lacing their fingers. "I'm all for a quick meal and then home to bed."

"Sounds great." She squeezed his fingers, wondering what he'd say if she suggested they skip dinner.

Matt arranged with his partner Tony to borrow his sailboat Saturday and that morning, Sara woke with a feeling of excited anticipation. She'd been looking forward to speeding across the Bay in the sleek craft since he'd first suggested the idea. She dressed warmly. Despite the sunshine and balmy temperatures for March, it would be cooler on the water.

When they reached the marina, Sara was surprised at the sleek, elegant boat. The mast towered above them. It was spacious, yet small enough for two to handle. When Matt gave her a tour, she found it had all the amenities of home.

After exploring the interior, she stepped out on the deck where Matt was studying charts. The gentle motion of the boat made her feel a little queasy, but she ignored it. This was another new adventure. She would have many to come with Matt. She wanted to explore everything that came her way.

"Aren't we just going sailing? Isn't the Bay deep enough for the boat, or are there channels we have to stay in?" she asked, looking over his shoulder at the charts with the squiggly lines.

He turned and pulled her close with an arm over her shoulders. "The Bay is surprisingly shallow in many spots. Not enough for the sandy bottom to poke up from the water, but enough we could drag a sand-bar if we didn't know where we're going. I thought we'd sail to Sausalito and have lunch there. Maybe go out beneath the Golden Gate Bridge later."

She looked across the expanse of water at the large nature preserve called Angel Island. They would get really close to that on the way to Sausalito. Maybe even see deer from the boat.

"Sounds great. What shall I do?"

Matt gave her very basic instructions and before long they cast off.

Sara had little to do once they were on the Bay and sat near Matt, enjoying the wind blowing through her hair. She still felt a bit queasy and tried to ignore the fact, but when they left the shelter of the marina, it grew rough. Tiny whitecaps topped the waves as they skimmed along, moving up and down as they headed for the Island.

Soon Sara was unable to do anything but try to concentrate on not being sick.

"Are you all right?" Matt asked, glancing at her.

"I will be," she said, taking another deep breath of the clean air. She couldn't be a bad sailor. This was something Matt loved. She wanted to do every-thing they could together. She'd get her sea legs soon, she just had to!

"You look sick."

"Oh." With that, she dashed to the small bathroom on the boat and lost her breakfast. Rinsing out her mouth, she held onto the small sink, looking into the mirror. She looked awful.

"Sara?"

She spun around. Matt looked in at her. "Are you seasick?"

"I think so. What are you doing here? You should be steering the boat." Visions of them crashing into something rose.

"I dropped the sails. We'll drift for a bit, but there's nothing nearby. I didn't think you'd be seasick," he said. "I'll see if Tony keeps any remedies around."

"It's my first time on a sailboat, I didn't know I'd react this way. I'm feeling better already," she said, embarrassed to be a problem on a day that had started out so promising.

"Want to head back?"

She shook her head, feeling miserable. "No. I'll conquer this, let's keep on to Sausalito. I can get something there for the return trip."

· In a short time Matt had the boat flying toward the Marin coast and the quaint, arty town of Sausalito. Sara stood near the rail, watching the distant horizon. She'd read somewhere that watching the horizon would help with seasickness. Only, it didn't seem to be working. She still felt awful.

She greeted their arrival with relief. Stepping on the dock, she took another deep breath, hoping the queasiness would fade now that she was on dry land. In only moments, she felt marginally better.

"I thought we could eat at a sushi bar near here," Matt said after the boat was secured against the slip.

The thought of fish almost made Sara's stomach revolt again.

"No. Not yet. I think I need to find my sea legs

before I could face fish. What I think I'd like is some-place where I could get a cup of soup.''

"There are a lot of restaurants within walking dis-tance from here. We'll find something to suit you.''

They wandered around the small village, perusing menus, commenting on the outdoor cafes. Sara took time to look over her shoulder at the skyline of San Francisco now and then. The air felt cool blowing from the Bay, but the sun kept the temperatures com-fortable. As she walked, she began to feel better. She dreaded the return trip, however.

Another disappointment. Maybe she wasn't as ready for life on the wild side as she'd hoped. She hoped Matt wasn't too upset. She felt as if all her plans were being extinguished one by one.

Matt took Sara's hand and headed up Bridgeway Street. He was disappointed she didn't take to sailing like he did. Tony rarely used his boat since his mar-riage. His wife's sister was wheelchair-bound, so they didn't go often. Tony made it available to Matt and Dex whenever they wanted it. Matt had thought about taking Sara sailing for an extended time, maybe tak-ing a trip down to Monterey, or up to Fort Bragg.

But if she was bothered by the light chop in the Bay, she'd never survive the larger swells of the Pacific.

They passed a deli, and he stopped.

"They have soup and sandwiches, let's try this,'' he suggested.

She smiled and nodded. "I want to eat on the patio,'' she said, nodding toward the outdoor tables and chairs on the side patio.

He couldn't gage if she was feeling better, or just

putting on a good face. He stopped her before they entered, resting his hands on her shoulders. ''If you're not feeling well, I can call Dex or Tony or someone to come get the boat. We don't have to take the boat back.''

''Actually I'm feeling much better. I'm sorry to be such a wet blanket. I never thought I'd be the type to get seasick.''

''Maybe you just need to get used to it.''

''I guess.''

He was struck once again by how pretty she was when she looked up, her eyes dark with concern. ''I really want to do this,'' she said.

''Give it time. If sailing doesn't agree with you, we'll try something else.'' He wasn't sure what. He loved the freedom of the boat. If he were in town longer between assignments, he might have considered getting his own. But the upkeep was too much with his erratic schedule.

''Let's eat and I'll see how I feel,'' she said.

After lunch, Sara declared she was fine. They wandered around the shops in the quaint little community. Matt bought ice cream for them and they sat in one of the many little parks, enjoying the view of the Bay and San Francisco. He didn't push about the return trip, but if she needed someone else to take back the boat, he wanted to call them soon.

She enjoyed everything they'd done since landing. He glanced around. Normally he wouldn't have spent so much time in such a tourist spot. But with Sara, he saw it with different eyes.

The town was clean and fresh and pretty with all the flowers and mini parks. With the bright sunshine, and the fresh breeze, the day was ideal. Slowly he began to relax. He would never have suspected a month or two ago that he'd be married and content to spend a day doing virtually nothing.

"Ready to go?" she asked, tossing her napkin in the nearby trash barrel.

"Want me to call someone to come get the boat?"

"Nope, I'm ready to sail the seas again!" She smiled and stood. "Come on, Captain, our ship awaits!"

Matt was relieved to see her enjoying herself on the return trip. It wasn't quite as rough with the wind behind them, and Sara even asked for a turn at the helm. He stood close by, not just to help, but from a need to be within touching distance. He had only know her a few weeks, but somehow it seemed like forever. He wasn't one to analyze relationships. Usually he'd been more the love them and leave them type.

But Sara was different. Around her, he was different.

He watched as San Francisco came closer. Tomorrow they'd go apartment hunting again. He hoped they'd find something they both liked. With most of her things at her apartment, it felt as if she was just visiting. She still stumbled over the his and ours when talking about his place.

He knew she was adjusting to marriage, he was, too. But he had no problem thinking of it as their place. Of thinking of Sara at home when he was away.

"This is great!" she called, laughing at the fun of it. She looked at the dock, coming faster than expected. "Oh, yikes! What do we do now? Are we going to crash?"

"We furl the sails, and take it in under power," Matt said, moving to begin the process. It was going to be all right. She had her sea legs now and they could do this more and more as the summer took hold.

Working together, Sara questioning every step, they secured the sails and headed for the slip under power.

When they docked, she flung her arms around his neck. "That was so much fun. I think I got my sea legs on the return trip. Can we do it again soon?"

He swung her around, liking the feel of her soft feminine body against his. He glanced toward the cabin, calculating whether they could use it or if he could wait for her until they got home.

"As long as Tony isn't using it. We could take a longer sail next weekend. Maybe even head out under the bridge."

"Wow, on the ocean? Let's explore around the Bay some more before we go there. I don't want to chance my luck."

He looked at her for a long moment. Her eyes were sparkling, her smile infectious and her cheeks kissed by the sun and wind to a rosy hue. He would like to always see her so excited and happy.

They found the perfect apartment the next afternoon, two bedrooms, a large living room and a kitchen big enough for them to move around together without bumping into each other. It was only two blocks from Matt's current one and had a view that matched. Since it was already vacant, they arranged to move in prior to the end of the month.

"Which gives us less than four weekends," Sara said as they returned home. "I'll have to spend next weekend going through things, and make sure Amber can get over there by then."

"Give a couple of months' notice. That'll give you plenty of time. Just because we can move in, doesn't mean you have to have everything out of your old place by then."

"Oh, good point."

She danced around the apartment. "I'm so excited. We're getting our own place."

He leaned against the wall and watched her. "We have our own place here."

She stopped and looked at him. "Sort of."

"But?"

"But at the new place, there won't be any memories of other girl friends," she said slowly.

He was taken aback. "You make it sound like I had orgies here or something."

"Did you?"

He shook his head.

"I'm being silly," she said, going to stand by the window to look. "But after Leslie's visit, I feel like I'm just one in a long line. I can't wait to move."

He crossed to stand beside her, unsure of what to say. He couldn't deny Leslie had been here. As had a few other women over the years.

"That's all in the past, sweetheart. If it makes you unhappy, we can stay at your place until we move."

She leaned against him. "No, I'll be fine. I'm just

happy we're moving. You won't have to go any where before that, will you? I don't want to do all this alone.''

''I'll make sure I'm here for the move.''

CHAPTER SIX

TUESDAY afternoon Sara almost fell asleep at work. She was so tired. They'd been packing since Sunday afternoon, staying up late to get things organized, then making love before going to sleep. She had more work than she could handle, but after the praise from her boss, she didn't want to disappoint him by asking to shift some of the load to one of the other accountants.

She got up and walked around, hoping to wake up. Maybe a soft drink with caffeine would help. She couldn't even focus on the numbers.

The phone rang. She lifted it up, still standing. If she didn't get something to wake up, she'd have to close her door and see if a quick catnap would work.

"Sara Tucker," she said.

"I like the sound of that," Matt said.

"Me, too. What are you up to? Is something wrong?" He rarely called her at work.

"Not wrong, just an inconvenience," he said.

She caught on at once. "Not another trip?"

"Stockholm. But just for a couple of days."

"You said you'd be here for the move."

"I will, that's a promise I'll keep. I'm taking one of the new representatives with me. Once I'm sure he'll manage, I'll return home. I probably won't be gone more than two or three days."

She didn't say anything. What was there to say? It was his job. She'd known it from the beginning.

Stockholm.

She looked at the piles of folders, printouts and tax books on her desk. Maybe she should just say good-bye now and take off for Europe with her husband.

She wanted to go so badly she could almost taste it.

"Sara? I'm sorry."

"Don't be, Matt. I just was wishing I could go."

"Ask for time off."

It was so tempting.

"Not now. I just can't. But I'll be writing my resignation letter earlier than I thought."

"Good. Quit. We'll get settled in our new place and then be ready to go when the next call comes."

"I hope you get another assignment in Paris soon."

"I'll see what I can do."

"You're not leaving before dinner are you?" she asked, suddenly wondering if that's why he called.

"No, we're leaving tomorrow morning. But I thought I'd get it over with, telling you."

"Gee, you make me sound like some kind of grouch or something."

"This way, you'll get your anger out and be loving when we're together tonight."

She laughed. "You'll be lucky if I stay awake long enough to watch you pack. I'm so sleepy this afternoon."

"We'll go to bed early tonight, I promise."

The conversation went a long way to waking Sara, and she plunged back into work with renewed enthusiasm. The sooner she finished, the sooner she could go home.

Amber called just as Sara and Matt finished dinner.

"Hi, honey," Sara greeted her daughter.

"Mom, Jimmy's leaving in the morning."

"Oh, so soon? I thought he had a little longer."

"I did, too, but they want him somewhere else now. I hope he has better luck staying in one spot with his next assignment. You'd think they'd have enough communication specialists over in Germany they wouldn't need one more right away."

"Is he there with you now?"

"No, he's on base. We said goodbye earlier. I'm bummed, but there isn't much I can do about it. I guess I just wanted to whine to someone."

"Whine away. It does seem unfair. But he'll be home in a few months and you two will be getting your own place together—like Matt and me."

"You found a place? Oh, tell me about it," Amber said enthusiastically.

Sara spent the next few minutes telling her all about the new apartment, their plans to move and Matt's assignment.

"I thought you were planning to travel with him, Mom. So far you've only been to London. Tell him he can take me if you can't go."

"What about school?" Sara asked sharply.

"I'm just kidding. Finals are in two weeks. But I'd love to visit Stockholm, or Paris or any place, come to that."

"I'll let him know. Want to have dinner one night while both our men are away?"

"Sure. Let's go pig out on pizza."

"I'll call you when I see how things go at work."

When Sara hung up, Matt asked about Amber.

"She's feeling lonely, I think. Jimmy is leaving tomorrow."

"She can keep you company while I'm gone," he said.

"We did make a date for pizza. And she said to keep her in mind for a junket to Europe—when finals are finished."

"The only one I want to go with me is you," he said, reaching for her.

By Thursday, Sara was convinced she was coming down with something. She plain didn't feel good. And she was so tired, despite getting plenty of rest every night. When Stacy popped into the office at one point, she looked at Sara with concern.

"You all right? You look like something the cat dragged in," she said with her forthright manner.

"What a way to cheer me up. I feel awful, actually. Maybe I should head for home," Sara said, leaning back in her chair. She was afraid if she closed her eyes, she wouldn't waken for a month.

"Yeah, well swing by the drugstore on your way," Stacy said.

"Flu medicines you think?"

"Pregnancy test, I think."

Sara stared at her, her heart racing. "We use protection."

"The only one hundred percent protection is not doing it at all. And I suspect from seeing that lusty husband of yours that is not the case. You could be coming down with a cold or the flu, but check it out anyway," Stacy said, taking a stack of completed forms and leaving.

Sara was rooted to her chair. *She couldn't be pregnant.* She'd had her family—Amber.

Matt didn't want children, or to be tied down. He

liked life in the fast lane, liked traveling to a new country every week. He liked sailing in sleek boats and skiing and doing who knew what else.

Oh God, she couldn't be pregnant. She couldn't go through that again, not at her age, not when she wanted to travel and see the world. They'd talked about moving to London—not about all the cares and responsibilities of motherhood. She wanted a chance to live for herself, not another child.

Feeling shocked, she grabbed her purse and headed for home—via the drugstore. She had to know. If it was negative, she was worrying for nothing.

But what if the test proved positive?

Trying to keep from panicking until she knew for certain, Sara hurried through the store and almost flew home. Once there she took the test, holding her breath as she waited for the result.

Positive.

She felt sick.

The last thing in the world she wanted was to start another family.

What would Matt say?

Bill had been properly receptive to the news she was pregnant, and then abandoned her after only a few months of a new baby in the home.

What would Matt do? He hadn't wanted children. They'd planned their future. He was already annoyed with her for the delay in resigning her job.

Oh, no. Another problem. Dare she resign now? What if she ended up a solo mother again? She'd need the income her job provided. And the security, seniority, stability.

Pacing the small bathroom, Sara tried to think. But

her mind was a jumble of thoughts and she couldn't focus on a single one.

She had to tell Matt. But how?

She'd have to decide what she was going to do. Stay at work? Travel as much as she could before the baby was born? Then what?

Did the new apartment even allow children?

Sara burst into tears. Her lovely plans for the future had just ended and she didn't know what to do.

For the first time since she met Matt, Sara didn't want to see him. She hoped his trip proved complicated and urgent and he stayed a month in Stockholm. Not that the situation would change between now and then, but maybe she'd come up with way to explain how everything they'd planned had changed.

Would he leave? Ask her to leave and keep his bachelor apartment? Would there be other lovely young women parading through like Leslie?

Soaking a wash cloth in cold water, she wrung it out and went to lie down with it over her swollen eyes. A baby should be a joyous event. Instead she was fretting about the future.

She remembered how scared she'd been when she'd found out she was expecting Amber. She'd been so young at eighteen, and had wanted to do so much.

Her second chance had come, and once again, she was pregnant.

There was a knock on the door.

Sara considered ignoring it. But it sounded again.

"Mom?"

Amber.

She hadn't even thought of what Amber might say.

Slowly Sara rose and padded across the apartment in her bare feet. They were supposed to go to pizza tonight. She should have called and postponed.

She opened the door.

"Hi, Mom," Amber said cheerfully, stopping when she saw her mother. "What's wrong?"

"Come on in." Sara felt the tears well again. This was a happy occasion, she had to remember that. She never wanted this new person to feel he or she hadn't been wanted. Even though the timing couldn't have been worse.

"Mom, did you get bad news? Is Matt okay?" Amber touched Sara's shoulder tentatively.

Sara shut the door, leaning against it for strength. "Matt's fine, I'm fine. I haven't had bad news, just news. Good news," she forced herself to say and tried to smile.

"If this is good news, I don't want bad," Amber said. "What is it?"

"I'm pregnant," Sara blurted out.

Amber stared at her. "You can't be," she said.

Sara gave a shaky laugh. "Thanks, but the pregnancy test says differently."

"Mom, you're too old to be pregnant!"

"I am not," Sara said indignantly.

"Obviously, but I mean, I thought you and Matt planned to travel and do things all over the world, not start a family."

"We do. Did." Sara pushed away from the door. "Want some tea?"

"I don't think tea is going to fix this. Should you be drinking caffeine?"

"One cup of tea isn't going to matter. And I need something."

"When did you find out? How does Matt feel about it?"

"I found out about a half hour ago and Matt doesn't know."

And she was scared to death to tell him. It would change everything. She wondered how long she could go before he'd notice? It would be the cowardly way, but she wanted his arms around her, she wanted his laughter and his sexy ways to wrap around her and make her feel desirable and wildly exciting.

For the life of her she couldn't envision that once he knew she was pregnant.

"Wow," was all Amber had to say.

"I don't want to go out," Sara said. "Want something here?"

"We can order pizza to be delivered. This is so weird, my mother pregnant. I'm going to have a baby brother or sister. I always wanted one, but not at this late date."

"Well you're getting one now," Sara snapped. She'd never known Amber wished for a sibling. Not that it had been possible with Sara's cautious attitude around men. The first time she cut free and let herself live and look what happened.

"Hey, Mom, I think it's great," Amber said, giving her mother a hug.

Sara clung. She wanted reassurance. She wanted something to hold on to. What would Matt say? The tears started again.

"Hey, Mom, be happy. Any cravings yet? We could order pizza with pickles and ice cream if you like."

Sara laughed, hugging Amber, then stepping away. "No odd cravings yet. Let's get our regular order."

* * *

Matt picked up his bag from the luggage carousel and headed out of customs and toward the long-term parking lot. He was dog tired but anxious to get home. The three day assignment had stretched out to a week. He'd missed Sara. He'd called her when he could, but with the time differences and their conflicting work schedules, the calls had been few and far between. And unsatisfactory to boot.

He didn't want to hear her voice, he wanted to hold her, see her enthusiasm when she spotted something new, or fascinating. He wanted to hear her laugh, watch her. Share places he loved, see if she'd love them, too.

As he put his laptop and bag into the car, he made up his mind. He'd force the issue of her resigning if she had not already done so. They'd talked about traveling together, if she was serious, he wanted her with him starting with the next trip, or the one after that for sure.

He understood loyalty, and admired her for wishing to help the firm through the busiest season, but there was no reason she couldn't give notice now for April 16 as her last day. It was only a few weeks away.

He wanted some show of faith in him from his wife. Was she afraid he couldn't support them? Maybe they needed a frank talk about finances. He had enough invested to see them secure the rest of their lives. Maybe if she understood that, and being an accountant, she'd be able to recognize it at once, she'd feel better about letting go her job.

In the meantime, he'd see if he could keep closer to home, maybe stay in the office for a while and get a better handle on some of the new representatives they'd hired. He wanted to check out their training program to make sure it wasn't lacking in any areas. The young rep who had gone with him to Stockholm had been fast and efficient, and thrilled to be on his first overseas assignment. But shaky on some of the company's protocols.

After a while travel became routine, as the new rep would find out. Since most of their clients were clustered in a few locations, he'd seen it all before, many times.

Being with Sara would make it all new again for Matt. New and different and far more exciting than he remembered it being in a long time. He wanted to show her the world.

He almost called her from the car, but he'd had enough of telephones. He'd be home in less than half an hour. With no assignment on the horizon, he could focus on packing up his place, helping her with hers and moving into the new apartment that would be their home for the future.

When Matt opened the door of the apartment a little later, he paused a moment, hearing the soft music, inhaling the tempting aromas coming from the kitchen, catching a whiff of Sara's special scent. His fatigue fled. He wanted his wife.

''Sara?''

''Matt?'' She came to the kitchen door, a radiant smile on her face.

''You're home. I'm so happy to see you!''

Her kiss was welcoming, ripe with a hint of things to come. He hugged her closely, delighting in the feel of her slim body, of the fragrance that she always wore. His finger threaded in her silken hair, treasuring the softness.

"I thought you'd call from the airport," she said breathlessly a few moments later. The pink color in her cheeks caused him to reach up and caress them with his thumbs.

"Phone calls are no substitute for the real thing," he said, kissing her lightly on her lips.

"Dinner will be ready in about twenty minutes. I wasn't sure if your flight would be late or not."

"Uneventful. What's for dinner, it smells good."

"Veal cutlets. Do you like them?"

"I haven't met any meat I don't like."

She laughed, and patted his arm, as if reassuring herself he was here in person. "And I bet you've tried some I haven't even heard of."

"Not too far off the mark."

"Are you exhausted?" she said as they walked to the kitchen.

"Not too bad. A night's rest will catch me up."

She fussed around preparing the dinner. Matt sat at the counter and watched her, delighting in her femininity. He'd always liked women, some more than others. But none before had given him that deep-down delight that Sara did.

"…home for a while?" she asked.

He'd missed the first part, but took a chance. "Home for a while. I said I'll be here for the move."

At the comment, she hesitated a moment, looked away. "That's good." She concentrated on checking the potatoes in the oven, squeezing them to test for doneness.

"Have you finished packing?" he asked, knowing she and Amber had been back to their old apartment a couple of times according to their nightly conversations.

"Not finished, but made some headway. There's so much we have to go through. It was easier to keep things than toss them before, but now I don't want to have to move things we no longer need.

"And treasures Amber thought she'd always want now seem silly. It was fine for her to leave them at her old room, but she, too, doesn't want to bother moving them and finding room in her apartment."

"I imagine she and Jimmy will have a simple set up if they plan to move every few years as the military does," Matt said.

"He's going to college once his enlistment is up. They'll only have a couple of moves I think. But it does make sense to streamline."

He took a sip of the coffee she'd prepared him, trying to keep awake. And trying to decipher if there was a change in Sara. He couldn't put his finger on anything specific, but she seemed to be avoiding his eyes.

She was busy fixing them dinner. She couldn't forever be looking at him. Though Matt admitted he wouldn't mind a little of that wide-eyed, hero-worship look she sometimes gave.

"Did you give your notice?" he asked.

She had her back to him. He could have sworn she tightened up.

"Not yet."

"When, Sara?" he asked. He was going to push. He wanted it settled once and for all.

"I told you I can't leave them in the middle of tax season."

"It's the end of March, the big thrust will be over within a few weeks. No reason you can't give notice for April 16 now, is there?"

He didn't imagine the hesitation this time.

"It's complicated," she said.

"No, it's not. Just write up a note saying you quit as of April 16 and turn it in."

She said nothing.

Matt felt a spark of anger. "Unless you don't plan to do so."

"I want to," she said.

Doubt pierced.

"You want to? What does that mean? I thought we *planned* to. I've been patient, I think, about this. You said you would quit, that we'd travel. So far I'm traveling and you are not quitting."

Did she want something else? He had never had a long-term relationship with a woman before. Sara had been so different from the women he'd known, he'd been smitten with her before he knew it. But they didn't have a long history together. Was this some convoluted way to get something else?

"Let's eat dinner," she said, taking plates down from the cabinet.

"I want an answer."

"I said, it's complicated. We can discuss it later if you insist."

"Now!" He rose and crossed the narrow space to stand beside her, turning her to face him. "What's going on? I thought you liked London. Are you having second thoughts about traveling? Don't want to leave Amber? What? I have money enough to take care of us, you don't have to worry about that. We can go over our finances later if you want reassurance."

"It's not that. Matt, I know you'll always provide

for us. Though I do think I should contribute as well, not be a drain.''

''Honey.'' He slid his hands under her hair, drawing her closer. ''You would never be a drain. We'll find something for you to do if you feel you need to contribute. I don't want to make you feel like a dependent. I just want you to go with me. Let's explore everything we can, see the sights most Americans only dream about. We'll go hiking in Nepal, sailing on the Nile, try rock climbing in the Dolomites.''

With that, she burst into tears.

Matt was shocked. He stared at her, totally out of his element.

''Sara?'' He pulled her into his arms, holding her while she cried. ''What's going on?'' he asked. Getting anything out of her was like pulling teeth. Something must be terribly wrong to have her cry like this.

Her hands clutched his shirt, he could feel the dampness from her tears soak through. Rubbing her back, he tried to think what he'd just said that would bring such a reaction. Had someone she known died rock climbing?

''Sara?''

''I want to,'' she said. Her tears blurred her words. ''I would love to sail on the Nile, but I got seasick. Only I don't think it was that. And I'd want to hike in Nepal, and rock climb but in a few months, I wouldn't be able to get close enough to the face to maintain any balance.''

''What are you talking about?''

She clutched his shirt even harder, burying her face against his chest. ''I'm pregnant,'' she said.

Matt felt poleaxed. Sara was *pregnant?* Never in

his wildest dreams had he pictured himself as a father. They'd used protection. He'd urged her to get birth control pills, but had faithfully donned a condom every time. Every single time.

"How?" he asked, stunned as the implications swept through. The plans they'd made crumbled. The life he'd known and loved was changing and there was nothing he could do about it.

"I don't know. Did a condom break? Did we remember every time? Perhaps one of them leaked. Does it matter how?" She still refused to look at him.

Matt gripped her arms and pushed her back enough to see her face, if she would lift it from gazing at the floor.

"Sara, look at me," he ordered. "When did you find out? Are you sure?"

She shrugged, and looked at hm. The miserable expression on her face should have eased his own frustration, but it didn't.

"I took a home pregnancy test last Thursday," she said. "It came up positive."

"God," he said, letting her go and turning to walk into the living room. He paced the space for a moment, denying this was happening. He wasn't father material. He hadn't planned on even getting married before he met Sara. No matter how hard he tried, he couldn't envision himself in a house with a yard and a role in the PTA. He liked traveling. He liked new environments, new locations, new experiences.

Well this was one hell of a new experience.

"You didn't want a baby, did you?" Sara asked from the doorway.

He spun around to face her. "I didn't plan on one,

if that's what you are asking. It'll take some getting used to. I never pictured myself as a father.''

"I think you'd make a good father.''

"Based on what? That I'm male?''

"You're intelligent, honest, honorable.''

"I know nothing about children.''

"Neither do any parents. They don't come with instruction books. We just do the best we can.''

"It'll take some getting use to,'' he said. A whole lot of getting used to. He thought about his uncle, how he'd never seemed to know how to talk to a kid. How hard it had been to get his point across when telling his uncle something he'd considered important.

How his uncle hadn't been much of a traditionalist or holiday man. Christmases had been austere, birthdays hardly noticed. School plays and sport events missed.

He could be a perfect father if he did everything his uncle had never done.

The buzzer on the kitchen timer sounded.

"Do you want dinner?'' Sara asked.

Food was the last thing he wanted. But he'd been hungry when he arrived. It had been a long time since his last meal. Might as well eat to keep up his strength. He was going to need it to come to terms with being a father.

"Let's eat,'' he said, heading toward the kitchen, unable to look at Sara.

Nothing about this homecoming was going as he'd hoped, Matt thought as he ate the delicious meal. The meat was tender, but could have been cardboard for all he savored it. The potatoes just the way he liked them, only he wasn't interested in enjoying his meal.

He was trying to come to terms with the shocking news Sara had dropped on him.

"When is the baby due?" he asked as the meal ended. Their conversation had been nonexistent.

"I don't know exactly, probably late November, around Thanksgiving," she said. He noticed she had hardly eaten anything. She was pushing a piece of potato around on her plate.

"Eat up, Sara, you're eating for two now."

Tears welled as she studied her plate. Damn, he hadn't wanted her to cry again.

"We'll manage," he said, hoping to end the tears.

"Will kids be allowed at the new apartment?" she asked.

"I have no idea. We'll have to call and check it out. It didn't come up in the discussion as I recall."

"It never came up in any discussion as I recall," Sara said, standing and tossing her napkin on the table. She turned and walked quickly into the bedroom.

It had not. There was no denying that.

CHAPTER SEVEN

MATT cleared the table and put up the left over food. He stacked the dishes in the sink and filled it with soapy water before heading to the bedroom to talk to his wife. He still felt stunned at the news. At the changes that would come with a baby.

Tired almost beyond belief, he wondered if he could muster his arguments. What arguments? It was a done deal. They just had to decide how they were going to handle it.

Sara was in the bathroom when he entered their bedroom. He paced for a few moments, wondering how long she would be. As the minutes stretched out, he wondered what she was doing in there. Maybe he'd just lie down for a few minutes and rest until she came out. It had been a long day, first getting things set in Stockholm, then the long flight home, then the startling news.

His head hardly touched the pillow before he fell fast to sleep.

Sara came out of the bathroom dressed in one of her sleep shirts a few minutes later. The bath had helped. She didn't feel as vulnerable as she had earlier. They had to talk, she knew that. She was not in the mood for any romantic overtures no matter how much she'd missed Matt over the last few days. But talk she could handle.

She stopped and stared, feeling chagrined to see him asleep, fully clothed. Her heart was touched. He had to be exhausted coming all the way to California from Europe. With the time delays at airports these days, long trips became nightmares of waiting. She took off his shoes, hesitating over whether to waken him or not, but elected to let him sleep. She took the blanket from the closet and covered him.

Then she checked the rest of the apartment, debating whether to do the dishes or not. Electing not, she flicked off the lights and went to bed. The homecoming had not gone like either of them expected.

Matt awoke to an empty apartment. He lay still a few moments, orienting himself to being back in his own home. Turning, he saw the imprint from Sara on her pillow. But she was not there.

He checked his watch, noticing he was still dressed. It was after nine. Sara had obviously already left for work.

Rising, he headed for the bathroom. He was getting too old to spring back instantly after a fourteen-hour flight and eight time zones. Hell of a thought.

By midafternoon Matt had tackled the urgent items in his in box and debriefed his trip to the managers involved. He and his partners had shared a quick lunch in Tony's office, then he and Dex had headed back to his own office.

"Need help moving?" Dex asked as they entered Matt's office.

"Might. Still got that pickup truck?"

"Yeah. We can get a couple of the new guys to lend some brawn."

Matt nodded, walking to the window and looking out over the other office buildings in the financial district. The wind must be blowing, he thought idly,

watching some trash skip along the gutter of the busy
street. People walking were few, but the cars were
endless.

"Something on your mind?" Dex said, leaning
against the doorjamb. "You've seemed preoccupied
all day. Was there something else we needed to know
about the situation in Stockholm, or how Davis handled himself?"

Matt shook his head. Slowly he turned and looked
at his longtime friend. "I'm going to be a father."

"What?" Dex was clearly taken aback. "You're
kidding!"

"Sara told me last night."

"I thought—" Dex stopped talking.

"Yeah, me, too. I've been nagging her to quit her
job so we could travel. Now this. What am I going
to do?"

"What do you want to do?" Dex asked cautiously.

"I want to take my wife and fly to Paris, then on
to Rome, or Hong Kong. Can you picture me changing diapers or attending a Little League game?"

"White picket fence, minivan." Dex chuckled.

"Glad you find it funny," Matt snarled. "Get out,
I've got work to do."

"Hey, it's not so bad. Millions of men do it every
year."

"I'm not them."

"It can't be all bad, look at Sam Bond."

"Who?"

"Remember him, from college. Sambo? He married right after graduation and he and his wife have
three kids."

"You're kidding."

"I kid you not. I get a card from them each

Christmas. Her doing, I think. Last year had a picture of the whole family. If he can do it, so can you.''

''He doesn't travel like I do. He came from a normal family. He obviously knows what to do about the whole scene.''

''So learn,'' Dex said, shrugging his shoulders. ''Hey, can I be an uncle?''

Matt glared at him and Dex held out his hands as if warding off a blow. ''Hey, old buddy, I'm happy for you, really I am.''

''Go on and get out of here, I have work to do,'' Matt said, going to sit behind his desk. He waited until Dex took off, then rose and closed his door. He returned to the window. He couldn't concentrate on anything. All he could think about was Sara's announcement last night.

His own childhood had been less than perfect. What did he know about raising a child?

Frustrated, he left work for home. He knew he'd get there before Sara, but he wanted to be there as soon as she arrived. They had to talk.

Sara drew on all her professionalism to make it through the day without screaming at the people around her. She was disappointed at Matt's reaction to her startling news. It was not something she hadn't expected, but secretly she had hoped that he would have been a bit more happy about the news. Nothing had been decided last night.

And the specter of his leaving wouldn't fade.

Her assistant came in toward the end of the day. She shut the door and pulled out a chair near the desk.

''Okay, boss, give. What's wrong?'' Stacy asked.

"Nothing." Sara looked at her for a moment, wondering where her acting had failed.

"You've asked me twice for folders that are already on your desk. That's never happened before. You are totally out of it and yet you have not sent the Reams account over to Mr. Pepovich for his final approval."

"You were right, Stacy. I'm pregnant." Sara threw out the words as if flinging down a gauntlet.

"Wow." Stacy sat back in the chair and stared at Sara.

"Won't this put a crimp in Pepovich's plans?" Quickly she did the math. "But not for a while. Are you planning to tell him soon?"

Sara shook her head. She wasn't sure what she was going to do about anything. Especially Matt.

"How are you with this?" Stacy asked.

"What do you mean?"

"Happy, annoyed, blaming that hunk you're married to, or what?"

"Happy of course," she said dutifully.

"And is he?"

"He was caught by surprise."

"You, too, I bet. Does this mean he'll stick closer to home now?"

"I don't know. He only got in from Stockholm last night. We didn't have a lot of time to talk." Sara knew she'd deliberately cut off any chance of a conversation, too afraid of what Matt's comments would be. But sooner or later, they'd have to discuss the situation.

"Are you feeling okay? No problems, right?" Stacy said.

"No, why should there be?"

"Well, no offense boss, but you're not exactly a teenybopper anymore."

"I'm not that old, either," Sara said, miffed her young secretary thought she was too old to be having a baby. Obviously that was not the case. Would her friends feel the same way? Amber had been surprised to find her mother pregnant at this age. How would Allie and Marian view this, she wondered, thinking of two of her closest friends.

None of it mattered. Matt was the only one she had to worry about.

Matt was already home when Sara arrived. She stepped inside the apartment and in only seconds was swept into his arms.

"I've missed you. Today was endless," he said before he kissed her.

She dropped her things to encircle his neck, giving back as much as he gave. Time stopped. Worries ceased. She could only feel the exquisite delight of being with this one man, of losing herself in his touch and soaring above the mundane world to heights only he could lead her to.

When the kiss ended, he lifted her in his arms to carry her to the bedroom.

"Dinner?" she asked breathlessly, almost giddy with joy.

"Later," he said, closing the bedroom door behind him with a quick kick. He set her beside the bed and kissed her again.

"Matt, are you all right with things?" she asked anxiously.

"I'm wide-awake, have had enough sleep and a little while to absorb the news. I'm okay with it. We can talk later, but first, I want to touch you, taste you and make love with you!'' he said, kissing her as his clever fingers made short work of the buttons holding her blouse in place.

The next morning both were rushed as they got ready for work. Promising each other to be home early, they said goodbye when Matt dropped Sara at her office. They still had to discuss things, but this evening was time enough.

For dinner, Matt brought home several cartons of Chinese food. He knew what Sara liked and didn't want her distracted by cooking and cleaning. They'd eat, rinse the dishes and talk.

She arrived home only moments behind him, a good sign both had arrived early, he thought.

''Oh, Chinese, you're wonderful. I'm starved. Let me change fast and I'll be right out,'' she said enthusiastically, giving him a warm kiss.

Matt debated following her into the bedroom, and decided not. He did want to give her some perspective on his feelings in the matter and another night of hot love in their bed would not lend itself to discussion. Time enough for that later, he hoped.

She was back in no time, wearing comfortable jeans and a pullover top in a buttery yellow. Barefoot, she walked across the kitchen and peeked at the food just coming from the microwave.

''Smells delicious,'' she said as she reached up to get plates. In short order they were seated at the small table and eating.

''How are things going at work?'' Matt asked, wondering if he dare bring up her quitting at this stage. His frustration in that regard hadn't diminished with the news of a coming baby. Surely she'd want to quit sooner.

"Hectic." Sara glanced at him and smiled, then concentrated on her food. "How about Aste? I bet Tony and Dex are glad you're back for a while."

"They manage fine without me, but yeah, I think they're glad I'm in town for a while. Watching the new rep in Stockholm gave me some ideas where we need to enhance our training and what's out of date now and can be scrapped."

"Are you in charge of training?"

"No, but I'll review the protocols with Tony and Dex and Josh. Josh is the head of training. He doesn't get into the field enough, I think, to see what's needed. It's mostly theory with him. I should take him on the next assignment."

She was quiet. He wondered if he should have mentioned another assignment. He wanted her to go with him. This time he wasn't taking no for an answer.

"Dex offered to help us move. He has a pickup truck. And volunteered some brawn from some of the new guys," Matt said, changing the subject. "Or we can hire professionals—whichever you want."

She looked at him. "Did you find out if we can still move to that apartment?"

"I called the manager this morning. There are no restrictions against children. It means the guest room will have to be a nursery, however. We wouldn't have room for Amber and Jimmy when they came to visit."

He watched her swallow, fiddle with her water glass. It was time.

"Sara, are you sure about this?"

"What do you mean?" Her eyes met his.

"I'm not going to be a good father. I have no experience in fatherhood, or even having a father around. I haven't been around kids since I was one. I'm not cut out for this."

She looked stricken. "So what do you want me to do about it?"

He shook his head. "I don't know. You caught me totally unprepared. I haven't a clue where to go from here."

She sat perfectly still, her eyes searching his, looking for what?

"Nobody has experience being a parent until they are one," she said slowly.

"But most people have experiences being a kid of a parent. Uncle Frank raised me. And if he's the best parent around, the world's in trouble."

"You mentioned him before when you told me your parents were dead. Still, he was a relative and took you in. He must have done something right, you're a terrific man."

Matt shrugged. He believed anything he'd accomplished had been his own doing, not as a result of Frank's parenting skills, or lack of them.

"Frank was a bachelor first and foremost. My mother's parents didn't want the responsibility of raising a child after her death. My dad's parents were divorced, his father lived on the East Coast and didn't step in. His mother was remarried to a man—" Matt stopped suddenly. She'd remarried a man who traveled a lot in his line of work, and she didn't want to stay home with her grandson and miss all the travel.

He'd been resentful as a child. Yet he wanted the same thing for Sara. He wanted her to travel with him and not stay home and watch some baby he hadn't ever planned for.

"Who didn't want children?" Sara prompted.

"Something like that. You have to see I wouldn't be a good role model for any kid."

"Well this isn't something we just say, sorry, not for us, and return to the store or something," she said with some heat. "I'm not exactly dancing for joy at this turn of events. I thought I'd raised my family. But it happened. And I feel sorry for a baby that neither parents particularly wants!" She tossed her napkin down and dashed from the table, running into the bedroom and slamming the door behind her.

Matt heard her crying—but he was unable to move. What a legacy for a child. It wasn't true. The whole situation just took some getting used to. She was right, there was no sending it back. For the rest of his life, he was going to be a father.

And he would never, ever, not even for one second, let this child think he wasn't wanted. Matt knew firsthand how hard that was to deal with.

Sara couldn't stop the tears. He'd all but said she had to do something with the child. But what? She had had longer to get used to the idea of the baby. She could feel the subtle changes in her body, foretelling major changes to come. One day she'd hold her son or daughter in her arms. Rock it, nurse it, love it.

Would the baby's father be anywhere around? Or would Matt have cut out long before then, convinced he'd make a bad father? Or too caught up in his fast lane life to stop long enough to visit his child?

She heard the phone ring, but didn't move. Matt was home, he could answer it.

Slowly the tears ceased. She lay exhausted, unable to get up, unable to move. She should go wash her face or something, but lethargy won. She closed her eyes, not falling asleep, just too tired and dispirited to move.

Matt knocked on the door, and the sound tore at her heart. This was his home, his bedroom, he didn't need to knock.

''Yes?''

He opened the door a crack and peered in, the phone in one hand. ''Tony and Dex are planning an impromptu sail this weekend. The weather is perfect. We're invited.''

The mere thought of the wide Bay and the bobbing boat almost made her sick.

''I can't go,'' she said quickly. ''Amber and I are packing tomorrow. Why don't you go, though.''

He hesitated a moment. ''You sure?''

''Yes, I'm sure,'' she said, keeping her eyes closed. It was dumb, but now that she had said it, she wished the words back. She didn't want him to go off on fun-filled adventures without her. She wanted him to say, no, I wouldn't have fun without my wife.

''Okay, then,'' Matt said. He spoke into the phone again. ''Sara can't make it. But I can. What time?''

He moved away, still talking. She felt a flare of anger that was totally irrational. She'd told him to go. He was just taking her at her word. Why did it make her angry?

Because she wanted to be the center of his universe, she realized. Just as he had become the center of hers. Tears welled again, but she damped them down. Rising, she headed for the bathroom.

Joining Matt in a few minutes, face bathed and

makeup donned, she smiled, hoping she could carry this off. He was sitting on the sofa, the TV playing softly.

"So when are you going tomorrow?" she asked.

"We're leaving at eight. When are you and Amber getting together?" He patted the cushion beside him, indicating he wanted her to join him.

"Not until ten. Will you be home for dinner?" Sara sat beside him, hoping he'd pull her into his arms.

As if he read her mind, he put his arm around her shoulders, and drew her close.

"Yes, I'll be home around four or so. Will you feel like cooking, or shall I pick up something?"

"I'll put on a stew that can cook all day while we work. Can we eat at my place? That way I can watch the stew as we work, and won't have to get it over here."

"I can be at your *former* apartment whenever you say," he replied.

Sara smiled, remembering how insistent he was she think of his apartment as home. Maybe with the new one.

If he stayed.

"What are you watching?" she asked.

"Travel channel. They are showing a segment on the world's best beaches."

Figures, even at home, he was longing for distant shores. Sara snuggled down beside him, watching as the exotic scenes played on the screen. She longed for them, as well. How could she fault Matt for being honest?

She couldn't fault him for anything. She loved him. He hadn't change a bit since she'd met him. He was wildly sexy, exciting, dynamic. He seemed to like spending time with her, though she didn't think she offered as much as someone like that blond bombshell who had showed up. Yet he was satisfied.

Or was he? They'd made such wonderful plans before they married. And so little had come about.

Due to her.

She should have quit her job. But if he left, where would she be without work? Maybe there was more she could do to live up to the plans they'd made, the ones she'd been as excited about as he. She doubted Mr. Pepovich would fire her if she took another week off. She had loads of vacation time on the books.

She would become the perfect wife, doing everything he wanted, so he would never wish to leave. And she wouldn't harp on the baby, nor bring the subject up more than she needed to in the normal course of events. Once the baby was born, he'd see he could be a great father. She hoped he would be willing to try.

What caused a man to leave a family? She'd never understood Bill's defection. He had never contacted her, never seen Amber after she was three months old.

How would she handle things if Matt left? How would she handle her life if he left?

The fear clutched her heart. She wouldn't be able to, she thought. In the short time they'd been together, he'd become an integral part of her being. The plans they'd made wouldn't come about now, or at least for another eighteen years. Would Matt be patient that long?

"We should have a housewarming party when we get the new apartment," she said.

He looked at her. "What brought that up?"

"The luau." She gestured to the scene on the television. "Reminded me of our move and new place. Don't you want friends to see it? I do. I'm excited about it."

"Whatever."

She smiled and patted his knee. "Maybe it's a girl thing."

"Like nesting. Are we getting a lot of new furniture as well?"

"Not a lot." Mostly baby stuff, but she didn't voice that. "I like this sofa and the chairs I have in my former apartment will blend in. We can decide before moving furniture."

She'd be agreeable, fun to be around. And they'd build such wonderful memories he'd never want to leave her.

Saturday proved difficult—sorting through her past with Amber. Sara had several boxes and bags for the trash or charity waiting by the door by the time Matt arrived for dinner. She and Amber had packed up most of the books and pictures; even some of the kitchen things. Sara wanted to go through Matt's kitchen before giving up any of her pots and baking pans. She suspected she'd want to keep most of it since his place seemed light on cookware.

Sara kept to her vow to be the best of companions. She kept the conversation light at dinner. Amber seemed to pick up on her mood and contributed funny anecdotes from college. Matt regaled them with the snafus he'd encountered in early trips. The time passed quickly and with all the fun Sara hoped for. She was pleased with her strategy.

Before they left to return to Matt's place, he walked through the apartment. "We'll get some professionals in to pack up the rest. You need to conserve your energy,'' he said.

''I'm fine.''

''Maybe. But tomorrow, we'll stay home and rest.''

She smiled in anticipation. The last time they'd stayed home to rest, they spent most of the day in bed—but not at all in restful pursuits.

However Matt meant exactly what he said. Sunday he brought her breakfast in bed, and left her to eat it, saying he had the paper to read. When Sara got up and dressed, he urged her to sit on the sofa to read or watch television. She didn't wish to do either.

''I want to spend time with you,'' she said, leaning over him at the dining table and looking at the crossword puzzle he worked.

''I'm here. I can rent a video if you like. We could watch it together.''

''Anything special you want to see?'' What was going on?

''No, what would you like?''

''I'd like to go for a walk. It's gorgeous outside. April is a lovely month in San Francisco, before the fog makes its daily appearance. Let's go to Golden Gate Park and visit the Tea Gardens,'' she suggested.

''Sure you don't want to rest up? You've been working hard lately. With the baby and all, I thought you should rest.''

Amber had asked Sara privately just before they'd left last night if Matt knew about the baby. No mention had been made all evening. Sara assured her he knew. But this was the first time he'd voluntarily mentioned it. And she didn't like it at all. She wasn't an invalid. She wanted to do something fun with her husband.

"I'm getting plenty of rest," she said.

"So no nap needed?" he asked.

She remembered other days when they had napped. Slowly she began to smile. Maybe she'd forego the park and spend the afternoon in Matt's arms instead.

CHAPTER EIGHT

THE next few days sped by. Sara didn't bring up the subject of the baby around Matt. He never mentioned it either. It was as if there was a huge elephant in the living room that neither admitted to. How long would it last?

The strain was starting to tell. She had accepted the fact of the new child and was growing excited. She wanted to talk about the baby, make plans, decide on names, look at furniture, buy a new teddybear. The list was endless.

But she tiptoed around Matt. They talked about work or about the move. Even the talk of travel had ended. Had he given up on her? Fear clutched her every time she thought about the future.

Wednesday afternoon, Matt called. Sara knew as soon as she recognized his voice that he had another trip lined up. He was calling to alert her.

"Sara?"

"Yes. What's up? You bringing home dinner?"

"What do you want?"

"Barbecue sounds good."

"I'll take care of it. Sara, I have a trip tomorrow. A short one, but I'm needed."

"Where to?" She caught her breath. How short?

"Las Vegas. One of our security setups at a casino seems to have a glitch. Can't tell for sure if it's a problem, or lack of training for the security people. I won't be gone long. A day or two at the most."

"I've always wanted to go to Las Vegas," she said slowly.

"So come with me."

"Okay, I will," she said, startling them both.

"You will?" he repeated. "I leave in the morning, won't be home before Friday night if then."

"Or we could stay over the weekend and see a couple of shows. Even go swimming. Isn't it always hot in Vegas?"

"I'll make the reservations. See you at dinner."

He hung up before she could say another word. Probably thinking she'd change her mind.

Sara replaced the receiver and drew a breath. She was committed. What would Mr. Pepovich say? He was likely to kick up a fuss, but so what? She had time due her and a day or two wouldn't break the firm. She'd take work with her if she could, but the firm preferred to keep the client's records on the premises. Still, she could make it up next week by working later. She'd been leaving at five every day Matt was home. Next week she'd stay as late as needed. It was only a week until tax day. She'd make sure all her work was finished the day before. Who could argue with that?

For this weekend, however, she was going to spend every moment she could with her husband, seeing the fabulous side of Las Vegas.

The weekend in Las Vegas was all Sara had hoped traveling with Matt would be. They swam in the luxurious pool at one of the largest of the magnificent hotels on the Strip where they were staying. They saw two shows, ate decadently and made love in the sumptuous king-size bed.

For four days Sara put reality away and enjoyed the life she had so hoped to have when she and Matt married. It was fabulous.

But reality returned Monday when she had to go to work.

"I'll be late tonight," she said as Matt prepared to drop her off at her office.

"How late?"

"Pretty late. Don't wait up."

He caught her arm as she started to get out of the car.

"What do you mean don't wait up? You can't work that late. Six or seven maybe, but not later."

"I have a lot of work to get through. Taking two days off last week means I have to get it down by working later to get caught up."

"What, are you planning to make up the sixteen hours you missed by working them through after normal business hours? Four hours a night?"

"If I have to. I told Mr. Pepovich I'd get the work done and Friday is the deadline."

"I don't want you working so late. You need to rest."

"I need to live up to my word and have the work completed on time. The clients are depending on us. On me. I won't let them down."

"You need to rest."

"I appreciate your concern, but Matt, I do know how to run my life."

"What about me?" he asked.

"I'll see you when I get home," she said, tugging her arm free and getting out of the car.

Some way to make herself indispensable to her husband, she thought guiltily, virtually ignoring him

while she plunged into work. But it was only until
Friday. She'd be caught up then and could spend
more time with him.

She could take a leave of absence for a few months.
To see what they could have had if the baby had not
come along? Wouldn't that make staying home that
much harder in the long run, she questioned as she
hurried to her office.

She yearned to explore different cities, visit places
she'd only dreamed about. Or even enjoy mundane
things like sleeping in if she wished, or staying up
late. Or shopping on Wednesdays when the stores
weren't crowded, instead of always on the weekend
when half of the city was also shopping.

Arriving at her desk, she quickly set to work. The
sooner she got started, the sooner done.

Sara was tired when she unlocked the door to the
apartment. It was after ten. Matt opened the door and
drew her into his arms. His kiss was sweet. She
couldn't have handled much more.

"Did you eat any dinner?" he asked, as she took
off her coat.

"Yes."

"Time for bed, then," he said ushering her into the
bedroom. In less than ten minutes Sara was in bed,
and asleep in less than two more.

The pattern repeated itself every day until
Thursday. At last—she was finished! Glowing with a
sense of accomplishment, Sara sent the last form off
for signing. She'd beat the deadline by twenty-four
hours. She was bone-tired, and almost groggy with
want of sleep, but she'd done it! Tomorrow would be
a piece of cake and then she'd have the weekend free

of worries. Next week she could approach Mr. Pepovich about cutting back her hours, or that leave of absence.

She called Matt at work, wanting to let him know she'd be home before dinner tonight.

"He's not here," his secretary said.

"Oh, will he be back before closing?" she asked.

"I don't believe so. Can I take a message?" the woman asked.

"It's his wife. I'll catch him at home later."

She wondered where he'd gone. He hadn't said anything about going anywhere, had he? They'd barely spoken over the last few days. She collapsed into bed the minute she reached home. He drove her to work every day, and insisted she take a cab home each night. Otherwise, their conversation had been decidedly lacking in any hint of intimacy.

The restraints of tax season were over. She could do more with her own life now, make sure she was the kind of wife he wanted to stay with.

Matt wasn't Bill. She had to remember that.

But Matt wasn't Matt, either, Sara thought Saturday afternoon. He seemed—distant. No other way to describe it. He'd been happy enough when she arrived home early on Friday, but beyond commenting he was glad she was cutting back her hours to a more normal routine, he had said little.

"Want to do some packing?" she asked.

He'd looked up from the paper he was reading and shook his head. "Time enough." He looked down again.

Studying him for a moment, Sara knew he wasn't

reading. His eyes almost bore a hole in the paper, but they weren't moving.

"Something wrong?"

He shook his head.

She didn't want to do chores. She was free from the exacting workload that characterized tax deadlines. She wanted to do something frivolous and fun.

But now that she was ready, Matt seemed not to care.

"We could go do something."

He folded the paper and tossed it on the coffee table. "Like what?"

"I don't know. What would you like to do?"

"We could go to the movies, I guess."

Sara wrinkled her nose. She didn't like that idea.

"Sitting in the dark watching someone else act isn't my idea of fun today," she said.

"What is? I thought you'd be tired and want to rest up."

She wasn't sure if that was a comment about her pregnancy or her work, both of which were touchy subjects.

"I don't. Let's do something fun."

Just then the phone rang.

Matt picked it up. Sara rose and went to the window and looked sightlessly out over the Bay. It shouldn't be as hard as this to get him interested in doing something with her. A niggling fear settled in her stomach. He was distancing himself. If nothing else, he should have suggested they spend the day in bed, as they had on their honeymoon. It wasn't that long ago.

Yet it was, a lifetime ago. Before the baby.

She sighed softly, tears threatening. Was she going to lose him because of their baby?

"Sara."

She turned around to look at him.

"Annie and Tony are throwing an impromptu barbecue today and want us to join them, up to it?"

She nodded. At least it would get them out of the apartment.

Tony's place was in the old section of town, a huge old home that had been built after the great 1906 earthquake and had been in his family for generations. The yard was guarded by a high wooden fence, the patio at the back of the house shaded by a trellis with a wisteria just starting to bud.

Sara had met Tony and his wife at the wedding. She greeted him and Annie. Tony and Matt were close and Sara wanted to do what she could to cement relations with him and his wife.

There were several couples already in the yard. She recognized Dex, leaning near a young woman flirting like crazy. She smiled at Matt, wanting to share the moment, but he was already talking with Tony in low tones.

"You two aren't working, are you?" she asked suspiciously.

"Only catching up on a couple of things," Matt said.

"That's their favorite theme," Annie said, laughing. "Come and meet my sister." She nodded toward a pretty woman in a wheelchair.

"What can I get you to drink first?" Tony asked.

"A soft drink," Matt said, putting his arm around Sara's shoulders.

"Right, the mother-to-be," Tony replied. He smiled at Annie, then reached over the bar and pulled out a cola for Sara.

"Matt, glad you could make it," a blonde of about twenty-five walked by, smiling at Matt, and nodding politely at Sara.

"Melody," he said with a nod of acknowledgment.

"Here you go," Tony said, handing Sara a tall glass.

"Is everyone here from work?" she asked taking a sip.

Tony handed another drink to Matt and glanced around. "Pretty much. A couple of the neighbors, but most are from Aste.

"Introduce her around, Annie."

"I intend to. See to it you two don't talk shop all afternoon. Come on, Sara, let's go see Julia before someone else arrives I have to greet. Are you totally thrilled about the baby?"

"Sure," Sara said, trying to smile. It was the standard response.

Annie looked around and then leaned close. "We're expecting, too, but Tony didn't want to tell anyone yet. But I thought another mother-to-be would want to know."

"How wonderful. Your first?"

Annie nodded. "Only Julia knows. We plan to tell folks soon, but for now, it's just family—and very close friends."

Sara wondered later if it had been a mistake to come. Everyone knew Matt. They greeted him warmly, exchanging insider jokes and comments. When introduced to Sara everyone was polite, but she imagined she could hear the question tumbling in their minds—what had he seen in her?

Despite the informality of the barbecue, the talk inevitably turned to business. Sara felt more and more left out as even the pretty, young women seemed to have a vested interest in the computer aspects, or the security planning.

After chatting with Julia, she wandered around the yard, noticing how meticulously it was kept. For a moment, she tried to visualize Matt with a rake in hand. The image wouldn't come.

She glanced at Dex, still flirting with that pretty woman. She couldn't picture him married. When she looked at Matt she tried very hard to see him in a yard pushing a little child on a swing. Neither the child nor Matt would appear.

''I'm Margot,'' a young woman said coming to stand beside Sara. ''Annie sent me over. I'm pregnant, too. It's my second, but I'm just as thrilled as I was the first time.''

Sara smiled. ''It's my second, too. But there will be twenty years between my babies.''

''Oh, wow, that's like starting completely over. How cool for Matt to be able to have a family. He's been such a lone wolf, I never thought he'd settle down. Have you picked out names yet?''

Sara shook her head, ''You?''

Margot was off and running. She and her husband had a list of names, and were thinking about giving the child several, not just a first and second. She then talked about her son, age two, her husband Brian who was ''over there somewhere.'' She motioned vaguely with her hand, never taking her attention from Sara. ''He loves these kinds of things. I'd rather stay home with Timmy. Want to find chairs somewhere? I'm ready to sit.''

Sara agreed, glad someone at the party seemed glad she was there.

The afternoon passed pleasantly with Margot. Sara enjoyed her company—especially since her husband seemed content to be in discussion groups from the office. The laughter that rang out from time to time made Sara wistfully wish he'd included her, but she was enjoying Margot's company.

Annie came by with her sister at one point and their discussion was lively and fun. Margot also knew the secret. Discussing babies proved to be better this time around, Sara thought. Her own excitement began to grow while exchanging hopes and plans with others in the same situation.

The food, when served around seven, was delicious. Tony commandeered several of the men to help with the meat. The salads and side dishes appeared as if by magic from the kitchen.

''For an impromptu affair,'' Sara commented to Margot, ''Annie and Tony sure have everything organized.''

''Tony's the organized one of the group. Matt is the computer guru and Dex is best at body guarding,'' Annie said. ''They play to their strengths.''

''Dex is a bodyguard?'' She looked at the man with the shaggy hair, trying to picture him in a tense situation, and failing. He looked too much like a boy-next-door type.

''Oh, he does other things, planning security, training in self-defense, defensive driving, and all. But yeah, he's their head for personal security.''

''What area does your husband work in?'' Sara

asked Margot, looking around for Matt. He was talking to the same blonde Dex had been talking with earlier.

"He works with Matt in computers. But he doesn't know as much, nor can he gain the customers' confidence as quickly as Matt can. It helps that he speaks several languages, though most of the international computer work we do is done in machine language."

They ate buffet style. Matt and Tony stood near the grill, keeping an eye on the second round of steaks while they ate. Some of the others gravitated toward them. Sara met Margot's husband then excused herself to join her husband.

"Hey," Matt said when she stepped up beside him. "Enjoying yourself?"

She nodded, holding up her plate. "The food is delicious."

"Some of us were talking about taking a sail tomorrow," Tony said. "You and Matt plan to join us. The forecast is for good winds and warmer temperatures."

"I don't think so," Sara said, remembering their sail a few weeks earlier. "But I'm sure Matt will be up for it."

"Might take you up on it," he murmured.

Not the answer Sara wanted. She kept her smile in place, however, not letting the disappointment show. She wanted him to stay with her on Sunday. This was their first time together in a while and separate plans for Sunday wasn't what she expected.

Early Sunday Sara awoke to find Matt all ready dressed. He suggested she take the day to rest up after her hectic week. He was off to sail with Tony and

Dex. She watched as he left, with barely a kiss on her cheek.

By mid morning, Sara had rested all she wanted. She left a note telling Matt she had gone to her apartment, then headed out to continue the sorting she'd begun. They were due to move soon. Somehow she hoped by leaving everything in her past behind, Matt would have to stay.

Would giving up her apartment be foolish? Or a way to cement their relationship even more so they would have to face the challenges ahead together?

She knew he had lined up some friends from work to help with the actual transportation of their furniture and boxes, but she needed to sort through a few more areas to make sure she only took things she wanted.

When Sara reached the apartment, she called Amber. "I'm at the apartment packing, want to come over?"

"I'd love to, Mom. I've been studying until I'm almost brain-dead. My finals are this week and I need a break before plunging back in," she replied.

"We could do something fun if you'd rather. Seems a shame for you to take a break and then end up working," Sara said. She was trying not to think of Matt spending the day away from her. She missed him. What if this was the beginning of a pattern?

Or the beginning of the end?

"I don't mind. I'll be there soon. Is Matt helping?"

"No, he's sailing with friends again."

Sara wondered if she should confide her doubts to her daughter. Amber was grown now. Sara didn't need to shelter her any longer. But old habits died hard. She didn't want Amber to worry about her and Matt. They would be fine.

She hoped.

Once off the phone, she tried to run from her thoughts as she began pulling down the dishes from the cupboards. Some she'd donate to charity, a couple of special pieces she'd take with her.

Amber breezed in a little while later. Sara had sorted most of the kitchen utensils, sorted through the food in the cupboards, boxing the spices and condiments, and putting the rest in bags to take home with her.

"Look what I got," Amber said, giving her mother a hug. "Fresh bagels from Manny's. Poppyseed for you, onion for me, plus lox and cream cheese!"

"That sounds great. I'm hungry."

"Well, you are eating for two," Amber said. She cleared a space at the small table and placed the bag on it. The aroma wafted in the air.

"My mouth was watering all the way here. You're lucky I didn't stop to eat mine on the way," she said cheerfully as she looked around for plates. "Where is everything? Are we boxing it all up today?"

"Only the things I want to give away. You can have first crack at anything you want. Matt has a set of dishes we're using. Now that we're married, we'll get what we want as a couple." She stared at the dishes, remembering Matt telling her to get what she wanted, that he didn't care that much. She wanted Matt to be as excited about setting up house together as she was.

"Who did Matt go sailing with?" Amber asked as they sat at the table as they had for so many years.

"He and his friends from work, Dex and Tony. It's Tony's boat."

"The sailboat you went on?" Amber asked.

Sara nodded, slathering cream cheese on her bagel and then placing some of the fish on top. Biting into it, she savored the delightful flavors.

"Guys only?" Amber asked before taking a bit of her own.

"I don't think so," Sara said, "I was invited, but declined. I don't need to feel seasick, I get enough queasiness from the baby as it is."

Dex's words suddenly echoed in her mind—playboy of the western world. Surely Matt would honor their marriage vows. He wasn't flirting with other women. They were happy. Or they were until she got pregnant.

"Mom? Are you all right? You have the most peculiar expression on your face," Amber said, looking at her in concern.

"I'm fine. Just thinking…" Thinking about the desolation she'd face if Matt decided marriage wasn't what he wanted. Especially one that now included a baby.

"I changed my mind," Amber said. "Let's finish lunch, and then go out. It's a beautiful day, not too hot, and with a steady breeze. We can go to Golden Gate Park, walk around, go to the Tea Gardens or something. What do you say?"

Sara looked around at the mess on the counters and floor. Just where she'd wanted to go with Matt. However, she'd take what she could get. "Sounds good to me. We'll leave this until next weekend."

"Or just leave it all behind. Start your new life with all new things," Amber suggested.

Matt leaned back, closing his eyes and shutting out the sounds of his friends talking. He let the wind whip through his hair as he absorbed the warmth from the sun. This was what he loved. If he had ever been able to figure out a way to make a good living from sailing, he'd have done that for his career. But the only ways he'd explored consisted of chartering the boat, offering fishing tours, or something that would have strangers in his personal space.

Better to do the job he was so suited for and splurge on Tony's boat when he got the chance.

And the chances were likely to become fewer and fewer.

He shook his head. He couldn't get past the fact he was going to become a father. Technically, maybe he was already considered one. But at least Amber could stand on her own feet. What did he know about kids?

He knew enough that most men who had children didn't take off sailing on a whim. Didn't plan to extend work trips by a few days to explore the neighboring towns and cities. He wasn't even sure he knew any men with children who went rock climbing or scuba diving.

Some of the men at work had families. They also had homes that took a lot of work.

Tied down for twenty years. Could he do it?

"Hey, man, come take a turn at the helm," Tony called.

Matt opened his eyes. Might as well enjoy the day while he could.

"What are you going to do?" he asked as he ambled over and replaced Tony at the wheel.

"Catch some rays. Talk with that pretty lady I brought." He winked at Annie.

"Fine. I'm heading out beyond the bridge," Matt said, nodding toward the Golden Gate Bridge that spanned the opening to the San Francisco Bay from the Pacific.

"Go for it, weather's great, the swells won't be too big." Tony went to sit beside his wife. Dex and his date were forward, enjoying the bow. Josh Pendar was the other man from work, he and his steady were lounging on the aft section.

Matt wished he'd stayed home, or brought Sara. But he didn't think she'd be up to another sail until after the baby came. She hadn't fared so well on the first one they took. Who expected then that she was pregnant? Still, the leg back had been fun. He entertained some thought to buying a boat for the two of them. He could take some time from work. They could have sailed to Hawaii or Alaska or something.

Unless they moved to London. Funny how they hadn't discussed that at all once he'd learned about the baby.

He studied the water ahead of them, turned into the wind a bit more, calling for Josh and Tony to trim the sails to capture the full thrust of the wind. Sailing usually completely drove any problems from his mind. It refreshed him.

Not today, however. He kept thinking of the future, wondering what he was going to do. He and Sara had not known each other for long. He'd thought they'd marry, and things would continue much as before for him—only he'd have his wife with him when he visited other cities and countries.

The reality so far had proved far different. And was changing even more with a baby on the way.

"Hey, man, you still need us to help move your furniture in a couple of weeks?" Dex asked.

"Hold off on plans," Matt said. "I'm not sure I'm signing the lease."

CHAPTER NINE

SARA and Amber enjoyed their afternoon in Golden Gate Park. They wandered the paths in the oasis of green surrounded by apartments and houses on three sides, and the Pacific on one end. The Japanese Tea Gardens were lovely, and quiet. They savored the ritualistic Japanese Tea Ceremony and browsed the gift shop before heading to the Conservatory of Flowers. Examining the exotic varieties of flowers and plants was fascinating, but Sara loved the butterfly exhibit best. Would her baby like to watch the small insects flutter around?

As the afternoon wore on, she grew tired. But she was determined to make the most of her day off as Matt was his.

"Want to eat dinner at the Wharf?" she asked Amber. Her daughter's favorite treat when growing up was to indulge in clam chowder at one of the hole-in-the-wall restaurants at the Wharf. Not the fancy ones flooded by tourists, but one of the smaller places that catered to locals.

"I'd love it. Want to call Matt and tell him where to join us or go home first?" Amber asked.

"I'll call him. I'm not sure when they were due back. Depends on how far they went, I guess."

When she dialed his cell phone, there was no answer—he was out of service range. She called the apartment and left a message, explaining carefully where the restaurant was so he could find it.

"I don't know if he'll make it," she said slowly when she hung up.

"It's weird, isn't it?" Amber said as they began slowly walking toward the Muni bus stop. The metro line would take them to downtown where they could catch the Powell Street cable car which would take them to the wharf. From there, they could walk back to Matt's place after dinner.

"What is?" Sara asked.

"Being married. For you and for me."

"It's sure changed things," Sara agreed.

"Not so much for me as for you. Jimmy was hardly here. We spent less time together than I expected. Did I tell you he wants to continue in the military? He mentioned it a couple of times when he was here. Yesterday I got another letter from him in which he says he is really thinking about it. He likes that kind of life. But I don't know if I will."

"You'd get to travel."

"Or he would and I'd be stuck in the States somewhere. It's a dangerous profession these days. He has the chance to get out in another year, why wouldn't he?"

"You two need to discuss it. Surely he wouldn't make a decision like that without telling you," Sara said.

"Who knows? I sometimes feel I don't know him as well as I thought I did. He's changed since we were in high school together."

"So have you. You know what you want to do, and are working toward a degree to enable you to teach. You can do that anywhere, so moving wouldn't be a hardship. I'm sure he's changed since being in the Army."

"Mom, you're the one who longs for new places

and new sights. I like living here. I don't want to pack up and move every few years. I sort of pictured us living here in San Francisco all the time. Like his parents do.''

''Tell Jimmy. He needs to know how you feel.'' Sara said, struck by her own words. Maybe she needed to share her fears and concerns with Matt.

But to what end? To have him confirm them?

The phone rang four times before the machine answered.

''Sara? It's Matt. If you're home, pick up.'' He waited a moment. Was she napping? Or was she still at her old apartment?

''I'm at Tony's. The sailing was great. We just got back and are having dinner in a little while. Call me when you get home and I'll come get you.'' He rattled off Tony's phone number and hung up.

He tried the other apartment, getting no response there either. Maybe she was between the two and would call back in a few minutes.

''Sara coming?'' Tony asked when Matt rejoined the others in the great room.

''She didn't answer. I'll try again in a bit.''

He tried twice more before dinner, leaving a brief message each time. He was starting to worry. It was already dark outside, she wouldn't have stayed out so late if she'd gone for a walk or something. Where was she?

As soon as he finished eating, he left. He wasn't worried precisely, Sara was grown and had taken care of herself for many years before meeting him. But he was concerned. Where was she?

*   *   *

"That was fun, Mom. Call me next time you want to pack up," Amber teased as she stopped at the bus stop. The next bus would take her all the way out to the university, near her apartment. A short walk and she'd be home.

"Next time we really have to pack up. We're due to move soon. We can't keep stalling," Sara said.

The big bus pulled into the curb.

"Gotta go. Love ya." Amber gave her mother a quick hug and stepped onto the bus.

It was only a few blocks to home. Sara turned and headed for the apartment. She'd done too much. She was so tired all she wanted to do was go to bed. But it had been fun to spend the day with Amber. They didn't do it often enough. She knew her daughter had her own life now. And she had Matt. But for so many years it had been the two of them against the world.

"You need a cell phone," Matt said as soon as she opened the apartment door.

"What?"

"I called you several times," he said from across the room. "And when I got home, I heard your message. If you had a cell phone, you could have contacted me directly."

"I suppose. Sorry you missed dinner with us," she said, taking off her jacket. Was he angry? He seemed distant.

"You missed dinner with us at Tony's. We went there afterward," he said.

"Did you enjoy the sailing?" she asked.

He shrugged. "It was all right. Would have been better if you'd been there."

A warm glow spread through Sara. She smiled. "I

was afraid I'd get sick again. It wasn't so great when it was just the two of us. I didn't want to be sick among a boat load of good sailors.''

"How's Amber?'' he asked.

"Fine. We started to pack some things at the other place, but decided to spend the day at the park instead. Then we ate at the Wharf. She has finals this week and wanted a break from studying.''

"I heard your message when I got in. You could have tried my cell.''

"I did, you were out of range.''

"You look tired,'' he said, studying her.

"I am. I thought I'd take a quick shower and head for bed.'' She might have been talking to a neighbor for all the closeness she felt with this conversation. Why didn't he come across the room and kiss her?

"I'll stay up a bit longer. Good night,'' Matt said, turning toward the computer he kept in the alcove.

Sara tried to ignore the hurt she felt, but it was impossible. "Matt, we need to talk.'' She had advised her daughter of the same thing. It was time she took her own advice.

"Not tonight, Sara,'' he said.

"Soon, then.''

He nodded.

Matt drove her to work the next morning, kissing her deeply before letting her out of the car. "See you tonight,'' he said.

Sara felt better than she had in a few days after that kiss. She planned to discuss a leave-of-absence with her boss before telling Matt, but if things went as she planned, she could tell him at dinner. It was spring in many parts of the world. She'd love to return to

England, or visit another country in Europe if Matt got an assignment there.

Mr. Pepovich wasn't happy with her request. He threatened to terminate her employment entirely. Despite the fear of that very thing, Sara held firm to her request. She hadn't told her boss she was pregnant, and didn't think her assistant has spread the news, so she was spared any discussion about what she was going to do long-term when he reluctantly granted her request.

With the promise of time off beginning at the end of the month, Sara returned to her office. She'd check in with the landlord of the new apartment next, once she cleared the crucial work from her desk, to see if she could start moving things in early.

Caught up in the client files awaiting her review, Sara didn't realize how much of the morning had passed until she picked up the phone when it rang at eleven-thirty.

"Sara, I've got to go to Brussels," Matt said. "The security setup for a banking consortium there has been breached."

"Brussels! For how long?" If she'd asked for her leave to start earlier, she could have gone with him.

"I don't know, a couple of days. I'll call you. I've got to run if I'm going to make the flight." He hung up.

Sara held the silent receiver for a moment, then replaced it. So much for sharing her news at dinner. It would keep, of course, until the next time they spoke. But she had wanted to tell him at dinner—face-to-face.

Returning early from lunch, Sara dialed the manager of the new apartment building. She could at least see if he was amenable to their bringing things over early. Even if it cost a bit extra, it would make moving easier.

''I still don't have the signed lease,'' the man said when Sara identified herself and made her request.

''But it was signed a couple of weeks ago. I signed it and gave it to Matt. He would have mailed it the next day.'' Had it gone astray in the mail?

''I don't have it. Did you keep a copy of the signed papers?'' Mr. Douglas asked.

She didn't know if Matt had or not. And until he called from Brussels, she couldn't ask.

''I'll check and call you back.'' Surely he'd call tonight when she got home from work. She'd ask him then and call the landlord in the morning.

''Actually, you will need to let me know soon, I have others interested in the apartment, you know.''

''My husband's out of town. As soon as I hear from him, I'll ask. I'll call you no later than tomorrow, Mr. Douglas.''

What had Matt done with the lease? If he hadn't kept a copy, would the man wait until Matt returned so they could sign a new one? She didn't want to lose that apartment. It had been so perfect.

Sara left work early, determined to be home when Matt called. She didn't want a message on the answering machine.

After changing into comfortable clothes, she went to his desk to see if he'd kept a copy of the signed papers. Rummaging around, she stopped suddenly when she found the original lease. Her signature was clearly on one line. Matt had not signed.

For a moment she felt stunned. The paperwork had

arrived the day after she'd told him about the baby. He hadn't signed it.

Sinking on the sofa, Sara stared at the form, as if it could give her answers.

Why hadn't he signed and returned the lease?

Sara waited until eleven o'clock before going to bed. Matt had not called.

The next day she told her assistant to be sure to put Matt through if he phoned. He did not.

Late in the afternoon, she called Aste to ask for Matt's location. His secretary didn't know where he was staying, but gave Sara the number for the bank. Unfortunately it was midnight in Brussels. She doubted Matt, or anyone else for that matter, would be at the bank.

Sara rose early the next morning and went to the phone. After endless attempts to locate him, she finally had to leave a message with one of the clerical workers who spoke English.

Twenty minutes later Matt called.

"Sara, is there an emergency? I'm right in the middle of something."

"I found the lease to the new apartment on your desk. The landlord said he needed it back right away or he's going to let someone else have our apartment. What's going on, Matt?" She would not scream her frustration, nor voice her greatest fear. Was he regretting their marriage? Regretting their baby? Was he already making plans to leave?

She heard his sigh over the lines. "We need to talk, but now isn't a good time," he said.

Her heart stopped for a second, then began to race. She had said the same thing on Sunday, but now she didn't want to hear what he had to say. She wanted him to tell her he loved her, that they would stand together through everything and face the future as a couple forever.

"When is a good time? I tried Sunday and you put me off," she said carefully, afraid she would dissolve in a heap if she didn't hold on tightly to her emotions.

"Not when I'm on a critical job, that's for sure," he snapped.

"Did you have any intention of telling me you didn't sign the lease? I've been packing, planning to move. When were you going to say something, the morning of the move?" Her voice rose. She was getting angry. She wanted to stay cool, collected. Even more, she wanted some answers.

"Sara, I can't talk from here. I'll call you later."

"You said that Monday, and didn't call. When are you coming back?"

"I don't know yet."

She wanted to rage in frustration. Why had he accepted this assignment? Why wasn't he home when she needed him?

"I want some reassurances, Matt," she said. Reassurances for the future. Reassurances he would stay the course. Reassurances he loved her!

"I can't give you any right now," he said, and hung up.

Gripping the receiver tightly, she blinked back sudden tears. *He couldn't give her any reassurances?* She loved him. She had married him planning to spend the rest of her life with him. But *he couldn't give her any reassurances.*

* * *

Sara went through the motions of daily life over the next few days. She didn't call Matt again, waiting in vain for him to phone. When Friday afternoon came around and she had not heard a word, she called Aste Technologies, asking for Dex.

"Hey, Sara, what's up?" he asked when he came on the line.

"Do you know when Matt's coming home?" she asked.

"Isn't he home yet?" Dex asked.

"Not that I know of. He was in Brussels."

"He handled that in two days. Finished up Wednesday, I know because he had some tasks he handed off to one of the techs here to handle. He can make computers do things even their inventors never thought of. He put a firewall in place that will still be working when we are long gone, I expect. But he was done on Wednesday. I thought he headed for home. Now that you mention it, he didn't come in today and I expected he would. Hold on, I'll check with his secretary."

Sara waited, already suspecting the worse.

"Sorry, Sara, she's out on vacation—took a few days since he'd be gone. The temp doesn't know anything. I expect we'll see him when he shows up."

She heard the perplexity in Dex's voice.

"I guess that applies to me as well," she said. "Thanks for the info."

Why hadn't Matt come home?

The weekend proved lonely. Sara cleaned, did laundry and shopped for groceries. She slept when she could. Napping helped pass the time, however, then she wasn't sleepy at bedtime. She tossed and turned, trying to rest, but worrying far into the night.

She checked the answering machine a dozen times a day in case he called. Nothing.

She baked cookies on Sunday afternoon, not wanting to be far from the phone. She was getting worried now about a possible accident. Surely someone would have notified her if that was the case, but what if he'd been mugged and injured with no identification?

The scenario that played itself out the most, however, was his walking away to a new life. He hadn't bargained for a baby. Hadn't been thrilled with the news when she'd told him.

When the phone rang, she ran for it.

"Hello?"

"It's Dex, heard from Matt yet?"

"No." Disappointment washed through her.

"I spoke with one of the managers at the bank in Brussels early this morning. He drove Matt to the airport himself on Wednesday afternoon. He should have landed in New York Wednesday evening. I've got people checking in New York in case there was an accident or something."

"Thanks, Dex. Um, would he have gone somewhere else? Instead of coming home, I mean. Was there another problem or something he might have gone to check out?"

"Not that I know about. Tony is working on it as well. We'll find him, Sara."

"If he wants to be found," she murmured.

"What?"

"Nothing. I appreciate your letting me know. I'll call you if he calls here."

She hung up and sat back on the chair. Granted she

hadn't known Matt long, but he was too honorable to just disappear. He wouldn't leave his friends and partners in the lurch. Nor was he the type to walk away without a word to her. He'd tell her to her face the marriage wasn't what he wanted and ask her to leave.

She glanced around. She'd never felt fully comfortable in the apartment. Or was it she never felt fully comfortable in the marriage? She and Bill had been sweethearts for years, yet he'd run out on her without a qualm. How much easier would it be for Matt to leave without the years of shared experiences to bind them together?

By Monday morning Sara was furious. Matt had better have a whale of an excuse for not calling and letting her know where he was. She would not be treated like this. Either he keep her informed where he was when he traveled, or she would end their short-lived marriage.

When she reached work, she discovered her secretary was out sick—just when she needed her most in order to wind up some matters in preparation for her leave of absence.

Sara began to jot down notes for the different accountants who would pick up portions of her workload while she was gone. She wished Stacy had been in, it would have made the day go easier.

As she worked her way steadily through the accounts, she began to wonder if she should bother. If she and Matt were not going to stay together, then there was no reason to take a leave of absence. In fact, she needed to work as much as she could in order to have some money saved for the first few months of the baby's life when she wouldn't work.

The thought of being a solo parent again tore at

her heart. She knew Amber had missed a lot with no man in her life as a child. If only her parents had been more forgiving, or Bill had at least kept in touch.

Would Matt want anything to do with his son or daughter? Or would he be too busy saving the computers of the world to worry about the child he'd help create?

The phone rang. Hope instantly rose.

"Sara?" It was Dex.

"Yes?"

"We heard from Matt. Actually, we heard last Thursday, but we had a temporary clerical worker who took the message and it got buried in some other paperwork. He said he had some personal business to take care of and he'd call. Told her to let his wife know. I guess he thought she'd find someone to relay the message, but she apparently just jotted it on a slip of paper and forgot about it."

"That's all, some personal business?"

"So he said."

"Like what?"

"I haven't a clue." Dex hesitated a moment. "You know his uncle is dead. He has no other family he keeps in contact with, so I'm not sure what he meant. It was our screwup, sorry for all the worry on your end."

"At least he wasn't in an accident."

"He should have called you directly," Dex said.

"Maybe he was short on time." She would not reveal the difficulties they were facing to Dex, no matter how close he was to Matt.

"If he calls again, we'll let you know right away. Sorry for the delay."

So Matt had at least tried to reassure her about his

delay. Not that taking care of personal business meant much. And where was he that he couldn't use his phone? He'd made a big deal of her carrying a cell phone. He could have called.

All worry now turned to anger. How dare he put her through so much for naught. If he wanted to try for the long haul, they really did need to sit down and talk—and one of the first things she would demand is he keep in contact!

She took a quick lunch, then distributed the folders and notes she'd made all morning. Her desk was the cleanest it had ever been. Some of her co-workers commented on her plans, wishing they could take time off to visit some of the world's capitals. She smiled, trying to maintain a calm demeanor when her stomach was in turmoil and her anger was barely kept in check.

When the phone rang around three, she picked up, wishing again Stacy had not been out ill today.

''Mom?'' It was Amber, and she sounded as if she were crying.

''Yes, honey. What is it?'' Had she failed an exam?

''Mom, can you come? Jimmy's dead.''

CHAPTER TEN

SARA willed the taxi to go faster, even though traffic was heavy. She knew the driver was doing his best, but her child needed her and she wanted to be there instantly.

Jimmy dead, how could that be? He was only twenty-one years old. He had his whole life ahead of him. Only, apparently no longer. Amber must be devastated. Sara wanted to push against the seat in front of her in hopes of pushing the cab to go faster, to get to her daughter.

Endless minutes later the cab pulled in front of Amber's apartment building, an older one near the university. Sara flung some money his way and dashed out and into the building.

Seconds later she knocked on the door.

Amber threw it open, tears tracking down her cheeks.

Sara was vaguely aware of two men who rose when she entered, but her concern was for her daughter. She took Amber into her arms, holding her tightly, feeling her own tears come.

''What happened?'' she asked, as Amber sobbed against her shoulder.

''He was killed,'' she wailed, sobbing harder.

''Ma'am,'' one of the men said.

Sara looked over, recognizing the Army uniform.

''I'm sorry we had to bring such bad news,'' he said.

He hardly looked old enough to wear the double bars on his shoulder.

"What happened?" she asked them, holding her daughter tightly.

"Woodworth's platoon was rotated into an incursion sector. He and three others were killed when the vehicle they were riding in was hit by a missile. His body is being sent home for burial. It'll be here in two days." He held out a manila envelope.

"He was stationed in Germany, there's no fighting in Germany," Sara said, stunned anew by the news. Trying to take it in.

"No, ma'am. But he wasn't in Germany. His platoon was sent to an area of conflict, they had just arrived when the attack happened."

He offered the manila envelop again. "This has all the information we have, arrival time of the body, who to contact to coordinate the funeral. Insurance matters. Who to contact with any questions you have that we can't answer."

She reached for it, and nodded, brushing her own tears away with the back of her hand. She couldn't let Amber go long enough to do much more. Her heart ached for her baby girl. She and Jimmy hadn't been married three months!

"If there's nothing else?" the man asked.

There were a million questions—how had he died? Why? What was her daughter to do with the rest of her life? Who sent mere boys into armed conflicts? How could any of this be happening?

But the man in uniform wouldn't have the answers. "No."

"Our sincerest condolences," he said formally.

When they'd left, Sara moved with Amber to the sofa.

"Oh, Mom, I can't believe it. He's never going to come home. We're never going to build a life together, go to school, get a house. I'd even go with him in the military if he'd been here," she cried, clutching Sara as if she could never let go.

"I know honey. I know." She felt inadequate to deal with all this. What would they do? She wished Matt were with her. He might have some suggestions. If nothing else, he would offer support. She needed someone to lean on.

"The Woodworth's need to be told. The Army notified me as next of kin. They have to know. Poor Virginia. She dotes on Jimmy. Doted," Amber said, tears streaming down her cheeks.

Sara's tears welled again. Amber obviously couldn't tell them. She'd have to. Was there anything worse than a mother losing a child? Jimmy was the only child Virginia and James had. This would be devastating news. Sara instinctively rested her hand on her swelling stomach.

"I'll call her now. She needs to know," Sara said.

Amber told her where the phone number was, and Sara went to dial, remembering Jimmy coming over after school to see Amber. Remembering the times they'd fought and made up. Remembered the plans they'd made, and the small wedding they'd had so recently. He had been far too young to die. And Amber was much too young to be a widow. They should have had their entire lives ahead of them.

Sara asked to speak to James when Virginia answered. He wasn't home Virginia replied. Sara couldn't think for a moment, then said she had a tax question for him, unwilling to give Virginia the news when she was home alone. She asked him to call as soon as he came in.

Then she went to prepare hot, sweet tea for herself and Amber. There would be so much to do over the next few days. But first, the initial shock needed to be dealt with.

Amber stopped crying, listlessly accepting the tea when it was ready.

"I don't know what to do," she said.

"We'll take it one step at a time. The Woodworths will want to be involved in the funeral plans, so we'll wait until they know before planning anything."

"I talked to him last week, when I was in the midst of taking finals. He said they were going somewhere for a few weeks, but not that it was a dangerous place."

"He probably didn't want to worry you," Sara said, wishing more than ever that Matt was here to help her deal with this. She ached for her daughter and the Woodworths.

"He didn't even ask after my finals," Amber said. "I had to tell him I was taking them. It seems so petty now, but I was upset my finals weren't as important to him as going to his next assignment." She started to cry again.

"Honey, he was a man, doing a man's job. He was focused on that. You were important to him. He loved you for a long time. Always remember that."

"The call was too short," Amber mumbled.

"If he'd known he wasn't going to get another chance to call, I'm sure he'd have stayed on the line for hours," Sara said gently. There was something to be said for not knowing when the end was coming.

"Maybe. But I don't know how I feel. Not very married. We only had a few nights together, you know. He was on base almost the entire time he was here. We never got to be husband and wife, shopping, doing things together. We were going to do all that when he got back. Now we never will."

"I know. I'm so sorry, sweetie." Sara would do anything to ease the pain her daughter was going through.

Amber rose and paced the small room. Her hand went to her stomach and rubbed gently. "What am I going to do?"

Sara stared at her. "Oh, God, Amber, are you *pregnant?*"

Matt opened the apartment. He was dog-tired, but more convinced of what he needed to do than he'd been in a long time. It wouldn't be easy, but he had no other choice.

"Sara?"

The quiet in the apartment indicated he was alone. He'd called from the airport, but no one had seen her in the office since about noon, and her secretary was out sick.

He took his suitcase into the bedroom. She was not napping in their bed, which is what he'd been hoping for.

Taking a quick shower to freshen up, he dressed casually and went back into the livingroom. There was no note. Of course not, she hadn't known he was coming home today. Hadn't even gotten his message about his visit to Sambo until this morning.

Dex had apologized a dozen times, but it didn't

make it easier. What had Sara thought when she hadn't heard from him in days?

If Sambo hadn't lived in the hills of Virginia, he could have used his cell and called out after that thunderstorm had knocked out the power and phone lines. The flash floods had made roads impassable for days. It had taken the local phone company until last night to get telephone service restored. He'd stayed as long as he could to help clear the roads, worked with the small town in getting its computers back up once power was back and retrieving as much data as he could from the damaged machines. Lightening and computers should never mix.

He'd thought Sara knew he was fine. Instead, she must have been sick with worry when she hadn't heard from him in a week.

"So where is she now?" he said aloud, dialing her office again.

No luck. No one knew where she was.

He tried Dex again, but he hadn't heard from Sara since that morning.

He dialed Amber's number, but only got the answering machine.

Who were Sara's friends? She'd spoken about an Abbie and a Marian, but he couldn't remember their last names. Rummaging around her things, he didn't find an address book. Probably still at her old apartment.

He saw the lease to the apartment they had picked together. He needed to talk to her about that. He should have done so already, but he'd been running scared.

Hell of a thing for a man to admit. The thought of

a baby had scared the life out of him. He wasn't father material, had never pictured himself as a father.

He tried Amber's place again. The phone rang until the machine picked up. He left a brief message and hung up. Nothing to do but wait.

And waiting was never something he was good at.

He went through the mail, keeping an eye on the phone as if that would help it ring. He got something to eat, and fixed a huge pot of coffee. He was tired, but nothing he couldn't handle. Flying in from the East Coast wasn't like coming home from Europe.

It was after seven when he tried Amber's phone again. Still no answer.

Impatient and worried, he headed out. He'd swing by Sara's old apartment. Maybe she was packing. Though he doubted it. Without the new apartment confirmed, Sara probably had given up on the move.

For a moment he wondered if she'd given up on him and moved back to her old place.

He drove the few blocks and was startled to see the lights on. He hadn't truly expected that.

Finding a parking place proved almost impossible. He was tempted to leave the car in the middle of the road and run up to her apartment, demanding to know why she was there instead of their place.

He found a spot about two blocks away. The walk back did nothing but fuel his anger. He'd been waiting for hours, had she been here at her place all along? What was she doing?

He knocked on the door, annoyed she hadn't even given him a key to her place. Her old place, he corrected himself.

Sara opened the door, shocked to see him. But it was nothing to the shock he experienced seeing her.

"Sara! What's wrong?"

She looked awful. Her eyes were swollen, and blotchy. She didn't have on a speck of make up, and her hair was pulled back as if to keep it out of her face with no regard for style.

"Matt? What are you doing here?"

"I came for you."

"Oh, Matt, Jimmy's dead." She burst into tears.

He stepped inside and drew her into his arms. "Oh, Sara. I didn't know. When did it happen? I would have come instantly if I'd known."

"You're here now, that's good," she said, leaning against him. "We just found out this afternoon. It's so awful."

He turned her slightly and picked her up, carrying her to the sofa where he sat with her in his lap.

"Tell me," he urged, holding her close.

"Amber is asleep at last. We came home because—" She stopped and looked at him, her eyes full of worry and sadness.

"Because this is your home, yours and Amber's. And comfort is what she needs now," he said. His place had never been hers. Would never be hers. He knew that now.

She nodded, her tears slowing.

"I didn't know you were back," she said, leaning her head against his shoulder wearily.

"I got in this afternoon. I tried calling you at work, but you weren't there."

"I found out about three. I went to Amber's apartment, but we didn't want to stay there. The Woodworths were devastated. I had to tell James. The Army notified Amber. I knew they would be heartbroken. How horrible is it to lose a child? I don't know how Virginia will bear it.''

''What happened?'' Three o'clock? He'd been at the apartment by four o'clock. He could have been with her all these hours.

He listened while Sara disjointedly told him what she knew. He didn't fully understand where Jimmy had been, but did it matter? The fact was the young man was dead and Matt's stepdaughter a widow at nineteen. Jimmy's parents had lost their only child. His wife was distraught, which couldn't be good for her or the baby.

And he hadn't been there when she'd needed him most.

She pushed back. ''I need to wash my face— again.'' She rose and went down the short hall to the bathroom. He heard the water running. Feeling frustrated, he rose and went to the kitchen. The tea kettle was on the stove. Cups were in the sink. Remnants of a meal were still on the counter, little eaten.

He began to clear off the dishes, stacking them in the sink, putting away the food. He heard her join him. She'd pulled a sweatshirt over her clothes. Probably for the residual shock since it was not particularly cool in the apartment.

''I can do those,'' she said dully.

''I can manage. Sit and talk to me. Tell me what you've decided for the funeral.''

She looked at him, a flare of anger showing.

''Where have you been? I've been out of my mind with worry, no word from you in a week. We didn't exactly end on a pleasant note in our last call—which by the way was initiated from me. Would you ever have called?''

"I would have," he said quietly. He turned off the water and turned to face her, leaning against the counter.

"When? How dare you waltz back in as if you'd only gone to the store."

"I had some things to see to. I wanted to…"

"Mom?" Amber appeared in the door. "Oh, hi Matt. I guess you heard?" she asked.

"I'm so sorry, Amber," he said, taking in her appearance. Gone was the vibrant happy young woman he was used to seeing. Her eyes were dulled from tears. She moved as if she were eighty instead of almost twenty.

"Yeah, me, too." She went to sit beside Sara.

"Can't sleep?" Sara asked.

She shook her head.

"Want me to warm up this food?" Matt asked. He wasn't sure what to do with two weepy females, but he'd try something. He hadn't known Jimmy well, but he couldn't believe the young man was dead.

She shook her head. "I don't want anything but to be with Mom."

Sara reached out and brushed her fingers against Amber's cheek. "It'll get better with time, honey. I know it doesn't seem like it now, but it will. I promise."

"It's getting through the now that's so hard," Amber replied.

Matt felt shut out. The two had a bond he'd never be a part of. They were a family. He was the outsider who had married Sara. Had the deck been stacked against them from the beginning?

He finished cleaning the kitchen, trying to ignore the boxes stacked against the far wall. Sara had been preparing to move, and he'd been stalling making that final decision and signing the lease.

What now?

He turned and leaned against the counter. The two women sat silently, watching him.

"Want to go into the other room where it's more comfortable?" he asked.

They shrugged almost in unison and rose, walking into the living room. Sitting side by side on the sofa, Amber then leaned against Sara. For a moment Matt could see a little girl, trusting in her mother, the only parent she had.

At least her childhood had held Sara, not the crusty old man who had raised him. Raised him, but not taught him how to be part of a family.

Matt felt as if this was a test. If he passed, he'd be allowed to make a niche for himself with them. If he failed, he'd be back on his own, only it would be worse this time because he'd known Sara and had a glimpse of what life with her could be.

"You needn't stay, Matt," Sara said, leaning back and closing her eyes. "We'll be fine."

"Sara, you're my wife, of course I'm staying." Was she trying to send him away? Didn't she want him to stay?

"Now's a fine time to remember. Where have you been?"

He glanced at Amber. She was looking at him, but he had a feeling she wasn't really seeing him.

"I had some things to work through," he said, sitting in the chair opposite her. He didn't want to have this discussion with a third party present. But he wasn't leaving, either. Not before he and Sara had their talk.

"Where there were no phones?" she asked skeptically.

"Actually, that's about it. I went to see an old friend. He and his wife live in the mountains of Virginia. Unfortunately there is no cell reception. And there was a storm. Power lines and phone lines were knocked out. I thought you got my message on Thursday."

"I didn't."

"I know, now."

"You didn't sign the lease."

He shook his head.

"Should I leave?" Amber asked, looking back and forth between her mother and Matt.

"No," Sara said.

"Maybe it would be better," Matt said simultaneously.

Sara glared at him. "She just lost her husband. Maybe I'm losing mine."

Matt felt sucker punched. "What are you talking about?"

"I know you don't want a baby, you've said so often enough."

"I have never said it once!"

"You have—"

"What I've said more than once is I can't picture myself as a father. Which is true. Actually, I never pictured myself as a husband, but you changed that. And now we're having our baby."

"And you're thrilled," she said sarcastically.

"Actually, thrilled isn't quite how I'd put it. Scared silly more like."

Sara looked at him. "Of a baby?"

He nodded. "I have never pictured myself as a father—mainly because I don't have a clue how to be a father."

"Being around goes a long way in my book," Amber murmured. "Mine never was."

"Babies don't know anything when they're born," Sara said. "Whoever they get is usually fine with them. And you don't become an instant father or mother. It takes time. I was so scared when Amber was born. Heck, I still don't know what to do all the time, look at this situation. But I wouldn't trade her for anything in the world!"

"You are a great mother," Amber said, hugging Sara. She looked over at Matt. "At least your baby will have his or her father. Just love the kid a lot and you'll be fine."

"I'll try to remember that," he said, tilting his head slightly and looking at Sara. If Amber weren't in the room, he'd sweep up his wife and take her to bed to try to erase the sadness that permeated her being. He hated knowing he'd caused some of it.

Sara studied him, as if seeking an explanation for what had to be a reversal of what she thought.

"I've had time to think about us, about the changes a baby will bring," he said. "And I'm okay with everything."

"Since when?" she asked.

"Since spending the weekend with Sambo and his wife and three kids."

"Who is Sambo? What kind of name is Sambo?"

"Sam Bond. He and Dex and I went to college together. He went back east, settled in a town in western Virginia, got married and has two girls and a boy. They are terrific kids."

Sara and Amber both stared at him.

"Cut me a break, Sara. I've never been around children before. I don't even have any friends who have kids, except for Sam. And he lives three thousand miles away. You know my background. Did you think I would dream of some day having a son or daughter depending on me? What kind of father would I be?"

"I think you will be a wonderful father," she said softly.

He was surprised at that. "You do?"

She nodded, smiling slightly. "I do. Just the kind I'd want my child to have."

"Me, too," Amber said.

"Both of you?" The thought shouldn't please him so much, but it did.

"And a terrific grandfather," Amber added.

He stared at her in dawning recognition. "Oh, no, Amber, you're not pregnant, too?" Now the words she'd said earlier made sense. Her own baby would never know his or her father.

She nodded. "I didn't even get to tell Jimmy. You and Mom are the first to know."

Sara smiled. "If you could see your expression. Imagine, becoming a father and a grandfather all at once. Bet you never counted on that!"

Tears filled her eyes suddenly. "If you're staying, that is," she said.

He shook his head, totally bemused. "What do you mean if I'm staying? Of course I am, I just needed to fix a few things in my head. It's a done deal. I spoke with Dex and Tony this afternoon. No more travel for me for at least a year. We'll have this baby together."

"No travel?" Sara asked. "But that's what you do."

"No, it's what I did."

"I thought you didn't sign the lease because you wanted to be in London, not San Francisco. And maybe wanted to be there unencumbered, without a wife and baby."

"I didn't sign the lease because I wondered if we needed a larger place—for our new baby and to have a room for our daughter and her husband to visit. Now I think we need a mansion to accommodate the entire family."

"The entire family?" Sara said.

"You, me, Amber and both babies. Where else will she live?"

Sara looked at Amber. "Where indeed."

"Once the funeral is over, I need to go back to school to finish this year if possible. Who knows when I can work on a college education with an infant to care for. I'll have to get a job. One day, I'll get back to it. But I can't live with you and Mom," Amber said slowly.

"We'd love to have you," Matt said, glancing at Sara for agreement.

She nodded, her smile almost as happy as he'd ever seen it. Only a tinge of sadness lingered. God, he'd do anything to have her smile be as radiant as it had been on their wedding day.

Amber looked between them again, then rose.

"I need to go to bed. Thanks for being here, Matt."

When Amber left, Sara spoke softly, "Thank you Matt. That was special to invite her to live with us."

"I meant it."

"I guess you did. It surprised me, however."

"Why?"

"I thought you had come to tell me you were leaving. That our marriage was over," Sara said slowly.

CHAPTER ELEVEN

SARA was gratified at the look on Matt's face. Obviously she'd been wrong.

"Well, you didn't sign the lease, you were gone without telling me where, you didn't talk to me, you went off with your friends, and you kept saying…" she trailed off as he rose purposefully and advanced toward her.

"I never said I didn't want the baby."

"You changed when I told you about it."

"You caught me totally by surprise. I do admit I've been angry you didn't quit your job and travel with me."

"I was afraid. Afraid you'd leave me and I'd be homeless and destitute."

"That doesn't make sense. I was never leaving you."

"We married so fast. I thought that if we couldn't do what we planned, you'd leave."

"I've told you before, I'm not your first husband. I would never leave you. Don't you have a clue how important you are to me?"

She shook her head slowly.

"Take a leap of faith, Sara. Believe me when I say I will never leave you. Not a baby, your job or anything else is going to separate us.

"It's too late."

"What's too late?"

"For me to quit and travel."

"Why?"

She blinked. "It should be obvious. Before long I'll look like a beached whale. I will need to be no farther than fourteen feet from a bathroom. I'll have the energy of a slug. Won't be able to tie my shoes, much less travel to Europe or the Far East."

"So?" He shrugged, sitting beside her, putting his arm around her shoulder, as if to anchor her next to him. "We'll deal with that when the situation arises. Did you know Sam and his wife go hiking on the Appalachian Trail every year, pregnant, infants and all?"

"What?"

"I've learned a lot these last few days. Pregnant women can do whatever they want—including visiting foreign locales. We'll have to make sure we're home in plenty of time for the delivery, but otherwise, if you want, we can still take our trips. But I've told Dex I'm not taking any business trips until this time next year. I'm not spending days away from my wife. I want to see all the changes the baby brings. And be here when he is born. By then we may be ready to take up traveling again."

"You love to travel, that's the best part of your job," she said.

"I do like to travel." He laced his fingers with hers. "But over the last couple of months, I've discovered, I like being with you even more. If we never left San Francisco again, I'll be happy with you, Sara. I never had anyone to share my life with—no one who wanted me just for me before. I realized in Stockholm and Brussels how little visiting those places means these days when you aren't with me."

"I requested a leave of absence at work. I was

going to tell you the day you left for Brussels. I'm ready to go with you,'' she said, overwhelmed with the burst of love that filled her heart.

He tugged her closer, and brushed his lips over her fingers.

''So we'll travel as time permits until the baby's old enough, then go back to our plan to settle temporarily in London. Think how worldly our child will be as he grows up visiting Madrid or Brussels or Tokyo.''

''He?'' She latched on to the one thing she could, her mind a whirl with the possibilities as Matt presented them.

''Or she. Or they.''

''They?''

''We don't want this child to grow up lonely, do we? I was an only, you were, Amber was until now. Didn't we all long for siblings?''

''You want more children?'' Sara's eyes were wide in surprise.

''First of all, I want you. Then, yes. I think I do want a family full of kids. If we ever decide to settle down we can get a house. But in the meantime, a large apartment, that someone can watch for us while we're traveling, will do.''

''So you want to stay married,'' Sara wanted that clearly stated.

''I meant what I said. You are more important than anything else I have or hope to ever have. I would do anything for you, Sara. I wish you believed that.''

He kissed her, long and deep. She came up for air and smiled at him.

''I guess I can try,'' she said.

''For the next fifty or sixty years. Just give me a

chance to show you I'm not some guy who is going to walk out on you. I'm in this for life. Our life together. Believe it, sweetheart,'' he said.

''I do.''

''Maybe this life we'll share isn't going to be the way we thought when we got married a couple of months ago. But that doesn't mean it won't be even better,'' he said.

''I wanted to be footloose and fancy-free. To travel and see the world. To go sailing, and exploring and learn a new language.''

''And you can. We can make it work however we want it to. As long as we're together—a family.''

''I love you Matt,'' she said.

''I love you, Sara.''

''You do?''

He frowned. ''You needn't sound so surprised.''

''You never told me before.'' She turned slightly, framing his face with both her palms. ''Tell me again, look right at me and tell me.''

''I love you, Sara Tucker,'' he said solemnly, then kissed her. When he ended the kiss, he rested his forehead against hers. ''How could you doubt my love?''

''At first I didn't, but then you grew so distant after I told you about the baby.''

''It was a surprise. I was running scared. And until I read that baby book on the plane ride home, I wasn't sure how much you and I could do exactly…'' He trailed off.

Sara laughed, her heart filled to overflowing.

''We can do anything we want, right up until the last couple of weeks.''

''I'm all for that, then,'' he said, tucking a strand

of hair behind her ear. "I meant what I said about
Amber. She might want to live with us, and that's
fine with me."

"Oh, Matt, thank you. We can let the situation settle a bit for Amber before making any long-range decisions. She may truly wish to be on her own for a
while, at least until the baby comes. Imagine, two
infants at the same time. I can't believe I'm pregnant
at the same time my daughter is!"

"I can't believe I now have to adjust to becoming
a grandfather before I've even been father. Life with
you, sweetheart, is not at all like I thought it would
be."

"But it'll be okay, won't it?" She still wanted as-
surances. He'd promised to love her forever. She figured that'd just be about the right time.

"It'll be better than okay. It'll be the greatest adventure we ever have. Now, what do you say we go
to bed. I want to make love to my wife," Matt said.

She rose and held out her hands to him. "I want
that, too. I need to feel loved and wanted and alive.
I'm sad about Jimmy. My heart aches for my daughter. But there is nothing more I can do for her right
now. Something live-affirming would be so welcomed."

He swung her up into his arms and headed down
the short hall to the narrow bed that would be theirs
for the night.

"I will affirm our life together every day. I love
you, Sara. You and our baby," Matt said as a vow.

The radiant smile she gave him was every bit as
good as the one on their wedding day.